THE CIRCUMSTANCE OF MARRIAGE

A novel by Mala Kumar

Cover Design by Mala Kumar
Back cover photo © Neha Gautam Photography, 2014

Library of Congress Cataloging-in-Publication Data

Kumar, Mala, 1985 –
The Circumstance of Marriage

ISBN-13: 978-1497333338
ISBN-10: 1497333334

To my amazing mother and father - Latha and Ashok Kumar. Thank you for having the strength and courage for letting me grow into the person I am.

To Kiran Kumar - the best brother one could hope to have. Thank you for your unconditional support.

To my resilient grandparents - Lalitha and Sri Rama, and to my aunts, uncles, and cousins around the world. Thank you for showing me true wisdom takes generations to contextualize.

To my insightful development editor - Mya Spalter. Thank you for your guidance. To my line editor - Keidi Keating. Thank you for your attention to the details.

To my inspiring friends - APS, AKF, AE, LV, ES, PB, JS, VSK, KP, NG, SA, KLW, AI, EAE, FBK, FC, JC, MM, HWGF, ZH, GS, MV, MTC, MLC, ST, JV, KAH, AEW, MJW, and LT. Thank you for your ever-present encouragement. This book would not have happened without your help.

Finally, to my 11th grade English teacher - Bear O'Bryan. You gave me one of the most important pieces of advice in my life:

"Mala, you really need to work on your writing skills."

Definitions of Commonly Used Terms

1. Amma – the Telugu (see below) word for 'mother'
2. Nana – the Telugu word for 'father'
3. Avva – the Telugu word for 'grandmother'
4. Pinni – the Telugu word for 'mother's younger sister'
5. Shudra * – the fourth of the Varna caste system, often known as the servant caste
6. Caste * – a social structure in India that divides the population into traditional labor roles
7. Chennai – a city in south India and the capital of the Indian state, Tamil Nadu. The former British colonialist name for Chennai was Madras
8. Bangalore ** – a city in south India and the capital of the Indian state, Karnataka
9. Telugu – a south Indian language spoken in parts of Chennai and Bangalore, among other places
10. Tamil – a south Indian language spoken in Chennai, among other places
11. Kannada –a south Indian language spoken in Bangalore
12. Beta – a word in Hindi that literally means 'son' that is used more generically to mean 'dear'
13. Standard (use: second standard) – a grade level in school
14. Lyon – a city in France
15. (Medical) residency – compulsory post-medical school training
16. LGBT(Q) – a acronym referring to the lesbian, gay, bisexual, transgender, (queer) community

* These terms have historically, economically, and socially complicated definitions that can vary greatly according to the defining source. Definitions provided here are simplified for the sole purpose to aid in reading *The Circumstance of Marriage.*

** Bangalore is the British colonialist name for the city of Bengaluru; it is used in *The Circumstance of Marriage* as it today remains the most commonly used name for the city.

Table of Contents

Ekam sat vipraha bahudha vadanti

Truth is one, the wise call It by various names

\- Rig Veda 1.164.46

Part I – *Lakshmi*

Chapter 1

I awoke to a crash loud enough to disturb the Gods. As my blurred vision came into focus, I saw my mother standing a few feet away from me, swearing under her breath as she bent over the contents of a small Tiffin container that bled streams of sambhar down its side. She cursed her clumsiness and began cleaning the mess off of the small plastic runner that served as our kitchen floor.

Trying not to make too much noise, I shifted in my cot to peer out of the door. A few warm sunrays lent enough light to show the first signs of life in our Chennai village. On the other half of my cot, I saw a tiny body curled up, resting peacefully. Careful not to wake baby sister, I pulled myself up so as not to disturb her.

"Morning, amma," I said to my mother.
"Good morning, my dear."

Her voice was strained.

"Can I help you, amma?"
"No, don't worry. You go get ready for school."

I lingered for a few seconds hoping she would follow with the most anticipated words that anyone in our village could hope to hear. On some lucky mornings, I ate before preparing for school. Amma telling me to go and get ready meant this was not one of those mornings.

At the other end of our dirt-packed six-meter house was my school uniform. Quietly changing, I heard my mother in the background stifling her cries. The sound of strain in her voice always sent a chill down my spine. I hated hearing amma cry.

Dressed in my sweat-stained uniform, I walked outside and saw our village was already abuzz at that early morning hour. The toils of preparing for the day had begun: walk half a kilometer, collect the water, build a fire, prepare the vegetables, cook the food. A few one-room houses down, I saw one of the villagers twisting his body in his dancelike bathing ritual. He was the only person I have ever met who could coat his entire body with less than two cups of water.

I made my way to our outhouse; it was a simple structure of scrap wood and a half buried plastic bucket, though it took us two months to scrounge the village for the materials. It was worth every painstaking minute. Our neighbors looked at us with envy for having a place to defecate so close to our house. Most of them were forced to walk a kilometer to the nearest public lavatory or cover their droppings like dogs in the wild.

I used the last of the soap in the tin cup hanging on the door. We were taught in the second standard the importance of washing. I still remember the absolute pride I had in standing up, and informing the other students that I already know this fact because my amma was the most intelligent woman in our village.

Back inside, I saw amma had cleaned up the mess, salvaging the bits of food that weren't completely coated in village grime. She was an excellent cook. I was sure the vegetables tasted like little treats from heaven, even with the dirt. Amma did not offer me any of the food; I knew she was not saving it for herself.

I softly called out to her that I was leaving. She turned around and gave me her usual radiant smile, which always lit up the village far better than the sun did.

> "Look at my daughter. You are the smartest person I know, my dear."
>
> > "Look at my amma. You are the wisest person I know."
>
> "Make nana and I proud, okay?"

I told her I would. Making my parents proud was the motivating factor that unlocked my every passion and desire for a better life. As I turned to walk out the door, my stomach growled. Spilling food was not something we could afford to do.

1950s India did not provide me with electricity. It did not provide me with running water, adequate nutrition, or public transport. In fact, it barely provided a roof over my head. The one thing 1950s India did provide me with was an education.

For ten years, I walked three kilometers each way to get to school. At the age of eight, I had my first terrifying glimpse of the world beyond the boundaries of my village. At age 12, it was a familiar playing ground to relieve tension before a long day of studying. At age 16, it was a stressful addition to my already busy life. At age 18, it was the stepping-stone to achieving the unimaginable. An education would bring a better life.

"Lakshmi! Lakshmi! Lakshmi!" I heard someone shouting.

As I approached the final steps, I turned around and saw my best friend running towards me. Her parents had chosen her name, Alpa, meaning 'small,' in the hopes that their daughter would grow up to be a tiny, fair-skinned princess. Much to their dismay, Alpa used her parents' relative wealth to stuff herself with candy. The extra weight slowed her down, prolonging her exposure to the sun.

We had nothing in common. She dreamed of an easy and tranquil life, whereas I dreamed of having enough work to support my family. She was at the bottom of our class, and I did everything in my power to ensure I stayed at the top. But Alpa had the kindest heart of anyone I had ever met. While the other students threw dirt in my face, stole my pencils, and called me a 'peasant girl,' Alpa stood by me.

"Chee. What did you get on your uniform?" I asked as she waddled up to me.

Alpa peered down at the dark stain on her stomach before looking back up at me with a smile. Of course the stain was chocolate, and of course Alpa did not worry that it ruined her uniform. For Alpa, life was much too fun to worry about such small problems.

I shook my head to demonstrate my disapproval of her habits. Secretly, I was just trying to distract myself from my growling hunger. Sometimes I was envious of Alpa and her carefree attitude about the world. Carefree was not something I could afford.

Alpa sheepishly looked down at the floor. She meant no harm. I apologized for being so mean.

> "I'm just nervous about final exams next week. Come on, let's go inside."

Made of a mix of mud, cement, sweat and tears, our school stood three stories high. Its sand-colored exterior matched the outside ground so perfectly that it was not unusual to hear someone had walked straight into the walls after the sunset. Eventually, our headmaster made the same mistake, and decided to use the government tuition money to have life-sized portraits of himself painted on the walls.

> *"The colorful exterior is a safety measure for the students."*

No one could question him - what could a villager say to rebuke the powerful headmaster? It did not matter that the tuition money was supposed be for books. Village children lived with what headmaster wanted, and headmaster wanted giant portraits of his face.

Our humble school hosted all twelve standards for the surrounding population of nearly 1 million people. Even as a poor village girl, I prayed that the building would not collapse under the pressure of the students' constant worry for their futures.

When villagers petitioned the local government to build another school, the official government response was always the same,

> *"Stop complaining. There is very little demand past the second standard."*

Very few families could surpass the limitations of poverty to keep their children in school past the second standard, beyond the age of eight. We could not argue either way.

My parents' childhoods had been no different. My father, my nana, had been pulled out of school in the first standard so he could help support the family. Amma had only attended school twice before her father dragged out by her hair and beat her for trying. At eight-years-old, amma decided to break that cycle with her daughter. She endured constant heckling from the villagers to have me married. In three weeks, I would be the first person on either side of our family to graduate from higher secondary standards. I was already the most educated person in the family - man or woman.

The rooms were crowded, we were four to a book, and had few other supplies. I knew no different. This building had allowed me to see wonders of the world that no one else in my family had ever had the privilege of knowing. The Pyramids of Egypt, Darwin's Theory of Evolution, the czars of the USSR...whatever the subject, I found everything fascinating.

In 1950s India, a desire to learn was rarely met with praise. Being a girl, being poor, and just being was never easy in India. Your character was the least important measure of your worth. Most people in school regularly put me in my place.

> *"Scheduled caste is the only reason you are here, Lakshmi. You don't deserve to go to school!"* the other students (except Alpa) would taunt.

Despite the constant reminders of my place in society, I enjoyed every minute of my education...until this year. Even in our common

Chennai village school, most of the teachers desired to impart knowledge on their students. They did not approve of my caste, they did not approve of my poverty, but they allowed me the privilege of learning without insulting me. That year, however, our teacher had dedicated her life to tormenting children.

Her favorite object in the world was the giant wooden stick she used as a cane, as a pointer, and above all, as a weapon to beat students. Questions aren't allowed in Indian schools, which was the reason she had a job. She did not know anything about most of the subjects she was required to teach. Unless the question was about M.K. Bhagavathar, her favorite film actor, teacher would not know the answer.

But teacher had the one quality all schools valued: a high caste. Her father had been a priest; her mother had come from one of the highest Brahmin families in all of Chennai. No one understood how she fell from grace and landed in the slums, though she never let us 'heathens' forget where she came from. She told us how lucky we were to have such a highly respected person as our teacher. She told me how lucky I was to even be allowed to stand in the same room as her, or to breathe the same air.

Teacher loved to torment the few impoverished students who had managed to survive until the last standard. While we ignored the hunger eating away at our stomachs, we had to hear about all of the lavish vacations and the endless quantities of food she had consumed while seeing the grand landmarks of *south* India.

"The beaches of Goa, the palace of Mysore, the…Taj Mahal!"

Teacher was an idiot, but teacher could not be questioned.

"Lakshmi!" Teacher shouted, hovering right above my desk.

"Yes, Madam?" I said as I stood up attentively.

I was poor, I did not speak Tamil at home, I was of an inferior caste, and I was smart. Teacher hated me.

"What is the date of Indian independence, Lakshmi!?"

Teacher's breath stank of stale onions. Teacher's brain stank of unearned privilege.

"15 August 1947, Madam!"
"Incorrect!"

She gathered a fistful of my hair and pulled me to the front of the class. Demonstrating to my classmates how to properly point and laugh, she hit me five times in the back with her beloved wooden stick for a correct answer.

Chapter 2

The beating teacher gave me burned beneath my uniform; I left without waiting for Alpa, who came waddling down the path, screaming my name.

"Lakshmi! Lakshmi! Lakshmi! Let's go to the cinema. They are playing a new America film!"

"American film. I can't, Alpa, I have to go to work now."

Even on my days off, I never went to the cinema. I could buy ten pencils - enough for the entire year - with that money. The disappointed look on Alpa's face made me feel guilty every time. I asked her to meet me after work so we could study together. Her face lit up at the suggestion, and she gave me a quick handshake before bouncing off. The handshake gesture was new. She probably learned it from watching American films at the cinema.

Two days a week I would tend a field of vegetables for our local village farmer. I had to pull out the weeds by hand, dig out holes for the new seeds, kill bugs that infested the plants, and chase away animals that tried to burrow in the soil. Already, I had a bad back, calluses on my feet, and more scars on my hands than I could count.

My second job was slightly more manageable. Four days a week, I assisted the seamstress in the next village over. We were all poor, but most of the customers were still far richer than me. For five to seven hours a day, I measured uptight mothers, fathers who tried to grope me, and spoiled children for new sari blouses, work shirts, or school uniforms.

Everyone watched their weight before coming to get measured, yet as soon as we recorded their measurements, the customers would stuff their faces with ghee, wada, idly, and dosa. It was I who heard their screaming when none of their new clothes fit.

Most days I didn't care. Without the work, I would have to drop out of school. Really, I was lucky, I told myself. How many people in India can go to school until the last standard and still be able to eat a meal everyday? By my age, amma had a child and nana had a family to support. Out of 207 children in my first standard class, 120 had not made it as far as I had in school.

That was the attitude I coached my mind into every day before work, even on a particularly exhausting day such as this one. An official from the municipal government had been given a bribe from a north Indian cotton salesman. As a result, the official forced the parents of the students in the primary standards to buy new uniforms less than a month before the holidays. My boss received much of the fitting business. After six hours of measuring hyper boys and girls and listening to parents scream about how they could not afford the cost, I finally made my way home after the sun had retired for the night.

In the distance, I could see nana. He was one of the tallest and strongest people our village had ever seen, though he used his physical stature solely to carry the most grain at his job in the fields. Other men might have used such power to control the weaker villagers, or to threaten physical violence.

"Hello, my princess," he called out to me.

The sound of his melodic voice always brought a huge smile to my face, and I ran to give him a hug. Though his leather-worn face always told me the answer, I asked how his day in the fields had proceeded.

"A special gift from God," he would always reply.

Amma and baby sister came outside to greet us. As I peered inside, my heart jumped at the sight of four brilliant green banana leaves arranged around two small steel containers. The smell of fresh vegetables and spices wafted through the house, and I sat down with great anticipation. Nana pulled the lid off of the containers and divided the food into four equal portions. I looked down at my leaf – a full cup of rice and a half-cup of vegetables. It was the biggest meal we had eaten in days.

Alpa came over after dinner so we could study for our final exams, which would start the next week. Her chubby little legs moved slowly as she peddled her bike down the path that led to our section of shanty houses. Completely out of breath, she walked over to baby sister for their usual exchange. It was understood that I would help Alpa study if she let baby sister use her bike.

My mind was clouded with a hard day's work, and Alpa had gone to the cinema after all. Instead of studying, she spent the night describing every detail of life in America while baby sister whizzed around happily on the bike. I listened to Alpa talk about the high-heeled shoes the women wore, the cigars the men smoked, and the fancy cars everyone drove. Never having seen anything that compared, I had no idea what she meant, though it sounded wonderful.

My stomach was full, Alpa and my family were resting comfortably, and both my mind and body had the rare pleasure of being able to relax at the same time. Nana must have carried me to my cot after I drifted off to sleep. I spent the night dreaming about pearls, diamonds, and a life of luxury that Chennai never offered. Invigorated with hope and rest, I awoke the next morning to start another special gift from God.

After two weeks of constant studying, my standard of Gandhi Matriculation Primary/Secondary School completed its final set of exams. Today was the most important day of our lives: results announcement.

> "Keep quiet!" teacher shouted with every angry bone in her body.

She banged her giant wooden stick on the desk. The sound echoed through the crowded room like waves of destruction.

> "We are announcing the top and bottom scorers for this year's final exams only. The rest of you will check your rank on the postings outside."

I held my breath. Last year, it was announced that as part of a new government initiative, the top scorer from our humble school would automatically gain entrance to the local university with all tuitions fees waved. It was my only chance at being able to attend higher education.

Teacher cleared her throat and spat on the floor. Still bubbling with her foul odor, it absorbed into the ground before she had a chance to humiliate the lowest scorer. I prayed that it was not my dear Alpa.

> "This year's *lowest* score goes to…Alpa!"

Teacher threatened to beat anyone who did not participate in her pointing humiliation ritual. I turned to look at my kind friend. Behind the safety of her desk, Alpa snuck a piece of chocolate into her mouth before silently bursting into tears. She would never admit anything, though I knew she tried to do well in school. Her brain simply could not hold the information.

"And this year's top score goes to...Lakshmi!"

Time slowed down as teacher spat my name. At the conclusion of the last syllable, I felt all the blood in my body go straight to my head. I must have been glowing, I was so elated. Before I even had the chance to thank God for the results, teacher slammed her wooden stick millimeters from my hand.

"Shut up!" she screamed at me.
"Get out!" she screamed at the rest of the class.

No one needed to be told twice. Alpa patted me on the back as she walked by. To that, teacher slammed Alpa's round bottom as hard as possible with the stick. Alpa shrieked and scurried out of the classroom as fast as her little feet could move.

"Stand up."

Teacher circled around me, her beady eyes looking me over. As she inched closer, I did my best to keep focused on the rat rummaging through a trash pile across the room.

"You cheated. How could a peasant girl get such high marks? A girl born to such a lowlife caste - dirty clothes, begs for tuitions money, can't afford a proper eraser for her pencil. You cheater. Your father can't write his own name. Your sister couldn't pass her second standard exams."

After a year of studying me, teacher knew exactly what to say to make me snap. How dare this pathetic, lazy human being who had never known a full day's work talk of nana and baby sister that way?

"And your mother. Your mother, who can't even afford to feed her own daughter…"

I silently screamed; I could not stop imagining how satisfying it would have been to snap that horrid wooden stick she cradled in her arms as though it were her baby. With one foul blow, I could break teacher's spirit. With one foul blow, I could destroy my future.

Teacher continued to circle around me. I inhaled, waiting for a beating that would leave scars until my next life. Miraculously, she did not raise her hand or her stick. After having me wait in desperation for what felt like hours, she threw my results paper in my face.

"Get out."

I picked up the filthy green bag amma had given me as a school sack ten years ago and ran to the door.

"Lakshmi!"

I stopped, careful not to turn around.

"Lakshmi, you know you have gained entrance to university with your score."

I smiled to myself. Yes, I knew. It was the accomplishment of a lifetime.

"But there are added costs that come with university. Books, supplies, uniform. Your pathetic parents could never afford those. A sad, dirty peasant girl such as you is not meant to go to university."

Chapter 3

I ran all the way back to my village, barely noticing the bushes and thick grasses of the south Indian terrain beating heavily against my legs. Teacher's words echoed in my ears without mercy. She was right. Amma and nana could not afford to pay for the additional costs and there was no way I could work while at university.

For a decade, I had imagined the victory of the esteemed accomplishment in achieving first-rank. The naivety of an adolescent brain simply overlooked the harsh realities of the world. So I ran. I ran as though my speeding legs could break the poverty barrier.

My feet pounded on the hard dirt path, making hollow slapping noises as I approached our house. By the time I reached the tip of our sanctuary, dirt covered my uniform, my hair was disheveled, and tears streamed down my face. Amma rushed over to me, catching my tired body as I collapsed in her arms.

"What happened!? Why aren't you at work!?"

In between my sobs, amma looked down at me with confused sympathy. Finally, I rummaged the results paper out of my nearly disintegrated pocket. She looked down at the paper with embarrassment. The letters on the paper meant nothing to her as an illiterate woman.

"What does it mean?"

I quietly told her.

"Oh my God! You got first rank, Lakshmi! You have gained acceptance to university, full tuitions paid!"

I tried to explain the problem of added costs and how I would never be able to go. Amma simply smiled back at me and told me to go rest.

"We will talk when nana gets home."

I wanted to keep telling amma about my problem, about how close I had come to achieving the unthinkable. Amma simply quieted me by singing my favorite children's song. Slowly, I drifted off to sleep, letting the sadness in my brain shut out the cruel world around me.

I must have slept for at least six hours. By the time I awoke, amma and nana were sitting on their cot talking. I tried my best to listen in, but baby sister saw me stir and shouted her song of delight.

"She's awake! Lakshmi lives!"

If there was anyone in the world who could make me smile through the pain, it was baby sister. No one in my family had ever seen a hospital or a health clinic. The midwife who helped amma deliver baby sister told us that amma was having a 'Cesarean' child. We did not know what this meant. Amma later told me baby sister was born with the umbilical cord twisted tightly around her neck. As a result, baby sister could not communicate as the rest of us could.

As amma passed me to get baby sister, she told me nana wanted to talk. I sunk back into the cot trying to figure out what I would say. My parents had worked so hard to put me through school. There were always more students than opportunities in India. Going to university and working hard did not guarantee me a job. It was too much of a risk. That kind of risk could not justify making my parents and baby sister continue to go without proper food.

"Nana, I got first rank of my higher secondary class, but..."

Nana put up his massive hand, motioning for me to stop.

"My child, your mother and I are highly proud of you. First rank is most impressive."

"Thank you," I sheepishly replied.

Society had taught nana to start each conversation with a list of his limitations.

> "I am an uneducated man who knows little outside of this village..."

> "Don't say those things, nana."

I did not believe in what society said of nana. My parents were my heroes, no matter what stigmas were branded on their bodies. He assured me that this time it was relevant.

> "The first time I held you in my arms, I knew you were special. I wanted you to find a good man and seek better opportunity. Your amma told me you were capable of far more. Your amma told me how brilliant you are. She made me realize you and your sister are the reasons I get up each morning and work a job that brings me constant pain."

His words washed over me, leaving a thick coat of shame. Nana had been working 13 hour days, six days a week, every week, for 26 years. I knew what was coming. He would tell me it was time I stop burdening the family. It was my time to get mar...

> "Growing up, we were taught to spend the money we earned as soon as possible. What if it gets stolen, what if the government takes it away? Your mother wanted to do things differently."

I looked up at nana with eager caution; afraid I had misheard the very likely reality as the impossible ideal.

> "For many years, your mother and I have been saving a portion of my wages."

Peering around me to make sure no one was coming, he pulled out a small steel can from the far corner of our house. Carefully removing the lid, he allowed me one small glimpse of the contents. Inside was a sparkling mountain of unblemished coins. It was the most money I had ever seen in my entire life.

> "You gained entrance into university, full tuitions paid. This will make sure that special gift from God does not go to waste. *You* will bring us a better life."

I was speechless. I was going to university.

Chapter 4

I had two months holiday before the start of university. The pile of money my parents had saved seemed enormous. After counting it all out, I realized that even if nana continued to set aside the same portion of money during holidays, I would still need to earn nearly Rs. 20 to pay for added costs.

After working twelve hours every day for three straight weeks, I saved up enough money to purchase an old bicycle to make the seven-kilometer journey to the university campus. Universities in Chennai required a uniform, though not like the little girls' uniform I wore through higher secondary school. Buying the material and getting fitted for the required university saris and blouses was expensive, so I continued to work for the seamstress to pay off the cost.

As expected, Alpa did not gain entrance into any university with her marks. She had eaten her way to morbid obesity and allowed herself to become very tanned. Without admission to a university, and with the work ethic of a sloth, Alpa's parents saw no choice but to get her married as soon as possible. The fact they had even allowed her to go this long without getting married was already a miracle.

She spent the days keeping me company while I measured my boss's customers and listened to their complaints about my 'peasant girl measurements' always being too small. Alpa would describe the latest film in the cinema, her newest candy obsession, or the fat, gross men her parents invited over as marriage prospects.

The worst of the prospects was Govind, or 'Go-wind' as the boys called him for his smelly gas. He was crass, he was mean, and had trouble figuring out how to put one foot in front of the other. He looked like a giant monkey - the swinging arms, the stupid expression.

We both knew that she would be able to secure someone better than Go-wind. As much as Alpa's size detracted from her physical beauty, it was a sign to the villagers that her parents had money. In between the numbers I furiously scrawled down at work, Alpa and I had a great time imitating Go-wind's smelly gas-passing sounds and his labored walk. Poor Go-wind. Poor Go-wind's wife!

I knew that I wouldn't be able to work for months once university started, and decided to earn my final wages on the last day of holidays. With the strange reluctance that comes at the end of a long journey, I gathered my few earthly possessions, and began the walk to the seamstress's shop. Amma called out to me as I left.

> "You're not going today. I was just at the shop to tell the seamstress."

> "What? Is something wrong!?"
>
> "You worry too much, Lakshmi. Come with me."

She grabbed my hand and led me to the path into town. In the distance, I saw the outlines of the other two most important people in my life. Baby sister cried out with joy in the midst of jumping up and down in the same spot. Nana let go of her hand, and she ran into my arms.

"Lakshmi! We are going to see Amrika!"

"What are you saying, baby sister?"

"We will see Amrika today!"

Nana smiled mischievously saying that he and amma had not given me a proper gift for all of my accomplishments. I started to explain that sending me to university was the most precious gift anyone could ever provide.

"Please Lakshmi. Let's just enjoy the cinema together!"

"The cinema? We can't afford to go to the cinema!"

"We are the parents. We make the decisions, and we are going to the cinema!"

He said it with such eagerness that I immediately realized this would also be nana's first trip to the cinema. For a man that worked so hard to provide me with food and shelter, I could not argue. The playful side of me did not even want to argue. This was easily one of the most excited moments of my entire life. It would be my first moving glimpse of a world outside of India.

At first glance, the cinema looked similar to the other sand-colored buildings in the outskirts of Chennai. As we approached, we saw colorful posters of the latest pirated Tamil and American films the cinema owner had purchased. Just underneath the film posters was a sign.

Tickets - First class, Rs.5
Second class, Rs.2
Third class, Rs.½

Important looking women and men stood tall as they bought their tickets. I stared poster of the movie we were seeing - *Father of the Bride.* It looked so sophisticated!

I knew nana was scared, but he marched straight up to the ticket vendor with a total confidence unusual for his normal demeanor.

"Give me four tickets, third class."

The vendor eyed nana, scanning his worn out, dirty sandals, the tattered lungi that hugged nana's hips, and the western style shirt that nana had received from Christian missionaries on one of their mass clothing distributions.

"Rs. 2 per ticket, third class." The vendor replied.

"What? The sign says Rs. ½ per ticket!" I cried out.

The vendor smirked at me with the same look of superiority teacher used to torment her students.

"Ah, peasant girl thinks she can read."

"I can too read! I am first rank..."

"Rs. 2 per ticket, third class to wipe your filth from the floor on which you sit."

"You fat bastard, how dare y..."

"Lakshmi, please," nana sternly said to me.

I could tell nana's heart was racing at the sudden appearance of every vein in his arms. Any other man of his stature would have flexed his muscles and threatened to kill the ticket vendor on the spot. Nana simply turned and whispered something to amma. She looked distraught at his words and was about to argue until baby sister came running up to her, pulling on her sari.

"Amma, shall we go and see Amrika?"

Amma turned back to nana and painfully nodded.

"Three tickets."

Nana threw the money on the counter as the vendor handed him the tickets. The vendor deposited Rs 1.5 into the collection bucket, and laughed as he openly stuffed the rest in his pocket. Giving the three tickets to amma, nana silently walked away from the cinema.

> "No! Nana! You have to see the film!"

I tried forcing my ticket into his hand, but he refused.

> "Lakshmi, it's okay. An uneducated man like me will not understand. I would rather hear the film from the mouth of my beautiful daughter."

Amma had to drag me inside the building kicking and screaming. I will never forget the mountains of defeat folded into the skin of nana's face. It burned into my brain as though the memory were on fire. In all of the suffering I had endured from the world, nothing hurt more than seeing nana publically humiliated by that miserable ticket vendor.

I spent the first 20 minutes of the film trying to comfort baby sister and stop myself from crying. The luxury flaunted on the screen served as the same insults of the selfish people sucking the limited wealth of our country. Why should we starve while they drape themselves in pearls? What had we done to deserve this?

It was only when amma drew me to her protective warmth and reminded me what nana had sacrificed that I allowed my mind to absorb the wonder of the dream that danced before me.

> "Don't let your anger prevent you from enjoying this opportunity, Lakshmi."

To amma and baby sister, the images before us were the window to America. To me, the words and the order were the window to America. I had only seen that level of equality between men and women, between the lowest and the highest, in my own house. In America, these were the standards that were lauded, not dismissed. It was too often the opposite of my society.

> *"Your parents are so obsessed with your education, Lakshmi. It is unnatural."*

By the end of the film, I knew why God had created someone like me to be born to parents such as amma and nana: it was I that was going to change what it meant to be a woman in India. Somehow, someway, I would be the one to make India a better place.

After the film was over, I carried baby sister out of the theater with amma following closely behind. As soon as she saw nana, baby sister leapt out of my arms and sped towards him.

> "How was it, my little darling?"
>
> "Nana! They don't even speak properly, and their clothes are sooo drab!"

Nana chuckled.

> "Is that right, Lakshmi?"
>
> "Oh, absolutely. They speak nothing of what we know in India!"

Nana nodded happily and motioned for us to start our journey home. A few minutes later, he was chasing baby sister down the path. Amma took my hand and gave it a kiss.

> "What did you think?" she asked me.

I drew her hand closer, and allowed my head to rest on her shoulder. That was the world I wished India to be.

Chapter 5

Registering for classes had been a difficult process. Most of the staff laughed to my face when I told them my caste and where I lived. Compared to the journey to reach university, however, their taunts did not discourage me. Still, by the first day of classes, I was absolutely petrified of what lay ahead.

Amma sacrificed her portion of food to make sure I had a good breakfast. Normally, I would scarf down every morsel. That morning, even a few bites made my stomach turn. With legs shaking from anxiety, I climbed onto the seat of my bike and peddled off to start a better life.

Riding up to the campus, I saw thousands of bikes leaning against the giant façade of the main building. I was 30 minutes early for the first set of classes; still, every student was rushing as though they had mere seconds to live. The air was charged with an energy and sense of competition that I had never experienced before. It was infectious.

University. What an invigorating word. Everything inside of the campus seemed to move at lightning speed. In two days, we reviewed my entire ten standards of schooling. By the end of the first week, I had taken nearly 100 pages of notes and had been assigned to read 500 pages. Total memorization of the material was required.

My professors spoke with precision and without pause. None of them ever slowed down and nothing would be repeated, no matter what the situation. Each of my professors was a leader in academia. Any professor with less than a Ph.D. was considered a joke.

Strangely, I found the volume of work comforting. If there was anything I knew for sure, it was my ability to memorize vast quantities of information, a sought out skill in the Indian education system. On the rare occasion a professor would stop to ask a question, I always knew the answer.

With so much material to squeeze in, no one had time to stop and dwell on caste. With my new uniforms no one suspected I had impoverished parents, or a learning-disabled baby sister. After a year of being under teacher's wrath, the anonymity of university brought me comfort. University was where I belonged.

Though studies kept me busy, Alpa and I saw each other at least once every weekend. Our usual meeting ground was by a small creek where we used to play as children. Alpa and I would find our favorite tree and sit on a patch of grass overlooking the water. She didn't much care for the subjects I studied, so she would do most of the talking – telling me about the latest 'America film,' while I reviewed my school notes.

One particularly hot Saturday, I arrived at our meeting spot early. The water was crystal clear, the sun was shining bright, and the shade of a tree brought great relief from the heat. Enjoying the serenity for a few minutes, I was startled back to reality when I heard crying behind me. I jumped up and saw Alpa walking toward me with tears streaming down her face.

"Alpa, what's wrong?"

"They…they…they…"

"They what?"

"They are…Go-wind…next month…"

We spoke at different levels, but we always knew what the other one meant. Her stuttered words could mean only one thing: her parents had decided to marry her off to Go-wind. I sighed, trying to find words of comfort for such a terrible prospect. Carefully guiding Alpa over to the tree, I asked her to explain everything.

"Oh Lakshmi! My parents brought many prospects. Some tall, some short, some ugly..."

"What happened, Alpa?"

"Every time we met someone, amma would make me wear my best clothes and serve tea. I tried really hard, Lakshmi. I want a good man!"

It was rare for Alpa to express concern about the future. Seeing a fresh set of tears emerge from her eyes, I handed Alpa my handkerchief to staunch the flow.

"Lakshmi, they would never come back. We went over to their houses to deliver sweets, but none of them came back. Only Go-wind!"

We sat in silence. It was one thing to make fun of Go-wind when he was the joke of the villages. It was another thing when Go-wind would be your husband. I could not imagine building a life with someone so despicable.

"Maybe he will get better once he is your husband."

Alpa blew her nose in my handkerchief. We both knew Go-wind's prime years were now. If this was his prime, we could only imagine his demise…

Alpa told me her parents were having the engagement party next week. The wedding would be at the end of December. Alpa's parents were tired of supporting her, and wanted her married into rich Govind's family with children as soon as possible. I tried my best to comfort Alpa by describing how beautiful she would look in an engagement sari.

"Everyone in the village will be so jealous! Think of all the gifts!"

For two hours, I set aside my studies and listened to her describe the details of his stupidity. Alpa wanted healthy, happy children who would be smarter than she. She wanted a husband who understood her jokes and who wanted to try new foods. Go-wind could barely function. He would not bring her joy.

We both knew the terrible prospect would soon become a reality. Doing my best to do what I did worst - keep the mood light - I wrapped my arms around the shoulders of my frightened friend, and walked her all the way home before parting ways. I left her in her room and told her everything would be okay.

Chapter 6

There were two kinds of people at university: those who were admitted on merit and those who paid bribes. Sahana fell into the latter category. Her father had been a businessman in Malaysia for a number of years. Being raised in Kuala Lampur made Sahana the worldliest person I had ever met. She was also the most arrogant. Having been placed in three out of four of my first semester courses, I saw Sahana five times a week, six hours a day.

I idolized our professors. They had dedicated their lives to the total comprehension of a subject of merit. Ask them anything related, and they could give you the history of some of the most fascinating topics on earth. To Sahana, they were old sacks with strong body odor that spoke with a lisp. If any other student dared to interrupt a professor during their lecture, that student would most certainly be kicked out of the class. With connections like Sahana's, she could mock the professors openly and not receive any punishment.

There was no end to her insults - the way professors dressed, the thickness of their glasses, their salaries, the quality of the food they brought to lunch, where they were born, who their parents were, caste, religion, language, everything. Honestly, if she had spent half as much time studying as she did giving insults, she would have made a fine student.

Sahana made it a policy to publically torment anyone who crossed her path. Needless to say, if the professors and the students of a higher caste were not good enough for her, neither was I. Avoiding Sahana became my first rule of university survival. Three months into the term, I had successfully failed to make my presence known to her. It was a tricky balance to demonstrate my knowledge of our subjects without becoming her target.

One afternoon towards the end of our term, we arrived to our Principles of Accounting class and took our seats as usual. Professor Gopal was running late, so the majority of the students took the opportunity to review their notes from previous sessions. Twenty minutes after the start of normal class time, one of the assistant deans walked in to make an announcement.

> "I have some bad news. Professor Gopal passed away last night."

> > "Ha! Finally died from the smell of his own body odor?" said Sahana.

The dean looked over at Sahana. Realizing who she was, he kept his mouth shut. As we only had two weeks before our final examinations, he assigned us the rest of the material to cover on our own. We were to write a summary of the material with the members of our groups, which had already been determined.

> "You are to report here for your examination at 1 PM exactly two weeks from today. Is that clear?"

Sahana scoffed aloud and commented on the dean's cheap polyester shirt. The rest of us simply nodded.

After the dean laid the stack of papers with the assignments out on Professor Gopal's table, a mad rush of students raced to the bottom to unearth the groupings. In an Indian university, working as a team was a rare luxury - only the death of a professor allowed it to happen.

There were four people to each group. Mine consisted of two I knew to be friendly. Together, we looked down at the sheet and silently panicked. Sahana was our fourth. The rest of us knew dealing with her would be far harder than completing the assignment.

Fortunately, she decided that without a professor to openly humiliate, there was no need to stay for the rest of accounting class. My two project partners, Nallini and Jayesh, and I debated a host of strategies to get rid of the evil queen. We decided to approach her the following day and gently ask how to proceed.

After classes, I somberly rode my bike home, debating whether to tell amma and nana my bad luck. Five kilometers from the house, I decided to keep quiet. Three kilometers away, I decided to tell them. One kilometer away, I decided I did not know what to do. Indecisiveness was not a typical attribute of mine. Striking a balance between being open with my parents and burdening them with my problems was the one exception.

By the time I got home, amma was already perched on the floor preparing the little food we would have for dinner that night.

"Hello my darling, how were classes today?"

"My accounting professor died."

It was not a typical response, and she did not know how to react. I rarely spoke of my emotions. She asked if I was okay. I told her I was sad to see such a respected person pass. Seeing she was not satisfied with my vacant response, I followed with the news of who I would be forced to work with on the report. Snapping her head up, amma looked at me with alarm.

"You must work with Sahana?"

"Yes. Why, you do not like her either?"

That was a stupid question. No one liked Sahana. Amma did not care for long lectures. She conveyed her complex thoughts in very few words.

> "Lakshmi, be careful. Sahana's father's money knows no bounds. They are powerful people. Don't get in her way, no matter how terrible she becomes."

From a very young age, amma told me I was capable of doing anything in the world. Staying out of the way of powerful, important people was the one limitation on life she truly believed. I assured her I would be careful. She examined my face to make sure I understood the message. There was no need for her to repeat herself.

Nana came home early from the fields that evening. After we all finished dinner, baby sister and I spent a few hours playing outside. She would run as fast as she could to tire herself out, take a break, tire herself again, take another break, and so on. It suited me well as I could study while she sprinted into the night.

While we were outside, amma told nana about my bad luck in being placed with Sahana. With a look of equal concern, nana made me assure him I would be extra careful around her. I told him I would, and that if necessary, I would do everything and put her name on the report. He nodded his approval of my plan.

> "It is hard, Lakshmi. They are born to privilege, yet we must do their work. Just be careful."

> "I know nana, I know."

Satisfied I understood the depths of Sahana's control, he asked me to tell him about what I had learned in university that day. He fell asleep to the soothing powers of the knowledge his daughter had acquired. The business principles, the chemistry, the English poetry, the world.

To impress Go-wind's rich family, Alpa's parents borrowed money from a loan shark to cover the cost of the clothes she wore for the engagement. Normally villagers would be very careful in letting others wear their jewelry, but everyone knew that Alpa was the one person who could be trusted. Under mountains of gold and precious stones, villagers helped cover up her pimples, scars, and tan with whatever makeup they could gather. By the end of their fussing, Alpa wore 4 meters of cloth, enough jewelry to weigh down a ship, and enough makeup to paint the village.

I thought Alpa looked like a clown, especially with fat Go-wind by her side. He had become so large that the local tailor had to use twice the normal amount of cloth to sew clothes that fit over Go-wind's giant belly. Standing side by side, Alpa constantly complained they were wider than they were tall. She might have been right.

By comparison, engagements are simpler than weddings. The priest says a few chants, the puja lasts less than two hours, and everything is done in one day. Still, the stimulus was too much for Go-wind. On three separate occasions, he got so frustrated that he tried hitting the priest, hitting his father, or stamping on Alpa's feet. I was sitting close enough to know he passed gas each time as well.

After the ceremony had finished and most of the guests had congratulated the newly engaged couple, Alpa waddled her way over to me.

"Lakshmi!"

"I know."

"They were sooo smelly, Lakshmi!"

She cupped her hands over her mouth and blew a spray of air through the cracks to form the perfect imitation. We doubled over in laughter at the sight of his animal-like shrieks at his aunt for not preparing his favorite sweets. In a mix of disbelief and giggles, Alpa recreated the sound of his gas to the beat of his monkey cries.

"Just think Lakshmi! In less than a month, that man will be my husband."

Chapter 7

"Okay, so we all agree on the plan?" I asked Jayesh and Nallini.

They nodded somberly. The three of us had decided to carefully approach Sahana and ask how she would like to do the project. We fully expected she would find a way to insult us all. We hoped that she would ask us to do the entire thing and leave her be. The less time we spent with her, the better.

We found Sahana after class sitting in the professor's common area. She made it a point to show the professors she was entitled to use their facilities at her whim. On her nicer days, she would even allow them to sit in her presence. As she thundered her way out of the room, Jayesh tapped her on the shoulder.

"Sorry madam," he began.

"What do you want, you vermin!?"

"I…uh…I…"

His body went rigid in fear. Her eyes could turn someone to stone. Giving the poor soul a break, I stepped in Jayesh's place.

"Hello, Sahana."

"What do you want, peasant girl?"

I cringed. No one had called me peasant girl since teacher.

"Jayesh, Nallini and I are your project mates for accounting, and…"

"So?"

As she eyed me with disgust, I became increasingly aware that I had not bathed in three days due to lack of water. Somehow I forced out the words asking how to proceed.

> "Well peasant girl, you will do the work and put my name on the report. FIRST."

She walked away without giving us a chance to reply. As soon as she was out of earshot, Nallini pumped her fists and jumped in the air for joy.

The report was much more time consuming than going to class and studying our notes. Jayesh and Nallini would take turns reading the material aloud, and I would write the main points down. The assistant dean assigned us 50 long accounting tables to complete. I finished each in fewer than five minutes. The three of us each reviewed the entirety of the report, making corrections along the way. On completion, we took care in copying Sahana's signature as the first author of the report. It pained me to do that, but I had made a promise to my parents.

Before the start of the final examination, the assistant dean came by to collect our reports. I had the report sitting in front me, and was prepared to hand it in myself. Sahana whizzed by and snatched the report from my hands, giving me a paper cut. As I looked at the blood creeping up from beneath my skin, Sahana threw the report pages at the assistant dean. I looked over at Nallini and Jayesh, who were both gripping their pencils so hard that their hands turned white.

The final examination was quite easy. In four hours, we were to complete a ten-page essay and 100 simple accounting problems. It took me two hours to fill in my examination booklet and another half-hour to check everything over. I knew I should use the last 90 minutes to ensure everything was perfect, but this was the last of my examinations after a long first term, and I was dying to go help Alpa avoid another clothing disaster for her wedding. With a few final flicks of my pencil, I finished my work and was the first person to turn my paper in. Sahana followed behind me.

"Giving up so soon, peasant girl?"

I did not bother to hear her insults continue. Placing my booklet down on the table first, I turned around to go find a true friend.

"What about this one?" Alpa asked as she held up a giant roll of silk fabric.

"No, you'll look like a mango."

"Okay, what about this one?"

"Who wants to wear a black sari for their wedding?"

Alpa sighed and threw the material on the floor, already frustrated with the duties of married life.

"Lakshmi, I hate this!"

"Black is not a good color, Alpa."

"No! Not that. Go-wind doesn't understand what is happening. Last night, he asked his amma when our engagement party will be!"

I couldn't help but laugh at the thought of monkey Go-wind demanding an engagement party and a banana.

"LAKSHMI! It's not funny!"

"It is a little funny."

Alpa pouted. It was the same expression she used when her mother refused to serve her a fifth portion of rice.

"Oh, come on. At least you will be able to do whatever you want. It will be so easy to trick Go-wind! Think of all the chocolate you can buy with his parents' money!"

Alpa stood tall like a national soldier at those words.

"Speaking of chocolate..."

She pulled out another bar, which had melted all over her things.

"Try it!"

The brown half-liquid looked disgusting. It reminded me of the public lavatory.

"No thanks."
"Okay, more for me!"
"Chee!"

I got up to wipe the chocolate from Alpa's hand, and told her to come find a nice wedding sari. Without solicitation, she sang words of gratitude in my direction.

"Oh Lakshmi, thank you for being my friend! I don't even feel sad when you are with me."

In the reflection of a pool of water that had gathered from the previous night's storm, I saw my dear friend happily licking her chocolate covered fingers. I could not help but stare with a humble appreciation at how easy it was for Alpa to find joy in the throes of such an awful prospect.

Amma and nana were such a guiding force of wisdom and tranquility in my life. Through the shaking reflection, I peered at my friend whose only guidance was a purity that bestowed her heart. She was the one having a lavish wedding. I was the one who was truly grateful for life.

Chapter 8

Exam results were in, and rankings for the university would be posted tomorrow. I had passed every one of my exams at or near the top of the class. All that stood in my way to first rank was accounting, which was my best subject. The assistant dean walked inside the classroom and heaved the score sheets onto Professor Gopal's desk.

"I need to see Lakshmi and Sahana. The rest of you, come and find your marks."

I looked over at Sahana. It was the first time I could see concern in her face. Out of the corner of my eye, I saw Nallini and Jayesh race to the front of the classroom and fight for their score sheets in a crazed fury. Sahana and I walked silently down the hall to the dean's office - a small, dark hole situated in one of the crumbling annex buildings. He closed the door behind us and told us to sit down. For once, Sahana did as she was told.

Reaching into a drawer of his rotting desk, the dean produced two blank sheets of paper and two pencils. He told us to write our names, dates of birth, and one paragraph about our favorite class. Very timidly, I asked permission to speak. He nodded somberly.

"Sir, I am not positive on my date of birth only. My amma said it was around 5 March on the Western calendar."

"What a pathetic peasant girl!" Sahana mocked.

The dean told me 5 March was acceptable.

I started writing without hesitation. Sahana demanded to know what was happening. Something gave the dean a new sense of courage, and he stood up to her for the first time.

"Sit down, Sahana!"

"I will not be told what to do!"

The dean argued no further. He grabbed my sheet of paper from underneath my busy hand and left the room, leaving us in total confusion.

She started pacing around the office. In between her groans and curse words, my mind was reeling with the possibilities of what could be wrong. Within seconds, I convinced myself that I was being convicted of a crime and Sahana was the only other suspect.

While I prepared myself for a mental breakdown, the dean and president entered the room. They were accompanied by an older man who was wearing a three-piece suit complete with a handkerchief and matching cane. He looked like one of the characters in the American film. As soon as Sahana turned to face the three of them, her confidence evaporated into the humid air.

> "What the hell are you doing here, papa!?"

My eyes widened to the size of coconuts. Why would they call Sahana's father to the university?

> "It seems that one of you has purposely failed the exam and one of you has received the highest mark in the class," the president said.

I stopped breathing for a few seconds. Sahana started to scream.

> "Well of course *I* was the one who got the highest mark. Do you think a lowly Shudra girl could beat me!? Someone who is practically an *untouchable*?"

I saw the silver arrow of the word 'untouchable' pierce through my heart. The pain and anguish that word contained was something Sahana could not possibly understand. Like so many others, she freely used it as a weapon of destruction.

The president cleared his throat. He turned to face Sahana's father saying he had collected a fresh sample of my writing.

> "It matches the writing on both the top examination and the report. However, the report and the exam list your daughter as its primary author."

I slowly sank into my chair. Nallini, Jayesh and I had signed Sahana's name thinking it would save us from misery. Now it might ruin my life.

Sahana's father demanded to see the papers, muttering something as the President handed them over. The sound Sahana's father's giant shoes made echoed like canons. He commanded me to stand. I did as I was told.

> "I do not believe in this caste nonsense as my daughter does. If you tell me this is your work, I will believe you. I will believe my daughter switched your names on the papers."

> "Daddy!" Sahana screamed at the top of her lungs.

She charged at him, stopping centimeters from his face. I was sure the fire from her breath could be felt all the way to Sri Lanka.

> "How can you believe a disgusting peasant over my words?!"

Her screams were so loud I temporarily lost my hearing. Sahana's father ignored the shrieking monster, keeping his attention focused on me.

> "Did you write these papers?"

It was the most scared I had ever been in my life. My mind flashed back to amma and nana's concerned faces as they begged me to stay out of Sahana's way. Nallini, Jayesh and I had spent nearly 100 hours pulling together that final project. We wrote Sahana's name to honor the promise we made to our pleading parents.

As the imposing man with the expensive Western clothes continued to stare down on my tiny frame, I thought about all of the sleepless nights of studying, the countless hours working, and the anguish of hunger amma and nana imparted on our family to save up so much money. My parents wanted me to appease Sahana, but this was different. If I gave Sahana credit once more, I would surely be rusticated from the university. I would be thrown on to the streets to beg like the peasant everyone said I was. There would be no better life.

Barely moving my lips, I whispered one word.

"Yes."

Sahana's father nodded. The look of disappointment in his face was one that let us all know it was commonplace. Sahana was her father's living regret. Without another word in my direction, he grabbed Sahana's hand and dragged her out the door. As they passed by the president, her father said one final sentence.

"My daughter will not be returning to university."

The president peered down at his shoes to avoid eye contact with the domineering and conflicting pair. Sahana screamed with an intense vile that she would never let this university live in peace. Halfway down the hall, she kicked her father straight in the groin, and managed to break free. Making it an arm's reach from me, she caught my eye, sending me an expression of unearned hatred that every impoverished villager has seen at least once in their life.

"You will pay for this, you peasant girl!"

I was awarded first rank that term.

Chapter 9

Alpa's wedding was beautiful. Though she was not the prettiest girl in her the village, she was the kindest person anyone had ever met. Everyone did whatever possible to make her special day the biggest and brightest celebration of the season. The food stretched out as far as the eye could see, reflecting the rainbow of decorations and ornaments Alpa's father brought from the fanciest stores Chennai proper had to offer.

Amma, nana and baby sister came with me to the wedding. As a gift to Alpa, we had picked out a book we found in an old colonial-era bookstore; it was about how chocolate was made. Considering the amount of food and sweets we were fed, the book was well worth the money. Baby sister entertained all of the guests with stories about how she rode Alpa's bike. Nana looked happy just to relax. Amma and I spent much of the wedding helping Alpa in and out of her six wedding saris.

A priest was hired from Chennai proper, who executed the puja at a pace even Go-wind could understand. Go-wind managed to survive all the way to the end of the first day before having any major outbursts. All was well until a guest accidentally stepped on his foot. He went crazy knocking over chairs, throwing food at the guests, and punching the air. Fortunately, his father managed to calm him down.

Despite Go-wind's tantrums, the air was generally jovial. By the end of day two, even Alpa seemed happy about the situation. We managed to sneak away from the guests for a few minutes before I had to leave. I brought our family gift along.

> "Oh my God! Lakshmi! It's perfect. Now I can make my own chocolate!"

>> "Well, I don't think it is so easy, Alpa. Maybe one day we will go to the real America and see how they do it."

Alpa jumped like a child at the suggestion, telling me she would count the days until our journey. Giving her a kiss on the cheek, I congratulated my newly married friend. We agreed to meet at our usual spot next Saturday. After one final hand squeeze, I watched Alpa waddle over to Go-wind, her husband.

My second term of university started soon after Alpa's wedding. Now that the halls were rid of Sahana, a new air of excitement and freedom overcame everyone. Strangely, the examination disaster affirmed my desire to specialize my studies in accounting. There was something satisfying about being in classes where the ultimate goal was to have total equality on both sides of the ledger.

Sahana had forever scared Jayesh out of accounting, but Nallini decided that she wanted to continue. We knew we worked well together, and we became close very quickly. She was of the same caste as me, which gave us solace.

As I became increasingly immersed in my studies, I noticed my relationship with Alpa slipping away. Our weekly meetings by the tree lessened to the point that seeing Alpa became the exception, not the standard. I tried a few times to go over to her and Go-wind's house. Every time I walked inside, burly Go-wind would stomp to the door to tell me Alpa was out shopping.

Second term finished without any major events or interruptions. For me, it was a semester of bliss. Nana had found a new employer who was paying double the normal wages, so I could afford to fully concentrate on my studies. Nallini and I had great discussions about all of the things we learned in school. Baby sister and amma kept each other company during the day, and were able to split much of the housework to lessen the load.

After another grueling set of final examinations, Nallini and I decided to wander to the cluster of shops that faced the university campus.

Her parents had given her a modest sum of money to buy a new pair of sandals as a gift for finishing her first year at university. A proper cement roof covered the shops in the interior. Knowing the sum of money Nallini had was too small to buy anything from the interior shops, I began walking in the direction of the cheaper stores that were grouped together under a massive piece of blue plastic. Nallini, a wild spirit, stopped me.

"We are in our university saris. No one will know we are poor," she said.

With the confidence of Nallini's boldness, we changed directions for the interior. We stopped in a shop too cheap for the richest that was still too expensive for us. Nallini wasn't sure what kind of sandals she wanted, and allowed the shop owner to spend a few minutes describing the different kinds he had in stock.

"What about this one?" Nallini asked me.

"I don't like the red..."

Before I had a chance to finish my reply, we heard a scream on the other side of the shop.

Running around, I gasped when I saw the scene.

"Alpa?"

Trembling like a leaf, Alpa turned her head and slowly picked herself off of the floor. Govind was standing over her. I struggled to catch my breath when I saw her face. Alpa had two black eyes and giant gash across her forehead. She grabbed her hip and inhaled, revealing a missing front tooth.

"Oh my God, Alpa!" I said, rushing toward her.

Govind stepped in between the two of us.

"You touch not my wife!"

He grabbed Alpa's hand and pulled her towards the door. I managed to wedge my way in between them to prevent Alpa from leaving.

"What happened?"

"I just fell on the floor over there, that's all."

The fat bastard dragged my injured friend across the store by her hair. When I tried to go after them, Nallini grabbed my arm and motioned for me to keep quiet. With strength I did not know he possessed, Govind pushed Alpa and disappeared into the crowd. I turned back at Nallini, demanding to know why she held me back.

"My sister went through the same thing. You were going make it worse for her."

Nallini made sure Alpa and Govind headed west before she let go of my arm to allow me to run east. Through the dizzying balls of light the milling shoppers transformed into, I ran as fast as I could. Above, the false security of the concrete turned into the familiar blue plastic roof before opening into a misleadingly calm sky.

I pushed my bike to its limits, slamming it to the ground with an uncharacteristic force when I reached home. Amma jumped up at the sight of me. Before she even had a chance to ask how my exams had gone, I described the details of the horrible scene I had just witnessed.

"Her face was black and blue, amma. What should we do?"

"Lakshmi...I'm so sorry. I don't think there is anything we can do..."

"What do you mean!? He's beating her, amma!"

Amma nodded empathetically as she peered outside in the direction of her old village. Without her saying anything, I could immediately tell she had gone through this with one of her friends. Afraid to hear the answer, afraid to not hear the answer, I asked what her friend had done.

"She tried to run away."

"What happened to her?"

"He killed her."

I slammed my eyes shut. I had to help Alpa. I had to save her.

Chapter 10

Nana and amma wanted to help, but without uncorrupt law enforcement, a reliable court system, or money, there was nothing they could do.

"How did your sister force her husband to stop?" I asked Nallini.

"She threatened to hire someone to slit his throat at night."

Even in Alpa's angriest state, I could never see her making such a threat. Govind would not understand, anyway.

After five failed attempts to get past the front door of Alpa and Govind's house, I finally caught a glimpse of her beaten face. Through Govind's best attempt to block Alpa from view, I shouted three key words.

"By the tree!"

I only hoped she knew what I meant.

She did. The following Saturday, Alpa managed to sneak out of the house to meet me at the creek. A few boys were playing close by. As

Alpa walked down the dirt path, one of the boys cried out at the sight of her.

"Gross! You have something growing on your face!"

Alpa looked down at the ground. When she was finally within reach, I stood up and gave her a hug. The something on her face was an open wound from Govind's latest beating. Without proper medical supplies, it looked like a giant leech had spurted from beneath the surface of her skin.

My loving touch opened a dam and Alpa's tears rolled without control. Govind had started beating her as soon as they had moved into the new house. She did not know how to cook like his mother, repair the house like his father, or sing like his aunt. He could not keep a job for more than a few days, and took his failures out on her. In the months they had been married, he had beat her all but eight days. Four of those eight days he was out of town.

Divorce was out of the question as that meant Alpa and her family would be ostracized from the community. She tried to tell her parents what was happening, but they did not know what to do. Between the dowry, the engagement party and the wedding, they were in debt and could not afford to help her.

It was unnerving to see Alpa so broken. We had known each other since we were eight. No matter how many times someone made fun of her weight, told her she was stupid, or announced how ugly she was, Alpa rebounded in minutes. She had a remarkable faith in people. Nothing had ever kept her down, until now.

She was not feeling well, and asked me to fetch her water from the creek. When I came back, she was leaning against the tree, vomiting.

"Alpa! Are you okay?"

"It has been happening for a few months, Lakshmi. I

think my stomach can't handle the beatings..."

Alpa told me Govind would beat her extra hard tonight for sneaking out. Still, we stayed by the tree for a few more hours. As the sun set on the horizon, we reluctantly picked ourselves off of the cool, soothing grass.

"Don't forget me Lakshmi."

"How could I ever forget you, Alpa? I will be waiting for you here next Saturday, okay?"

Her once pure and smiling face now carried the emotional and physical scars of a broken spirit. With a heavy heart, I clutched my hands to my chest as she turned and walked back to the injustice.

For the next three Saturdays, I waited for Alpa, but she did not come. Soon after, I started my second year of university. It was so difficult concentrating on anything knowing that Alpa lived in a constant state of fear. How could anyone be cruel enough to hurt someone so sweet and unassuming?

I would spend hours replaying the terrible scene from the shoe shop - seeing Alpa pick herself up from the floor, and defend the man who was making her life a living hell. What would Govind do next? How could Alpa reason with someone who had so much anger, and so little compassion?

Nearly a month had passed since Alpa and I last met by the tree. The turmoil of not knowing how she was took my brain hostage. One moment I was sitting quietly by Nallini, the next I found myself outside Alpa's house. After surveying the ground, I spotted a heavy branch, and practiced swinging it a few times.

Any other Indian household would allow guests to walk straight inside. I chose to knock on the dark wooden front door. Expecting Govind to answer, I held the branch up, ready to hit him with the strength of every woman, ready to kill the bastard.

Alpa opened the door. Just six months prior, she had the reaction time of an ostrich. Now, she instinctively scurried away like a mouse. Finally realizing who was at the door, Alpa gave me a big a hug and told me to keep quiet. Govind was sleeping. I motioned for her to step outside.

"How are you!?" I asked urgently.

"I'm pregnant."

I gasped and looked down at her belly. Due to her size, it was impossible to tell.

"How many months?"

"Almost five, I think. I was scared to tell Govind. He has been a lot better since I did."

I expelled the breath I had been holding in for weeks. I wanted to stay with Alpa longer. I wanted to bring her home with me for safekeeping. She assured me that was not necessary. Govind had barely touched her since she told him about the pregnancy.

"Come back in four months to see my baby!"

I told her I would, knowing all I could truly do was pray my friend into safety.

Chapter 11

Despite the gravity of Govind's past behavior, eventually my studies began to overwhelm everything else. Doing well in school was a matter of life or death.

Every professor I had ever met made it a point to remind the class how fierce the competition was in India. If we screwed up even one term, we would not get a job. There were literally millions of

Lakshmi's and Jayesh's and Nallini's in India to replace us.

Nallini and I did not take these warnings lightly. The majority of the students in our university, in every Indian university, were men. Many offices openly declared they would not hire a woman for any position other than a secretary. Whatever the competition was for our male classmates after graduation, it would be exponentially harder for us. Women had to prove much more than mere scholarly achievements.

Nallini and I devised a system of perpetual studying. We would take turns reading aloud the information we had so vigorously written down during class. After going through the entire set of notes, we would pick random pages and ask each other to fill in the blanks. Every time one of us got even one word wrong, we restarted at the beginning. Our brains became walking repositories of all the information presented.

Our hard work paid off. In the third term ranks, I once again placed first, and Nallini came in with a close second. By December of 1958, we were on our way to achieving the unthinkable: claiming the top two slots in the entire school, as women. Together, we felt like we ruled the university. We felt like we ruled the world. I knew we would be the women to change India.

I knocked on the door. Once, twice, thrice. No answer. Peering over to Alpa's room, I saw the window was covered. I walked around the entire building looking for any sign of life. There was nothing. With a tired sigh, I set down the small dish of sweets amma had sent over. Alpa's mother had stopped by a few days prior to tell us the good news. All toes and fingers in place, responding to sound and light – Alpa gave birth to a healthy baby girl. Her mother was elated.

Her mother asked me to visit Alpa the following weekend. Govind would be out of town visiting relatives in Madurai, leaving Alpa and her mother alone with the baby. So there I was.

Eventually I conceded home. Much to my surprise, Alpa's mother was at our house. By the puffiness of her eyes, I could tell she had been crying for quite some time. Quietly, amma stood up and guided me away. She told me to go to Alpa's parents' house immediately. Alpa was there. She would explain.

> "Amma, what is going on?"
>
> "Go to Alpa, Lakshmi. This is something I have no right to tell you."

Not bothering to take off my sandals, I ran through the door and straight to Alpa's old room. She was curled up in a ball at the foot of her cot in the same way baby sister would to block out the world. Except for belabored breaths, there was no sign of life in her body.

The room had the unmistakable stench of despair that was all too common in our lives. I called out to Alpa, hoping my voice would be enough to prompt even the slightest hint of movement. There was nothing. For hours, we sat in total silence. It did not take long for me to notice her baby girl was not in the room.

Alpa spoke without warning.

> "He killed her, Lakshmi. Girls are worthless, boys are best, Govind said. He screamed when she cried."

Her breathing quickened such that I thought she was hyperventilating.

> "First he slapped her on the face. That would make her cry more. Then he put a cover on her nose to stop the noise. That would make her cry still more. I begged him to stop, Lakshmi. He didn't care; he didn't want to hear the baby's cries."

Alpa stayed awake with her precious baby for two straight days and nights. Govind's cruelties resurfaced as soon as he saw it was a girl that had exited the womb.

> "Lakshmi, she was so warm, so nice. But I felt very tired the third day. I fell asleep. When I woke up…there was so much blood, Lakshmi. Govind went away. I don't think he's coming back."

Alpa rolled over and fell silent again. I left the room before sinking to the floor and breaking down into tears. In all of the violence I had seen the police inflict on the villagers, in all of the killings employers committed against farmers, in all of the rapes and cases of domestic violence women cried about openly in the streets, nothing hit me as hard as Alpa's words.

That week, I missed class every single day. Alpa's mother and I would take turns staying in the room with her - reading to her, sitting with her, being silent with her. Alpa would not eat, she would not drink, she would not move or talk. It was as though her body were an empty container.

I begged her to come back to me. All of my love and gratitude for my dear friend did nothing to revive her listless body that had lost the will to live. After five days, Alpa left her bed only twice. The first time I was there to help her vomit the only food she had eaten in three days. The second time was the one hour her mother and I accidentally left her alone.

Alpa walked to her parents' tiny kitchen, found their biggest knife, and slit her own wrists. Her mother found her unconscious minutes later. None of us had the money to bribe the hospital staff to admit her ahead of the other patients.

On the steps of a government hospital, G.R. Alpa Krishnan, my best friend in the whole world, died on 29 January 1959.

Chapter 12

Food lost its taste, school seemed meaningless, and the voices of the people I loved were empty and distant. It hurt to touch people, yet it also hurt not to be touched. I could not bear to stay awake for more than a few hours, yet I could not sleep for more than a few minutes. My mind was stuck somewhere between earth and hell. Govind's family bribed the police to not file a report, and to make sure the courts would never hear the case. There was no recourse in that world. That was India.

Though she immediately recognized my torment, amma also knew the pain would eventually become tolerable. At some point, she knew I would want to resume living. Despite having attended school for only two days in her life, amma understood there would be major consequences if I continued missing classes. She borrowed my bike one afternoon and rode to the university. Finding Nallini in the massive crowd of students, she explained what had happened. Thanks to amma and Nallini, I received medical leave for the term without having to set foot on school grounds.

Emerging from that bout of depression was like learning how to walk again. Some days I could make it through without help. Other days I was less stable and required constant attention. I would often have a day that made me question the point in living. Why fight so hard when everything that matters is so easily stripped away?

Baby sister did not understand what had happened. She did, however, understand how sad I had become, and spent my days of depression singing to me or stroking my hair. Every night on his way home from work, nana would stop by the creek and bring me one single flower from the riverbed.

It took the collective efforts of my amma, nana and baby sister to ensure I would not let myself die. Slowly but surely, my family resuscitated me from devastation.

One afternoon, nana came home early. I was having one of my better days, and offered to prepare him some tea.

"Could we take a walk instead?" he asked.

"Of course, nana, to anywhere you wish."

Spending time alone with nana was a rare treasure.

We walked into the fields, continuing as the footpath faded. Nana made a few light remarks about the weather, the crops, and amma's excellent cooking. After nearly 45 minutes, he turned into the thick brush, leading us farther into the countryside than I had ever ventured.

We came upon a small abandoned shack in the middle of the thicket. The roof was a patchwork of ancient metal scraps, straw, and mud. Two of the three walls had fallen, exposing an interior filled with random assortments of cloth, paper and trash. A family of bush rats had burrowed through a remnant of cloth, leaving the tattered remains a haven for mold and grime.

It took me a few moments to realize the crumbling structure meant something to nana. He stared at the remains with an intense look of contemplation. His massive hand was not enough to shield me from the tears I saw stream down his worn face.

"Lakshmi, this is where I grew up."

Nana never spoke of his childhood; it was amma who had recounted his stories to baby sister and me.

"There was once a small river that ran through these woods," nana said.

His father grew up in the heart of the city slums.

"At a young age my father decided to move out here, to

return to nature. I would have to walk an hour to find odd chores to save for a school uniform."

The same school I had attended, amma had told me.

"One day, my father returned home early and caught me with my prized clothes. He did not know that I had quit work for an education. He beat me to a pulp and dragged me all the way to the headmaster. *'Don't you **ever** let my son back into this house of lies!'* he screamed."

"I'm sorry. I didn't know..."

"It was a different time, a different life. I do not wish to make you feel guilty. I am so proud of you, Lakshmi."

Simply replying with a 'thank you' was insufficient for the power those words carried. I slowly turned my head to gaze at my incredible father, who was lost in the crumbling shack before us.

"Lakshmi, after my father pulled me out of school, I did not want to carry on living. It was the same when I lost my two brothers. When Alpa died, a part of you died with her spirit."

He was right. It felt like a piece of my heart was missing.

"What you must remember is that Alpa also gave you a piece of her. One day, someone will live their life with a piece of you."

"What do you mean, nana?"

"Lakshmi, sometimes we do not live this life for our own opportunities. Sometimes, we live this life for the opportunities we bring to others."

Chapter 13

At the end of the term, Nallini came by to tell me she made first rank.

"It was easy without you getting in the way!"

We spent the next few days catching up on all of the university gossip. The lightness of our conversation felt so natural. Long walks on the beach, exploring different parts of the city, enjoying an occasional snack on the street - spending a carefree month with Nallini was exactly what I needed to start enjoying life again.

Just as quickly as the holidays came, they ended. Nallini had advanced a semester ahead of me, which meant we would not be taking any more classes at the same time. Even though she had given me a thorough explanation of all the upcoming material, I was determined not to become lazy.

Before my first class back started, I reached the classroom early. I sat at a desk in the front and center, closed my eyes, clenched my fists, and did my best to…

"Excuse me…" someone interrupted.

A wide-eyed man my age was staring down at me.

"I was wondering what you were doing just now?"
"Clearing my thoughts."
"Ah, I see. Is it okay if I sit down?"
"You already did."
"And you are?" he asked, ignoring my comment.
"Um, Lakshmi."
"I'm Ram. Pleasure to meet you, *um* Lakshmi."

It was strange to be approached by someone of the opposite sex. I looked around and saw a few people staring at me. Rumors would certainly not help my concentration in my first term back. Thankfully, the professor walked in and immediately started the lecture.

After 90 minutes of dutiful note taking, I gathered up my things and ran out of the classroom, hoping Ram would not pursue me.

"Lakshmi!" Ram shouted.

I kept walking, hoping to find Nallini. She was nowhere in sight.

"Lakshmi, wait!" Ram shouted again.

This time, he grabbed my arm.

"What are you doing!?"

Realizing he caused a public commotion, Ram put up his hands like a criminal caught robbing a jewelry store.

"I'm sorry! I keep forgetting people don't do that here."

"Where is here? Chennai?"

"No, India. I just moved here with my family. I'm from London."

"Oh, I didn't know...your Tamil is really good."

He explained how both of his parents refused to speak to him in English in case his father, an industrial engineer, was ever transferred back to Chennai. The transfer had happened a few months back, and Ram reluctantly followed since he could not afford London, otherwise.

"I am really sorry for grabbing your arm like that."

"No, it's fine. Don't worry." I answered with an unusual air of forgiveness.

"Look...I'm new to Chennai. Is there anyone who can show me around?"

My body temperature rose quickly. Ram was handsome, tall and fair, I noticed.

"I could show you around," I said without thinking.

"Great! I'll see you this afternoon? 4 o'clock outside the main campus entrance?"

Ram smiled and took off in a gallop. I only managed an incoherent sound before realizing the trouble I had landed myself in.

"Are you crazy? You can't go alone with him!" Nallini exclaimed.

"Okay, so you'll come then?"

"One day back and already you've found this mischief!"

"Great, so it's settled, you'll come with me!"

"I missed you, Lakshmi."

Nallini was always excited for an adventure. Ram looked surprised but happy to see us walking arm-in-arm towards him after classes.

"Am I lucky enough to have two tour guides today?"

"Oh my God! He's so handsome!" Nallini squealed in my ear.

We spent the afternoon showing Ram around the university. He had only been to India twice before moving back, and found everything fascinating. Why do some neighborhoods speak Telugu and not Tamil? Who decided to make Chennai the capital of Tamil Nadu? No one had ever asked us such difficult questions; we were rediscovering our own home through the eyes of a stranger.

It was close to dusk before the three of us decided to part ways. Ram graciously thanked us for showing him around and putting up with all of his questions. Nallini let him give her a quick kiss on the cheek.

I settled for one of my dear Alpa's American handshakes.

School in the UK was much less focused on memorization. After a year of studying with Nallini, I realized I worked much better in the company of another person, so Ram became a regular fixture in my study routine. Together, we would spend hours sitting in the small, cramped library, pouring over our lecture notes and copies of the textbooks Ram's father could afford to purchase.

As time passed, I noticed an undeniable physical connection…between Ram and Nallini. Though he made a good study partner, and though I had no experience in the matter, I knew Ram and I were not a good match. He needed someone with a better sense of humor, more attitude, and more spontaneity. I needed someone with more security.

"Will you tell anyone about me and Ram?" Nallini asked.

"Of course not!"

And so Ram and Nallini commenced a risky "love romance." I did not have a clue what they did behind closed doors. All that mattered was that I had the support of two loyal friends. Together, we formed a perfect triangle of security.

Chapter 14

Ram and I were in the university library reviewing our exercises from a particularly difficult lecture. Nallini sat next to us studying notes for a more advanced class. Right as I was about to solve the hardest problem from the set, I heard a bang at the other end of the hall. Mukesh, one of the boys in my village, stood up from a pile of books he had knocked over.

"Lakshmi! Lakshmi! Come quickly!"

"Mukesh, what's wrong?"

"Just come quickly, Lakshmi!"

Not wanting to slow me down, Mukesh gave me directions on where to go. It sounded like the field where nana worked. I was not sure I wanted to see what lay ahead.

After a 20-minute ride, the dirt paths began to melt away to thick grass. Nana's old house was less than a ten-minute bike ride from where I eventually came to a halt. In the distance, I could hear vacant wails that signified deep sorrow. The voice was unmistakable – it was amma.

Time slowed down and every noise of the Indian terrain was amplified to deafening levels. A huge crowd formed a circle around the wailing that was coming from the center.
Hundreds of whispers and clicking tongues rang through my ears as I forced my legs to continue carrying me forward.

"Let me through. I am Lakshmi," I could barely say.

Unable to digest the scene at first, I felt my body crash to the floor as my brain processed what was happening. Amma sat in the middle of circle, crying and rocking her body in an uncontrolled trance. Her sari was caked in dirt that had mixed with blood to form a death-filled mud. She gently stroked nana's lifeless head, which exposed amma's blood-soaked sari through the gaping hole in the center of the forehead.

My nana, my hero, died on 20 September 1959.

Chapter 15

It was obvious that nana had been murdered. When the villagers stormed the police station insisting on an investigation, the officers threw everyone out and demanded nearly a year's wages in bribes before they would lift a finger. Having no other choice, two of nana's friends took some twine from a nearby oxcart and strapped nana's body to my bike to wheel him back to our house.

After a two-hour journey, I helped amma into some clean clothes, and begged her to take rest. September in Chennai is one of the hottest months of the year, which left me no choice but to work fast. Nana's body would soon start to decompose.

It took all night for me to properly clean our house and wash a fresh set of nana's clothes. At dawn, I grabbed the can that held my parents' life savings and emptied every last coin. I walked into town and suffered the usual taunts and insults of being a poor Shudra woman as I made the arrangements to give nana a proper funeral. He deserved to pass into the next world with dignity.

The priest instructed me to remove the bloody shirt nana was wearing and bring the body down to the beach to be prepared for cremation. As I lifted the shirt from his torso, a small piece of paper fluttered out of the breast pocket. I grabbed the paper and threw it on nana's side of the cot. Two of the neighborhood boys helped me carry nana to the beach where the priest was waiting. Amma managed to hold herself up and come with baby sister.

After a humble puja, the priest gathered and placed nana's ashes in a blessed urn.

"Let us spread his ashes in the ocean," amma said.

"No, amma. Nana should be spread elsewhere," I replied.

It did not matter that the river of nana's childhood had been reduced to a tiny stream. Nana had become a man and discovered his purpose in life at the site of his childhood. The piece of nana that I now held within me was telling me he wanted to pass on to the next world there.

It took amma a few minutes to summon the courage to open the urn.

Slowly pouring the last physical remains of my father, she collapsed into a heap and cried to the high heavens. The three of us remained with nana through the night, afraid of what lay ahead.

Eight months prior, amma slowly nursed me back from depression. Now, it was my turn to do the same for her. Taking care of her barely gave me enough time to think, let alone feel sad. Thankfully, the neighbors, and Nallini and Ram spared food, clothing, and water. It was enough to allow me to spend every minute by amma's side for the first few months after nana died.

If part of me died with Alpa, half of amma must have died with nana. Her eyes became an empty black, and her hair turned completely gray. She lost a third of her body weight that season. I did my best to feed her, bathe her, and change her clothes. Nallini brought me books from the university library, which I would read to amma every day. But after three months, amma's eyes were as vacant as the day nana died. I did not lose only nana that afternoon. I lost amma, too.

"What do you mean you are quitting school?" Nallini asked.

"What other choice do I have?" I replied.

"Shall I ask my father if you can borrow money?" Ram offered.

Ram was being kind in the gesture, not understanding why I could not accept. Taking loans to stay in school was not an option. Debts in the UK were managed by a bank. In India, debts were managed by a person's whims, and a person's whims were too often brutal. I could not put my family at that kind of risk.

My old jobs at the seamstress' shop and the farm did not pay enough to feed three people every day. Field workers were paid by the amount of grain and rice they carried. There was no way I would make anything close to nana's wages with that job. Besides, I had an education, at least by relative standards.

I went through amma's modest sari collection, and picked out the nicest outfit I could find. With a lot of scrubbing and some twine, I was able to patch my only pair of sandals to be passable.

As I pleated my sari, I noticed something on amma and nana's cot. It was the piece of paper that had been in nana's shirt, which I threw in my bag. Lightly whispering to amma and baby sister, I grabbed my bloodstained bike and rode into town.

My first stop was the university. Surely they had to have some kind of administrative job available to former students. Reaching the familiar campus entrance, I marched upstairs to the offices and asked for a job application. The man behind the desk looked me over.

"What are your qualifications, madam?"

"Higher secondary, first rank. Three terms here, first rank, sir."

"Why did you drop out?"

"Sir, father passing. I must earn wages to support my family."

He laughed as though I were an imbecile.

"You are not a man. Go get married. It is your husband's duty to take care of you and your family! Next!"

He looked right past me waiting to help the next person who shoved their way to the front of the queue. I mentally slapped myself out of the insult. Waving my hands in front of the man's face, I repeated myself.

"Give me a job application."

"You are not so ugly; you can find a decent suitor."

This time, I screamed at the top of my lungs.

"GIVE ME A JOB APPLICATION."

The man looked startled and embarrassed. Deciding not to question further, he turned and grabbed a form from a giant pile and threw it at my face.

"Place it in the corner box when you're finished," he instructed.

Inside the box lay at least 500 applications. There were two positions being advertised.

As I left, the man behind the counter whistled at me. I turned to face him, expecting another offense directed at my gender.

"What subject did you study here?"
"Accounting."
"Then why are you wasting your time? Go be an accountant!"

It was an obvious point that I had neglected to see. That day, I tried two newspapers, seven shops, and five government offices to see if they had any accounting jobs. The newspapers and government offices laughed me out of the door at the proposition that a woman could handle their precious finances.

The wealthiest and those of the highest caste are often not the same people in India. Though I had amma's best sari on and I spoke intelligently, a lifetime of being a lower caste was not easily disguised. Four of the shops interrogated me about my status as soon as I approached. Only one would let me inside when I finally confessed my background.

"How dare you bring your Shudra filth into the air we breathe!?"

In all of my years of schooling, professors and teachers emphasized the nature of a massive population vying for very few work positions. That day was the first I truly understood the gravity of competition.

Chapter 16

I had no choice but to take my old job with the seamstress. Working fourteen hours a day, six days a week barely brought enough money to buy food for the three of us. Eventually, the cries of hunger from baby sister forced amma back to earth. She became a robot that cooked and did the household chores. Nana's death had killed her spirit. The once vivacious and loving woman was reduced to a mere shadow.

As I settled into a routine of poverty without hope, I felt the depression wash over me once again. The mindless work gave me hours to lose myself in thought. My best friend had been driven to suicide and my father had been murdered. Eleven years of hard work in school had not allowed me to progress to the better life nana had hoped I would have.

That November saw the end of a particularly intense monsoon season. The rain flooded nearly half of the village, bringing any activity in the area to a near standstill. The seamstress closed her shop for fear her materials would get blown away or damaged. That meant I could not work. That meant we had even less to eat.

For five straight days, our daily portions were whittled down to a half-cup of rice and a handful of lentils. By the sixth day, the hunger overtook our bodies. I tried to comfort baby sister through the noise of the storm. An unforgiving clap of thunder made baby sister shriek, causing amma to knock the last of our rice into the dirt.

Amma collapsed in a heap, and began to cry with a pained desperation. I put baby sister down in one of the cots and rushed over.

"It's okay amma. It's okay, we'll get more food tomorrow."

We both understood it was a promise I could not keep. Amma spoke her first words in months.

"I am so tired of this life. I am so tired of being defenseless against people who hurt my family. I am so tired of watching my children go hungry."

I wrapped my arms around her; I tried to find the words of comfort I felt I had no place in saying. There was nothing I had to offer.

"Lakshmi, promise me you will leave this village, leave India, leave this life. Promise me Lakshmi."

She had never spoken such words to me before. She had never suggested I give up on our world. For her to ask me to abandon my dream to change India, her spirit had truly broken. It was the worst awakening of my life.

"I promise you amma. I promise."

I finally managed to get amma and baby sister to sleep. The rained pounded heavily well into the night. It used to be a sound that brought me comfort for a healthy crop season. Now all it did was remind me how little work I would be able to secure the next day.

Unable to sleep, I found our little kerosene lamp. Reaching into my bag for matches, I rediscovered the small slip of paper that had been in nana's shirt the day he died. Carefully holding it to the light, I read words that made my head explode.

The note was written on the stationary of a company called Malaysian Agrimetrics. It contained one single line:

"I said you'd pay."

It was Sahana's handwriting.

Chapter 17

I begged and pleaded with the police to open an investigation. The deputy said he would not move a muscle unless I had "unequivocal proof" that the sheet of paper had come from my father's shirt, and that Sahana had written the note.

> "What if someone stole the paper from her father's office?" he told me.

> > "And why didn't the police look at the body when your father died?" asked another deputy.

I told him the police wanted too much money. We could not afford to pay. The two deputies nodded their heads. I had my answer.

Our neighbors were sympathetic, but everyone warned me to stop pursuing the matter.

> "He will have his daughter rusticated from university, no problem. But he will not let Sahana go to jail," they all said.

> > "That is a powerful family, Lakshmi. Even if justice finds Sahana, she can have you killed," said Nallini

> "I don't care."

> > "Well...she can have your amma and baby sister killed too."

That convinced me to drop the case.

I knew it was time to leave India. Without a proper education, without money, and without connections, there was only one way to escape:

Marriage.

One of the newspapers that did not accept job applications from women did accept personal ads for people wanting to marry. The last of our money would only be enough to buy a newspaper, so I prayed with all of my might that someone worthy had taken an ad in that week's edition.

The same clerk who rejected my job inquiry was sitting behind the counter. He gave me a mocking smile when I asked to purchase the personal ads for the week.

"You finally see you are a woman?" he said.

I stepped outside to read through the selection. Most of the ads were trash. Rich families placed many of the ads in the hopes of finding someone for their Govind-like sons. Some of the ads were for foreigners wishing to find someone in India. Amma taught me long ago those ads were code for being sold into slavery.

Tucked away in the far bottom corner, one ad caught my eye:

"Young doctor from Bangalore seeks a new life with intelligent bride. Must speak Telugu."

It was too perfect to be true. Without a moment of hesitation, I ran back inside the newspaper office to leave my reply.

Chapter 18

He responded in less than 24 hours. Through a series of messages at the newspaper office, we agreed to meet at the local canteen the following week. He said he would be wearing a bowler hat. I did not know what that was. I told him I would wear a green sari. It was the one amma wore at her wedding.

I arrived at the canteen first. The busboy pointed out a free table, and I sat down to wait…and wait…and wait. More than an hour after we agreed to meet, Shankar finally arrived, along with two of his cronies.

"Sorry I'm late," Shankar offered.

"Oh, this one is always late, better get used to that!" said one of the two.

"Just ignore him."

Not two seconds later, his other friend chimed in.

"So why do you want to marry this idiot?"

Laughing never came easily to me, and I did not know how to respond. Shankar's friends were distracting and rude. They carried on, not giving Shankar and I enough time to exchange even a few lines.

"Enough! Get out!" Shankar said to the two of them.

"Bad start buddy," one of them replied.

Shankar let out an exasperated sigh, and pushed the smaller of the two off of the bench they were sharing.

"Sorry about that," Shankar said once they finally left.

"Why are they your friends?"

I cursed myself at asking such a direct question; assertiveness was not highly regarded by suitors. Shankar did not seem to mind.

"Our fathers are childhood friends. I see them often, whether I want to or not."

"I see. Are you three taking a journey through South

India to find a bride only?"

I was serious. He thought it was a joke.

"We just finished our final medical school exams and decided to take a holiday here. They made me place the ad on a dare."

My heart sank.

"So you're not looking to marry someone after all?"

"No, well, I don't know. I'm still trying to decide where I want to work, so it depends on what I want…what we…would want."

His face flushed at the word 'we.'

Shankar called the busboy to order food. As he brought his hands up from beneath the table to start eating, I noticed how badly he was trembling.

Over the next few days, I learned that he came from a middle-class family in Bangalore. His father ran a moderately successful grocery store in the heart of the city, enough to provide Shankar with the comforts of modern life, though not enough to guarantee a life of luxury. His mother was uneducated and kind. His father was uneducated and judgmental.

Most of the girls Shankar had met 'made him cry from boredom.' Either they only cared about superficial things such as clothes and jewelry, or they only cared about beating everyone in final exams. He had never met a single girl who just liked to learn for the sake of learning.

"That's why I let my idiot friends place the ad in the paper," he explained.

The only thing his parents cared about was elevating their status through his marriage. The only thing Shankar cared about with marriage was being happy.

> "I don't care about caste or religion. My kids have to speak Telugu, though," he said.

I told him about the evils poverty had laid on my family.

> "That's why for many years I was one of those robots you detested."

My motivations were not superficial, though. They were out of the desire to find something better. Yet all of my efforts had only led me down a path of misery and disappointment. In another world, in another life, my education would have solved my problems. In this world, in this life, finding a husband would have to be the answer.

Meeting Shankar made me understand what Nallini and Ram had spoken of in their 'love romance.' Shankar and I had an obvious connection. On 8 December 1959, G.M. Shankar Deva asked for my hand in marriage. We wed a month later in a small ceremony attended by less than 20 people. Shankar never asked for a dowry, and I never offered one. Six months later, I was pregnant.

Chapter 19

With my pregnancy, amma's purpose in life was renewed. The color flushed back to her face, the song in her voice was restored, and the dance she performed with each step resurfaced. If I had not been constantly nauseous, I would have celebrated with her.

Shankar agreed immediately when I suggested we move to the United States or Canada. Ram and his father were very patient in explaining the concepts of 'passport,' 'visa,' and 'sponsor.' I do not think Shankar and I would have made it through the paperwork without their help.

The only place to accept Shankar's application was in a small city outside of Philadelphia called Youngstown. They were in desperate need of new medical residents, and agreed to sponsor Shankar for a temporary visa.

> "We can't keep you past your residency, you understand?" they asked him.

We had no choice but to be confident Shankar would find a job after. When we applied for the visas in January 1960, American laws did not grant automatic sponsorship for an immigrant's family. The hospital's advice was to hire a lawyer.

But who could afford such legal fees?

It cost half of my daily wages to place a reservation with the international operator. After waiting for hours, sometimes days, my call would be scheduled. With the time difference and general hustle of the hospital, only one in three of my calls would be met with someone on the other line.

No amount of my arguing convinced the hospital to also sponsor my baby and me. They would always reply saying they could not understand what I was saying, or that they had no need for a woman that had not completed a university degree. Finally, Ram offered to use his British accent.

> "Hallo, this is Nigel calling from the New York City office of London's finest international law firm. If you don't grant Mr. Shankar Deva's wife and daughter visas, we'll call American immigration services for a thorough sweep of your facilities."

It worked like magic.

There was one condition: I had to wait until after the birth of my child before leaving India. That meant the earliest I could go was December. Shankar had to start work by August. He was devastated at the idea of missing the birth of his first child, but in the end we decided it was worth the sacrifice.

Shankar's father felt the humiliation of his son marrying a peasant girl would only be cancelled out if Shankar went to America and became a successful doctor. It was for this sole reason his father paid for our trip to the New Delhi Indian embassy to collect our passports and visas.

Compared to Chennai, Delhi was a madhouse. Cars, bikes and auto rickshaws packed the uneven streets, never conceding a single centimeter of space. Child street merchants selling foreign contraband trinkets bombarded anyone who dared take their eyes off the road. Delhi was packed with foreigners. It was by far the most cosmopolitan place I had ever seen. If Delhi was this grand, I wondered what must the United States be like?

Chapter 20

Shankar left for America on 1 July 1960. He took the train from Chennai to Hyderabad to Mumbai. From Mumbai, he flew to London, then to New York City where he spent the night with a friend of his father's. From New York, he took the train to Philadelphia, where one of the hospital administrators picked him up and dropped him off at the apartment the hospital had arranged for us.

I counted the time of Shankar's journey down to the minute. As soon as he reached our new home, I hired a rickshaw to the calling station where I carefully placed a call with the operator to the number the hospital instructed us to use. After seven hours, the scheduled call went through. More than three days after he departed, I finally spoke to Shankar.

"What is it like? How is the apartment? Where is the calling station? Is it safe?"

He laughed. I imagined the expression on his face trying to figure out how to tell me all the details.

"The apartment is large, and the best part, Lakshmi, is that I am talking to you from *inside* the apartment!"

"You are speaking from the apartment only?" I asked him in English.

"Yes! The administrator told me everyone in America has their own phone!"

It sounded so perfect! I could talk to amma and baby sister with my own private phone!

"And tonight there will be something called fireworks for the American Independence Day!"

Fireworks. American Independence Day is July 4th, I noted. I had only seen fireworks once - at the university. I imagined those would be nothing compared to the fireworks of Youngstown.

With the time difference and my growing belly, I was only able to talk to Shankar four more times before December. The first call came a few days after he started work. Though he made everything sound like a dream, I could already hear the strain in his voice. By October, Shankar said the weather had gotten extremely cold.

"Colder than anything we have ever known in India."

In Youngstown, snow fell and stuck to the ground nearly every other day. Shankar slipped a few times, carrying painful bruises to work. I heard the regret in his voice at not being present for the birth our child. It must have been so hard for him being there completely alone.

All of the money Shankar was able to remit back to Chennai went to pay for my expensive train fares and airline tickets. With nothing to spare, private hospitals and clinics for my delivery were not an option. Public facilities were less sterile than our house. I would be giving birth to my child on the same floor on which I slept.

My water broke on the evening of 8 December 1960. Amma sent baby sister to stay with one of the neighbors, and gathered all of the clean material and clean water she could find. Amma's friends took turns staying by my side, singing to me, rubbing my belly, and putting a handkerchief wetted with cool water on my head.

The labor felt like it took an eternity. Amma later told me I gave birth in less than 3 hours. A midwife was called at the end, and she and four other women sat around me, coaching me through all of the incomprehensibly painful pushing and breathing. With each heave, I held Amma's hand tighter.

One year after Shankar asked me to marry him, our little baby girl, Pooja, was born. The midwife stayed to help amma clean Pooja off and to cut the umbilical cord. Properly wrapped in a fresh cloth, amma handed me my precious daughter.

> "Lakshmi, just think. Soon you will leave this misery behind. Your next child will be born in America," amma said.

Chapter 21

On 13 January 1961, Pooja and I landed in America. Pooja had been thankfully quiet for the entire journey. As soon as we entered the New York International Airport terminal, she began to cry. The stimulus was too much for her tiny ears and eyes to handle.

I set down the small bag I brought with me on the plane, and found a seat to readjust her wrapping, hoping it would calm her down. I did not want Shankar's first memory of his daughter to be her sobs. By the time she finally quieted, I realized all of the other passengers had gone ahead. Shankar's instructions had been to follow the flow of people until I saw him. I tried telling myself this was just like discovering another path to school.

My calming tactic did not work. Feeling panicked, I grabbed Pooja a little too forcefully, and she started crying again. I felt thousands of white, black, and brown faces sneering, beckoning me to turn around and fly home. My head started to spin, and I felt my arms go limp. At that precise moment there was a tap on my shoulder. Shankar's calm face looked back at me. He brought me close to his chest, and bent down to give his daughter the first of many kisses.

Our plan had been to stay with the friend of Shankar's father. At the last minute, they had called Shankar and apologized.

> "Our son is sick. We do not wish to risk your baby catching the infection."

Shankar asked what kind of illness their son had contracted. They did not give an answer, and instead hung up the phone. I understood. Even in America, having a peasant girl in your house was undesirable.

Shankar made a reservation at a hotel in Manhattan. It was far more expensive than we could afford, but he wanted to impress his wife and daughter. Though the January cold of New York was unbearable, as we crossed the bridge from Queens, Pooja came to life. Holding her up so she could see through the glass window, she wrestled her hands out from underneath her coverings and laughed for the first time.

> "We are home, amma," she was telling me.

Chapter 22

The first 18 months were difficult. Shankar worked 80 hours a week, leaving me alone to care for Pooja, tend to the apartment, buy the food, and do all of the cooking.

We could only afford to buy one car. In India, one car was a world-class luxury. In America, where everything is spread out great distances, one car was not enough. An Indian community raised a child; in America, childcare was expensive. Without family nearby, caring for Pooja became my full time job.

She grew with each day, and it soon became unreasonably expensive to send for material to make her Indian clothes. Shankar heard a few of the hospital nurses mention a store called 'JC Pennies,' which was where I would take Pooja to buy American clothes when we felt confident enough to bear the cost.

One lovely spring afternoon, I took Pooja for a walk. She looked pretty in her new white dress. Pooja loved birds. I let go of her hand for a few minutes so she could chase a blue jay. The women in the street would always stare at the two of us. I hadn't grown accustomed to the idea of wearing pants like a man or American skirts that exposed one's legs. Instead, I continued to wear my saris, even though they attracted attention.

That afternoon, one of the staring women decided to approach me.

> "Um, Ma'am?"
>
> "Yes?" I replied, with my best smile.
>
> "Ma'am, your daughter is only wearing a slip."
>
> "A what?"
>
> "YOUR DAUGHTER IS ONLY WEARING A SLIP."

Why did Americans always scream when we did not understand the meaning of their words? I was Indian, not deaf. She saw the confusion on my face and looked as though I was refusing to understand her advice. Frustrated, she walked away.

I decided to take Pooja to the store for an ice cream and pick up a new container of snow. At the time, I did not know that what we Indians knew as 'snow,' Americans called 'facial lotion.' As we walked in through the doors, I spotted the new catalogue for JC Pennies.

"Look Pooja! We will buy you something next month when nana gets paid!"

I took the catalogue, but I couldn't find the lotion.

"Excuse me, where do you keep the snow?"
"The what?"
"The snow. It is usually near the soap."

The cashier gave me the same look as the other woman as she inspected my clothes.

"Lady, what the hell are you talking about?"
"I need snow!"

The cashier snorted and turned to another employee.

"Hey Donna! This woman wants SNOW!"

Donna started laughing hysterically and pointing at me in the same way teacher had encouraged the other students to respond to my beatings.

"Lady, come back in December if you want snow!"
"Oh and by the way," the cashier said, grabbing the catalogue, "Your daughter is only wearing a slip. You brought you daughter out in her *undergarments*."

Both women started cackling so cruelly that I became scared for my safety. Upset at my sudden change in body language, Pooja gripped the ice cream so hard as though it were a shield. It took force I never wished to show my daughter to remove the container from her tiny hands. I picked her up and ran out of the door, leaving my dignity melting alongside my daughter's treat.

Was this progress?

Most days Shankar would be so tired, he came home, ate a small plate of food and went straight to sleep. On the rare occasion we had a chance to talk, I could see the sparkle in his eyes was slowly fading. The closest Indian family lived nearly 30 kilometers away. Very quickly, we grew lonely.

It didn't matter how carefully he spoke, how many times he apologized, or how hard he tried. If anything went wrong, Shankar would always be blamed. Doctors would insult Shankar in public, nurses would tell him to find Christ, and patients would spit in his face. The hospital administration refused to pay him for an entire month because they accused him of stealing a bottle of aspirin from the pharmacy. All of the other residents were guaranteed two weeks paid vacation. Shankar was downgraded to three days without explanation.

The worst part was that there was nothing we could do. We did not know the law, we could not afford to hire someone who did, and we did not have an advocate. By the end of the two years in Youngstown, we had reviewed Shankar's contract a hundred times. Being absolutely sure we were safe, we called every hospital in Philadelphia. One rainy day, we got a call back from a private one that would be willing to sponsor all three of our visas. Without telling a soul, we rented a van, packed up the apartment, and left Youngstown the day after Shankar's contract expired.

Chapter 23

I loved Philadelphia! Shankar's salary was more than three times what he made before, but the city was not three times the cost. We moved into a spacious apartment in a safe, quiet neighborhood. Soon, I was remitting weekly sums to amma. She used the money to buy a small house near the shops across from the university. Airline tickets and long-stay visas were still very expensive, but amma and I made plans for her and baby sister to come visit us in Philadelphia the following year.

While Pooja played in the park, I would sit with my Turkish, Brazilian and Egyptian friends and listen to stories about their homelands. Everybody I met in Philadelphia wanted to go to India. To them, I had not grown up in a slum. I had grown up in a fascinating world of colors and whimsy. I did not dare crush their idealized dreams of my homeland. It was much too fun to pretend to be someone better than anyone in India told me I was.

Joanne, the mother of Sarah - one of Pooja's friends - quickly became a close confidante. The first day we met, Joanne looked at my sari, though not in the hurtful way the people in Youngstown did.

> "Oh my God! What are you wearing! It's so beautiful!" exclaimed Joanne.
>
> "Thank you," I said, elated and embarrassed.
> "I'm Joanne," she said with a huge smile on her face.
> "Lakshmi."
> "Lakshmi! That is so pretty! Just like you, Lakshmi!"

No one had ever told me I looked pretty.

Joanne taught me so many things. She bought me my first set of make up - a box of lipstick with 20 different shades! She gave me confidence to wear Western fashions, and took me to my first beauty parlor to get my hair cut in the style of Jacquelyn Kennedy.

We would buckle Pooja and Sarah in the back of her car and ride all around the city while listening to the radio. She even convinced me to try my first chocolate bar. Oh how I thought about my dear Alpa as I unwrapped the delicate brick of sweetness. This was certainly a moment that was worth living for someone else.

Joanne and her husband showed Shankar and me the pleasure of hiring a nanny a few nights a week. They took us to the opera, the natural history museum, and even to a baseball game. Shankar and I thought baseball was an easy version of cricket, though we still enjoyed the atmosphere.

Pooja loved the city too. She found everything fascinating. Every dog, flower, child, and building had to be inspected. Thanks to Joanne, I discovered walking to be much easier when wearing pants and closed-toe shoes. On our daily stroll around the neighborhood, Pooja would point out tall buildings, short buildings, and odd looking buildings. One of the local shopkeepers loved Pooja, and would give her a postcard of a different city every time we passed by.

"That girl is gonna be an architect!" he told me.

By December 1962, Shankar, Pooja and I had firmly settled into Philadelphia. The city provided us with a life of steady food, clean water, proper clothing, and a dignity and respect that we had never been afforded. Together, we enjoyed many luxuries of a life that I had once assumed was limited to film stars; the life of stability and happiness spoke far more to the girl I was back in the Indian theater.

That year, one of our neighbors invited us for our first Christmas party. I was not sure what to wear. Joanne advised on the elegant new skirt I had just bought, a red blouse, and a green and gold flower broach. Shankar put on his nicest suit, and I dressed Pooja in a slip *and* a beautiful gold dress. As he looked at the two of us, the sparkle in Shankar's eyes lit up the entire room. He gently pulled us over to a mirror, and the three of us smiled back at our reflection.

Chapter 24

Of course, I dearly missed amma, baby sister, and my friends back in India, but Shankar's work would allow for many reunions, of that, I was sure. With minor exceptions, Philadelphia had been incredibly kind to us. It was hard to imagine we were anything but invincible. The problem with a perfect life, however, is that there is nowhere to go but down.

4 August 1963 started out as any normal day would. As usual, Shankar was in the hospital by 8 AM. Two hours later, a patient came to the hospital with his eye completely swollen shut. Normally, this would be a case for the emergency room doctors. As it was an exceptionally busy day, the nurses dispatched for the best internal medical doctor on staff - Shankar - to help.

"Make sure you take the patient's medical history," Shankar instructed.

According to the chart, the patient had had a minor surgery on his arm a few years back. No allergies, no history of heart problems, nothing wrong with the brain. Shankar looked at the patient's infected eye, and determined from the tests run that the patient had a bacterial infection.

"What's the treatment?" the nurse asked Shankar.

"One dose of penicillin."

After being apart from Pooja so much the first few years, Shankar always came home for lunch between noon and 2 PM. When the clock struck 2:30, I assumed he was simply delayed. As the clock reached 3, I began to worry. When I still had not heard from him an hour later, I dressed Pooja and called a taxi to take us to the hospital. I associated American hospitals with strength. In India, any minor injury can cause death. Life in America was not that fragile.

The hospital secretary told me that Shankar was in the medical coordinator's office. After pointing me in the right direction, she shot me a smile. Nearly three years in the country had taught me American smiles could mean many things. I knew this smile was not out of happiness.

Shankar was sitting alone in the office, his face buried in his hands. Pooja shouted happily, startling him out of a daze.

"Nana, lunch?" Pooja asked Shankar.

"No beta, not today," Shankar replied.

"What happened?" I asked.

Shankar shook his head slightly, tears gathering in his eyes.

"Nana, don't cry!"

Pooja put her hands up to his eyes to catch the tears as she had done for me so many times in Youngstown. He called in a nurse.

"Can you take our daughter to get a juice box?" Shankar asked the nurse.

"Orange, nana?" Pooja asked.

"Whatever you wish."

Pooja happily walked off with the nurse, giving us a few minutes alone for Shankar to explain what I felt could only be devastating.

"I told her to take the patient history."

"She forgot?"

"It was incomplete."

Not knowing the patient was allergic, Shankar administered the penicillin and left the room. The hospital had been so overwhelmed it took a few minutes for anyone to notice the patient had a massive seizure.

"He was probably epileptic," Shankar guessed.

The patient died shortly after.

The police took a formal report from everyone who had had contact with the patient. Shankar told them he did not know the patient was allergic to penicillin, and showed the chart as proof. After questioning the nurse, the police informed the hospital that she denied Shankar tasked her to take the medical history.

> *"I double checked, he said he'd do it!"* she claimed.

The hospital administrator knew Shankar was a competent doctor, but said he had to protect the hospital.

> *"It's a question of liability."*

They put Shankar on unpaid leave, and advised us to hire a lawyer immediately.

Looking at the trauma on Shankar's face, I realized why God had allowed us to find each other as life partners. Many falls from grace ensured I had the strength to gather my family and assure them everything would be okay. My words were enough to convince them, if not myself.

Chapter 25

The hospital sent us a list of the best medical malpractice lawyers in the city. Only one that fell in our price range would take on the challenge of representing an immigrant. Her name was Yael Stein.

> "You remind me of my parents. They survived The Holocaust," she said.

Hiring Yael meant sacrificing the money we were saving to bring amma and baby sister over. Breaking the news was nothing short of heartbreaking; by August 1963, it had been nearly three years since we had seen each other. I felt as though I had abandoned my family after all they had done for me.

Shankar's family was more upset that their son might not become a successful doctor than they were about Shankar himself. Whatever happened, they forbade him from returning to Bangalore and further humiliating the family.

> "First you marry a peasant girl, now you will go to jail? What did I do to deserve such disappointment in my family?" said his father.

Shankar stopped phoning his household after that conversation.

With Shankar's contract was on hold, Pooja and I would be illegal immigrants after six months. Because criminal charges might be brought against Shankar, he could not leave the country. Six months in misery felt like a lifetime; six months to save one's family felt like an eye blink.

Pooja spent much of the time at Joanne's house while Shankar and I helped Yael in any way we could. Much to our financial dismay, we were forced to hire a second lawyer for our immigration purposes. Though I always favored saving money for future protection, we knew there would be no future without the sacrifice.

Yael's preparation covered our statements on every possible question the judge might ask.

> "What did Shankar have to eat that morning? Was he well rested? Was he stressed? Did he get along well with the nurses? How clear is his English?"

We wrote down every piece of information and memorized how best to phrase the answer. The memorization part was easy for me. Knowing how to apply the information was much more difficult.

With the immigration lawyer, we produced copious notes detailing our every move since we landed in America.

"Immigration will leave no detail unnoticed!"

What were our intentions in coming to the States? Did we live within our means? Did we have an ulterior motive for coming here? Who, what, where, when, why, and how for every move we made. Day and night, we met with our lawyers. Every little detail, every fond memory, every painful event was relived, dissected, and catalogued.

Yael did her best to obtain records of the hospital staff and administration. We paid for her to fly across the country to bring back copies of the records. Meanwhile, our immigration lawyer spent a week in Youngstown to confirm Shankar's employment record. It was not until then that I realized the gravity of our initial lie to get Pooja and me into the country.

Finally, our big break in the hospital case came with Yael's final trip out of town - to Kansas City, Missouri.

"Our nurse in question went to school there," Yael informed.

"What did you find?"

"Turns out she married last year there and changed her name."

Due to a clerical error, the records under her new last name were filed separately.

"Mrs. Edith Bennett, née Conner, did not pass a require course: medical record keeping. She is an illegally licensed nurse."

The case was dropped against Shankar with a mere ten days to spare.

The immense relief that came with dropped charges was temporary. The entire ordeal had proven quite embarrassing for the prestigious hospital. They formed a case against Shankar in violation of the acceptable hospital behavior clause in his contract. Shankar was officially fired a few days later.

"You have the right to appeal," they argued.

But not before we would be required to return back to India.

Working around the clock more out of pity than for the money, our immigration lawyer pursued every possible solution. He spoke with officials from the office of diplomatic affairs, chased down ambassadors, wrote to the United Nations, and appealed to two-dozen members of the US Congress.

"If Kennedy hadn't been shot, I'd even write the President."

With 48 hours until deportation, we were unsuccessful. Making one of the hardest decisions of our lives, Shankar and I conceded we would have to return to India. We packed up our most prized possessions and visited our closest friends to say goodbye. Joanne was hysterical. She cried and begged us to not give up.

"They'll take you over my dead body!"

"Where are the fucking police? Why can't they do something?" her husband shouted.

My poor Pooja had little understanding of why everyone was so upset.

"Amma, don't be sad. Shall we get ice cream?"

Shankar, Pooja and I spent our last few hours alone in America in our apartment. We unplugged the phone, drew the curtains tight, and curled up in bed, using the comforter to block out the noise of the outside world. Pooja, unaware of the turmoil that was about to uproot her life, slept peacefully between us.

Humiliated by the situation, Shankar could not bear to make eye contact with me. He rejected my offered hand of support, and I wondered if this rejection would continue in our life back in India. It was not the first time in my life that my world had fallen apart, but with a daughter to care for, it destroyed me more profoundly than anything else.

Chapter 26

There was a heavy banging on the door. Immigration was early. In our six-month probation period, they had delayed answering each of our questions. On the day we were to be shipped off like criminals, they showed up early.

Shankar still had his arms draped over Pooja. Both were asleep, so I carefully inched my way off the bed, not wanting to disturb them in their final moments of peace. I put on my shoes and prepared to let complete strangers invade our house and ruin our lives. I opened the door, and was shocked to see our immigration lawyer staring at me, panting heavily.

"We did it!"

Waving a sheet of paper in his hand like a Wall Street trader, he continued to shout well after I managed to usher him inside.

"We did it! It's over! You're safe, we did it!"

Hearing the noise, Shankar came rushing downstairs. As I unfolded the paper, my heart pounded so heavily that my entire body swayed in motion, like a ship fighting to avoid capsizing in the ocean. The letter was written on gorgeous blue and black Congressional stationary. Our lives hung in the balance of five paragraphs.

Dear Dr. and Mrs. Deva,

I was saddened to hear of the unfortunate circumstances surrounding your employment contract termination at the St. Augustine Hospital in Philadelphia earlier this month. Our legal system is in place for the ultimate protection of our citizens and residents; however, it does on occasion result in unfair outcomes, as in your case.

It has come to my attention that your residency status is contingent upon employment with St. Augustine. As such, the US Immigration Services scheduled you to be deported back to your native country of India on February 5, 1964.

I have brought your case to the attention of several of my colleagues, and it was unanimously agreed that there is no legal precedent by which you should be removed. As such, my staff has contacted the US Immigration Services and instructed them to not execute your order of deportation.

As a US Senator, it is my job to encourage growth for the betterment of my country. Dr. Deva, as a physician, I believe you can serve an important need of our community. Dr. and Mrs. Deva, under a provision afforded to me as a US Congressman, I have put forth piece of legislation that will allow you and your daughter to secure permanent residency so long as Dr. Deva provides his services as a medical doctor in an underprivileged area of my state of West Virginia for a minimum of ten years.

My staff has been in contact with your lawyer, and will expedite the process to ensure your full protection as soon as possible. It is my pleasure to be at your service.

Sincerely yours,

Robert C. Byrd
United States Senator, West Virginia

Senator Byrd personally drafted a bill allowing for our permanent legal stay and had it passed through the US Congress. Shankar, Pooja and I were awarded our green cards two months later. In ten years, Shankar and I would be eligible to become citizens. Pooja would be eligible as soon as she turned 18.

Chapter 27

West Virginia was like Youngstown in many ways. Shankar and I, however, were stronger and wiser people. Disillusioned with hospital administration, Shankar took out a small loan and rented a three-room medical office within walking distance of our house.

Though a brilliant doctor, Shankar had neither the time nor the knowledge of how to run a business. It presented itself in such an unpredictable way, but I finally found use of my accounting knowledge, acting as general manager for Shankar's medical practice. University had taught me how to be a master money handler. Life had taught me how to be kind. Shankar's practice served some of the poorest people in the country, and I soon made it a common practice to write off the bills of patients who could not otherwise afford service.

Professionally, Shankar and I found solace. Personally, we were once again alone. Our town in West Virginia had a population of less than 25,000. We were the only Indian family.

When I found out I was pregnant again, we decided to use our savings to bring amma and baby sister over for a year. Buying airline tickets in a small town of West Virginia became a huge challenge. It took five trips and nearly three months to coordinate the schedules, file the correct paperwork, and make sure amma understood the instructions.

"When shall we have them come?" Shankar asked.

"We can only afford mid-February."
"You're due in early March."
"It will be fine."

I could barely move the last few weeks of my third trimester, so Shankar and Pooja left for New York to bring amma and baby sister without me. Giving my large belly a final kiss, Shankar half-walked, half-slid through the snow to the car, and started the four hour journey to the nearest airport that could connect them to what was now called John F. Kennedy airport, the same airport Pooja and I had passed through more than four years prior.

I watched them drive into the white winter curtain. Looking around the house, I realized this was the first time in my life that I ever had total and complete privacy. I took full advantage of this on the first day. No sleep schedules, no cleaning, no cooking. Just total relaxation.

The Indian mind is not trained to be alone; by my second day of solitude, I was already growing restless. As patients, West Virginians were easy to get along with. As friends, I had none. I tried calling Joanne, but her husband told me she was out of town visiting her parents. I tried watching television. American programs never held my interest. The weather was terrible, or I would have gone to the library. Having nothing to do and no one to talk to, I feel asleep on the couch.

I was startled awake a few hours later by snow that fell from the a tree onto the roof. For a split second, I thought the snow had fallen straight through the house. It took me a few moments to make the uneasy discovery that my pants were wet. My water had broken.

An OB/GYN was by my side soon after I entered the hospital. My brain spiraled back in time to the extremes of my life. I saw flashes of Alpa dying on the stark white steps, of seeing Pooja playing happily in the parks of Philadelphia, of the gaping hole that was once my father's wise mind. With a final jolt of pain, I squeezed the nurse's hand, and emerged in a parallel time.

"AAAMMMMAA!" I screamed at the top of my lungs.

One of the other nurses asked what I was saying, which returned me back to reality. I looked around and rediscovered the painful truth that merely a room full of strangers surrounded me.

Chapter 28

"What shall we name her?" baby sister asked.

"Lucy!" Pooja shouted.

Amma looked radiant as she gazing down at her elder granddaughter; she was so proud Pooja could understand Telugu. Pooja proposing a name from her favorite cartoon series, *Peanuts,* was all the more endearing.

"You must decide before you leave the hospital," the nurse told us.

"Chee! Such an important decision," Shankar ticked.

"Who's a woman you admire? Someone you owe?" the nurse prompted.

I translated what the nurse said to amma. She leaned back with the knowledge of what our past had entailed. Other than amma herself - who was not an option, as she was thankfully still with us on earth - there was but one name my life could truly offer. We left the hospital with baby Alpa an hour later. Pooja was elated to have a little sister.

Having amma and baby sister with me was the exact relief I needed from an emotionally draining journey. Pooja and baby sister spent the entire year playing. Amma looked after baby Alpa during the day so I could tend to the office. Every evening, we would have an excellent south Indian dinner, and spend the night swapping stories, discussing the latest films, and simply enjoying each other's company.

The six of us saw all of the attractions in the state. The Smokey Mountains, the famous coal mines, the University of West Virginia campus. We even made a trip to Senator Byrd's West Virginia office in the capital. Shankar and I closed the office for a week to take amma and baby sister to Washington and New York. After the emotional trauma it had inflicted, we decided to skip Philadelphia.

We bought amma and baby sister brand new suitcases to fill with toys and gifts for the villagers in Chennai. Amma loved spending hours going through discount stores and buying four of everything - toilet paper, key chains, fly swatters, crayons, chewing gum. A new JC Pennies opened that year, and Pooja was thrilled to finally have someone to chase around the maze of aisles. Baby sister became a huge fan of socks, and bought at least 40 pairs to take home.

Saying goodbye to amma and baby sister was so difficult. Only the heart is superior to the brain, and my love for Chennai grew exponentially knowing I would not be joining them on the return journey. But seeing the two of them looking happy and healthy, holding new suitcases and the equivalent of a year of Chennai wages reassured me that Shankar and I had made the right decision to come to America.

The idea of being the woman to change India still roared in my soul. In another life, I swore to make it happen. In this life, I knew Chennai had not let me progress. It was not a place to raise a daughter. It was not a place to be a woman.

Chapter 29

In the fall of 1966, Pooja started the first standard, and Shankar and I decided to have a family outing to celebrate. We went to the only

Italian restaurant in town, and split a giant bowl of spaghetti and a pitcher of Coke. Alpa made a huge mess of her food; she was too independent to let either of us help her eat.

"Not hungry, beta?" I asked Pooja, who had barely touched her food.

Pooja shook her head, on the verge of tears.

"Is there something wrong?" Shankar gently asked.

"Nana, amma, I'm scared about school."

"What's the matter?" Shankar asked.

"What if the kids don't like me?"

I smiled at Pooja, thinking of all the friends she would make, and all the happiness she would find in learning. America would let her learn with the same passion as I had and with the same happiness in life as my dear friend, Alpa.

"You are a good, kind person, and many people will want to be your friend."

She was not convinced. It would take time for her to get used to the idea of going away every morning. With an ease that still made me quiver with excitement, Shankar and I immediately offered to see a fun film after dinner. She brought her head up to our gazes and told us that would make her very happy.

"Four, please," Shankar said to the ticket salesman.

Glancing up from his newspaper, the salesman looked at Shankar and over to the rest of us. I recognized that look immediately. It was the same look of lower class hatred I had seen many times in Chennai. Before the salesman said anything, I walked to Shankar and said in Telugu that we should leave. The salesman overheard me speaking.

"What the fuck is that?"

"Nothing. We are leaving," I replied

"But amma! I wanted to see the movie!" cried Pooja.

The salesman looked down at my precious daughter with a disgust that made me enraged enough to kill.

"What did she just say? What the hell is amma?"

Never having lived a life of poverty, Shankar showed his anger for treating his daughter that way, and walked as close as he could to the glass window. His India had not taught him the necessity in simply walking away.

"Four tickets!"

"I ain't giving you no tickets! We don't sell to your kind!"

Before I could stop him, Shankar started screaming at the top of his lungs. The rage in his voice shook little Alpa into hysterics, which in turn made Pooja upset. Seeing the frightened looks on my children's' faces, I finally grabbed Shankar's shirt and pulled him back to the car. Strapping in Alpa and Pooja, I got into the passenger's seat, trying to collect myself before turning around.

"Why was he so mean to us, amma?"

"I don't know, beta. Some people are just bad seeds. Shall we go get ice cream?"

Pooja hiccupped a few times as she caught her breath. I turned around to wipe the last of the tears from her eyes. She grabbed my hand and brought it against her warm, scared face as she pulled herself together from her first battle of discrimination.

"No amma, I just want to go home."

Pooja became increasingly distant as she grew up. Her early years of school were marked with constant teasing and insults from the other children. They did not understand the food she brought for lunch, the language we spoke at home, or the reason we did not celebrate Christmas. Eventually, she turned on us as the cause for her pain and suffering. Even when she agreed with the bullies, they would not let her live in peace.

"Why do we have to be different!?" she would scream.

"It is who we are, Pooja!"

"I hate who we are!"

"You hate how they treat us for being who we are."

"The effect is still the same!"

Everything we did was different, and different was bad.

The constant teasing lowered Pooja's self-esteem. She told us the reasons she had few friends was because most of the people were 'idiots,' and the few who weren't wanted to go out to parties, take weekend trips to the countryside, and go on dates with boys. Of course, I would not let her do these things. I did not trust American boys with my precious daughter.

The loneliness took its toll on her, and Pooja's grades suffered as a result. She barely placed in the top ten percent of her school. I constantly warned her that this would affect her future. She would merely roll her eyes.

"Stop being paranoid, *mom*," she said.

The idea of competition did not mean much to her, but my life had been shaped by both the destructive and miraculous nature of its power. Though the life Shankar and I had built in West Virginia was better than anything I could have provided in Chennai, it still lacked the opportunity and the fairness I needed for my girls.

When Pooja was 18, she came home with her final report card of the fall term. Half As and half B+'s. I knew she was proud of what she had achieved. As a mother, I was scared. Shankar and I discussed the situation in private. By the end of the night, I knew what I had to do for my precious Pooja.

Chapter 30

> "You haven't explained why you are RUINING MY LIFE," Pooja screamed at me.

It was an upsetting statement coming from her mouth. I had felt confident she would understand.

> "Pooja, we are…"
> "Save it, mom! There's no justification!"

The shadow the lamp casted across our skin confirmed the dark feelings brewing inside my daughter. She stood up with such force she knocked over her heavy wood chair, and caused a crash so loud I was sure the foundation of our lives had crumbled. I hesitated at the look of pure anger that washed over her face. It reminded of the rage that fueled so many of the evil forces in my life - Sahana, Govind, teacher. Pooja stormed out of the room without another word.

Shankar stopped me from running after her.

> "Why doesn't she understand?"
> "She will. Just give her time."

I waited a few minutes before going upstairs to try again. In between sobs, I could hear her talking on the phone describing what had just happened.

> "They want to destroy my life, Sally. My mom thinks I'm some stupid idiot who can't take care of herself. What did I

do to deserve this?"

It was heartbreaking to know you were the cause of such a deep pain your child felt. That was certainly not my objective in the matter, though it was something that was unavoidable. I could not risk gambling with my daughter's future, knowing how close my life choices almost ended the very existence of the people I sought to protect, and how close I came to destroying my own future. I could not let Pooja make the same mistakes I had made.

Pooja needed to start a life with someone who could work with her to find the opportunities Shankar and I had failed to provide. Pooja needed to marry for a better life, just as I had done 20 years prior.

Part II – *Pooja*

Chapter 1

Even at its worst points, never once during my childhood did I consider my life would devolve from an undying hopefulness to bitter hopelessness. As soon as mom uttered the word,

> *"Marriage."*

I saw my innocence leak with each staggered breath in an emotionally charged retreat to my room.

> "It's not fair. My mom is trying to ruin my life! What am I going to do!?" I screamed.

> > "Don't worry Pooja, me and Bobby got a plan. We'll get you out of this!"

In that little town in the middle of nowhere, I could count every friend I had ever made on one hand. At the age of 10, it was our neighbor, Sam, who led me on his top-secret missions in the West Virginia outback. That lasted until I found out his top secret missions consisted of burning ants to a crisp using a magnifying glass. We stopped talking soon after. Sam became quarterback of the football team last year, and now dates the homecoming queen - Peggy - who enjoys cheerleading and telling me how ugly I am. Sam never stops her.

At age 15, it was dark-haired Nicole, who quickly became my friend after she realized I was the only one not making fun of her foreign food, foreign looks, or foreign family. Less than a year after moving here, her parents packed up the family and moved to Chicago to join the growing Greek community there. I asked her to write me a letter. It still hasn't arrived.

When I turned 17, I met Sally. Her mom was divorced, and Sally had to deal with a lot of whispering behind her back; Sally understood what it meant to be different in a place that hated different people.

Her boyfriend Bobby was stupid.

"But he has a truck!" Sally said.

She immediately offered to drive the hour with Bobby and me to the Greyhound Station. Though cumbersome, the roads from there led to anywhere in the country.

The only trips outside of the area my parents permitted were straight to India, so I surveyed my closet as though looking at the contents for the first time. I had no idea what to pack; all I knew was that I hated hot weather. The gross pieces of garbage mom bought for me at the local consignment store - sweaters with tassels, bellbottoms big enough to envelop me whole - most certainly did not make the cut.

Twenty minutes later, I dressed myself in a gray shirt with one low-hanging shoulder, a pair of tastefully cut jeans and a black blazer. Jennifer Beals wore something similar four years later in *Flashdance*. I always had a great sense of style. I belonged in New York, I decided.

Carefully hoisting my bag off the ground, I walked around the edge of my hardwood room floor, praying the creaking wouldn't wake up my insomniac of a father or blabbermouth sister. I wished I had time to write dad a note, but wrestling over the right words wouldn't be a quick task. He shared my love of postcards, though. I knew he'd be excited to receive one from his own daughter.

I wouldn't have to pass by mom and dad's room if I took the kitchen staircase. The screen on the front door always slammed so quickly. Just a few more steps and...CRASH!

"Aaah!" I screamed.

"Shit!"

"Dad?" I asked to the dark blob across the room.

"Pooja? What are you doing?"

He flipped on the light. When the scene came into focus, I saw a broken glass and a pool of milk on the floor just inches away from dad's fuzzy whale slippers mom had gotten as a deal with my tasseled sweater. Between the slippers and his milk moustache, dad looked like a little kid. He stared at me fully dressed, complete with a big bag slung over my shoulder. I stuttered a few words trying to find an excuse. Dad put his hands up.

"Can we talk before you go?"

I bit my lip, mulling over the options. If mom had been the one in the kitchen, we would have been knee-deep in an excessively loud argument by now. I decided to let dad say his piece before heading off, knowing he'd give me more of a head start if I did. He had always been the peacekeeper of the family.

"Okay, only for a few minutes."

"Just leave the bags by the door."

"Here, put this over the milk," I said to him as I handed over a few paper towels.

He did the infamous Indian head nod in response. I assumed this nod meant, 'thanks.'

"Come, we'll go sit in the living room," he said.

There was no way mom could listen in if we talked there. Good.

He motioned for me to sit down using his patting gesture. It was the same kind of paw-thumping a dog did when you scratched behind its ears. I wanted a dog when I was a kid. Mom always said that 'those beasts' would be too much of a distraction to my studies.

In the corner of my eye, I saw the headlights of Bobby's car as he and Sally pulled into the driveway. What they possessed in brawn they lacked in brains, leaving the headlights on full blast as though blaring yellow beams wouldn't attract attention at 2 AM on a Sunday night.

As usual, no sooner had Bobby put the truck into park did they start making out behind the glare. I had never even kissed a guy - my brown skin and aggressive mother made sure of that. But I knew greater things lay ahead in New York. Dad started talking in the midst of my thoughts…

"Look beta," he said.

There was that old Indian word again, 'beta,' which my family used to mean 'dear.' I had to admit, it was better than the Southern convention of describing each other as food. 'Honey, sugar, sweet pea, dumpling.' When I was in first grade, I thought you could use any food to describe someone. I got into my first fight when I called a kid in my class 'marshmallow.' Dad had to come and pick me up that day.

"Do you want to run away?" he asked (again).

The short answer was yes. The real answer was let me live my own life and go to college. Then no. I might even come home for the holidays.

"Dad, I don't want to get married to some greasy Indian guy."

A small smile crept over dad's face before his famous eye sparkle emerged in disarming force.

"Hey, be careful, I was a greasy Indian guy once!"

I rolled my eyes in response. Every time I complained about mom and dad's head nods, dad told me the American equivalent was an eye roll. At least our eye rolls weren't ambiguous.

"Your mother is one of the strongest people I have ever met. I could have never done half as well without her."

"I know, but I want to do so many things with my life."

He told me he understood, and so did mom. I doubted the second part. Mom had treated me like a helpless, blind infant since I was born. My guess was she was tired of taking care of me, and too arrogant to let me do anything for myself. One time-honored Indian tradition was the need to feel irreplaceable.

"We want you to have a successful career *and* do all of the wonderful things we know you are capable of doing."

"Thanks," I muttered back.

A compliment was rare in that house. Sally complimented me more on my new blazer than mom had my entire life.

"The reason we want you get married is to *help* you be who you are, Pooja."

"Marriage ties you down, dad!"

"Pooja, we don't want to force you into anything. Do you think you can just give it a try...for me?"

Usually when he asked for a favor, he pouted. This time he looked dead serious. I turned to look away, trying to block his expressive face from my mind as I figured out the quickest way to end this conversation and climb into Bobby's truck.

"Dad, this is a really big deal."

"It is, which is why you must be okay with the decision."

"Does this really mean a lot to you?"

He nodded again, but this time in a very American, somber way. A clump of snow fell on top of the truck, startling Bobby and Sally out of their make out session. It was so cold that time of year. New York was expensive. What if I couldn't afford an apartment with heating? What if the public schools there were worse than they were in West Virginia? I questioned if I even had what it took to survive out there all alone.

"And you really want me to have a successful career?"

"Of course."

"And so does mom?"

"Especially your mother. She just doesn't know how to tell you. What do you say, beta? If it doesn't work out, I won't argue."

"What if I say no?"

Dad dropped his head at the sound of the question. I saw a few tears stream down his face. The only time I had seen him cry was when his mother died. The disappointment on his face was enough to make me walk to the front without my things. I couldn't believe I was doing this. Pulling open the doors, I shouted over to Sally.

"Go home! It's okay!"

My hand felt like a dead weight as I waved to her. I reached out to close the wood door, but forgot to catch the screen. BAM! It went.

Within seconds, mom rushed downstairs. In a half-English, half-Telugu panic, she screamed to call the police.

"Burglar! Robbery! Get the jewelry! Where are the girls?"

Talk about priorities!

"Mom! It's fine, go back to bed."

After one look at dad, she immediately calmed down. They

exchanged head nods that seemed to communicate the entirety of the situation.

I returned to the kitchen to clean up the milk and retrieve my suitcase, half expecting it would ask for an explanation as to why we weren't going somewhere other than India.

All I could muster in response were four disappointing words.

> "We were so close."

Chapter 2

As expected, I graduated at nearly the top of my high school class with stellar recommendations from all of my teachers. Ever since grade school I had imagined the regalia of high school graduation and all of the praise for my hard work that would follow. Instead, the last few weeks consisted of listening to my classmates comparing notes about required classes, college boys, and how they would decorate their dorm rooms. Sally summed up the situation best, in her own benign way.

> "But Pooja, you're so smart and stuff! You should go to college too!"

I couldn't pretend there was a logical explanation for letting everyone who I knew was of an inferior intellect move forward in life while I resigned myself as a married woman. Every time I tried to muster enough courage to have a serious conversation about backing out, dad would appear with his world-class smile, complimenting me on how well I had done and how proud he and mom were.

For the many difficult moments they caused in my childhood, deep down, I still wanted to please my parents, especially dad. He constantly assured me I would still get the chance to do everything I wanted. I believed him; I had to.

All I wanted as a graduation gift was a new bike. I imagined peddling around a gorgeous, expansive campus with my dark hair whipping around in the wind. It wasn't exactly a scene out of *The Mod Squad,* but for once the thickness of my mane would work in my favor. Instead of a bike, mom bestowed a different 'gift' - a trip to JFK airport in New York. Not New York City, mind you, just the airport.

Five previous times in my life, I had been dragged to JFK to go to India. To me, JFK was a place to jealously look onward at the lucky kids who got to go to one of those amazing destinations I learned about in school. Paris, Rio de Janeiro, the Pyramids in Egypt, or even California. I hadn't been to any of those.

Growing up, while I stood in the security line to help mom count our suitcases full of toilet paper and plastic bags, I would stare into the distance at the husbands happily pointing at the packet of information the Trip Advisors at the local AAA put together on all of the exciting landmarks they'd see. The kids would excitedly gather around their parents.

> *"Let's go to the Eifel Tower first, or the Champs Elysées!"*

The moms couldn't wait to expose their children to all of the interesting foods and cultures.

> *"Think of all the French croissants, the Brazilian steaks, and the California oranges you'll get to eat, Johnny!"*

For us, going to JFK always meant the same thing. Drive two hours to the closest regional airport, fly to New York, spend a night in the cheapest motel close by, then come back to the airport and start the 48-hour trip to either Bangalore or Chennai. It would have been a lot better if we actually *did* something while we went. In five trips to India, I had never even seen the Taj Mahal! Neither had mom!

We'd always spend a few days in Bangalore seeing dad's family.

They'd use the entire time to comment on how fat I had gotten, even the relatives that were big enough to blend in with the cows walking through the crowded streets. No trip to Bangalore was ever complete without dad's family making snide comments about mom. Bangalore always made us both miserable - it was one of the few things we agreed on.

The rest of the time was spent in Chennai. Mom's family was incredibly nice, but spending three to seven weeks in a slum and using a wooden box as a bathroom was not exactly an American teenager's version of an ideal summer. Overall, I hated our trips to India even more than I hated West Virginia.

"Pooja, your stupid wedding is ruining my summer! I wanted to go band camp!" Alpa cried out at me.

"How do you think *I* feel!? At least you don't have to get married to some gross Indian guy!"

In the distance, I saw dad shaking his head, as though the marriage prospects in India planted little microphones around the airport and were listening to my every word. Knowing India, there were 40 spies packed on each bus, and the surveillance equipment was from the 1950s.

Trips to India were so tiring since mom and dad insisted on taking Indian Air. All of the other airline check-ins went smoothly because the passengers understood that wearing every piece of jewelry they own slows down getting through the metal detector. On other airlines, people waited their turn in line, refrained from spitting in the hallways, knew how to use the bathroom, knew how to eat with utensils, and to cover up the awful stench of their own body odor. On other airlines, the staff actually answered you instead of replying the same way to every question.

"Yes, madam." ::Head nod::

Indian Air was a gross slice of actual India. We *always* flew Indian Air. Never drink the orange juice.

I looked down at the elegant flower watch I had Sally buy for me on her last trip back to visit her father in Nashville. It was worth every painstaking minute of babysitting the previous year. Still, even the shiny black face couldn't quell my headache; it was still another 5 hours to London. Then we'd have a 12-hour layover, and another nine-hour flight, four hours in the Bombay airport, where we'd have to go through immigration, get our luggage, ride an overstuffed bus across the city to the regional airport, and finally fly to the tiny Bangalore airport.

Every exhausting landing in the Chennai or Bangalore regional airport would be met with mom and dad forcing us to change into Indian clothes so our family could start their 200-point inspection. Just thinking about the next two days made my head spin. I closed my eyes and painfully slid back into the plastic seat that stuck to my skin.

"So are you nervous?" Alpa asked.

"Why? You don't care."

"You're my sister. You should get a nice guy. I'll help you find him, okay?"

I laughed at the thought of skinny Alpa sitting on a throne with reading glasses, a clipboard and giant pencil in hand, interviewing a long line of Indian guys to make sure the important questions were asked.

"What are your thoughts on The Brady Bunch*? Marsha or Jan?"*

We landed in Bangalore nearly 34 hours after taking off in New York. Our blurred vision gave the entire airport that same surreal look of when a negative is overexposed to light - everything is fuzzy and outlined in red lines. Even in the wee hours of the night, the area around the airport was always abuzz. Thousands and thousands of people would pack as close as possible fighting for space to greet family, friends, and random rich Indian-Americans who had just landed.

Mom loved this part of the trip. She'd wave to the crowd as though they were the audience and she was Miss Universe.

> *"Thank you, thank you. You are all too kind! I dedicate this to world peace!"*

Within seconds of walking outside, five young men jumped over the gate and offered to carry our bags. I had never paid attention to them before. This time, I looked at them with a strange mix of anxiety and curiosity. I knew mom would only allow really well educated people to be considered, but all Indians looked the same to me. What if the guy trying to make extra cash carrying my luggage would be my future husband?

Chapter 3

Mom made finding marriage prospects like the hiring process at a competitive company. The quantity of candidates wasn't met with comparable quality. After placing an ad in the local newspaper, nearly 500 guys responded within a week. I would have loved to see the look on racist Melissa Barker's face!

> *"You can't run for homecoming queen, Pooja! Brown people aren't meant to be beautiful!"* she once said.

Mom placed the ad in English, and immediately discarded all of the replies that were written in anything else. From those, she tossed out all of the 'applicants' who didn't have at least a Masters or professional degree in business, technology, medicine, or law. Of the 124 left, she had me go through and pick out the top 50. From the stupid responses, my judging criteria weren't very selective.

1. Did he spell the 'United States of America' correctly?
2. Is he older than 17 and younger than 40?
3. Did he avoid calling himself 'the most greatest' man?

After vetting the top 50, we realized only 20 could actually speak English. They each come over for an interview.

Number 13 was talking. His number was worthy of its unluckiness. Even overlooking the *Saturday Night Fever* suit, the crumbs that were sitting in his Burt Reynolds-esque moustache danced like lice as he moved his arrogant mouth up and down to praise himself. He hadn't said a nice thing about anyone else since he had arrived. Who walks in through the door demanding to know how much the dowry will be, because:

"The house looks quite run-down."

Within two minutes I knew I couldn't listen to number 13 any longer. Certainly this meant I couldn't marry him. Deciding I deserved a break, I looked over to the other side of the room and saw Alpa stick her finger in her throat. Those were my sentiments exactly. Before I made it halfway across the room, bad-body-odor-number 13 decided to leave. Mom made me stay inside for the next Prince Charming.

Number 14 was way worse than 13. After mistakenly going to the neighbors' house, he terrorized an old woman in the midst of her afternoon nap. Realizing there was no food, he then squeezed his 350-pound self through the door of dad's family's place, where we were staying. He looked like a rogue 'Mr. Potato Head.'

Before I could ask how on earth he had made the final cut, mom rushed in between the two of us and demanded he leave. It took him a few seconds, but he finally understood what she said when she made a weird motion as though to hit him in the head with a bat.

"Mom, this isn't working! That guy looked like he wanted to

eat me!"

"You're right."

It was a rare concession. We had been at the application process for nearly two weeks, and the only thing to show for our efforts were pounding headaches.

Alpa and I managed to let our foul moods melt away by sitting in the garden. Bangalore was so peaceful - it was known as the "Garden City" for good reason. The street dad's family lived on was quiet and centrally located. Trees lined both sides, kids had a ton of park space to play in, and people in the neighborhood even had small yards.

"Hey!" someone next door shouted.

A guy peered at us through a few trees. He was speaking in Telugu. At one point, Alpa and I had spoken the language at home, but mom and dad never knew when to stop in public. The staring and pointing from the locals of West Virginia eventually got to us, so we tuned out everything except English.

Standing up, Alpa and I gave the guy a blank look. He shook his head at us. We shook our head back.

"Sorry, I thought you were from here, you're wearing Indian clothes. Do you know if the owners of the house are home? I borrowed this book from them and I want to make sure they get it back," he said.

Alpa and I were taken by surprise. Any of the applicants we had seen so far would have phrased the same point completely differently.

"Hey! Vhy dooon't you speak Telugu? Vhy pretend be Indian? Give this book to uncle. Bring me tea! I 'most greatest' man!"

We both perked up at the thought of an ally who could actually communicate without insulting us. I joked to myself that if this guy had a car, I'd marry him.

"The owners are my dad's parents. I can give it back to them," I offered.

"Great, thanks," he said back, giving me a big smile.

His perfect white teeth and intense eyes matched those of dad. I glanced down at the thick book he handed me. The cover said *US Medical Residency Directory*. My usual shyness around strangers decided to make an exit.

"Are you a doctor in the States?" I asked.

"Not yet! I just got accepted to a program in Brooklyn. I leave next month."

"Congratulations!"

"Thanks, I'm really excited. Are you two visiting?"

"Yeah, to find me a husband."

My heart pounded at my unnecessarily candid answer. Surely he thought I was crazy. I didn't feel otherwise describing my ridiculous situation out loud. What kind of American girl lets herself have an arranged marriage? He echoed my thoughts precisely.

"Ah, I see. I thought Americans have love marriages though?"

Love marriage, what a funny term. In America, marriage implied love. In India, there was only one synonym for love - gold.

"My parents are special...but at the rate we're going, I'll be going home single."

"Give it time, it'll work out. Thanks for returning the

book."

I smiled, suddenly aware I hadn't been to the dentist in two years.

"I'm Anand, by the way."
"Pooja. Nice to meet you."

The bright sun of the Bangalore afternoon cast a long, deep shadow on his retreating figure. I silently praised India for demonstrating the caliber of man we had been searching for.

Chapter 4

The final six suitors showed no sign of promise. Mom was dying to get down to Chennai to see her family.

"Shall we continue the search down there?" dad asked.
"Absolutely not, it is out of the question!" mom shouted back.

Her intense negative reaction was odd considering how prideful she was of her culture. She merely played it off by claiming that continuing the search without a break was too exhausting. I didn't argue. Finding a life partner was becoming less annoying and more terrifying by the minute.

After the sweltering 2.5-hour train ride, we found an autorickshaw and let mom direct the driver into the thicket of the Chennai slums. Avva, mom's mom, greeted us with her usual smiles and cheek pinching before telling Alpa and I we had grown so tall and pretty. It was hard to imagine how a woman so animated could produce a person as stoic as mom.

Chennai brought out a relaxed and happy side of mom that we rarely saw. In Chennai, she was always doing something fun - shopping, going to temples, playing games with her sister, or catching up at the neighbors' houses. It was a nice departure from her 'work now, work more later' attitude in West Virginia.

Soon after mom and dad started making decent money, mom remitted a small portion every month back to avva. The money went to good use - building a new house. Though a welcomed move, the new house still qualified as the slums by my standards. I never got used to the lizards and spiders that shared the space.

For a few weeks every other year, dad, Alpa and I would be left to fend for ourselves while mom went off into the streets of Chennai. As the anxiety of finding a husband continued to build, I encouraged mom to take all the time she needed. By the look of her reaction to dad's suggestion, no Chennai man would ever be my husband. I prayed I could convince mom to spend the rest of trip in her childhood city, and I could return back to the States uncommitted to anything except myself.

Like the calculated machine she was, mom put an abrupt stop to her pleasure at the end of July, precisely as planned. We soon found our way back on a train through the sweltering heat straight to the Garden City. Avva was famous for her dramatic goodbyes. This time, she calmly hugged me and smiled, as though she knew she would be seeing me soon. It was a terrible sensation.

Back in Bangalore, we interviewed another hoard of guys. All of them made a concerted effort to point out their precious gender roles had been swapped.

"It is usually the man who decides who to marry, not the woman," number 22 said.

"I passed the US citizenship test on my own. *I* should demand a dowry," I snapped.

"Pooja!" mom spat at me.

There were no arguments on her side when I decided to sit out the interviews of numbers 23 - 27. I returned in time to see number 28 enter the room. He was tall, light-skinned, and handsome. Mom started out the meeting as usual.

"What are your qualifications?"

He was an electrical engineer, loved the actor, Amitabh Bachchan, and wanted to have three boys. To sum up: unequivocally boring. Mom was smitten, though, due to his graduating 'first rank' from both pre-university college and engineering school. The conversation quickly started repeating itself like a broken record.

"I graduated first rank from engineering university."

"I graduated first rank from accounting university."

I was half-tempted to demonstrate the country line dancing I learned the previous year in school. That would have certainly made mom happy.

"Look at my daughter. First rank in cowgirl school!"

Alpa was sitting outside in our usual spot making up one of her new card games. She swore she was going to get rich by inventing the new Gin Rummy. What aspirations my little sister had!

"What's he like?"

"Mom loves him because he graduated at the top of his class."

Before she had the chance to respond, we heard someone laugh.

"Who's there?" we asked at the same time.

"It's me! Sorry, I couldn't help but overhear you." the voice said.

I stood up and peered over a clothesline full of laundry that separated the two properties. Anand was sitting outside reading a textbook.

"Why did you laugh?"

"That chump! My father and his father used to do business together."

"Yeah, so?"

"He went to one of those private colleges."

Anand looked at me waiting for a reaction with the same force as the tone of his voice, the same look as when Christian missionaries 'informed' me that I was going to hell for not believing in Jesus. Their obvious point was met with my indifferent reaction.

"That guy is an idiot."

"No way, our mom got first rank. She worked non-stop for her grades!"

"Your mom and I both went to a government university, which are based on merit...mostly. Many of the private schools are worthless. They appeared after your parents left India."

That time it was my turn to give Anand a look of incredulousness. I landed on a very valuable playing card out of this marriage mess. Gin rummy!

Chapter 5

"But mom! I don't like that guy!"

"Pooja! He is coming from a good family only."

Mom using Indian sentence structures meant she was dead serious.

"Did he ask a single question about me?"

"That will come later, Pooja. He will get to know you once you are married!"

I wasn't surprised to hear mom's decision to go with Number 28. In her mind, 'first rank' trumped all other characteristics short of criminal. Even so, I saved my powerful information for one more round of argument.

"I don't want to marry that guy."

Mom threw her hands in the air in her typical 'why doesn't she listen?' way and looked over at dad.

"Talk some sense into your daughter!"

Dad closed his eyes and scratched his head. Alpa and I joked he was trying to shake the right words loose from his brain.

"Pooja. Raj...number 28, is coming from a good family. He graduated first rank..."

"Enough with the first rank! He bribed his way to the top!"

"What? Who told you that?" mom asked.

"Anand, the neighbor's son. He told me India now allows non-merit private schools. Anand said Raj is an idiot."

"You have been talking to our next door neighbor?" dad asked.

I thought about lying. It was a valuable piece of information though. Anand was the most normal Indian guy I had ever met. In a dream world, I thought he might even be able to talk some sense into mom and dad.

"Yeah, he's really nice. He's moving to the States in a few weeks."

Their faces fell. Dad mumbled something to mom in Telugu. They finished their conversation in a series of Indian head nods and words I couldn't understand. Before I could interject, they walked out of the front door and left me in a total pile of confusion.

Without mom and dad to act as our normal buffers against our criticizing relatives, Alpa and I decided to eat dinner that night in our room. Apart from India, where else would cookies and a bag of chips be acceptable as a meal? A few hours after drifting off in a diabetic semi-coma, I awoke to loud whispering coming from the first floor. Grabbing my sandals, I wandered down the dusty red staircase out of half-curiosity and half-fear.

Mom and dad were sitting in the living room with Anand. He didn't look physically harmed, thank God. Dad opened his mouth as though he wanted to say something. He wasn't used to taking the lead when mom was around.

"Pooja, could you go out with Anand? Maybe sit in the park or get an ice cream?"

"Why...what's going on, dad?"

On their behalf, Anand cut in and said he'd explain. We agreed to take his car to Cubbon Hill. I had been stuck in the house all night and desperately needed some fresh air, anyway.

It was gorgeous outside; the humidity and heat disappeared on a good Bangalore night. The kind of car Anand drove would have prompted me to demand a state inspection in America. In India, all I wanted to do was take advantage of the precious privacy of the moment.

We drove for 20 minutes through the main streets before veering off the side dirt path that led up to the Hill. At the top, we found a peaceful vantage point overlooking the entire city. Not many people in Bangalore had electricity. Tiny specs of light dotted our view.

Neither of us knew what to say. I didn't mind not talking. Anand seemed uncomfortable. Sometimes silence is a good thing in the States. Silence in India is an invitation for someone to start yelling. The agony of the quiet got to him.

"How many times have you been to Bangalore?" he wanted to know.

"Six. We usually spend most of our time in Chennai. Have you lived here your entire life?"

Anand leaned back in his seat, clearly more relaxed without the vacant sound space.

"Yes, I've lived in the same house my entire life," he replied.
"Me too."
"Really?"
"Well, I don't remember anything except West Virginia."

"What's it like? The States?"
"It's hard to describe. It's really diverse, you know?"

"Just like India?"
"Even more so."

It was an ironic thing for me to say, seeing as I had grown up with two types of people: uneducated white coal miners and uneducated black coal miners. Still, I knew the vast possibilities American could offer.

"What's it like where you grew up?" he asked.

"It sucks."

I blurted out the word before I could stop myself. There was one strict order for every trip to India: 'No cursing!' Having thoughts or opinions about my own life was also unofficially banned.

"Sucks?"

"It's terrible. The people are really close-minded. They secretly hate anyone who is different. What are the people like here?"

Anand turned to stare into the distance. He was one of the few Indians I had met that measured his thoughts before deciding what to say. I liked that.

"The people here are also closed-minded, and they also hate people who are different. But they don't keep it a secret, they tell you straight to your face!"

We both laughed. It was so true.

"Are you excited about moving to Brooklyn?"

"That's actually why your parents asked me to take you out."

"Oh no, what did they do?"

"Don't worry, it wasn't bad. They wanted to know...well...if I'd be interested in marrying you."

If had been in a TV show, that would have been the shot where I spat out my drink. I never had a soda when I needed one.

"What did you say to them?"

"I told them we needed to talk first. It's not a decision I can make alone."

It was the perfect answer. Despite the fact that the most promising

Indian man I'd ever met was entertaining the thought of filling the role of my arranged husband, I still wanted to leave India single. My valuable information card had completely backfired.

> "What about New York?"

As desperate as mom was to see me married, I knew hell would freeze over before she'd consent to me moving to Brooklyn. There wouldn't even be enough time to have a ceremony before Anand was due to start working; an elaborate wedding was non-negotiable to mom.

> "It's a great opportunity that I'd have to give up, but I can start another program later. It'll be easier being married to a citizen."

I hadn't considered Anand could find another job after getting married.

> "Look, Pooja, I think we'd get along well. If it doesn't work...divorce is more common in America. I'd have a job. We'd both continue on with our lives."

My thoughts narrowed in on the last words of his explanation. At 18, I didn't feel like I had started a life to be continued. What if mom forced me to marry number 28, or number 14, or any of those other jerks? What if I refused to marry anyone and disappointed dad to the extent of losing the one relationship in my life that gave me strength?

It took every ounce of courage I had to make a decision; I barely had enough left to give Anand his answer.

> "Okay. Let's get married."

Not once did it occur to me to ask why he agreed.

Chapter 6

We went out several times after that crisp first night to get to know each other better. Anand was an amazingly articulate person, and more importantly, a great listener. He was never patronizing, always interesting, and possessed the same worldly spirit as me, despite only having left India for a week to take an exam in Hong Kong. His relatively privileged childhood was something he did not take for granted, and the fact that women were treated as second-class citizens was a huge motivation for leaving the only country he had called home.

On our third 'date,' we went for a walk and a coffee in Gandhi Bazaar, one of the oldest neighborhoods of the city. As we rounded a street corner at the footsteps of a massive temple, I felt a tug at my shoulder and realized my purse had just been stolen.

"Hey you, stop!" Anand shouted.

Anand chased after the thief with the speed of a tiger!

For three years, I had been in love with our high school track star, Ken Johnson, and had found recurring excuses to stay after school to catch glimpses of his gazelle-like body running as though there were no tomorrow. Anand's gallops through the flickers of light that dotted the dark night had that same butterfly-like effect. It took mere seconds for him to chase down my belongings.

Between his general hygiene, good looks, first rank in medical school, and wealth, Anand had been one of most eligible bachelors in Bangalore. As he gave me my purse and grabbed my hand out of concern, I couldn't help but relish the herd of girls in the background swooning with jealousy at the sight of us. I had my first kiss that night. It was as memorable as I had hoped it would be.

Dad was truly elated with Anand being a part of the family. There was an ease in his body and voice that none of us had ever seen before.

"He's from my city! It's such a pleasure!" dad exclaimed.

Mom and dad spoke the same language, but they were from different parts of the country. Living in an American town of 25,000 for all of those years had clearly had an effect on my parents. The idea of a local Bangalore boy being a quick phone call away was music to dad's ears.

A woman of very few words but predictable sentiment, I knew mom was happy with Anand as well. I took her approval as an added bonus to the situation. Nevertheless, it was bittersweet seeing her sing words of praise for a man she barely knew when she rarely complimented her own daughter.

I had come to India that summer of 1979 in the hopes the country would fail to produce any man good enough to be my life partner. Anand easily disproved that suspicion. Though agreeing to marry him was the least of the evils, I genuinely felt that a man like Anand meant dad was right - it would be within my power to reach my life goals. It would not be a love marriage, at least not in its true sense. Love, however, would come by circumstance, by the circumstance of marriage.

Chapter 7

Since Alpa had school, the marriage ceremony couldn't take place until the winter holidays. In typical fashion, mom found a way to besmirch the contentment I had found by turning a lovely fall season into 'Basic Training: Indian Bride edition.' She spent the four months until Christmas spouting unsolicited lessons of how to cook south Indian food, how to wrap a sari, how to celebrate Hindu holidays, and the 'art' of entertaining Indian guests.

She didn't understand her aggression only made me question

everything all over again. Marrying Anand would unfortunately rule out meeting boys at parties, but surely all other aspects of college life would be there? The fascinating classes, long discussions in coffee shops, lounging around on campus…every time mom spoke about my 'duties as an Indian wife,' those simple scenes mutated into a list of lofty fantasies.

"Not like that! You'll ruin the chapatti!"
"Stop reaching over me!"

I had to step back to swat mom's arms away. She was going to make me burn myself, I swore. Her boot camp sessions had gotten worse; this last one involved me waking up at 6 AM to prepare a mountain of food on an ordinary Tuesday. Who eats all of this food so early in the morning? Who takes three hours to cook? I announced I was taking a break.

"Where are you going?"
"To rob a bank and get some ice cream."
"Pooja, wait! You must learn how to properly roll chapatti!"

Not bothering to reply before walking out the door, I let the screen slam shut. One silver lining to the situation was being able to talk back to mom since she got what she wanted. Her typical threat of:

"Do this or I will send you to India!"

didn't make sense anymore, not with an Indian man who agreed to marry me on the condition he moves to America.

I walked out the door and headed for the small corner store at the end of the neighborhood. Even though it was really close to our house, I was 12 the first time I went. Mom refused to enter, always muttering about how its white and yellow exterior reminded her of a store she knew back in Youngstown. Since she told me, I had been going there whenever I needed to get away from her. The store got a lot of my business over the years.

The streets were quieter than usual. Everyone was at work or school. I was sure the rest of the town assumed the same was true for me. I still hadn't decided if I liked the near anonymity of my situation.

My teachers all tried their best to convince me to go straight to college; they couldn't grasp the cultural implications that it was not my choice. Imagine going to college with no money, no help, and against the wishes of your family? There was no way my classmates would understand, so I never told anyone outside of Sally.

It was lonely not having anyone to talk to. Sally and I tried speaking a few times. The wonders of West Virginia University quickly made that too much of a commitment for her to continue.

Inside the convenience store, I decided on a peanut drumstick ice cream. Normally flashing the item in my hand and tossing a quarter on the checkout counter was one fluid motion. This time, a shout knocked me out of rhythm.

"Pooja! What are you doing here? Don't you have classes?"

It took me a second to realize it was Bobby. Sally had dumped him her first week away when she found out he had failed summer school.

"Hi Bobby. How are you?" I asked.

"Everything's fucked up. I can't believe Sally's gone. I was going to marry her."

"Yeah, I miss her too."

"Why are you here, Pooja?"

He hit every nerve in three lines. I did my best to calmly respond.

"I had a change of plans, Bobby. I'm..."

"Oh yeah! *You're* getting married! Now *that* is fucked up! Didn't you get into Duke?"

I couldn't believe he remembered. Mom and dad had never given me permission to apply, so I never told anyone except for Sally and Alpa I got in. It was the very definition of bittersweet.

"Why are your parents so dumb? It makes me laugh," he continued.

"Shut up, it's not funny, Bobby."

"I bet you'd be good at doing wife shit. Are you good at folding laundry?"

My head burst at that moment; I could see tiny specs of red straight ahead, as though the store were on fire, burning into ash. Bobby, one of the dumbest people I had ever met, was making fun of *me*. The worst part was I had nothing to say back.

How could I defend what mom and dad were doing? How could I explain I had picked the best choice? Or did I pick the best choice? Maybe I should have gone to Duke against their will, taken out loans, moved myself to the campus, and prepared myself to never talk to my family again? Maybe this was a result of me being weak and scared?

Somewhere in my fit of thoughts I caught another glimpse of Bobby doubled over in laughter. It tapped a rage in me I didn't know I had. Before I knew what was happening, I shouted with the force of a lifetime of frustration. The same words came out in succession:

"SHUT THE FUCK UP! YOU'RE A WORTHLESS PIECE OF WHITE TRASH!"

The other five customers in the store immediately scattered, sending the manager out in a fury. Bobby was fired and I was officially banned from the store. I couldn't have cared less. I didn't leave the house much after that day.

Chapter 8

Mom was perfectly satisfied to plan the entirety of the wedding on her own, which gave me solace from her basic training. With nothing else to fill my days, I took to hiding in the local library as I had done so many times during high school. One of the librarians noticed the constant sullen expression on my face, and became a great ally in providing me with quality reading material. Though I never asked, she always hand delivered any new brochures on college campuses. I didn't bother to pay them attention as I had before.

Time became a blur until Christmas. The days were so indistinguishable that it was Alpa who had to remind me to pack for my wedding.

> "Pooja! We're leaving in 3 days, dummy! Listen to mom, go get your suitcase!"

My lack of purpose in the previous few months gave me a numbing effect. I was the bride, yet I seemed to be the last thing on everyone's mind. Mom was vicariously living her dream wedding by executing everything for me. Dad was preoccupied with welcoming Anand to the family, and Alpa did nothing but remind me how my wedding had ruined her summer and now her Christmas.

Anand came to greet us when we landed. Dad ran up to him to shake his hand, and Anand bent down to touch mom's feet as a sign of respect. As he stood up, he caught my eye. His sparkle that had charmed me a few months ago now made me feel uneasy.

> "Hi Pooja, how was the journey?" he asked.
>
> > "Your suit is really ugly," I replied, referring to the polyester ensemble he had on.

Mom looked like she was about to kill me. He simply smiled back and assured me this was the best 1970s India could produce.

"You have great style, Pooja. You need to take me shopping in the States."

I was taken aback. No one in my family had ever made that observation.

"Yes, of course. Sorry."

"No problem. How are you?"

I had no response; it was the first time in months someone had asked me how I was doing.

The night before the wedding was like watching a state fair being coordinated on a stage meant for a ballet. Thousands of strangers poured into the house. Most of the women came to find the answer to one key question.

"Who is the woman that finally landed Anand?"

Mom and avva covered me from head to toe in impossibly ornate saris, jewelry and makeup. Some of the strangers nodded approvingly; others flapped their mouths in bewilderment that their daughters weren't judged as lucrative.

One concession everyone must make is that Indian weddings are truly beautiful, and mine was no exception. A giant tent was pitched and lined on two sides with black onyx statues of Hindu deities. Workers painstakingly hung garlands of exotic looking flowers through the entire roof of the tent. In the center of the seating area, a small fountain served as a monochromatic break in the sea of colors the 1,000 plus guests at my wedding showcased.

I managed to smile for the pictures, act happy to see distant relatives I had never met, and pretend that pleasing my new husband had already become the number one priority in my life. The truth was that my numbness persisted throughout the entire three-day ceremony. Feeling nothing was occasionally interrupted by feeling sad at the sight of mom's unequivocal happiness. She had met none of my accomplishments in life with pure joy - there was always room for improvement, always something more I could have done, always an extra effort she felt I should have made. My wedding was the first time there was nothing that could make the way she perceived the situation better. In her eyes, Anand was the first perfect thing about my life. He was the first perfect thing about me.

"Pooja?" someone called out.

I already recognized the sound of his voice. I chose not to turn around. Anand waited a few seconds before timidly taking a seat by my side.

"You look beautiful," he complimented.
"Thanks," I muttered.

He made a few more attempts at starting a conversation, all of which I shut down with one word responses.

"You've been very quiet since you got back," he concluded.
"This is me, I'm a quiet person."
"That's not true! We talked so much last summer."
"Now it's different. Now I'm quiet."
"I don't understand. What happened?"

Approximately 37 minutes before Anand sat next to me, I officially became a married woman and was expected to build a life with this man. But I felt like I had no life to build off of.

"I feel the same way," he offered.
"You do?"
"Absolutely."
"So what do we do now?"
"I suppose we have to figure it out together."

I had never thought of it like that. Anand confessed his life had been prescriptive. His best scores were in science, so his family told him to be a doctor. Everything else, including this wedding, had gone precisely as his parents had planned. Anand just happened to be good at what Indian society told him to do.

"But it hasn't made me happy. I need something different."

His uncertainty put me more at ease. While my parents and wedding guests assumed that Anand and I locked the door to the bedroom that night to consummate as a married couple, we spent the hours devising a plan for the future.

I took comfort in knowing we had both figured out how to be firsts in our lives. I was the first one to grow up in the States; Anand was the first in his family to get an education. Anand wholeheartedly supported me in making my own decisions, so I would be the first woman in our family to have a job outside of the family business. He would be the first in his family to live in a foreign country.

We knew they were accomplishments many others had made before, and some of them were accomplishments we had yet to actually make, but they were ours. You have to start somewhere to build something out of nothing.

Chapter 9

It took three extra weeks for Anand to get his initial visa to come to the States. I used that time to repeatedly return to the library to execute my part of our plan. Crouched in the depths of the catalog cards, I found my trusty librarian and her vast collection of college materials.

Anand had already sacrificed residency in New York. I had already sacrificed Duke. We now had to figure out a place that would satisfy both of our needs. By the time he landed on January 4, 1980, I had a list of schools across the country that I wanted to attend and had the credentials for admission. His first point of order after stepping off the plane was to help me talk to mom and dad.

> "Pooja, my wife, has the right to apply to all of the schools," he said.

> > "I have the right to apply to all of the schools," I repeated.

This time no one argued.

Our first weeks as a married couple were less than exciting. There was no honeymoon, no celebratory parties or mingling with other couples. Anand spent most of his time by the phone or at the local hospital trying to set up as many appointments as possible to interview for the next round of residency openings.

I didn't mind. While he tracked down leads, I worked diligently to compose perfect college entrance essays. Duke had admitted me based on a paper about the generational journey it took for me to be able to approach a serious academic institution as a young Indian woman. Somehow that journey seemed disingenuous after conceding to marry. Talking about building my life with a near stranger eight years my senior would never transcend cultural boundaries.

February 1980 ushered in two months of Anand's residency travels - he had managed to schedule twelve interviews in nine cities, most of which were within easy commuting distance of the schools I had chosen. Two of the interviews were in cities that had no decent school options for me. He had been approached by the hospitals, and was questioning whether to even make the trips.

On the last day of the month, I mailed out my applications for entrance into the following semester. Instead of returning home, I made my sixth trip in three weeks to the Roanoke regional airport to pick up my…husband. The first few returns, he described everything - the buildings, the cars, the people, the hospitals. Novelty wears off quickly, and I figured his increasing quietness with each trip was a sign he was growing accustomed to his new environment. This time, the silence was laden with pessimism.

"What did you think?" I prompted him.

"There were many tall buildings."

"That's Atlanta."

"It wasn't my favorite."

"There is also a lot of history to the region. And good schools."

Including a school that would receive my application in a few days. He knew I had posted my work, and I expected he'd ask about my admissions essay topic. Instead, he retreated back to his silence. It was the first time since we'd met that I got a sense he wasn't sure of himself. That made me nervous.

"Are you okay?" It was my turn to ask.

"Pooja…" he said softly.

He asked me to pull to the side of the road so we could talk for a few minutes. By the tone of his voice, I knew our plan was just a plan. Our plan would not be reality.

Chapter 10

Every interview Anand went to started out the same way. They'd be impressed with his perfect American accent, charm and good looks, swearing that a new era had begun and doctors from overseas were welcome with open arms.

"Our Swiss, Japanese and Argentinean colleagues have contributed a lot to the local medical community," they all assured.

My childhood had taught me that India was still an unknown, even in bigger American cities. Despite all the passion and knowledge he possessed, once the interviewers understood how poor India still was, they dismissed Anand and his education. The names of the cities where he did his fieldwork were too long, the techniques he had memorized were too antiquated, and his professor's credentials were deemed unworthy.

Like a dog whittled in shame, Anand told me with his tail between his legs that all of the interviews so far had ended in an unequivocal rejection. The good ole' Southern boys of Atlanta had practically laughed him out of the room when he told them the name of his medical school: 'Medical College of Basavanagudi.'

"What are our options?" I asked.

"I could wait a year and apply again."

"I don't want to get stuck here for another 18 months."

"Or I could go to these last two interviews even though they're in cities that weren't part of our plan."

Detroit and Orlando. Those were the choices - different manifestations of hell. Detroit was a city riddled with crime and drug use; they were willing to hire anyone who resembled a doctor. Anand would get a residency position because they were desperate; the city had little amenities or safety to offer.

Nearly a decade before, Orlando had solidified its status as a theme park destination, effectively doubling the city's population overnight. An announcement had been recently made about a second theme park to be opened within the next few years, and everyone - hospitals included - were anticipating a major spike in demand for just about everything. It was a boon for last minute applicants like Anand.

The gravity of the situation hit me like a boulder, forcing me out of the car in a stammering heap of hysteria. Anand gave me a few minutes to let out my tears before walking over to apologize what must have been a hundred times. Words like,

> *"I'm so sorry"*

had long lost their meaning and did little more than to enrage me. Everyone was so sorry for me all of the time. No one did anything to make it better or to get out of my way and let me make it better for myself.

> "How the FUCK did you get into a residency program in Brooklyn last year?"

He took a deep sigh, trying his best to stay calm.

> "I asked the same question after my interview last week. How could I get into New York and not Boston?"

A native New Yorker who was sitting in the room took one look at the address of the hospital that initially extended Anand the offer, and snickered.

> *"Son, that hospital is in Crown Heights."*

Anand found out later that the neighborhood of Crown Heights was infamous for gang related violence, hardcore drug addicts, extreme poverty and murders. It would have been infinitely worse than anything Detroit had to offer.

Guilt washed over me because I had no way to hide my total disgust for Anand not being able to secure a position in any of the cities we had agreed on, where I had school options. Anger took over as I once again replayed the list of empty promises mom and dad had made in forcing me to get married. Shame for America wove its way through my body for not producing people who were able to see how brilliant and deserving Anand was. The three combined to form a thick layer of immobility. Much like I had made the decision to marry Anand, I would again be forced to pick the least of all evils.

A tiny whisper of defeat escaped Anand's lips, and I saw he too was crying. The last time he grabbed my hand, he was the hero. This time, he was the victim.

> "Pooja, I'm so sorry. If you move with me to Detroit or Orlando, I promise you the next place we go will be for your career."

I brushed away his tears and fought back another round of mine.

> "It's okay, Anand. We'll make it work somehow."

Anand received his official offer from Memorial Hospital in downtown Orlando a month later. In April 1980, we packed our moving van and left West Virginia. I got into all ten schools I applied to.

Chapter 11

With every mile we drove south, I felt myself sinking further into depression. At a pit stop somewhere in the middle of Georgia, a woman called me out in front of thirty people while I was waiting in line for the bathroom.

> "My lord," she said, pointing at my ring. "Aren't you way too young to be married?"

Before he started work in the summer, Anand tried his best to cheer me up. We'd take day trips to the closest beach, he'd coax me to go to Disney World, and even offered to go dancing at a flamenco bar a few blocks away. Most importantly, he shielded me from mom.

She was infamous for starting every conversation with the same sentence:

> *"Pooja, I have had a very difficult life..."*

With the same conclusion:

"You must not be lazy."

As though my life situation had resulted from my lack of will to make things happen. I quickly became adverse to telling her anything about Orlando. Anand, still feeling guilty for not following through on his end of the bargain, made an excellent filter in those first few months.

"Pooja is very busy; she cannot talk right now," he'd lie.

Once Anand had to start work, I had to deal with the phone. I approached it with many trepidations, until I finally figured out mom would let it ring precisely four times and then hang up, deciding it wasn't worth the effort to wait any longer. On its sixth or seventh ring, I'd pick up and promptly tell dad or Alpa I had to go or the caller had the wrong number. My system worked for a while. We never got any other calls.

One week in July, I heard the phone ring. My heart would usually pound with brute force until the ringing made it over the fourth hump. Ring number seven was approaching. I picked up the receiver, mentally rehearsing my routine.

"Hello, you've got the wrong num…"

"Hello? Hello? HELLO?" a thick Indian voice shouted in succession.

It was Anand's mother. His dad usually directly called the hospital for her.

"Yekka da Anand?" she demanded.

I took a deep sigh. I hadn't heard Telugu in months. I was starting to have a visceral reaction to the sound.

"He's not here. Can I take a message?"

"Yekka da Anand?"

"He's not here! No! Not here!"

"Anand letha?"

"No!"

I heard some shuffling on the other side.

"Hello? Anand not there?" his father asked.

"No, can I take a message?"

"You don't speak Telugu? Vhhhy don't you speak Telugu!?"

On hearing that primeval question, I slammed down the receiver with such that the apartment rumbled with pity.

After that day, I decided the best solution to the phone was not to be there when it rang. Since Anand was still making peanuts as his salary, going to Disney World and flamenco bars quickly became too expensive. The entertainment of Orlando was tacky, anyway.

It didn't take long to exhaust the very limited public library resources of central Florida. The region was known for its rollercoasters; people didn't go there to study. Instead, I began visiting Anand in the hospital for lunch. With the commute on the bus, it was upwards of a four-hour round trip, the only four hours a day I did anything.

"Would you like pudding?" he asked one Thursday.

"That's apple sauce."

"How about French fries?"

"You mean onion rings?"

"Pooja!"

He was getting frustrated. It was understood given the situation that he had no right to ask me to cook, maintain the house a certain way, or fulfill any of those stupid lessons from mom's basic training. We never discussed how long that agreement would last. The impatience in his voice implied that he felt it would not be much longer.

I never asked about his work even though I could tell he really liked it. The other residents were friendly, the staff was supportive, and administration was grateful to have filled every slot. My presence was a dark cloud over the literal and figurative sun Orlando brought for my husband.

That day, one of the Department Heads of Surgery decided to join us. Like a lion celebrating his newly killed prey, Anand puffed out his chest in victory at the gesture. It was rare for someone so high ranking to pay any heed to a resident. The Head made one feeble attempt to engage me in conversation.

"How do you like Orlando?"

"I hate it."

Anand was mortified. I decided to skip the hospital tour he said he'd give me. He decided to skip coming home that night.

Chapter 12

"Pooja, are you ready?" Anand shouted down the hall to me.

I thumped my foot against the floor, staring at my closet. Putting yourself together is always easier when the outing is a welcomed occasion. After deliberating for a few minutes, I landed on a blue dress that draped nicely around my waist and landed tastefully at the calf to show off my legs in the heat of the Florida summer. Bold colors were in that year, and I picked out a bright green bag to do the talking for me. Everyone assumed those who sport color were happy people. I needed that assumption made tonight.

Anand and I had our first real argument when he came home a few days after I told the Head I hated Florida.

"Why can't you make any effort!? When are you going to stop

punishing me? Why do you refuse to be happy?"

Our life together was very new, but that man was one of the few people I had ever truly started to get to know. Anand was my only advocate and friend in an isolating city. You can't just pull yourself out of depression, though I had learned how to feign interest many times in my life. When he nervously asked if I would accompany him to the Chief of Medicine's house party, I had no choice but to go, and I had to make a good impression.

During the car ride, we sat in the same strained silence as when I had picked up Anand from the airport six months prior. This time, our roles were reversed. Topics for an interesting conversation evaded my head, as I hadn't picked up a newspaper, turned on the television, or had a real conversation in weeks.

"Should we go home?" he asked, interrupting my thoughts of nothingness.

"Yes."

His shoulders slumped.

"I was being sarcastic," he replied.

"So was I."

"No you weren't."

"No. I wasn't."

"For what it's worth, I think you'll like her."

"Her?"

It turned out the Chief of Medicine was a woman. She had grown up in Washington DC, attended medical school in Virginia, and eventually decided to move to Florida to be closer to her Trinidadian grandparents. Finding out the Chief was a female gave me an unexpected spurt of energy that even Anand noticed.

By the time we pulled up to the hostess's driveway, he was happily describing all the fascinating things the Chief had done in her life. His humming in the backdrop was dwarfed by the sight of the massive house that contained a grand foyer straight out of a Humphrey Bogart movie. A gold tint shimmered over the entire space as though someone had taken a giant paintbrush and turned everyone into a Sepia photograph. Anand caught a glimpse of the expression on my face.

> "We'll have something like this one day, you know," he said to me.
>
> > "Maybe if I go unconscious and dream this place alive."
>
> "I'll give you everything you've ever wanted, I promise."

I knew he wanted to believe it. The problem was that all I wanted was to leave the one thing that he needed.

For the next hour, I dutifully followed Anand around while he mingled with various hospital personnel. Growing up in an environment familiar to medicine gave me enough substance to know when to nod, smile or tick my tongue in sympathy for a struggling patient or frustrated doctor.

Anand was aware that I had not even the slightest interest in going into medicine myself. On the way to the fifth set of conversing people, he flashed me a quick side smile of gratitude and said he'd understand if I wanted to step outside.

Grateful to make it to the fresh air, I had a chance to sit back and take in the beauty of the garden. Mom and dad were hoarders of any wealth they had accumulated and never spent money on aesthetics.

> *"Money is meant to be saved!"* Mom would always dramatically declare.

Seeing someone make investments into what they owned was something I appreciated.

"Would you care for a glass of white wine?" a woman standing next to me asked.

"Are you saving it for someone else?"

"I grabbed an extra by mistake. It's all yours."

I turned to face her - she was an impressive looking person, exuding confidence that was both calming and unnerving. At 19, I could count the number of times I had drank alcohol on one finger. Desperate to not come off unhinged, I brought the cup up to my lips without letting a drop in.

"How is it?" she asked.

"Bitter."

"Bitter? I thought it was a Riesling?"

I had no clue what that meant, so I changed the subject.

"This place is enormous!" I exclaimed

"Enormous is a relative term."

"My guess would be 9,000 square feet. That's enormous to me."

She pursed her lips as if to consider what I had just said, then asked me how I came to that estimate.

"Well, the land in this part of the country is generally very flat and soft, so any hidden or underground basement is unlikely. It's easy enough to guess the length and width of the exterior. Assuming there are no major enclosures, multiply by three floors, and I get about 9,000 square feet."

I barely had time to react to the expression on her face; I was equally stunned I had just said that!

She paused before speaking, finally asking what I did as a profession.

I felt myself blushing beneath the thankful haven of my dark skin. It was obvious I was young. I'm sure she knew as soon as she handed me that glass of wine.

"I'm…uh…between…I…" I stammered.

"Follow me," she replied.

We walked a few paces over to a man I hadn't yet met. Without hesitation, she broke between his sentences.

"Jonathan, I'd like to introduce you to…" she started, glancing in my direction.

"Pooja," I finished, voice shaking, beyond nervous.

"Pooja just made the most brilliant observation about our house. I think she would make a fine addition to your program."

Our house? I thought. My only goal that night was to make a good impression. How could I not know I was talking to the Chief?

"My wife doesn't say these kinds of things often, you know," Jonathan said to me.

"I must be serious," she asserted.

Without further warning, she spun on her heel and walked back into the house, her silver dress catching the moonlight as though the sky purposely configured itself in her favor.

Jonathan didn't let me take an extra moment to process what was happening. He gave me the next half-hour to describe a million thoughts on building facades, landscapes and open spaces. They came so naturally; I found an autopilot of thinking I didn't even realize I had.

"Pooja, I'd be thrilled if you came in for an interview," he said.

"I've never had a job…"

"No no, don't be silly. Allow me to introduce myself properly…" said Jonathan, Dean of Architecture at the University of Florida, Orlando.

He gave me his card, making sure to write down his direct line on the back.

"I'll have my secretary schedule you in first thing Monday morning."

Back inside the house, I found Anand by the drink table. I still had the glass of wine in my hand.

"Found a friend to sneak you alcohol?" he playfully asked.

"You'll never believe who," I replied.

"You'll have to tell me all about it during the car ride home."

I nodded, surveying my scenery. The faint glow that persisted throughout the halls of the house had ignited something brilliant within me.

Chapter 13

Jonathan emigrated from his native Nigeria to the States as a student at Virginia Tech to be 'something practical' - as his parents put it - like an engineer or a doctor.

"I was less compelled by people as individuals than people as communities," he said.

Despite his parents' wishes, he accepted admission to the School of Architecture, and landed a job in DC after, which is where he met the

Chief, Christine.

"Marrying a doctor was still not out of the question."

He built an impressive career over the next 20 years. When Christine decided she needed to be closer to Trinidad, Jonathan took the unanticipated move to create something new - a Department of Architecture at a school few had heard of. Within a year, it became accredited; within five years, it became one of the top 20 in the country.

"What made you think of those observations about our house?" was his first question of the interview.

"I don't know. It came naturally."

Of course the sole architect behind its design was its owner, and Jonathan took kindly to the implicit flattery behind my attention to his work. We talked about the history of American and African architecture, principles of negative and positive space, and how elements from our everyday lives can influence how a building is designed.

"I noticed you're into fashion, that can play an important role in inspiring one's work," he continued.

"Thanks for noticing, it's something I've always taken to heart."

In high school, my classmates knew me as the weird brown girl who always did her homework. Everything else about me was unappreciated; my classmates didn't know the difference between chic and shit. Jonathan could relate as an immigrant African at a college in rural Virginia.

"Pooja, I won't pretend Orlando is the metropolis you've been searching for."

"I've come to that conclusion."

"Despite its location, we've been able to create a great program. I'd love for you to be a part of it."

Jonathan told me that for him, architecture was about creating spaces for bettered human interaction. What he said made total sense. There was a distinct feeing of comfort in using my life to plan how people interact, and how a family functions and communicates.

Time flew by as we spoke, and two hours after I had first stepped foot in his office, I left with an official invitation for automatic enrollment into the Department of Architecture. Classes started the week after.

"Hi, mom," I said.

"Where are you?"

"At home, where else would I be?"

"How would I know? You never pick up the phone."

That era was over, I knew. I finally had good news to share.

"Guess what? I am starting architecture school!"

"Is Anand home? Are you making proper Indian dinner?"

"I'm starting architecture school next week!"

"The key to chapatti is to let the dough..."

"MOM!!!"

I screamed with such intensity I thought I would have a brain aneurism. This was the most significant thing that had happened to me in a year; I was furious she didn't care to listen.

"What is it?" she finally conceded.

"I'm starting architecture school next week. I'm really excited."

"Architecture? I thought you were going to be an accountant?"

She always had a way of projecting her desires as mine. That weird obsession with accounting was one of them. I knew this conversation was over before it had even started. With my newfound insight into buildings, I blamed our terrible West Virginia house for never creating the space for proper interaction. I had her pass the phone to dad before my mood was completely soiled.

He, of course, was thrilled at me finding a new passion, and for making the most out of a bad situation.

"I'm so proud of you for figuring this out on your own."

His words of gratitude were all I needed hear to refuel my excitement.

"She will realize very quickly we all got what we wanted," he assured.

Fortunately, I didn't have time to dwell further. There was less than one week before classes started, which meant I needed to get a hundred things in order. The mental block of doing mundane tasks like applying for a Florida driver's license disappeared when it was part of a greater process to register for classes.

On August 23, 1980, I finally lived out one of the recurring dreams of my life - I entered my first college class. Though it hadn't happened as I had hoped, the time I had invested in my higher education already had me thinking that this was the beginning of something truly amazing.

Chapter 14

"And that is why buildings in Washington DC and Paris have such similar façade structures," I concluded.

"Bravo!" Anand shouted, clapping his hands with emphatic gestures.

"Thanks for listening."

"Are you sure you don't want another student's opinion?"

I let the question hang in the air just long enough until I was sure it was safe to change the subject. Classes had gone really well my first year in Orlando, and I was genuinely looking forward to the next day when my Intro to European Architecture section began. Jonathan was a guest lecturer and had asked me to make a special presentation. I was thrilled, until he told me the reason.

"Pooja, I'm afraid that our students have trouble finding connections to foreign things in their own lives."

"I second."

"Could you put together something to bring a European city closer to home?"

Because I was one of the few people in the university who owned a passport, Jonathan needed my help relating to students who refused to pick up a book that was not required.

"I'm going to be a lot busier as a second year resident..." Anand started.

"I understand," I assured, not wanting to get into this conversation again.

Anand, dad, Alpa and even mom on occasion had no shortage of praise for my academic performance. I made the Dean's List both semesters, and I was easily one of the most recognized faces among the Architecture Department professors. Everyone knew I was going to go far in this field.

Socially, things were different. Thankfully, I wasn't still considered that weird brown girl who did all her homework; I was just married. At its core, UF Orlando was still a party school. My peers were more concerned with drinking and Greek life than they were about excelling at their work. That intimate circle of friends I was hoping to cultivate through coffee shops and dinner parties didn't exist in a place like that.

My one attempt to assimilate in the popular culture of the school was a disaster.

"What's your name?"
"Pooja. You?"
"Poo-WHAT?"
"Poo-JA."

The guy smelled of stale beer and stupidity. But he was the first person who came over to talk to me, and I was still trying to salvage the night.

"Want to make out?"
"I'm married."
"Knocked up?"
"NO! It's cultural."
"How many kids you got?"
"Zero! It was arranged!"
"That's a fucked up arrangement," he said, before stumbling away.

Statements like those put me in a limbo. 'That's a fucked up arrangement' was a line I would have thrown in mom's face two years prior. At the start of my second year of college, I didn't know what to think. I was neither Indian nor American. I was a student without a student's life. I was a wife without a wife's life. But, I loved the content of my classes and the professors that came with them. It had become secondary that the only thing outside of my academic life was my husband.

I looked back at Anand and offered a few pacifying words to end the conversation.

"Don't worry, I love what I do, I'll be fine."

"Thanks for stopping by, Pooja," Jonathan said.

"My pleasure."

I looked around his office. The family photos were updated regularly, and they always looked gorgeous. In my mind, equal in beauty was his overstuffed drawer of contacts.

"Thanks to a few professors in the department, we have come across some funding," he continued.

"Congratulations! What will it buy?"

"Mostly new supplies. And a paid research assistant."

Doing my best to be conspicuous, I shifted by body slightly forward, desperate to not miss a word of what was coming.

"If you would be amenable, we'd love to take you on three days a week."

The smile of my face must have stretched a mile wide. There were 500 students in the architecture program. Being hand picked as a research assistant meant that I was the best; great things were indeed yet to come.

"I would be honored!" I screamed, still not sure if I had

conveyed the depths of my happiness.

"Excellent. I know Orlando wasn't where you saw your..."

I waved my hand in a dismissive motion. Landing an opportunity like this was enough to quell the last waves of bitterness that sometimes surged through me on particularly stressful days. It took a while to get to a point where I understood that Orlando not being forever didn't mean Orlando shouldn't be as good as possible. Such an offer meant I was making that happen.

"I'm glad to see things are getting better. This position would be contingent on your commitment to complete the program."

"Absolutely! When do I start? I'd be ready early next week!"

Jonathan chuckled with an air of experience. Funding in academic institutions was rarely quick moving. The position would start in three months. He was intent on making sure the role would fit both the needs of the program, and give me solid experience. We discussed a few topics that would bolster the profile of the school. Everything French was in style.

"Please keep the following information quiet," he said at the end of our meeting.

"I can keep a secret."

"Some of the faculty would like to visit a field site this summer. We'd of course bring the Research Assistant."

The whole campus must have felt the atomic reaction that caused my heart to explode. My first work trip would be to Paris!

Chapter 15

That afternoon was the first time in more than a year that I skipped a class. As soon as I left Jonathan's office, my mind began playing out beautiful scenes of what lay ahead. Working side-by-side professors, finally having my days filled with intellectual conversations in coffee shops, only in *France*. Thirty minutes in Jonathan's office had given me more inspiration than the rest of my life combined. How quickly I had been able to work my way up in Orlando was impressive. I had to celebrate!

None of my classmates would appreciate how much of an honor this offer was. Alpa was too young and mom and dad turned every conversation about school into a cultural tug of war.

"These American universities do not make sense!"

The one person in the world I wanted to tell was Anand. I knew he never meant for me to end up here, and I knew he wanted me to do well. This news was a way to move past those nasty first months and to finally congratulate ourselves for doing so well despite what we had been given.

After tracking him down at the hospital, I told him to be home by 8. Being such big news, I wanted to reveal the surprise over dinner, not quickly tell him in between patients.

I swore to never tell mom that I was actually grateful for her boot camp sessions. I borrowed the car for the afternoon, running around the central Florida region tracking down ingredients for a proper south Indian meal. Timed perfectly, by 7:30, all I needed to do was let the idli cool and set the table. The setup was beautiful; Anand would love it.

It took every ounce of patience for me to not sit by the phone the first 20 minutes he was late. By 8:30 I was pacing. By 9 I was crying. By 10 I was angry. He pushed through the door around 10:30, clearly exhausted.

"Where the hell were you?"

"The head of internal medicine called me in, I couldn't get away."

"I spent 4 hours cooking you dinner."

My voice was shaking; I was so livid. He followed the direction of my pointed finger and saw the feast I had prepared sitting on the table. The steam that had gracefully risen from the dishes was now replaced with cold food that had a grayish appearance.

"I'm so sorry, Pooja! I had no idea, you never cook."

I flinched at the last part. It was a reminder I was a bad wife, exactly what I had been hoping this dinner would lay to rest.

"I'll go wash my face and we'll sit and eat together," he decided.

There was no better solution. I nodded, and told him I'd wait on the couch. 10, 15, 20 minutes later and he still hadn't emerged from the bedroom. The noise of the hand on the clock behind me grew with each second until I was sure my eardrums would explode.

"Anand," I said, trying to wake him from our bed, where he had passed out.

"Anand!"

"ANAND!!"

He stirred enough to rub his face with his hand.

"Pooja, I'm so tired. It was a 16-hour shift."

I didn't care. The most exciting news of my life was supposed to be celebrated over that dinner I took such trouble in preparing. How were we supposed to start over if he couldn't even find two hours to spend with his wife at dinner?

A moment of quiet was all it took for him to fall back asleep. Dejected, I closed the bedroom door with me on the other side and spent the night on the couch, falling asleep to the sounds of late night TV. He was gone by the time I woke up the next morning. The untouched food was still on the table, as though it were an exhibit in a museum.

Chapter 16

We tried working on our communication skills. Anand made the case that had I been clearer with the effort I intended to put into that dinner, he would never have agreed to go into the meeting. Regardless, he said he should have called and let me know how late he would be.

Using very direct statements, unambiguous instructions, and a lot of phone calls, we managed to schedule times to see each other over the next few weeks. Inevitably, one of us would cancel at the last minute, realize we had unfinished work that needed to be done and either leave or simply fail to show up at all.

All the open communication in the world could not change how busy he was and how little I was willing to compromise on school to accommodate his erratic schedule. I realized in mid-October that I still hadn't told him I had been awarded the Research Assistantship.

The drift apart was slow and steady. One day we woke up and realized how far from each other we were. We were both new to our careers and grew each day. The more we grew as individuals, the farther apart we grew as husband and wife.

I got a call from the pushy owner of our apartment complex in November that year. Construction of the new theme park addition was near completion, and investors were hoping to start welcoming guests within six months. Because of the proximity of our complex to the parks, our owner had gotten a lucrative offer.

"I'm being offered three times what I paid! I need you out by Christmas!"

"We signed a lease, you can't kick us out. We don't have time to find a new place."

"Ain't my problem. Your lease is nullified if I sell. Read the fine print!"

He slammed the phone down before I could argue further. Annoyed but not panicked, I dug out the lease and read the masses of pages I had neglected to look over before Anand and I had co-signed. Our aggressive owner was right, he could sell and we'd have no recourse.

I sighed and looked up at the calendar. It was less than a month to finals. Then I had a lot of research to get through before the start of the next semester. How was I supposed to find a new apartment before Christmas? With only a few minutes before I had to catch the bus to campus, I left Anand a note telling him to keep the weekend open so we could start looking. I had no desire to become homeless.

We caught each other the next Saturday afternoon.

"I saw your note," he said.

"We should start looking today. When will you be ready?"

"We need to talk."

"Okay, I'll get the keys. I found some listings already."

"Pooja, we need to talk."

"Grab the newspaper for me, would you?"

"NOW!"

It took me a few more seconds to realize what he was asking in between my lines. We were becoming progressively worse at listening to each other.

"You know residency is only a two year program, right?" he asked.

"Then a few years of fellowship, I know."
"I decided on what my specialty will be."
"What is it?"
"Neurology..."

His voice trailed off as though that word held some hidden meaning. It was an impressive specialty, I thought. Beyond that I had no opinions.

"Why are you silent?" I prompted. He gave me a few more seconds to make the connection myself.

"Orlando doesn't have any hospitals with a neurology fellowship," I finished.

"We're moving in May, Pooja."

The way he said that word - *we* - brought back all the same emotions. Why was it okay that his needs were prioritized over mine?

"*WE* are not moving anywhere, Anand!"
"We have no choice!"
You have a choice, Anand. *We* do not. I am not moving again."
"You hate it here!"
"Not anymore!"

A small look of recognition crossed his face and I knew he finally saw the considerable rift between us.

I told him about the Research Assistant position and all of its glory. It was a fantastic opportunity that had not existed until then. My timing was impeccable.

"And it's contingent on me finishing the program here."

"I had no idea, congratulations."

"So you see I have to stay here. Now let's go find an apartment!"

I found it so ironic the conversation had evolved me wanting to stay in a city that I had once violently hated.

"Pooja, no."

"No?" I asked, visibly insulted.

"Your Research Assistant position is a great opportunity…"

"But?"

"But this is not up for discussion. This is my career, our financial security."

"What does that mean? That I don't get to be a part of the decisions?"

"You are always a part of my decisions!"

"*Your* decisions, Anand! What about what I want?"

"Pooja, you're just a kid…"

I saw myself shrivel down to a puppet, the marionette strings sprouting from my shoulders. Anand grabbed the wooden handles attached, whipping me around for the pleasure of the audience.

"My first act will be 'Dance of the Pooja!' She'll serve coffee after the show."

I couldn't bear to see his face anymore. Fifteen minutes after jumping in the car and leaving him bewildered in the apartment, I found myself driving in the direction of Jonathan and Christine's house.

Chapter 17

"Pooja? What are you doing here? Is everything okay?" Christine asked.

I pushed past, forcing my way into her house as though we had been close friends for decades. The fact that she was Anand's boss and her husband was my boss didn't even cross my mind. If she noticed, she didn't mind.

"Is everything okay?" she repeated.

I tried to speak and instead felt my throat melt in anger. As though she knew there was a fiery war waging beneath the surface, she walked over to the kitchen and poured me a glass of water. There was no air of hurriedness that usually covered my apartment in a dense fog. One of the busiest doctors in the entire Orlando area had more time to talk about my feelings than my own damn husband.

Her kindness was overwhelming; I told her everything. The lonely little girl who passed her days conducting the orchestras in her head, building cities out of paper, befriending plastic dolls, and dreaming of a time when life would be much better. The hardworking student who prioritized studying over breathing, yet still developed a voice and a style. The now young adult who constantly felt the only options in life were her happiness *or* the happiness of everyone else.

Of all the reactions possible, I was not prepared for the one thing I had yearned to hear for so long.

"Pooja, you're absolutely right."

Christine told me about her and Jonathan's experience being decades deep into their marriage. Having two people who are passionate about their career can be very difficult to balance.

"The hospitals I needed were not located in places conducive to Jonathan's work."

"He chose you over what was best in his profession?"

"Often, yes. But he still built an incredible career."

She stopped short of saying it was something I could do too. Neither of us knew if that was true. And both of us knew there was an inherently different motivation behind what Jonathan did and what my relationship with Anand entailed. Anand and I did not marry because we fell in love.

"All I can say is that Anand believes in you," she offered.

"That's doubtful."

"It isn't. How do you think I knew to introduce you to Jonathan?"

My mind reeled with that last statement. The whimsical child in me had written off the encounter as fate. Christine told me in his first few months of work, Anand was fascinated with the possibilities of careers in America. He wanted to know more about everything.

"He saw that the kind of observation involved in architecture was something you have."

"Why didn't he tell me?"

"Maybe he wanted you to make the decision on your own."

Christine walked over to me and gently put her hand on my shoulder. She told me that for all of the brilliance Anand possessed, he still had some growing up to do.

"He is smart beyond his years, but you are wise beyond your years."

"You're saying having me will benefit him?"

"Absolutely, and he knows that."

"What about me?"

"Maybe you would have found architecture without his support. Maybe something even better."

But that was a hypothetical question no one could answer. All that was certain was everything I had built in less than two years and Anand's role in enabling that to happen.

Christine called Jonathan into the room. Jonathan was empathetic to my situation even though it meant he'd be losing his Research Assistant. They assured me that they'd take the next few days to think about cities that had both the fellowship program Anand needed and an architecture program for me.

"Pooja," Jonathan said, "You will make it to Paris. You will make it anywhere you want."

Jonathan's words gave me calmness about the sacrifice I was about to make. I gave him my verbal resignation of the Research Assistant offer, praying with every ounce of will that I had not made the biggest mistake of my life.

Chapter 18

I decided I needed time to organize my thoughts before approaching the same topics with Anand. In the meantime, I simply said I would move with him to a city that had a good architecture program. He decided on a last minute trip to India for the winter holidays; I was so grateful we didn't have enough money for two tickets. Like the unfamiliar roommates we were, we said a lukewarm goodbye and parted for the month. For once in my life, I couldn't wait to get to

West Virginia.

Alpa and I spent most of the last two weeks of December sitting on the couch and watching TV. Letting my mind atrophy with the mundane entertainment of daytime television was exactly what I needed to balance out an intense 18 months of self-reflection and evaluation.

Growing up, mom always had a belittling way of dismissing my problems. Everything had always been in comparison to her traumatic life events - her father being murdered, her best friend committing suicide, nearly getting deported for something that was not dad's fault.

*"**Those** are reasons to be depressed, Pooja."*

This trip, she was thankfully easy on me. I didn't know what had prompted the change, but the few details I had shared with her about my life in recent months actually seemed to register. She knew I was passionate about my work, and a part of me wanted to believe she was remorseful for letting Anand take away the opportunities I had been able to create.

Dad was his in usual good mood, and even participated in Alpa's and my cookie baking marathon, movie watching with hot apple cider, and pillow wars. Being out of the house had given my parents a chance to see that I could be my own person. As much as mom must have thought our uncharacteristic fun was nonsense, she let dad, Alpa and I have carefree moments. I needed a stress relief, and I was grateful I could finally turn to my childhood home for that comfort. Together, the four of us rang in New Year's 1983 with the comfort I had wished for so many nights as a kid.

Chapter 19

A few days after the New Year, I decided to resume my old habit of getting the mail. Running to the little black box was one of my favorite things to do as a child; it was one of the only connections I felt I had to the outside world.

As I walked back to the house, I flipped through the contents even though I knew there would be nothing for me. It was a typical stack - a few bills, two Christmas catalogues, a flyer for the new Piggly Wiggly store, and one large envelope from Georgetown University…for Alpa.

The envelope was ornately covered in fine ribbons of black and white against a blue inset. I remembered getting promotional materials featuring smiling students outside on a grassy campus or raising their hands to be called on by a professor. When I was in high school, I was so taken with the atmosphere they created. Looking back on the quality of some of schools that were advertised now only made me cynically smile.

> *"College you've never heard of: We have students. Some of them can read."*

Taking a second look at the envelope, I realized it looked nothing like promotional material. It was a letter. Even though it was a total invasion of privacy, I couldn't help myself. In slow motion, my hands ripped wildly at the seam while the other pieces of mail crashed to the snow and left gaping holes in smooth surface. I couldn't believe what I saw inside.

> "Dear Ms. Alpa Deva,
>
> We are pleased to inform you that your early admission application has been successful for the Fall 1983 semester. Please find your admission packet enclosed. Congratulations on your hard work. We look forward to seeing you this September."

Not bothering to pick up the rest of the mail, I ran back to the house without the slightest care of the commotion I made. This time there was no mom running downstairs in a panic. This time it is me who pounded heavily on the staircase, demanding to know answers. Alpa was sitting in her robe, brushing her hair.

"What the fuck is this? Mom and dad let you apply to college!?"

From my past secret applications, I knew that if Alpa had done the same, the letter would have gone to a friend's house. Receiving a response at home meant mom and dad knew what was happening.

"Pooja, I was going to tell you!"

"To hell you were! I've been home for three weeks!"

Her tiny body began to shake; her hand flapped like a bird trying to escape its captor.

"Why didn't you call and tell me?" I demanded.

"What could I say? Mom and dad are letting me apply when they forced you to get married?" she could barely whisper.

"Yes! No! FUCK!"

I collapsed into a heap on the floor. In the background, Alpa cried, saying she was so sorry. Everyone was always so sorry.

"Pooja, I love you so much, I'm always on your side."

"I know…" it was my turn to whisper.

"I don't know why they changed their mind for me. When I found out I'd be skipping 10th grade, I guess we had to talk about it sooner."

"What did they say?"

"You should talk to dad. All I know is that I got lucky."

I knew she was right. My 16-year old sister getting married wouldn't do anything to change my situation. We sat in silence for nearly an hour before she had the nerve to ask to see the letter. Her glee of getting in was clearly marred with the sadness and anger my presence brought. Mom and dad would be home from the grocery store any minute. Despite my instincts to punch a hole through the wall, I slowly stood up and locked myself in my room.

For two days, I stared at the white wall that defined my childhood existence. No photos of friends, no happy drawings of ponies…no real sign of life reflected the sad state of the first 18 years of my life. The only toy mom would have permitted was a jack-in-the-box shouting her favorite word,

"Competition competition competition!"

Yet despite everything I did to adhere to her principles of hard work over pleasure, all she wanted was for me to get married. She never listened to what I wanted, about what growing up in America meant, or what I had learned it took to be successful. She was never willing to listen to anything that went against what worked for her and dad, until now, until Alpa. Why did Alpa get that chance and not me? What was wrong with me?

On Monday night, I heard a faint knock. I knew by the sound of the breathing that it was dad on the other side of the door.

"I brought sandwiches. I thought you might be hungry."

He was right. I hadn't prioritized eating in the last 48 hours. I told him to set it by the door and waited until I knew I wouldn't have to see anyone before carefully pulling the tray inside. Dad anticipated as such; folded under the plate was a note. Against my first instincts, I saw what it said inside.

"Write 'yes' if you want me to get rid of mom and Alpa so we can talk. Write 'no' if you don't want to talk before you leave on Wednesday."

I deliberated for a few minutes, trying to imagine how I'd feel returning to Orlando knowing what I did without getting any answers. Before depositing the empty tray back in its place, I returned the slip of paper with one word written on the other side.

Yes.

"How did you get rid of mom and Alpa?" I asked dad.

"I tried to convince your mom to let me talk to you alone."

"Big mistake."

"Yes, big mistake. Then I gave Alpa $10 to ask mom to take her to the Smokey Mountains."

"But she just kept the money?"

"But she just kept the money."

"Finally I told your mom she doesn't have to go with me to Bangalore on our next trip to India. That worked."

We let out a chuckle before returning to the awkward silence. It was apparent neither of us knew how to start the real conversation. I took to compulsively checking my watch - as if I had anywhere to go - and dad kept scratching his chest.

"Are you okay?" I asked.

"Maybe it's gas. I have indigestion."

"Ew!"

"Sorry."

The scene was reminiscent of every visit to India I had taken during childhood. We'd travel 8,000 miles to spend two months sitting on a couch trying to figure out how to relate to our own flesh and blood. It never worked. Dad must have been on the same wavelength, which scared him. It was one thing to not know how to talk to a cousin you see once every two years; it was another to not know how to talk to your own daughter.

"Pooja, I'm sorry you found out about your sister going to Georgetown like that. I know that can't be easy for you."

"No, it wasn't. Is she your favorite child?"

I wasn't there to mince words. Dad cried out in surprise as though it was a ridiculous proposition.

"How could you say that?"

"What am I supposed to think?"

"You and your sister are three grades apart. We have learned a lot in that time."

"You guys changed your life philosophy in less than three years!?"

I could tell I had hit a nerve. I was surprised to find out the reason why.

"It was not my philosophy!" he cried out.

"Then why did you get me married off?"

"Pooja, your mother has had a really hard life..."

"Enough! That isn't a justification for everything!"

I was so tired of that reasoning. My parents had been in the States for more than 20 years at that point. How dare dad suggest the first 18 had made no impact, that they had an epiphany in the last three!

"You're right," dad conceded.

"What changed?"

"Nothing. Your mother wanted Alpa to get married as you did."

"And you stepped in this time?"

He hung his head in shame. The guilt his tired body stirred in me was not enough to make me regret the accusation.

"Pooja, I'm so sorry."

So sorry, all the time.

"Your mother and I came to this country with very different expectations than what ultimately happened. We wanted to move to a place that would offer much opportunity for you to flourish, for you to be anything you wanted to be *regardless* of whether you got married. We thought…your mom still thinks…that the only way for you to have a better life is to get married."

"Dad, this is America. It doesn't work the same way as in India."

"I know. I knew that a long time ago. You worked hard in high school. People still tell me how talented you are! But we forced you…"

He said that when he heard people speaking of Alpa in the same way, he finally found the courage to stand up to mom. Alpa and I didn't need to get married to become successful. That was clear after how well I had done with what little I was given in Orlando.

Dad stood up to give me a hug. As soon as his warmth enveloped my body, I felt myself start to quiver as I began the long process of expelling a lifetime of remorse. Dad held me close, apologizing through the embrace.

"I'm so sorry, Pooja. We should not have forced you to get married."

As he uttered the words I had waited so long to hear, I saw the stars in the night sky shining down on me with the sympathy of the entire universe. Dad's apology brought a mix of validation and disappointment my body could barely allow. For two years, I had been trying to swallow my feelings towards school, towards Florida, towards mom, towards Anand...towards myself. Hearing dad say those words out loud meant that I was not selfish for being angry. My life had become someone else's life against my will.

We spent the rest of the night talking about my situation. Dad offered his own experience - medical residency was one of the hardest periods of his life, and Anand was probably going through something similar. His American resident colleagues were worked to the bone for very little money or respect. As an immigrant, it was ten times worse.

> "As immigrants, we don't know what food to eat, what things to say, what clothes to wear, or who to turn to. It can't be easy for Anand, either."

Dad offered to help by calling Anand to help convince him to pick a residency program that had options for me.

> "I can't give you the last two years back, but I will do everything I can to make sure the rest of the years are as good as possible."

In the end, dad and I both decided that two years was not enough time to see if a marriage would work. Things were currently not going well between Anand and I, but I knew that hadn't always been the case. The fact that dad gave me his full support regardless of what I did made my decision to keep trying with Anand more empowering.

Mom and Alpa returned a few hours later. I knew mom's instincts were to offer her input on each point of my conversation with dad. She knew better. Like any good little sister, Alpa simply hugged me, saying how much she loved me.

Before I left for Florida, dad brought me two belated Christmas gifts - the first time I had received a present from anyone. He bought me two books on Parisian architecture. Mom gave me an old green and gold broach. I left it on their kitchen table.

Chapter 20

My flight and Anand's got in an hour apart, so I killed the extra time by sifting through the limited selection of the one airport store.

"Thought I'd find you here," I heard Anand say.

I turned around to face him, not quite sure if it was a happy occasion.

"How was West Virginia?"
"It was...interesting. How was India?"
"Also...interesting."

The tiredness in Anand's eyes told me to wait to bring up anything serious. We chatted about mundane things like the weather while collecting his bags and stopped to grab a pizza on the way home.

His time with his family was mediocre as expected. It was his friends he had been dying to see. He told me that despite everything that had happened, he still felt like a kid when he was around his 'old buddies.'

"Some things never change," he finished.
"Some things constantly change."

He agreed, and stood up to clear the dishes. I caught his wrist, gently grabbing the plate out of his hand.

"I'll take care of it. You have a long week ahead of you."
"Yes, thank you."

There was a brief moment of hesitation before he turned back one step to squeeze my hand and give me a kiss on the cheek. It was the first time in months I could remember an entirely positive interaction between the two of us.

It took a full two weeks to finally say aloud what was on our minds. I recapped the conversation with dad, first admitting that I knew I had never taken an interest in Anand's work, or asked him how he was faring in a foreign country.

"It hasn't been easy," Anand replied.
"I should have been there for you."

Anand told me Christine had approached him with a list of cities that had what we both needed. He assured me the fellowship programs he'd apply to over the next few weeks would all be for programs located in those places.

"I appreciate the effort," I assured.
"I appreciate the patience."

We researched our top destinations and compiled a short list. With our credentials and references, we had no reason to believe it wouldn't work out in both of our favors. Together, we drove to the post office and wished our applications a bon voyage. I told myself I'd see one of the following destinations in the fall: Ithaca, New Haven, Baltimore, Chicago, New Orleans, or New York. This time I was so confident it would happen.

Chapter 21

It was New Orleans. Jonathan was elated at the move, personally calling and telling me all of the wonderful things Tulane's architecture and urban planning department had to offer.

"A city as diverse as NOLA will be very much to your

liking!"

He was right. Soon after Anand and I settled into our tiny little apartment in the Upper Garden District, I received my course list. The classes covered subjects I hadn't realized existed. Maybe it was the charm of the St. Charles streetcar, maybe it was the infectious energy of the city, or maybe it was the idea of being somewhere I had chosen. Regardless of the reason, starting over in a new city quickly went from a burden to a blessing.

"Hi everyone, my name is Jeff, and I am your new instructor this semester. I know, groan, a TA teaching a 300 level course. On the bright side, cultural references to anything before 1965 are now permitted."

We all laughed heartedly. Though a highly respected scholar, Professor Chang was rumored to have zero tolerance to references to anything before the year he immigrated to the States. Even so, a TA teaching a 300 level course was usually undesirable. With Jeff, I doubted that would be the case.

After living in NOLA for more than a year, I finally felt like I had found a home. Words had always come naturally to me, so I added a second major - English Literature. It showed how much I enjoyed where I was, electing to tack on another year until I completed my degree. The last visit back to West Virginia had been exhilarating; people seemed genuinely jealous of my life. I knew that I was finally living the dream.

Jeff instructed us to write our names on the blank cards he passed out so we could address each other directly. I wrote my name in big block letters, adding a small explanation underneath (it's pronounced like it's written).

He officially welcomed us to the course 'English Theory of the East.' Professor Chang assigned Edward Saïd's 'Orientalism.' It was by far one of the most interesting pieces I had ever read. I couldn't wait to give my perspective, though I wanted to wait for the perfect moment.

"So, what are some initial reactions?" Jeff asked.

A guy on the other side of the class raised his hand.

"Yes, Scott?"

"I think Saïd is really bitter about his childhood."

"Can you expand on that?"

"It's very obvious that colonialism scarred him as a kid. He writes about Western perceptions of the East as though they are invalid."

I contained myself from shouting my reaction to that gross misinterpretation, and instead raised my hand.

"Yes," Jeff said, staring at my card.

"Pooja."

"Just like the Hindu religious ceremony?"

That was impressive. I had never met a non-Indian who knew that.

"Well that form is usually spelled with a 'u,' but yes, exactly."

"So what are your thoughts, Pooja?"

Jeff shifted to give me his full attention. I had to allot myself a few seconds to catch my breath before starting. I couldn't help but notice how attractive he was.

"I agree that colonialism has deeply affected Saïd, though not how Scott claims."

"Can you elaborate?"

"I think what Saïd is saying is that we apply our cultural

norms to foreign environments. In the case of European colonialism, colonists didn't recognize non-European advances in society, and instead focused on what they thought was lacking."

I looked around the class to make sure they were not lost in the discussion as the student body of UF Orlando surely would have been. Everyone was intently listening.

"Resulting in?" Jeff prompted.

"Resulting in colonists who thought they better understood and were superior to the societies they invaded."

A few of the students in the class turned to say they agreed with me. I peered over at Scott, who was busy weaving his web of grievance at being stood up by my commentary. He began crawling back and forth like a spider, waiting for someone stupid enough to get lost in the discussion and find they were caught in his trap.

Jeff made eye contact with me and followed my gaze to Scott spider.

"Black widow?" Jeff asked.

"Tarantula," I replied.

The class stared at us like we were insane.

"Very astute observations, Pooja," Jeff said.

I felt my heart caught in my throat.

The first week of classes was always a mad rush of people on one side of campus trying to get to the other. After half an hour of waiting behind a guy who wasn't sure if he was actually enrolled at Tulane, I finished straightening issues with my student loans just in time to see the last bus that could take me across campus to the streetcar drive away.

"Shit!" I cried out.

The first assignments I had for architecture classes required me to take home nearly all of my drafting supplies for the weekend. Trying to balance the metal instruments, the drawing materials, and the giant slabs of paper made me crumble under the weight.

"Pooja!"

I looked up to see Jeff running toward me. He moved gracefully for being so tall, displaying a curious level of athleticism compared to the average bookworm PhD student. Briefly forgetting not to openly gawk in public, I regained control of my brain as he padded up to me.

He offered to give me a hand with my clunky materials, which were now spread out over a wide expanse.

"What's with all the stuff? Are you a targeted kleptomaniac?"

"Worse, double major. Architecture."

"I want to again compliment you for your astute observations on Tuesday."

The eye contact worked like a weight against my arm, and I once again spilled the supplies we had just collected. One relief in being a brown girl who grew up in West Virginia was the powerful mask of dark skin. It was the ultimate weapon against embarrassment.

"Where are you headed?" he asked.

"I just missed the bus to take me back to the streetcar."

"Let me give you a ride! That's on my way home. My car is just over there," he said, pointing to the adjacent lot.

A breeze fluttered his partially unbuttoned shirt, briefly exposing a muscular frame underneath.

"I'm married," I blurted out.

"Okay...do you want a ride?"

"I...uh..."

"I'm a nice guy, Pooja."

Against my marital judgment, I accepted his offer and followed him back to his red Mustang.

"It has an automatic retractable roof," he said.

"Don't put it down."

"You sure?"

"Yes. My hair."

In the open air, my hair would have quickly morphed into a giant ball of weeds. Retractable roofs are not meant for Indian girls. The top closed with a satisfying 'click,' commencing what I could already feel would be many moments like this together. I saw Jeff worked with a delay trying to comb through the palpable tension that was enclosed by the intimate space of his car.

"When did you move to NOLA?"

"14 months ago with my husband, Anand. You?"

"Three years ago without a husband, Anand."

I silently told him he was lucky to move here unattached.

"I know I am," he answered my unspoken thought.

"Where are you from?"

"Mississippi."

"Why did you leave?"

"A lot of reasons. The people there are superficially welcoming to strangers, but close-minded with locals, you know?"

Our time must have been cut short with a wrinkle. A normal 15-minute ride was reduced to a few seconds. Pulling up outside of my apartment complex, Jeff jumped out and helped me carry my things to the door. The faint scent of cologne tickled my nose with the subtlety of a feather.

He gently kissed my hand to say goodbye. Before we had even made full contact, an electric bolt surged straight through my arm, bestowing me with a shiny new coat of confidence. By the way we had already connected, I knew that armor would only grow stronger with time.

Chapter 22

Partially due to my workload but mostly in the hopes of encounters with Jeff outside of class, I spent increasingly more time on campus. It didn't take me long to figure out his teaching schedule. Our synergy was so apparent that I took my newfound confidence as opportunities to often 'accidentally' bump into him. When the five-minute exchanges became insufficient, I asked him out to lunch.

> "Where would you like to go? I asked him.
>
> "I'm actually kind of busy…"
>
> "I won't take no for an answer!"

I made no effort to hide my disappointment at his initial response.

> "Okay, you win. Do you like Creole food?" he conceded.
>
> "I've never actually tried it."
>
> "You live in NOLA and you've never had Creole food? You must try it; it's imperative!"

The beauty of New Orleans is that it took mere minutes to reach a completely different atmosphere. We pulled up to a small hole-in-the-wall restaurant on the east side of the French Quarter. Health inspections weren't standard in the city.

"Everything is deep fried. You don't have to worry about getting sick from spoiled food," he assured.

"Oh so that's why they do it!"
"Indians too?"

The walls of the place were plastered with photos, memorabilia, and old jazz records. It looked as though someone had tired of keeping the contents of their life on a bookshelf, and decided to staple gun everything for public viewing.

"It's the owner's collection. He was in one of the most famous Louisiana jazz ensembles back in the 60s," Jeff explained.

"What happened to the group?"

Normally confident, never-at-a-loss-for-words Jeff hesitated in his response.

"There were some internal disagreements."

Before I had the chance to ask for elaboration, the waiter came over and Jeff jumped up to give him a hug. My body quivered at the thought of Jeff being so comfortable with physical affection. When I first married Anand, I thought he was a gentleman in his restraint. Over the last year, I had begun to realize that Anand was just a prude.

"Edward! You're still waiting tables at your own place!" Jeff exclaimed.

"Jeff, my boy, how are you?"
"Doing well, still…um, living with Charles. You?"
"Glad to hear. I'm still with Tracey. Who's this pretty lady?"

Edward held my eye contact for a second too long before letting his gaze wander down my torso to my legs. The idea of the old man checking me out gave me the creeps.

"Pooja and I are colleagues."

I loved the sound of those words. It made me nostalgic for the Department of Architecture back in Orlando. Working my way up to the same status at Tulane in either of my majors would take more time than before; the students were smarter and the school was better here.

"Sorry for that long sidebar," Jeff apologized as he sat back down.

"That guy was gross; he was staring at me."

"You look lovely, but I doubt that was the case."

The comment was equally offending as it was flattering. Jeff stared down at his silverware, which somehow kept his features in perfect proportion. I couldn't read what he was thinking.

"He is really committed to Tracey."

"His wife?"

A round of beers came out to interrupt the conversation. Grateful to change the subject, Jeff made good use of my still obvious ignorance of alcohol.

"This is one of the best the Bayou has to offer," he explained.

I took my first swig and nearly spit it out.

"Beer isn't for everyone. We'll find you your drink."

Anything implying future social interaction was all I needed to reorient myself. The food was absolutely delicious and helped set the mood back to what I had intended for this lunch.

"How did you decide on an English, Architecture double major?"

"Well, Anand, my husband, had to…"

"I asked how *you* decided, Pooja."

He emphasized it in such a way that I immediately noticed how often I structured my answers to questions in the context of Anand. It was antithetical to my deep-seated desire to assert my independence in our marriage.

Careful to express my opinions in a way that fit only me, we spent the next hour talking about Louisiana culture, life in South, and what I thought of Tulane. It wasn't until we got up to leave the restaurant that I realized that was the longest conversation I had ever had about my thoughts and opinions.

Jeff paid for both of our meals. We spoke at the same time.

"You get the next one."

"I'll get the next one."

On the way out, he told me about a new bar that had just opened up near campus and asked if I'd like to get a drink with him that Friday night? Until then, the sweaty, swarthy imbeciles of Orlando nightlife had swayed me away from trying the NOLA bar scene. I completely threw those thoughts in the trash as soon as Jeff asked me out.

"I would love to," I replied.

The wrinkle brought our friendship to a point that normally takes years to reach. Time flowed like water with Jeff. Within weeks, I thanked the world on a continual basis for bringing me someone so intelligent that could relate to growing up in a small, isolated town.

"Ironically, Americans perceive India as backwards. Really, your husband and parents grew up in environments that could be considered more cosmopolitan than where we are from," he once observed.

"That sounds like something Saïd would say."
"You read my mind."

Together, we explored the depths of New Orleans with the same avid curiosity of someone who had never laid foot on its beautiful steps. We painted ourselves into French Creole murals. We tamed the wild alligators of the Bayou swamps. We explored bookstores that contained the writings of languages long lost. We picked the brains of culinary avant-gardes. We stayed up late, we rose early, we appreciated the conversations, and we relished the comfortable silences.

With a simple graze of a touch, Jeff conveyed more intensity of emotion than I had ever felt from anyone in my life. My conflicted reality reminded me that I was a married woman, and therefore Jeff had to stay a friend. His loyalty and patience were unyielding, and he never demanded more. We understood the humor in the pain and the pain in the humor of the life we had to live. Our minds were at a convergence, and with each passing moment we spent together, I could feel my intense and profound attraction to him growing.

Chapter 23

We made it a habit to give a unique occasion to our frequent outings. In a tribute to exploring my drinking preferences, we planned one night to go to a bar named 'Brigista' to test Jeff's theory was that I was a martini girl.

Though we had both passed it on our own without a second thought, together, we discovered the sophisticated beauty of a black lacquered bench by the English building. For its odd and convenient presence, it became our usual Wednesday meeting spot.

He was a few minutes late that night, finally emerging looking distracted by a disappointing site - another person. Not wanting to lose his attention even a second longer than necessary, I called out. He slowly turned his chiseled face, the moonlight giving a haloed effect to his person. Two months of seeing him nearly every day had only elongated the breath he stole from my lips.

"Hi Pooja!"

The man by Jeff's side trotted up to me.

"So this is the famous Pooja! I'm Charles, Jeff's…"

"Roommate," Jeff finished.

My disappointment grew at the thought of Jeff finishing someone else's sentences.

"Hi, nice to meet you," I replied.

"Is it okay if Charles comes with us?" Jeff asked.

I was afraid this would happen. Jeff and my time alone had become semi-sacred, though it was the kind of sacredness that could be easily broken at the behest of either party. As much as I wanted to scream at Charles to go away, I only had one option about what to say.

"Sure, no problem."

Fighting off my discontent, I turned to eye the roommate. Charles had on the same style jumpsuit Michael Jackson wore in the 'Thriller' video. Draped over the suit was a sparkling black sweater. A bowler hat sat on his head to round off the outfit.

"Isn't he the unequivocally most stylish person you've ever met?" Jeff asked me.

"Unequivocally," I had to agree.

Charles thanked us by doing a quick spin in Mr. Jackson's honor.

"How does it feel to have this bozo as your instructor?" Charles asked me.

"It's hard to get through to that initial layer of stupidity, but once you do, there's no going back."

"Oh sassy! I can see why you like this one!"

Jeff looked elated to see the three of us getting along so quickly. Jeff was happy. That made me happy.

Charles, dance instructor extraordinaire, played the perfect balance off Jeff and my serious conversations into the meanings of life. The harmony the three of us quickly struck was infectious, and soon, I was surprisingly grateful to have a regular third to complete our solid triangle of outings.

Jeff's alcohol knowledge paled in comparison to Charles's, who was also an ex-Miami bartender extraordinaire. Within a month, I had learned much about the fine art of red wine and could make the perfect Bloody Mary, which turned out to be my drink. On one particularly crazy night, Charles even showed me the dangers of Long Island Iced Teas!

The two of them were avid jazz fans, and brought me along to their various extravaganzas. Excited to finally have a dance partner, Charles taught me the finer points of swing. Together, we flapped our hands and threw our legs in the air like every moment was worth celebrating.

With his two left feet, Jeff stood in the corner, admiring the courtship practices his best friend used to lift me off the ground. As Charles and I danced the night away, the three of us were elevated into a heavenly ecstasy. Night after night, Jeff stole glances in my direction of a pained and beautiful attraction. I couldn't remember another time in my life that I had been that confident, that happy to be alive.

Chapter 24

"What do you mean you're not coming!?" Anand shouted at me.

"Calm down!" I replied.

"Just answer the question!"

Two years ago, I would have given a long explanation right away. Jeff and New Orleans had taught me how to be assertive in my personal life. It had taught me to deal with Anand more directly.

"I'm not having this conversation until you calm down, Anand!"

He had booked two tickets to India for the winter holidays without asking; I had already signed up for a January session course, and Alpa was coming to visit in between classes.

"I already went to India once by myself. Everyone will think we're having marital problems if you don't come," he tried to reason.

It wasn't as though that was entirely inaccurate. Anand's neurology program wasn't what he had expected. For the first year in New Orleans, I tried reaching out to him and supporting him in a way I never offered in Orlando. He'd always mutter something about how I didn't understand. Soon after I met Jeff, I stopped caring.

Instead of progressing in our relationship, our limited interactions were mostly reduced to arguing. Since moving, I could count the number of times we made love on one hand. Anand had become more repulsive than desired.

"Since when do you care about what people in India think of you?"

"You're such an ungrateful bitch!" he shouted.

It was a line he used often. The words rolled off me. Jeff and I had plans that night, so instead of engaging Anand further, I did what I had learned worked best - I left.

"Get back here! We're not finished!" I heard in the distance.

Alpa flew down to NOLA the day before Anand left for India. I took Alpa out for some sightseeing the morning after she arrived. Anand didn't bother to stick around to say goodbye. He didn't even leave a note. The only sign of his departure was a missing suitcase.

The fact that Anand and I were apart for our anniversary and my birthday didn't register in my thoughts. His absence was completely dwarfed by the scenes I played out in my head of Jeff meeting my little sister.

Jeff joined us for a day of sightseeing, and that night the three of us had plans to go to the newest and most exclusive restaurant in the city for dinner. Jeff must have apologized a thousand times for Charles being out of town. Secretly, we both knew how exciting it would be to spend the night alone with the company of family.

"Oh my God, you weren't kidding, he's so hot!" Alpa squealed at me.

Jeff had wandered a few steps ahead to take a picture of a new statue of a street performer the city had just unveiled.

"I know! It's so hard to control myself sometimes!"

"You guys haven't...you know?"

"I would never cheat on Anand."

The words sounded insincere even though I knew they needed to be true. It was becoming harder to reconcile the gloomy state of my marriage with the increasing strength of the idea that Jeff was my soulmate. Even though Jeff and I had never technically discussed the nature of our relationship, I knew being married to Anand was the one thing holding us back from moving beyond something plutonic.

Jeff called us over.

> "This statue is amazing! The clothes represent the perfect symbiosis of Bayou culture and Aquitaine troubadour."

> "I don't know what that means, but it sounds wonderful," Alpa dreamily muttered.

Jeff smiled at her, and playfully grabbed my hand.

> "Well this one understood."

Alpa let out another squeal of jealousy. It was the perfect response to juxtapose to the much deeper nature of my reaction.

The restaurant Jeff picked out for my birthday dinner turned out to be an old manor house set far back in the Marigny district. It was so exclusive the establishment was not even listed in the phone book. Only people who were well connected could get a table; Jeff had known the owner for a long time. He was a dignified older man who had a peculiar resemblance to Rock Hudson.

> "That's not the only thing we have in common," the owner said.

Jeff swatted the owner's arm away at the comment, complete with an embarrassed smile.

> "Pay no attention, he's just…"

"Drunk," Alpa finished.

"Exactly."

I was surprised Alpa of all people had a better sense of what was going on than me. I joined in on their laughter nonetheless, not wanting to ruin a single moment of this perfect night. Jeff topped off the occasion with a toast in front of the entire restaurant in my honor.

> "To Pooja, my love, my darling. Happy birthday to the best friend a man could ever wish for."

My birthday gift to myself was inwardly making a simple word substitution in his toast.

> *"To Pooja, my love, my darling. Happy birthday to the best ~~friend~~ wife a man could ever wish for."*

Another wrinkle in time concluded Alpa's visit just minutes after she arrived. Jeff had vaguely mentioned that he did not get along with his family, and decided to spend Christmas with Charles in New Orleans. When he arrived at my apartment to drive us to the airport for our flight to West Virginia, I asked him to join us, stopping just short of offering to pay for the ticket.

> "I love your humor! Imagine the look on Charles's face when he finds a note saying I left him for West Virginia!"

"He'll understand you left him for me!" I exclaimed.

"That would take a LOT of explaining!" Jeff replied.

Alpa and Jeff burst out into laughter, leaving me behind in the dust. Without further mention, the two of them loaded our things into Jeff's car and ushered me inside. The interior felt constraining for the first time.

"Don't be a sour puss about going home. Your parents will

be happy to see you," he told me.

I realized he thought me soon seeing mom was the source of my sudden quietness.

"Besides, I got you a present. Open it on the plane."

Determined to honor his request, I practically pushed everyone who stepped in front of me out of the way to get to my seat.

"What is it?" Alpa asked once we were settled.

I clutched the small gift to my heart, letting its subtle power absorb into my blood stream. It was a mini replica of the St. Charles streetcar.

Chapter 25

After ten days of arguing with mom about how I needed to make choices that suited my needs instead of Anand's, I returned to New Orleans for my winter class. Basking in the peace of a husband-free apartment, Jeff came over several times for late nights of feisty debating over red wine.

We made plans to go out to our favorite jazz club to ring in the New Year, but Charles came down with a cold at the last minute. He insisted and I quickly agreed to go out without him. Jeff was not convinced and persuaded me to come over to their apartment instead. Though I was highly disappointed, curiosity got the best of me.

"I can't believe this is the first time you've been to our place!" Jeff exclaimed.

He bent down to swallow me up in his famous bear hug, which this time was shorter than usual. I was beginning to think all of our affection was getting to be a bit uncomfortable for Charles.

"How do you like the place?" he asked, sounding nervous.

"It's great! Minus that pea color wallpaper."

"Thank God, that means a lot. What color do you think is better?"

Charles came out in a slow march at the sound of our voices. His normally high-pitched sing-songy voice had been reduced to the sound of something grating against sandpaper. Jeff reached out to rub Charles' shoulders before turning to get him a bowl of chicken noodle soup. I dug into my first glass of the many planned wine tastings for the night.

"How was your Christmas?" Charles scratchily asked.

"Mom spent the entire time screaming at me for not supporting Anand."

"Just because you didn't go to India?"

"And because 'I'm ruining my life wasting time on English studies.' "

Charles rolled in a fit laughter at my mom imitation, telling me about the heart attack he nearly caused his dad when he declared he was going to be a professional dancer.

"It was almost as bad as when…"

"Here's your soup!" Jeff announced, walking in from the kitchen.

We watched as poor Charles managed to get down a few bites before being overtaken by a fit of sneezes. He lumbered back into his bedroom shortly after, leaving Jeff and I alone with more than three hours to count down to midnight.

"Was it really that bad?" Jeff asked me about West Virginia.

"I feel like what I need and what's expected of me is

always mutually exclusive."

"I know the feeling, trust me."

Jeff didn't offer many details about his life back in Mississippi, but I knew he was talking about how his parents hated his decision to do a PhD instead of a career that involved hard manual labor. He came from a long line of construction workers. His parents thought a PhD in English was a worthless, lofty pursuit he couldn't afford. We had that in common, though for very different reasons.

"What if you went into medicine or law?" Jeff asked me.

"It doesn't matter. The English degree is just another excuse to criticize. My mother wants me to blindly follow Anand around, regardless."

Jeff pulled me to him, letting my head lay against his chest. The sound of his heartbeat was always so calming. I called it my reflection spot; epiphanies about life always came naturally when I was in that position.

"You said you got in to all the schools you applied to out of high school?" he asked.

"I did."

"What was your application essay about the second time around?"

No one had ever asked me that before. I had shuffled away the tear-ridden words to the back of my brain long ago. Dusting them off and showing them was not something I was sure I wanted to do, even with Jeff.

"It's not important."

"It is to me," he assured.

"It was…it was about gender equality."

I had written about mom and how she was my biggest adversary in me finding equality as a woman. All of Anand's smooth talk about progressive ideas convinced the teenager me to marry him. My passionate essay was about the cultural irony of my mother needing a man to tell her that her daughter should be allowed to be independent.

In four years of marriage, I had never told Anand what I wrote. Despite all of his promises about us having equal roles in our marriage, I had come to realize Anand loathed the idea of having to answer to his wife before making big life decisions.

"I know now Anand hates that."

"But not then?"

"No."

"And you think your mom knew that then?"

"Yes."

"I don't think you should be with Anand."

"WHAT?"

Of all the things we about which advised each other, relationships were never included. It was out of character for Jeff to be so frank.

"Where did that come from?"

"Oh my God, I shouldn't have said that."

I was more upset he didn't follow with what I wanted to hear.

"You should be with me."

He tried explaining that the holidays always made him think of his family.

"I can't imagine giving up your dreams for someone you don't even love."

"What makes you say that?"

"It's just..."

His voiced trailed off as he let his gaze settle in the direction of Charles's bedroom. I peered up to see he was staring at a clock. For once I had no idea what he was thinking.

"Forget I said anything. Just promise you won't give up on you."

"I promise."

I settled back into my thinking spot. Jeff's heartbeat was a steady reminder I was resting against the person I felt closer to more than anyone else in the world. We fell asleep just moments after watching the hands on the clock make it to midnight.

Chapter 26

"Wake up, dummy."

"What happened?"

"You fell asleep on the couch."

Jeff gently nudged me to get up. I groaned, complaining that I couldn't move. Satisfied when he swooped down to pick me up, I let him carry me outside to give me a ride home.

"Pooja, I'm really sorry for blurting out you shouldn't be with Anand. I had no right to say that."

"It's okay. We were just…."

"Drunk."

"Exactly."

We managed to laugh off the very serious conversation that could have easily transpired. Despite avoiding the potential debacle, something shifted in that moment. As he drove away, I felt the elasticity of our bond had been compromised, and I lingered with a great apprehension for the final snap that would separate our connection.

Unsure whether it had happened, I stepped inside and nearly fainted when I saw Anand quietly staring at me from across the room.

"What are you doing here? You're not due back for another two weeks."

"You sound disappointed," Anand replied.

"I'm surprised. What are you doing here?" I repeated.

He started pacing violently, shaking his finger and spewing incoherent sentences in a mix of Telugu and English. All I was able to catch was that he had come back to surprise me with great news, but now he wasn't sure what to do.

"What are you talking about?" I asked.

"Don't give me that. Don't think I don't know."

"Don't know what?"

"Here I was, ready to surprise my wife with the news of great riches!"

I immediately knew what he meant. We had spoken so infrequently that I didn't know the details, but the words 'great riches' coming from an Indian could only mean he landed a high paying job.

"Anand, congratulations!" I said with genuine appreciation.

One thing we did still have in common was our work ethic, and I knew that he deserved the successes he received. My warmth in the response calmed him down enough to speak properly. He was as relieved as I was that this didn't turn into another taxing argument.

"I can't wait to get out of this tiny apartment," he said.

I wholeheartedly agreed. We had been living like paupers for nearly four years.

"I was thinking of getting a place over the bay!"

"You mean river?" I called back from the bathroom.

"The starting salary is $150,000!" he continued.

That was an impressive number. I was sure his chest was puffed out like a mountain at the thought of commanding that kind of money.

"Imagine all the things we can buy!"

"Another car for sure. I'm surprised the hospitals around here could offer that much!"

"They can't."

My heart started to race. I prayed that I had misheard the very possible nightmare instead of the impossible ideal. Anand saw the moment of confusion on my face as the opportunity to clarify what I was most afraid of learning.

"The job is in San Francisco. We're moving at the end of the April."

The words came out in slow motion, each hitting me like a rock against my body. One more stone surely would have killed me.

"I have school."

"Berkeley is accessible by train and they have an architecture school. Besides, I already accepted the offer. We're going to be rich!"

In all the ways I had grown since we first met, not being preoccupied with material possessions was the most obvious. His glaring negligence of that fact sent me into tyrannical rage. How dare he use money as an excuse to not consult me?

"I don't fucking care about the money!"

He was taken aback by the force of my words, but his combative nature didn't stop to appease my anger. Instead he hurled a series of insults that he had clearly been saving for years. As progressive as he sounded when we first married, I knew he still measured his success in wealth. My apathy about dollars stirred an equal fury in him.

"You're lying, all you care about is money!" he accused me.
"Have you even met me?"
"Don't pretend it's not true!"
"Don't pretend you know me!"
"You think I don't know you? You think I don't know what's going on with you and your fucking David Hasselhoff look alike!?"

I wasn't cheating, and the implication that I had sent me further into the maniacal rage. How dare Anand accuse me being unfaithful? It took every ounce of my being to stay loyal, and for what? Four years of marriage and all he thought that mattered was the material possessions.

"It's all you ever talked about when we first met each other!" he claimed.

"I was lonely. And is that all you recall about me, your wife?"

"You're just like all the other Indian girls."
"Why did you marry me, Anand?"
"No matter what I do for you, you want more."
"Why did you marry me, Anand?
"I was the one who turned you to architecture…"
"Why did we get married?"
"I came to this disgusting city so you could be happy…"
"Why are we still married?"
"I never say anything about you going out alone!"
"WHY DID YOU MARRY ME, ANAND?"

I saw him sway at the turbulence of my question. He tried finding his orientation by sitting down. His hand was lying limply on the table, his face looked pale.

"Pooja, this is a great opportunity for my career. I will be able to take care of you for the rest of your life!"

"Anand, please just answer the question. This is a conversation we should have had a long time ago."

Since the day he had arrived in the States, a part of me wanted him to feel guilty. Finally seeing him in that state didn't bring the satisfaction I had hoped for. This was not the way he thought his announcement of self-worth would go. Seeing him so dejected made me feel like a monster.

"I don't know," he finally answered.

A few tears streamed down his cheek. It was a humbling moment for both of us.

"You know I was all set to go to Brooklyn for my residency."

It felt like yesterday and a lifetime ago at the same time.

"When your parents came to my house, they made sure my parents were also present."

"I didn't know that."

"Marriage in India, it's like, it's like..."

"Buying a pair of shoes?"

Anand snorted at the comment. I had always been good with analogies…it was the product of a boring childhood.

"Yes, like buying a pair of shoes. Those girls in India, they just care about money, caste, status."

"And you didn't?"

"Not like they did. I cared about doing well in school. Money clouds knowledge."

I stopped to let him understand the irony of the words he had just spoken. The moment passed without a conclusion.

"Even though marriage wasn't a priority to me, I knew those girls were out of the question. They just didn't...fit. But *you*, Pooja. You grew up here. I thought you would be different than those girls."

"Thanks."

Catching my sarcasm in the reply, he assured me he meant it as a compliment. Anand was proud of his accomplishments. He was ready to come to the States on his own and figure everything out alone. His mother, however, was scared for her son. She never said anything positive about him leaving the country. When his father suggested the two of us get married, for the first time, Anand's mother seemed happy about him going to America.

"Do you have any idea how it felt to have my own mother ignore all of my accomplishments in life, only to congratulate me on a marriage proposal?"

The words were expelled with such a deep-seated bitterness that I was not sure who had put them out into the open. I looked into the eyes of the smart, successful, honest man I had married and was appalled to see my own reflection.

I could tell by the way he continued that the morbid discovery was completely one-sided. He started talking about his desires to start a family, to build a distinguished career for his sake and for mine. His success meant my success, he thought. I know he didn't see it the other way around.

"This job is a huge step in my career."

He sounded so mechanical. When I failed to concede, he asked if I would consider staying in New Orleans on my own until I finished school and then join him later.

"Pooja? Do you think that could work?"

I thought about if we had been exactly the same people, only he had been born the female and I the male. Would I have done things differently for Anand if I were the one in control? Would Anand's happiness have factored into my steadfast, tunnel-vision desire to conquer the world and reap the praise of a thousand generations? For Jeff, the answer would have been yes. For Anand, the answer was,

"No."

"What do you mean no?"

"Do you love me, Anand?"

"What? Of course I..."

"Be honest. Do you love me?"

He paused. We both knew what his silence meant.

"The love will come later. It did for my parents; it did for my sister and her husband. Right now, you need to join me in San Francisco so we can build our future together. Will you do that, Pooja?"

It was then I knew why he asked the same questions over and over again. I reached up and softly stroked his face. The sparkle in those gorgeous Bangalore eyes was dying. I wanted that sparkle to come back, but that sparkle had already cost too much of my life.

Chapter 27

Our divorce happened quicker than our marriage. When it became apparent that staying together would mean sacrificing his dream job, Anand stopped begging me to reconsider. Because we split on mutual terms and we had no children, it only took a month to get the paperwork finalized. Without hesitation, he evenly split everything we had in the bank, and even offered to support me after the divorce. I decided it was time to be my own person and politely declined.

Staying true to his word, dad did not protest when I told him the news. He demanded no explanation and kept his promise to not question my judgment. I had given the marriage four years of mental exhaustion; dad understood if I could give no more.

Mom's silence conveyed more disappointment than any words she had ever spoken. To her, Anand held the key to my future, and giving up on my marriage was synonymous to giving up on my life. She had not been captured by Anand for the same reasons as me. She could not understand why I had to let him go.

I decided not to talk to Jeff during the divorce process, knowing that if Jeff were at the front of my thoughts it would seem as though he were the reason I wanted a new life. He wasn't the reason I wanted to divorce Anand. I wanted to divorce Anand because we were not meant to be together. Whether I was meant to be with Jeff was another question altogether.

The emotional distance that had grown between Anand and I meant that I did not have to wait long to mentally move to the next stage. Within a few months after the divorce being finalized, I retrieved the shelved bond of friendship with my soulmate. It was time to finally start a relationship for the sake of love, not circumstance.

Chapter 28

Jeff stepped through the door of *my* apartment like a dignified prince about to escort his bride into the kingdom of an unknown, yet perfect future. His compliment of me in my dress caused me to curtsy like a townswoman admiring her majesty. He was wearing a sharp pair of pleated khakis and a navy blue polo shirt. His clothes always perfectly framed his strong body. His mind always perfectly framed his strong body.

"What's the occasion?" he asked, eyeing the dinner spread.

I had to chuckle at his attempted nonchalance. We had had coffee breaks that were more glorified than the effort it took on the phone for me to have him over. I playfully clinked my glass against his to keep up the charade. I was dying of anxiety inside.

"I was surprised to hear from you. It has been awhile," he started, back on the serious path.

I explained the reason he hadn't seen me on campus was because I deferred for the semester. Going back to being single after four years was harder than I had thought. I had to figure out how to operate as an individual person for the first time in my life.

As I described the convoluted process of finding my own footing in New Orleans, I sensed an unusual and unwelcome agitation growing in the atmosphere. Three months apart had clearly put some distance between Jeff and me. In the midst of the complicated silence, I could barely make out the thought bubble floating above Jeff's head.

"I made the right decision," I replied.
"It was the right decision."
"*I* made the right decision," I reiterated.

I told him to take the timing of his New Year's outburst and Anand's announcement as coincidence. Jeff wasn't entirely convinced. I did my best to recapture the feeling of euphoria Jeff had brought into my life so many times in the past year. Rechanneling strength from his cherished birthday toast, I started the speech I had rehearsed a thousand times.

"I wanted to talk to you about something, Jeff."

"Of course. More wine?"

"Sure, thanks. It's about us."

"I'm glad to have you back. Do you want to eat?"

Him changing the subject was not a good sign. But I had come this far. I had finally made the bold choice to divorce a man for whom I felt nothing, despite the inevitable repercussions. Stating my obvious love for Jeff was supposed to be the easy part.

"Okay, let's eat. I love you Jeff."

I had said I love him more times than I could count. Why did he look so frail?

"I love you too, Pooja. You know I do. More salad?"

"I really love you, Jeff."

The leagues of distress in my voice echoed in the clangs of his fork hitting the ornate china plate I had picked out precisely for this occasion. Now my effort at the details sounded an intense harshness through the neglected big picture. I could have stopped. I should have stopped.

"Pooja," he quietly whispered.

"I love you, Jeff," I continued.

"Pooja, stop."

"I'm *in love* with you, Jeff."

"I *know...*" his voice trailed.

All matters of love were applicable to Jeff. I loved him in every way that was possible and acceptable. His violent emphasis of the word '*know*' told me that the depths of his love could easily be measured in finite containers. I was too scared to make eye contact; I was afraid my dreams would crumble and bludgeon me to death with the pieces that used to form the basis of my existence.

He got up and walked over to my side of the table. Putting his warm hand on top of my leg, he uttered the words I never thought to dread.

"I love you like a sister, Pooja. You just got divorced; you're lonely."

"No Jeff, I know you feel the same way I do."

He told me that even if we could be together, now was not the time. I had just gotten out of a four-year marriage. I needed some time to be single.

I neglected to hear the conditional form: 'could.'

"So you'll wait for me to be single for awhile. Then we can be together, right?"

My newfound assertiveness was not only for Anand.

"Answer me, Jeff."
"We can't be together."

'Can't' rung in my ears, threatening to shatter me from inside.

"Why don't you want to be with me!?"

I could see tears brimming in his eyes. He had the most pained look of regret saturated deep into his face. It cut straight through my soul and burned my heart to ashes.

"WHY?" I screamed with all of God's fury.

"Pooja, I thought it was obvious."

"You thought WHAT was obvious?"

"You didn't pick up on any of the signs? Our one bedroom apartment, spending Christmas by ourselves..."

"What the fuck are you talking about!?"

My shining knight let his sword collapse to the ground, claiming he did not have the power to bring me back to his castle. The muddled incoherent apology finally ended in one sentence I never expected.

"Pooja, Charles is my boyfriend. I'm gay."

Chapter 29

Losing Jeff was harder than losing Anand. A part of me died the day Jeff picked up his keys and walked out of the door forever. It was more than I could handle. I went insane ransacking my own apartment, throwing dishes, breaking the TV, destroying clothes. I prayed to the Gods I never believed in, prayed to the spirits that had danced in my soul for the feeling of self-destruction to go away.

After a week of drowning in my own misery, I knew that Tulane, the entire city of New Orleans, would forever remind me of the one person I had dared to love. At the end of April, the same week Anand moved without me to San Francisco, Alpa flew down to New Orleans to help me leave the city for good. I couldn't stand to be there anymore.

"Do you want to come out tonight?" Alpa asked.

I shook my head. It hurt to speak.

"Pooja, just come out for one drink. The bar is very close."

"I don't want to!"

"Geez, okay. Let me know if you change your mind."

I didn't bother to respond.

I knew better than to tell mom the reason why I ultimately left NOLA. Instead, once I gathered my composure well enough to go two minutes without crying, I made up a list of excuses about how Tulane was never a good fit for what I wanted. I claimed I moved there primarily for Anand's benefit. Had mom known a man other than my husband had played such a central role in my life, the blame that would ensue on the cause of my divorce would last a lifetime. Being reduced to an impulsive child who acted on a little schoolgirl crush would have broken me.

Dad didn't ask for an explanation, nor did he suggest I return to West Virginia. Mom probably forbade him to offer. With nowhere else to go, Alpa offered to let me stay in her dorm. At 18, living in a dorm room was a dream. Now it was an absolute nightmare.

Alpa did her best to include me with her adolescent friends. Somewhere in the back cellar of my damaged spirit, I appreciated the gesture. But the realities of being in my mid-20s weighed down by a lifetime of emotions made even basic conversation taxing. Being around someone even a few years my junior brought a constant reminder of how quickly I was forced to reckon with the battles of adulthood.

"Divorced at her age? What a failure," they all thought.

"How much pain they've yet to endure." I mentally replied.

Alpa's friends were three calendar years and one lifetime younger than me.

"Oh my God, are you alright!?" Alpa asked me.

I could barely lift my head away from the toilet bowl. Half of the time since I landed in DC had been spent vomiting. I thought I was reacting to the trauma of everything that had happened, as though my emotions needed to be physically purged from my body.

I asked Alpa to run to the local deli and buy me a bottle of lemonade. Before she made it half way to the door, I felt my knees give out and a distant thump of my head hitting the floor. By the time I awoke, I realized I was in a stark white room connected only to other stark white walls. At first I thought I was dead. I hoped it was true.

"Nurse!" I heard Alpa scream.

"What happened?" I asked.

"You passed out from dehydration."

"You had quite a fall," the nurse said.

The first sip of water she nudged down my throat felt like glass. It seemed a cruel punishment considering the necessity of the act to gain my strength back. Giving me a few seconds of mercy, the nurse quietly asked Alpa to give us some privacy.

"Am I dying?" I asked.

"Quite the opposite."

"What's the opposite of dying?"

"Birth."

By May 1984, I was in my second trimester of pregnancy. The extreme stresses life had recently dealt me ensured that the normal symptoms - weight gain, fatigue, dizziness - had gone entirely unnoticed.

My connection to Anand and our marriage's end was mediocre, unattached and unemotional. Yet the overwhelming feeling that came over me when the nurse broke the news of my pregnancy was happiness. I knew I might never again fall in love as I had with Jeff, but at that moment, I knew I would never again be alone.

Chapter 30

Dad's efforts to acquiesce mom were immediately dropped after I phoned them with the news. Within a day, he had made arrangements to indefinitely shut down his practice and drove the 7 hours to DC to personally escort me back to West Virginia.

Somehow, in the chaos of completely reorganizing his life, he convinced mom to respect my wishes not to tell Anand the news. We slept together so infrequently during our marriage that I had stopped birth control soon after moving to NOLA. One fleeting moment of Anand's sexual desires did not warrant him being brought into the conversation before I had decided what role I wanted him to play.

Dad caught me in the kitchen during one of my long nights of mental planning. Unlike our last chance encounter, he did not try to convince me to listen to his advice.

> "Look at what our choices for your life has made happen."

Instead, he assured me that he would financially support me and my baby as best as possible for as long as possible.

> "Does mom know you offered?" I had to ask.
>
> > "It doesn't matter, beta. I don't need her permission to help my daughter."

It was a relief to hear. It would be money without mom attached, and without Anand attached.

Though the practice was shut down, mom spent all of her time crouched over the office accounting books crunching phantom numbers to avoid having a real conversation with me. Any flicker of hope I had that my pregnancy would bring her closer to her firstborn daughter remained a fantasy.

I peered over at my alarm clock and saw it was past midnight. All attempts to fall asleep the past two hours had failed, so I threw my legs over the side of the bed with surprising grace for being in my third trimester. My baby was a good kicker, but my baby was surely small. I wasn't showing much.

Eating whatever wanted whenever I wanted was a pregnancy luxury I was quick to cash in. After serving myself a huge portion of chocolate ice cream, I settled in the family room to a repeat of *Saturday Night Live*. Billy Crystal was hosting. He was funny sometimes, funny enough for the middle of the night at least.

I put the TV on mute and walked back to the kitchen to replenish my bowl. Behind the buzzing of the freezer, I heard shouting coming from upstairs. Quietly approaching mom and dad's room, I made out mom screaming something in Telugu. Not surprisingly, a few key words told me she was complaining about money. As though she knew I was outside and wanted me to understand what was going on, she switched the conversation to English in the midst of violent paper shaking.

> "What about these loans she took out? Who is going to pay back $20,000!?"
>
> "I will go back to work after the baby comes!"
> "That barely covers Alpa's tuition! It will take our life savings to pay off these debts!"
>
> "You don't charge a third of our patients!"

He said the last part with a distinct undertone of bitterness, a feeling I had long come to recognize. They entered familiar territory of whether dad's poorest patients should be denied service because they couldn't afford to pay. I had heard the same argument before my stupidly extravagant wedding. At the time, I was rooting for mom not charging patients in the hopes they would decide against marrying me off. Now I could only sympathize with dad. I knew how it felt to be underappreciated for hard work.

"You would rather give them free service than support our own daughter!"

"You do not understand what it is like to grow up in poverty!"

"That's the same reason you have given for every important decision we have ever made!"

Mom muttered something in Tamil so dad wouldn't understand. It was a sure-fire way to know she was angry. I imagined what she was saying:

"Now this is all my fault? I am the one who told Pooja to take out loans to pay for an expensive school? I am the one who told her to get pregnant and then divorce the father who is now making a huge salary?"

Dad stammered in the background, trying to find a line of reasoning against the words he couldn't understand coming from mom's mouth.

"We forced her to get married. This is her child…"

"That she can't afford!"

"In her own time, she must decide with Anand what to do with the baby."

"She must go back to Anand, Shankar."

"All we have done so far is tell her what to do. Look where that got us."

Mom's rattled breathing heightened as she started again. I slid to the floor with a revolting sense of awareness. Though delivered in her hallmark insensitive manner, mom jolted me to the reality that I was young, hadn't finished school, and didn't have a job. Dad's money would only buy me limited time before mom called for Anand's reinforcement.

Chapter 31

The next morning, I took the car keys from dad's jacket and went out to buy baby clothes and a crib. I decided that flashing tangible objects in mom's face would be a more salient way to drive home the point that I was prepared to raise my baby on my own and figure out how to get my life together. I cashed in all the money I had left to my name for the outing - a whopping $120.

The other car was gone by the time I got back to the house. It was the first time in months I had been alone, so I took advantage of the privacy to map out my argument. I would have gone straight through the day had the phone not rung three hours later.

"Hello?"

"Pooja. It's mom."

Her normally monotone voice sounded alarmed.

"Mom, it's fine, I just went out to get some baby clothes."

"Pooja, come to the hospital now."

"Did you hear me? I went to go get baby clothes…I've decided to raise this child on my own."

Two-hundred minutes of planning how to break the news and I accidentally slipped three seconds into a phone conversation. Mom didn't notice.

"Just come, Pooja."

I expected anger to bubble after such a dismissive reaction, but her tone told me not to question and to simply listen. A nurse directed me to the fourth floor. Dad's shifts of hospital duty immediately came to the forefront of my mind; the fourth floor was the ICU. Completely panicked, I thudded up the stairs to save time, and saw mom waiting. She was alone.

"Mom!"

"Pooja!"

She ran over to give me a hug, a rare occurrence throughout my entire life.

"Mom, what happened?"

"He had a heart attack."

"What!? Is he okay?"

The next five words changed my life forever.

"He died ten minutes ago."

Chapter 32

The spot on dad's chest that had been bothering him wasn't indigestion; it was a sign of heart problems. Dad suffered a massive heart attack that the doctors could not explain given his diet and lifestyle.

"Our technology is not good enough. There's nothing we could have done."

Alpa called us a few hours later to tell us that a friend was giving her a ride home the next day. Mom's usual emotionless voice cracked constantly in the five-minute conversation. That day her tears came down so hard we left the hospital in one car because she couldn't steady herself enough to control the wheel.

Having already lost the one other man who had made a significant impact on my life, losing dad effectively shut down my brain. I barely registered as I watched mom, a usual steadfast being, fall apart under the loss of her life partner of 25 years. Dad had been with mom for more than half of her life. Dad knew mom better than mom knew herself. With dad gone, I lost my interpreter to mom.

Thankfully, just hours after the obituary in the newspaper was distributed, hundreds of dad's loyal patients rushed to our support. One sweet old woman even came over to do our laundry. I took the opportunity for a confession.

> "I don't remember people around here being so nice."
>
> > "He was a good man. No one took care of us like your dad did."
>
> "No one took care of me like dad did."

With all of the help around the house, Alpa and I made arrangements for dad's memorial service. More than 750 people in a town of 25,000 came. My OB/GYN told me it was unsafe to fly at my late stages of pregnancy, so I offered to go to the travel agent and book tickets for mom and Alpa to take dad's ashes back to India. Mom refused, speaking her first words in days.

> "This country was his home. He would want to rest here."

In the summer of 1984, mom, Alpa and I drove to the heart of the Appalachian Mountains and spread dad's ashes in a tiny creek overlooking one of the largest valleys in West Virginia that went just beyond the reach of society. The serenity of the mountains was a perfect representation of the calm, solid, soothing person dad was.

Staring out into the abyss of the mountain range, I knew that the pain I had suffered during the course of my pregnancy would take years to truly sort out. A tiny creek carried the remnants of my father away from me, and I prayed, as I am sure he had done for me. I prayed that my baby would have a better life than I had. In a final bid to the strongest man I ever knew, I closed my eyes tight and whispered the words I should have told him when I had the chance.

"Your belief in me will make me a better mother."

Chapter 33

I triple checked the number before turning the phone dial to the last digit. He answered on the third ring.

"Hello?"
"It's me."
"Pooja! I'm so sorry about your father! Are you okay?"
"Yes…I will be. I miss him so much."

He could not empathize. His father was not a good man.

"I miss you, Pooja."
"I need you to come here, to my parents' place. We have to talk."

"I'll be on the first flight."

He was there within eight hours.

I stepped back to let him inside. A bottle of wine he brought as a token of appreciation made a hollow clang as it found its resting place on the table. Thinking it was another patient who had come to pay respects, Alpa walked over to say thanks.

"Anand! What are you doing here!?"
"It's okay Alpa."

Anand held up the wine bottle, suggesting we talk over drinks. It was so unnatural to hear him speak of anything recreational.

"I brought some wine…I know you love red wine."

"It's all for you," I replied.

"Not drinking?"

"I can't."

He thought it was out of caution for dad's passing. Being Indian, he was accustomed to the phenomenon of clandestine alcohol to deal with emotions.

"I'm so sorry, Pooja. Shankar was a better dad than I ever had."

He was genuine in those words. Dad's elation in me marrying the boy next door was mutual with the boy next door.

"Anand, I need to talk to you."

"I still want to make this work."

"It will work in a different way. I'm pregnant."

The glass in his hand soared out, splattering blood-colored spots over the patchy carpet that outlined the room.

"Is it mine?"

"Yes. I'm positive."

"I can't even tell!"

"I haven't gained much weight."

Before he misinterpreted the situation as a concession to annul the divorce, I made it clear I wanted him only as a part of my baby's life. The look of defeat was unmistakable; a part of me realized in our time apart that he had begun to love me, despite our conversations. But having this child together didn't mean that we were meant to be together.

"I don't want to be your wife as much for your sake as for mine."

"I don't understand."

"It doesn't matter if you do."

He told me he needed me to know he was truly sorry. His first years in America had been really lonely, and he felt more lost than ever after the divorce. He came to this country to build a life, and to have a family.

"Please know that I will do everything I can to support him."

"Or her."

"Or her. Having a child means more than anything else to me in the world."

We had that in common. Though Anand had not made me happy, with this baby he had given me happiness. I knew that I would give my baby the love I had never had. And I knew he would give her the money he had intended to use to buy my love.

Chapter 34

My daughter, Deepa, was born on September 3, 1984. At just over 7 pounds, she was the smallest, fully gestated baby the hospital had seen all year. Jeff was the first person that could send a shiver straight to my heart. Deepa was the second.

"You are my angel, Deepa. Mommy will always respect your choices, your thoughts, and your opinions. Mommy will never make you get married before you are ready, before you have found the right man."

Part III - *Deepa*

Chapter 1

"That's one theory why some people are born gay!"
"I like almonds too. Hey, I gotta go."

She trotted away in a skipping gallop that accentuated the extra baggage hanging over her overly stylized Japanese jeans. Sights like this always made me tremble with both excitement and fear at the power of persuasion. How did stores successfully pass off clothes made for the meatless East Asian body to crowds of American tourists who fainted at the sight of vegetables?

"Can it at least be deep-fried?"

Out of the corner of my eye, I saw the reason I was dragged out on that miserable night talking to a tall blond guy in the corner. She was barely visible through the thicket of swaying drones that came out for the explicit purpose of posting status updates on their social media pages bragging about their 'awesome night' rather than to actually have an awesome night.

"There you are! I thought you'd left!"
"I came to get a drink."

By the way her eyes narrowed, I could tell Gloria was trying to figure out how many 'a drink' I had so far. It was usually a straightforward calculation factoring the hours by the bar and how closely my face resembled a French bulldog. I hated this part of the examination.

"You were talking about your little stress theory, weren't you?" she asked.

How did she know?

"I know because you always look stressed after that explanation."
"That explains it."

"What? Whatever, let's dance."

Gloria started to sway to the music in exaggerated movements. It was supposed to be a joke on how ridiculous the scantily clad women of Daddy Yankee videos looked, but I knew she was also doing it because those moves really did turn me on. It was an odd position to be in as a feminist.

The 'Happy New Year 2008!' sign behind her was distracting. I always had to stop and think about whether those kinds of signs were referring to the year they were bidding farewell to or the one they were welcoming in. There really ought to be a line of explanation at the bottom.

"Hey, I'm down here!" Gloria shouted.

"Sorry, just thinking."

"What's wrong with you tonight?"

Gloria said that to me so often as if to imply that something being wrong with me was the norm, not the exception.

"5! 4! 3! 2! 1! Happy New Year!" everyone cheered.

Gloria jumped into my arms and gave me a huge kiss. The five drinks I had made the catch a near fall.

"Happy New Year, baby," she whispered in my ear.

"Jesus, it's 2008."

"You're supposed to say Happy New Year back."

A woman across the bar stared me down with daggers in her eyes. She had approached me the previous year with an aggravating sense of entitlement.

"How about a kiss?"

"Sorry, do I know you?"

"No, but I'm Indian, you're Indian…"

I motioned for her to shoo. She told to me fuck off. There were 1 billion Indians on this planet, dear. We couldn't all be expected to live out her fantasies. I took the open hostility as a sign I should be going.

"Are you leaving?" Gloria asked.

"Yeah, I'm taking off."

She started her usual whining ritual. Three stomps of her right foot, brush aside a stray lock of my hair, and complain about how it would be no fun without me, all in the hopes that I would stay and she could complain about how it was no fun with me.

"I hate gay bars on New Year's; everybody always acts like an idiot."

"That's every bar ever."

"That's why I wanted to stay in."

"Fine, I'm coming," she said in an exasperated tone.

"No, stay."

It had taken her three hours to apply her makeup, yet somehow she was across the bar at the coat check within seconds. I gave the poor soul manning the booth my last two dollars. Gloria had conditioned herself to dramatically sigh at the sight of my wallet. She had tried to forcibly upgrade me my previous two birthdays. Personally, I didn't see any problems with its bright red *Snoopy* aesthetic. It was my thing.

Gloria took my cold-induced vibrations as a cue to cuddle-walk. I wasn't in the mood to be touched.

"What's with you tonight? Thinking about your dad?"

She could read me like a book.

"No, I'm not."

"Then what's wrong? Your bitter bitch of a mom?"

"Watch it! My mom is a good person."

"To *you*."

Gloria's father claimed he was 1/32nd Native American and found the whole tradition of American Thanksgiving 'utterly despicable.' Out of pity in forcing her to listen to his stupid manifesto again, I made the tragic error of letting Gloria come back to avva and mom's place under the guise of being 'my cool Dominican friend.'

I thought with adequate preparation, Gloria could get along with mom. For hours we studied the detailed nuts and bolts of mom's inner thinking: the pauses, the sighs, the hand waves, and deep yearnings. Gloria was an excellent student and a thorough note-taker who mastered full comprehension of several case studies. Even so, her lifetime of sarcastic remarks could not be tamed for a straight 72 hours.

"Gloria, that is quite a short skirt you have on for the dinner table."

"Sorry Ms. Deva. Would it be better if I changed?"

"The damage is done. Too bad life does not come with a CTRL+Z command!"

"Buy a Mac."

Gloria was immediately moved to the top of mom's black list. I estimated the statute of expiration was 200 years.

"So what's wrong?" Gloria asked.

"Nothing! I just think it's interesting that…"

"Studies have suggested excessive stress during pregnancy can lead to a hormonal shift causing the unborn fetus to mature into a person of a minority sexual orientation. You've said that a hundred times."

It was worth repeating. Gloria's newfound physical distance should have made me happy, but I knew it was the opening credits to her favorite show: *As Deepa Turns.*

"You have a problem with homosexuality," she said.

"Then why do I work for an organization that promotes gay rights?"

"I'm not saying you have a problem with gay people. You have a problem being gay yourself."

"Now you're being the bitch."

"Baby, I call it like I see it."

She ended all hurtful exchanges with that line, as though her brutal honesty was like declaring an Italian shirt on your customs card. It shouldn't be allowed just because it's publically stated.

We stopped in front of the Christopher St 1 train stop. Centered perfectly such that no one could pass, a young couple was making out like the next day was Armageddon. Gloria lived off the 1. I lived off of the F. Across the street there was an 'Original Sal's Pizza.' I lived three blocks from another one. So did Gloria.

"You go ahead. I'm gonna get a slice and head home."

"Why the fuck did I leave the club?"

"I told you to stay."

Not bothering to give Gloria a chance to let this develop into another public argument, I popped the collar of my pea coat and dug my hands deep into my pockets. It was a terrible night to have forgotten gloves. As I ran across the street, I could hear Gloria commence her complaining ritual: stamp her left foot four times, right hand on hip, state in Spanish a summary of my inadequacies. Too bad I took French.

"That your girl?" the guy behind the counter asked.

"Indeed. One pepperoni, please."

"She's hot."

"And smart."

"And crazy?"

Absolutely. Anybody who has ever dated in New York knows that of the three - hot, intelligent, sane - only two are possible in a potential partner. An unequivocal whole in each of the three does not exist. If you think you have found one, think again. They are either a robot or a felon in hiding.

Gloria's post-ritual phase composed mostly of unabated waiting began as I made my selection. It was mean to watch her suffer through the cold. I knew she'd concede soon enough. The low was 10 degrees. Even her heart froze below 25.

"$3.75."

"You take cards? I'm out of cash."

"Minimum is $15."

He followed my gaze out the window. Gloria was still waiting.

"It's on the house."

"Thanks man, you saved me."

"No worries, Happy New Year."

"Happy New Year back."

I always ate my slices on the go, challenging myself to stuff it down my gullet with the fewest possible bites. That night would not break any records. I meticulously sprinkled each of the condiments, grabbed a few napkins, and took forever to pick out a table.

"They all look so inviting!"

"Puta!" Gloria shouted before storming off.

I waited a few seconds to confirm the train rattling below had her person safely contained. On the way to the F, I passed by the usual assortment of New York New Year-er's: The grad student who is devastated because she'd thought she'd be married by now, the middle aged guy who realizes his life has no meaning, the drunken frat boy having anonymous gay sex by the dumpster, and the angry tourists who finally understood that $500 in the City on that night only got you a tiny corner table in an overrated club.

"Hey Deepa, back already?"

"Yeah, it's miserable out there."

"Oh no! I'm about to go out to a party."

If Julie was prepared to wander into the frozen abyss, the apartment must have been nice and warm the entire time. By my obvious disappointment at a squandered cozy night in, it took her all of 10 seconds to figure out Gloria and I got into another fight. I always maintained Gloria just understood me. Julie maintained I just found Gloria attractive. Fortunately Julie's normal lecture on destructive relationships was thwarted by New Year's sympathy.

"Hey! I never read that piece you wrote to submit to the paper. Can you read it to me now?" she asked.

Julie hated my writing; I must have looked suicidal, but I wasn't above capitalizing on pity.

Here it went:

One of the most common questions we queers get is,

"So when did you know you were gay?"

My answer:

Birth.

I knew I was gay before I knew what gay was. When I was

eight, I went to my first sleepover. My friend told everyone to close their eyes and think of the guy in our class they thought was the cutest. Truth be told, I thought red-haired Amy who sat two rows up from me, who loved butterflies and wanted to sing in her church choir was the cutest person I'd ever seen. As the girls at the sleepover began to name the boys, I realized that perhaps thinking of another girl isn't so normal.

And so the next ten years were filled with made up crushes, fake fantasies, and the pronoun game. "Yes, I have a crush on *someone*, but I'm not telling you who *it* is."

Somewhere in between that first realization of 'abnormality' and the pronoun game came the moment of self-realization, which presented itself in the form of an article about the movie remake of "The Brady Bunch," although I'm sure Robert Reed would have endorsed a gay equality episode in the original series.

My mother gave me the article, only half-glancing at its contents before cutting it out. Apparently in the first version of the script, Marsha is way too receptive of her best friend, Maureen, who is clearly in love with Marsha. In the first version, Marsha seemed like a *lesbian.*

"What's a lesbian?" I shouted to my mom.

"What!?"

"They said Marsha seemed like a lesbian."

"Uhhhh…A lesbian is someone who doesn't like men."

Finally, being an Indian nerd came in handy. I pulled out my giant dictionary and flipped to the right page as my mom nervously called out that word she didn't want me to know so young. 'Lesbian' sat on page 317.

It read:

lesbian, *n.* - of or relating to sexual relationships between two females or female homosexuality.

I almost fainted. There's a *word* for this! I must not be the only one! Judging by my mother's reaction, I could tell she was not fond of the word or the persuasion, so I kept quiet.

Two weeks later, I turned 12.

Julie twiddled her thumbs with such fervor you'd have thought it were the very motion holding the earth in balance.

"What do you think?"
"It's funny..."

I reminded myself to take Julie off my list of people to call in case I needed someone to talk me out of jumping off a bridge.

"It just seems so...distant. I think you need to make it more personal."
"It's just supposed to be a light piece."

"Deepa, to get an article published about something as *common* a subject as homosexuality you have to be more exposed!"

She lingered on the word 'common.' Being gay was too common. I did my best to hide my disappointment to her reaction, despite watching my mood tumble from bad to worse. A kiss on the cheek was all Julie offered as consolation before leaving me alone in our apartment.

"Happy New Year back," I said to no one in particular.

Chapter 2

Even when I didn't feel particularly social, I was still a slave to the electronic technology-laden 21st century daily regime. Checking my phone was the last thing I did before going to bed, yet somehow I had six missed calls by the time I woke up the next morning. Three were from mom and three were from Gloria. Mom probably thought I was dead and Gloria probably thought I went home with someone else.

Gloria's last attempt at communication was a text.

"Brunch at 12? Same place as usual?"

The amount of time I spent staring at the phone was long enough to tell me that I didn't want to see her. Relationships are about compromise, however, so I sent her a message that would simultaneously comply with her wishes and piss her off.

"Ok."

She hated those replies.

"Can't you vary the damn message!? How about 'I gotcha,' or a 'Great, that sounds good.'"

Mom made her fourth phone call as soon as I stepped out of my building.

"Hi mom, Happy New Year."
"What happened!?"

I let her scold me for five minutes about my lack of communication. Reading between criticisms, I took this to mean she did not have a good night. Her neighbors of ten years found the courage to invite her out for the celebration. Mom accepted, and promptly used the rest of the week to complain about commitments. She cancelled on them at 8 PM New Year's Eve.

"Grace was being so childish I was forced to stay in with your grandmother."

"Childish how?"

"She wanted to go to some restaurant and have drinks. Deepa?"

"Still here."

Judging from the conversation, her pattern of breathing, the time of year, and the emphasis on my name (dee-PAH!), the ensuing pause sounded like it was of the second persuasion: 'Ask me about what I am doing.' It was one of the earliest varieties, originating in the mid-90s and second only to pause of the first persuasion ('I want to talk about how your father ruined my life.')

I first spotted pause of a second persuasion after mom took up a hobby of a rather bizarre nature. She would sigh and mutter, drop newspaper articles, and leave the TV running to showcase subject matter of relevance. Its guilt tactic methods were entirely to draw me into her latest obsession.

1995:

"I simply do not understand why you are not as passionate about saving the manatees as I am, Deepa."

2000:

"I simply do not understand why you are not as passionate as getting Dr. Brown elected as city comptroller, Deepa."

2005:

"I simply do not understand why you are not as passionate about scrapbooking as I am, Deepa."

Mom was almost at breath 15 of a pause of a second persuasion. Beyond 20 was dangerous territory in a forest that no one dare enter.

"How is your Foucault book club going?" I gingerly asked.

"Terrible. They're all Neanderthals reading like he's from the Stone Age."

I had no idea what that meant. Mom always had a tendency to express her discontents with life in seemingly random combinations of words. Left unabated, this conversation could last until the following day.

"I gotta go. Say hi to avva for me. Love you!"

"You know, Deepa, you really don't give me enough time to express my thoughts…"

I hung up before she finished. Not two steps ahead, my darling girlfriend used her X-ray eyes to inspect the contents of my brain.

"Was that your mom?" Gloria asked.

"It was my grandmother."

"Bullshit."

Over Thanksgiving, mom told me at least ten times in front of Gloria to give her time to express to her thoughts. Mom thought she was being assertive. Gloria thought mom was being immature.

Whatever chord mom struck in Gloria's nerves had not quelled in the six weeks since. Gloria used anything as an occasion to list out her top grievances.

"Your mom is codependent, has low self-esteem, is homophobic…"

"My mom is not homophobic!"

"Then why haven't you come out to her?"

No matter how many times Gloria forced this conversation, my points seemed to disappear into oblivion. It was not easy for the Indian community to accept an idea such as homosexuality.

> "Like it's easy for *any* community! You think my Dominican parents were happy to hear the news that their precious little girl dates other precious little girls?"

> "At least Dominicans *talk* about sexuality!"

The idea of marriage in Indian society wasn't predicated on love or attraction. Being enamored with your life partner wasn't a desired quality of an Indian marriage. Progressive as mom was in not forcing an arranged marriage on me like her mother did to her, mom could not relate to the basic explanation.

> "I can't even use the idea of being in love with someone of the same sex because my mom doesn't understand what it means to fall in love!" I argued.

> "Your excuses for that woman are eating you alive!" Gloria retorted.

By then the five vodka sodas I had the previous night were beating a hole in my head. This would inevitably be followed by cannons being shot into my stomach, and a round of grenades set off in undisclosed locations. A toilet served as the perfect surrender flag. I found out the previous year that Gloria was a double agent for the enemy.

> "This was a bad idea. I'm leaving." I told her.
> "Fine, run away!"
> "That's affirmative."

Chapter 3

In New York, the first day back to work after the New Year was always a cluster of emotionally conflicted people debating whether their urban dreams in the concrete jungle were worth another year of grime-covered insults. Every year, a mass of New Yorkers fled to the respective corners of the world they once called home in a desperate attempt to make the nostalgia in their heads come true. And every year, that mass of New Yorkers returned to the City after a week that reminded them how hard it was to function outside of the five boroughs (if you counted Staten Island). No other day showcased this conflicted pilgrimage better than the first day of work after the New Year.

I was no exception. Every time I told myself it was time to leave the urban maze, a quick visit back to Maryland confirmed that New York City was the only place in the world I had ever been where being me wasn't questioned. Where else was a gay Indian-American woman with a penchant for German pop music and a divorced arranged-marriage mother so easily accepted?

For the third first day back to work after the New Year, Brian was waiting for me in the office like a sadistic cat. Normal people start out the post-New Year conversation with something like,

"Hi! How was your holiday?"

Brian's method was different.

"Thinking about your dad's abandonment? How was your mother's annual horrid phone ca..."

"Hey Brian," I said to cut him off.

Brian stared at me for a few seconds as though I was about to combust.

"Your dad?" he continued.

"What about your dad?" some guy asked.

"Who are y..."

It was Brian's turn cut me off.

"Her dad left the States because..."
"Nope!"

I interrupted the inevitably awkward conversation by asking who the new guy standing before me was? He was wearing the standard average white guy uniform: khaki pants, a light blue dress shirt, brown loafers, and a tan belt.

"This is Garrett, my new intern!" Brian exclaimed.
"What about your dad?" Garrett asked.
"He moved to an ashram in India exactly three years ago," Brian said.

"What's an ashram?"

Garrett asked in a slow moving, old man kind of way that made me laugh out of pity.

"Why'd he move?" old man Garrett repeated.
"Because Deepa told him she's gay."

Garrett was unmoved by the story and lumbered off to get coffee. Brian let his eyes wander to Garrett's ass.

"That was unnecessary," I said with an air of grievance as to how 2008 had started.

"Did your mom call for her usual pity party?" Brian asked.

Brian joined Gloria in the mom-haters club. Our freshman year of college, he had just escaped the gay detention center of Kansas, and made no concessions in unleashing the suppressed effeminate in full force. I hadn't yet solidified the first syllabus for my crash course on mom. He greeted her for the first time wearing an ensemble of short shorts, a pink pin-stripped shirt and a beret. She commented on his 'howler monkey' voice and choice of clothing ever since.

It was Brian who fed Gloria her favorite line after my stock public defense of mom.

"She's a good mother."
"Just a highly temperamental person."

The effeminate was not temporary, and he waved me off with a cat claw and an order he gave every day since we had first joined the office:

"Transfer to the LGBTQ division! Fight the straight power!"

The interior of The Justice Coalition office was peppered with a litany of non-profit trademarks: overworked staff, squeaky orange felt chairs, a carpet that was last replaced around 1987, and of course, rows of paper-covered faux wood desks. Above mine that morning hung a sign that most certainly was not brought in by any veteran staffer.

"Welcome back fighters of immigrants' justice!"

Anyone who worked full time in that office lost enthusiasm for their job within a year. Out on the street, Justice Coalition workers were a socially aware (often extreme), progressive contingent fighting for people who could not fight for themselves. The opposition, the pressure, the backlash were equally frustrating as they were motivating. In the office, we were all of more or less the same opinions, and thus spent our time fighting over details that would never become part of the real mainstream dialogue.

It killed the drive for those of us who were consistently behind a desk. Sometimes it was enough to make our non-profit salary seem insulting, so we'd quit. Sometimes it led to a higher-paying promotion. Most of us fell in between.

"My name is Deepa. Welcome to purgatory."

"Hello!" someone said behind me.

She introduced herself as Carrie, the new junior associate for this section, and very obviously the source of the overzealous banner.

"I'm Deepa. Welcome to pur…err…I'm one of the senior associate researchers."

"Barbara told me that I should report to you for the duration of my work."

"How long are you here?"
"Six months to start!"

Barbara was a great boss and the reason I stayed so long. The one thing I couldn't stand was that she always hired new junior associates without warning and listed me as the immediate supervisor. All of a sudden, I'd be responsible for writing recommendations, giving professional advice, and trying to keep them busy. It added to the monotony of my life without paying any real returns. I didn't sign up to be a teacher; I signed up to be a researcher.

I assigned Carrie lengthy background information and some briefs I wrote on a series of cases in Florida, in which five legal Hispanic immigrants were deported due to US government screw-ups at customs. She seemed content even though I knew my assignment was garbage.

After a day of sorting through 400 emails, I heard the same voice pipe up, this time timidly in the background.

"It's time for me to go. Thanks for your help, Deepa."

A few years ago, I had gone to a party in completely gentrified Brooklyn neighborhood close to the train. As I was leaving the apartment, a girl asked me to wait for her so she could find her purse and walk with me.

"Are you kidding? It's two blocks away."

"Please? Just wait?"

Against my normal tendency, I complied. Once we were in the station, we split in different directions. She thanked me for waiting with such genuine appreciation that I felt evil for how frugal I was with my time. This city did that to you.

Carrie thanked me in that same way and I realized that I was responsible for already killing her enthusiasm. Not needing to contribute to the problem, I asked her to stay for a few extra minutes to type out a summary of what she was interested in doing. Within ten minutes, I had a detailed and well-organized list of actual cases and subjects. For the first time in my supervising history, it appeared I had someone who would actually be an asset.

It was nearly 7. We were supposed to meet at 6:30. Like every pretentious restaurant in New York, the hostess wouldn't seat anyone until the entire party showed up. It was a tactic to drum up sales at the bar. It worked.

"Another vodka soda," I told the bartender.

"Make that two," I heard her say.

"Hi pinni!"

"Please, call me Aunt Alpa."

She had used that as a running joke ever since we figured out 15 years earlier that the only two Telugu words I ever said were "avva" and "pinni." Somehow "mom" made it through the familial references.

Pinni had on her corporate boss regalia. That night's ensemble included black three-inch stilettos, a perfectly tailored light gray suit, and a black dress shirt that likely cost more than my entire outfit. The hostess immediately noticed pinni standing table-less at the bar, and apologized profusely for not seating her earlier.

"How was your New Year's?" I asked.

"Good! Amir's sister offered to watch the kids so we could go to a party."

"Where?"

"Just a few blocks down from us on 8th Ave."

After pinni and her husband, Amir, sold their second start-up consulting firm for a gigantic profit, they upgraded from their Brooklyn condo to a huge loft in Chelsea. Normally the grandeur of such a lifestyle was a turnoff for me. They redeemed themselves by establishing more than 200 college funds for at-risk youth across the city, students in Amir's native Tehran, and back in West Virginia.

The local West Virginia newspaper did a five-page article on the computer lab pinni set up in her old high school. One of the features was the plaque emblazoned with her dedication quote:

"Through the depths of time, education remains the portal of my success."

Mom hated that plaque.

"My God, was Alpa trying to make people gag?"

After selling the company, pinni tried the stay-at-home mom thing for all of five minutes, but took a Senior Managing Director position at McKinsey soon after. Amir, on the other hand, loved being at home with the kids.

We spent the next half-hour talking about our New Year's fiascoes.

Hers involved champagne and Dance Dance Revolution. Mine went without saying.

"Gloria is not good for you, Deepa."

Her assertion was not unfounded. Every time I saw pinni was either just after or just before a major argument with Gloria. What could I say? It was hard to find someone who held my interest past the second date. Crazy was often interesting.

"Wait until marriage to be in the midst of a constant battle," pinni said with a little wink.

"Whenever that's allowed."

"It doesn't matter if you can't get legally married."

Pinni was of the ten percent of the country that at the time favored marriage equality, though she didn't view its necessity at the same level as I did. How could she? How could she understand what it meant to not be let into the hospital past visiting hours to attend to your life partner, or what it felt like to have to adopt your own child, or how insulting it was to mark 'single' on an HR form after being committed to someone for 30 years? That was the prospect I was faced with. Of course the law mattered.

"How's the rest of your life going?" I asked to change the subject.

"A special gift from God."

Avva loved to use that expression. Its depth always seemed way too pronounced for me. Pinni insisted we were all blessed enough to use it without hesitation.

"How's your mom?" pinni asked.

"Mom is mom."

"And her new book club?"

"Good!"

I lied about mom at least once per conversation. As the topic of discussion, all things related to my parents usually died quickly. They represented subjects that were either superficial or too mentally consuming; there was no in between.

Pinni and I poured through a heaping pile of appetizers and entrées. As usual, she threw down her credit card for the entire meal. I told her again that I'd eventually make my way to the private sector and buy her dinner back. She simply smiled and told me to take my time.

"There are plenty of years to make piles of meaningless money," she said.

Chapter 4

Gloria called me the next afternoon. She apologized, using the familiar set of excuses, including a sound byte about how she crossed the line with mom. I agreed to meet her over the weekend, insisting it be the new performance art-inspired exhibition in SoHo. Better to talk in public where the sympathetic queers abounded.

She greeted me with passive-aggressive statements about dragging her out in the cold. Somehow it was okay for her to bully me into dealing with the New Year's insanity, but I was chastised for wanting to leave my apartment on a Saturday afternoon. I used my own passive-aggressive skills to remind her art galleries are typically under a roof.

"How hard is it to wait inside?"

"Hello, not with those 80s era heroine addicts," she said.

"It's a performance art-*inspired* exhibit. They're *90s* era heroine addicts."

She smiled and threw her head slightly back in a laugh. It made her look like a candy dispenser. I think she would have been strawberry flavored.

Like most SoHo exhibits, everything was crammed into a few small rooms in a half-intentional, half-neglectful way. Gloria hated going to these kinds of shows.

"I love the raw emotion the asymmetry of this piece captures," someone observed.

Gloria leaned in to whisper to me.

"Honey, that isn't the product of raw emotion, that's the product of a stroke."

I laughed a little too loudly. Thirty people in black shirts and Italian framed glasses turned and glared. Following Gloria's examples of exasperation, I rolled my eyes, looked at my watch, and brought my gaze to a completely empty corner, muttering about the cultural warfare that inspired such dynamism. Gloria pretended to scold; the opportunity to make fun of those talentless souls was too good to pass up, even I had to admit.

"Thisss is a thSoHo art gallery, thisss is a thsserious placthe of businessth!"

Using her best lisp, she spat each word with false purpose. My snort was so loud it echoed through the entire gallery. Before the walking stereotypes had a chance to do it for us, we excused ourselves from the gallery in total hysteria.

"Oh baby, when we're good, we're terrible," Gloria said.

"Indeed," we said at the same time.

"So we're okay?" she asked.

"Yeah. It's a weird time of the year for me."

"I didn't make it any easier."

An acknowledgement of the fact was the closest she would come to an actual apology. That and brunch, which she offered to buy me to make up for last time. Our favorite place was a quick train ride away.

We were seated almost immediately. It must have been too cold for people to want to go outside.

"Yet here we are," Gloria said.

Not wanting to get into another argument, I let the comment slide.

"I don't know why you wanted to meet outside today."

Still quiet.

"Only a masochist would want to go out in this weather."

Everything was so difficult with this woman.

"Why do you like me? You complain 75 percent of the time we're together." I finally replied.

"Because the other 25 percent of the time is fucking fantastic sex."

"Keep it down, Gloria."

"It's New York City. Lesbians are allowed to say the word 'sex.' "

Saved by the waiter. He asked for our drink order; I responded in automatic pilot.

"She'll have an apple juice and coffee, cream on the side. I'll have a Bloody Mary with extra Tabasco and a glass water."

As the waiter walked away, Gloria managed to catch my gaze, telling me this was why she liked me.

"Cause I remember your drink order?"
"Yes!"

The first girl I ever dated told me she liked me because of a weird hair growth pattern on my head. Until this moment, that was the worst explanation for someone liking me. Fortunately, Gloria had other small additions:

"You are a good listener, you're kind, you're smart, all of that."
"There are a ton of people who are all that."
"True. But you're one of the most unique."

That was doubtful. It had already been established that there were more than 1 billion Indians on the planet. Julie said that being gay is too common in New York. Ergo, I was a common subset of a common population.

"What do you like about me?" Gloria asked.

I hesitated for a moment too long. On the timeline of appropriate responses, there was certainly no other alternative to making a joke.

"Fucking fantastic sex," I replied.

Julie and pinni were right. I couldn't think of one decent reason why Gloria was good for me. She must have realized the same thing with my pregnant pause at the most inopportune moment. As with every one of my previous girlfriends, there was no giant falling out in the end. We merely stopped contacting each other. By the end of January, we had effectively broken up.

Chapter 5

Barbara called me into her office a few weeks later. She was the only person I knew to have both a regular drip coffee maker and espresso machine side-by-side. The office aesthetic was completed with her own personal industrial copier that she used to create massive pools of paper.

"We have a predicament in the Florida case," she said.

I didn't have to ask which case; Barbara spoke in the same outlined format as a formal research memorandum.

"It's the case in Orlando. It appears the green cards we believed were illegally disregarded may indeed be invalid."

"What? That throws out our entire argument!"

"Apparently Pedro and Jorge are not brothers. They're long-time partners. I'm sending you and Carrie down to help."

"You're sending me down because they're gay?"

If there was one thing I absolutely hated, it was being pigeon holed to gay issues because of my orientation. There was more to me than being queer.

"Deepa, we're so progressive we'd like to *not* send you because you are gay. This was already your case and Carrie can help."

"How long are we going to be gone?" I asked.

"Personal troubles?"

"Just curious."

"As long as it takes, kid."

Before I had a chance to disagree, Barbara took off to print a 400-page document to add to the pool.

"Aisle or window seat?" I asked Carrie.

"Window. I get plane sick sometimes."

"Not a fan of flying?"

"Not at all. I'm from Connecticut. I went to England once. That flight was traumatizing."

I found that ironic given her interest in immigration rights, though the majority of our cases were not about people who found their way to America on a jet plane.

Conversations on the subject of travel made me happy. What I lacked in material possessions I had made up with in international excursions: India, South Africa, and a year in France were my most prized memories. It was a huge added bonus when the travel conversation ended with my all time favorite question:

"Do you speak French?" Carrie asked.

Showing off my French skills was the one arrogant thing I openly did. It made me feel confident, especially coming out of Gloria's slurred commentary in Spanish. She always knew how to smash the words such that the only thing I understood was 'puta' and 'mira.'

I offered a few sentences in a verbose response to say,

"Yes."

"Impressive! I bet you get all the ladies with those skills." Carrie replied.

My face immediately turned to stone in a shade of brown that was highly coveted as the façade of a house.

"How do you know I'm gay?"

"I guess it's obvious? It's not a big deal..." she trailed off.

'Being obvious' wasn't something I aimed to achieve. I wore women's clothes, and I even went through the charade of donning makeup on my face. I thought I did a great job of finding a comfortable balance between being who I was and not letting society take one look at me and make assumptions.

I cooked in my annoyance for the duration of the flight, swatting off Carrie's attempts to go over the case. By the time we landed I was undoubtedly pissed. Part of that job, however, was learning to suck up one's own problems and focus on the lives to save. I had no choice but to push off my existential crisis for later.

Carlos Hernandez, a field investigator and Spanish interpreter from the Miami affiliate office, picked us up from the airport.

> "We're glad to have you two here! This case is much more complicated than we had anticipated."

> "What's the general sentiment?" I asked him.

He explained the gay community of Miami stuck to one part of the city. Even the more conservative areas knew what an economic boon it was to have them around. Orlando was a much different story.

> "Outside of theme park entertainers, they're not so welcome around here," Carlos said.

Patricia Sanders, an Orlando-based lawyer, agreed to take on the case last year when it was an open and shut matter of INS negligence. She contacted The Justice Coalition to garner publicity on what was supposed to be a big win against the constant demonization of the Hispanic community.

In 1978, Dr. Pedro Ramirez, a Ph.D. in Mexican Literature from Universidad de Santa Fe, Mexico was hired by the University of Florida, Orlando as a Spanish professor. The university quickly recognized Dr. Ramirez's talent, and fast-tracked him through the department. A few years later, they offered him a full tenured position. He accepted on the condition that UF Orlando brought his brother, Jorge, over to the States.

Under the Immigration Act of 1965, the National Origins Formula was abolished, making immigrants' skills and family relationships with citizens or residents the primary criteria by which residencies were granted. It was under this law that Jorge was admitted as a permanent resident to the United States. Pedro eventually became a citizen of the United States, though Jorge never did.

"Due to a gross clerical error, the INS threatened to deport Jorge in 2007," Patricia reminded us.

What was supposed to be a simple clarification turned in to several months of fighting. The Governor of Florida and President Bush wanted to make this a national example for illegal immigration and launched a full investigation. That's when Pedro called Patricia. Her firm traced the problem to the INS 'losing' paperwork from a required background check from the Mexican Government.

With successive stalls courtesy of the court system, the INS finally found something even they were not expecting. An investigator with the State of Florida uncovered evidence that Pedro and Jorge were not brothers as they had originally claimed. Tailing both, speaking with Pedro's former students, and an illegal entry to their residence all suggested that Jorge and Pedro were actually long-time partners.

"Lovers, if you will," an associate lawyer said.

I cringed at that word. A wife would never refer to her husband as simply her "lover."

In cooperation with the INS, the local police brought Pedro in for questioning. The authorities were allowed to hold both in detention indefinitely. A court-ordered DNA test - technology that became available long after Jorge had settled in the States - was conducted, confirming there was no blood relation between the two.

Same-sex partnerships were not recognized under the Immigration Act of 1965, providing grounds for deportation of Jorge. Federal charges were placed against Pedro for smuggling in an illegal immigrant under false pretenses. Both were being held in federal prison pending Jorge's immigration hearing and Pedro's criminal trial.

I heard echoes from the past generations of my family - what a total clash of problems - avva's immigration battle and my fight with gay rights discrimination. All I needed to hear was that Jorge and Pedro were forced into a same-sex arranged marriage.

Chapter 6

Barbara was right in sending me down to work on the case. Had Pedro and Jorge not been Hispanic or had they been an opposite-sex couple, there was no way the US Government would have made such a spectacle of their lives. Finding a way to establish precedence for them to not be deported required understanding how the overlap of two communities produced one result. That was something I could understand.

Despite the throes of research Carrie and I conducted, and despite the level of detail Carlos put into his investigations, weeks of our efforts left us in more or less the same place as before. Carrie and I were slowly discovering there was not much we could do to bend the odds in Pedro and Jorge's favor. The law was not on our side.

> "We've been at this for eight hours. Want to get a drink?" Carrie asked me.

"I don't know, I really…yes. Let's go."

I didn't bother to ask mom if she had any favorite places to go out while she lived in Orlando, although I could imagine what she would have said.

> *"Nightlife in Orlando? You mean a boom box playing Jimmy Buffet and case of cheap beer?"*

An online search told me there was a highly rated bar a few blocks from our hotel. We walked inside and found the reviews pleasantly accurate. A few people in suits were enjoying martinis at a far table, a group of students were discussing something intently over a bottle of wine, and two lone individuals were quietly getting lost in themselves at the bar. The place was decorated well and the vibe was chill. I needed more places like this in my life.

"A vodka soda and..."

"A white wine, please," Carrie finished.

Carrie got the first round.

"I want to apologize about what I said on the plane," she started.

"It's fine."

"No, it's not. It'd be one thing if we knew each other. I shouldn't have assumed."

"Don't worry."

"I don't like people thinking they know me because of my appearances."

"Like you only listen to 'Indie' music and exclusively buy food marked 'organic'?"

I blurted out the last line without thinking. She managed to sidestep her offense at my quick 'white person' assessment. That awkward moment of silence appeared in which the people involved are deciding whether the playing field is now level or whether this will evolve into a 'friendship' of backhanded insults. Teenagers called this 'frenemies.' Her chuckle seconds later told me this would thankfully be the former.

"You never told me what you think about this case," she continued.

"What? It's all we discuss!"

"We talk about our research. I want to know what *you* think!"

There were a thousand things to be said about everything, but I didn't know how or to whom to tell.

"Fine, I'll start. It's bullshit same-sex partnerships aren't recognized under the law!" she offered.

"Definitely. That needs to change."

"Immigration laws are fucking worthless!" Carrie shouted.

"Don't say that! They're not all worthless!"

She looked down at my tightly clenched fists and immediately apologized, though I could tell she had no clue why.

"Why so sensitive?" she quietly asked.

"It's just family stuff."

I was always one of those people who could dance while totally sober. Talking was another issue. She answered that call by buying another round of drinks.

"Why should I tell you my family history? What's in it for me?" I teased.

"I'll tell you mine. Four-hundred years ago, a big boat carried a bunch of British people over to North America. The end."

"Nice try."

"If you tell me yours, I'll set you up with one of my friends."

The few set ups my friends had provided were all with someone who was taking ungodly amounts of anti-depressants, or who weighed 300 pounds, was kind of mean, 'but had a good heart.' Carrie assured me her potential match was attractive, sane, kind, and interesting. It was an unlikely scenario, but I hadn't eaten since noon and I felt the alcohol in my bloodstream loosening the vault that was my mouth.

"My grandparents got married because India was a hard life. But they were of different castes and from different parts of the country. My grandfather's family banished them from returning for yeeeearsshhh."

The harrowing tales avva told me of her childhood greatly formed me as an adult.

"Imagine working like a dog your entire life, only to end up in the same cruel place at death as you came in at birth?"

"What does this have to do with the Immigration Act?"

I told Carrie their story - how they got married in 1959. How they had to lie to initially get avva and mom into the country. How the Immigration Act of 1965 would have changed so much of that.

"As it always goes, my grandfather, the *immigrant,* got blamed for something that was not his fault."

"There was an investigation?"

"Yeah. If the INS had discovered their lie, my grandmother and mother would have been deported. My grandfather would have gone to jail."

My voice trailed off at the end of the last sentence. Nearly 50 since avva immigrated, and Pedro and Jorge were in the same situation. I remembered so vividly the layers pain and humiliation on avva's face when she told me her story.

> *"I had seen much suffering in my life, beta. But nothing shook me more profoundly than the thought of my baby Pooja returning to the desperation of poverty I promised my amma I would escape."*

I decided at that moment to dedicate myself to immigrant rights. I thought I could bring justice and hope to the lives of people who were trying to escape the unbreakable cycle of despair that abject poverty imparts. Yet somehow my life's passion and hard work was failing for gay people like me.

"So it worked out?" Carrie tried to finish.

Perhaps an English major would have considered the story a classic happy ending, but the suffering to get to the conclusion and the characters that remained often made that idea such a false statement.

"It worked out for my grandparents, but for my mom, it culminated in a profoundly unfulfilled life."

"I thought arranged marriages are common?" Carrie asked.

"In *south Asia*! Not in America! She got divorced. My dad paid for everything, but my mom raised me. We were close when I was a child."

"Not anymore?"

That was enough of a life confession. I turned the subject back to the Ramirez case and asked Carrie to elaborate on her opinion.

"Excuse me, are you gals talking about that UF Orlando professor who might get deported?" someone at the bar asked.

We saw a young couple looking back at us.

"Yes!" I shouted.

"I couldn't help but overhearing your story, that's so remarkable about your grandparents!" the woman chimed in.

It meant a lot to hear a positive affirmation from the majority population.

"This Ramirez issue is an insult to hard-working immigrants," the man said.

"Absolutely," Carrie and I agreed.

We learned the man and woman married a few years ago. Both were from the Orlando area and had many close friends who were Latin American immigrants. Some of those friends were brought over illegally by their parents in pursuit of the common goal of most immigrants - a better life.

"Your grandparents didn't work hard to come here, build a family, and contribute to society only to have the issue turned into a blasphemous joke by these *fags*," the woman continued.

Carrie and I froze in shock. I felt the fleeting moment of hope and warmness of the situation dissolve as though someone had shot a bullet at the red balloon in which the bar was contained. Deepa of a sober dimension would have fought the shamefulness of those assholes. Deepa of an inebriated dimension didn't have the mental bandwidth to make that happen.

"Let's go," Carrie whispered to me.

She grabbed her purse. Together, in a disappointment that can only come from realizing what you had was for naught, we slammed the bar door in the faces of ignorance calling out behind us.

"America is the land of the brave, not the land of the gays!"

Chapter 7

Patricia came into the office to tell us the first trial to determine Jorge's immigration status was set for a month away. The general feelings of dejection were palpable in the room, and Patricia's best efforts to instill enthusiasm went nowhere. For Carrie and I, the already monotonous tasks of reading and cataloguing thousands of pages became overwhelming with the acute realization Orlando lacked the mental and emotional comforts of New York.

Patricia and Barbara agreed to let us return a few weeks before the first trial. Our work couldn't continue indefinitely; the Florida Justice Coalition offices needed to take over. Before we were to leave, Patricia asked if we could do one last thing.

"It would be great if you could visit them in person," Patricia said.

"You want us to talk directly to Pedro and Jorge?" Carrie asked.

"We're not lawyers," I added.

"We're hoping a fresh perspective will help," Patricia replied.

After the mental gymnastics I had done on this case, I hardly felt fresh. Patricia assured us that the questions had all been preplanned and had well documented answers; she was merely hoping a new detail or two would emerge if Pedro and Jorge had someone different to talk to.

"I'm really nervous to meet these guys," Carrie remarked the next day.

Those were my sentiments exactly. Three years of being a glorified report writer had left me feeling no closer to helping the avvas of the world find the peace they deserved. All of a sudden I felt like I was the last hope for these two men.

As soon as we entered the prison, the hooting and howling from the inmates began like every movie that had ever depicted the scene. Obscene comments were made, tongues grossly dancing out of mouths, and clothes were dropped and tossed. All of my societal reasoning didn't quell the one politically incorrect thought I let freely bubble to the surface.

"Thank God I don't date men."

Our passes worked without hindrance and we were shown to a dark questioning room. I had watched enough bad cop shows to know to expect a dimly lit interior with a fake mirror on the side. The room did not disappoint. A few hours in a place like this, and I would have been be ready to confess whatever was asked - true or not - to get me the hell out.

Two elderly men were sitting quietly at the table and holding hands. At this stage, there was no point in denying the true nature of their relationship. Despite having their lives turned upside down, Pedro and Jorge looked incredibly calm. I could see, however, that prison had aged them greatly. They looked ten years older than the picture that was taken of them the past November.

They greeted us with lively handshakes and a kiss on the cheek. Pedro was a full foot taller than Jorge. He had white streaks running through his thinning light brown hair, a finely tuned moustache and wore glasses. Jorge was much darker. From his features, I saw he had Native American blood running through his veins. His brilliant black hair looked like that of a child - disheveled and playfully running over his forehead. It was ridiculous to think that anybody believed they were brothers.

The questions we presented had been asked many times. With minor exceptions, they repeated verbatim what we had on file. Pedro came from an upper class family in south Mexico and received the benefits of a fine education. His parents wanted him to be a doctor, but he found passion in words.

"I compromised by becoming a doctor of literature."

One boiling summer day during his second year at university, Pedro met Jorge, a local auto mechanic. The connection was instant and earth shattering.

"A shock raced through my arm the first time I touched Pedro. It doesn't take an education to recognize love," Jorge said.

Being gay in south Mexico in the 70s was forbidden at best, and the two quickly became skilled at hiding their relationship. To help keep their cover, both Pedro and Jorge publically 'dated' two closeted lesbians. After Pedro was accepted to start his Ph.D. in Santa Fe, he convinced his and Jorge's 'girlfriends' to move with them to continue the charade. The plan worked, and Pedro and Jorge were able to carry on their relationship until Pedro was hired by UF Orlando in 1978.

"Once I was sponsored for a green card, it was easy to convince the gringos we were brothers. We have been together in the States ever since."

Being thoroughly versed in every detail of their lives, Carrie knew we already had all of this information. She kindly thanked them for their time, visibly shaken after hearing their powerful story in person.

"Coming?" she asked, motioning for us to leave.

"Could I ask you a few questions in private?" I said to Pedro and Jorge.

It was unconventional and probably not allowed, but Carrie knew better than to question me and excused herself without protest.

> "Why risk everything? Why not stay together in Mexico or break up?" I asked.

Jorge laughed and congratulated me for being the first person to ask that very obvious question. Finally, they went off-script with the responses.

> "We constantly asked ourselves that question. Each time we lost faith, we were reminded by a simple touch," Jorge answered.

> "I don't understand," I responded.

Pedro said that he and Jorge went through a lot together in Mexico before Orlando. It is never easy to break off a long-term commitment, especially with the kind of intense love they had for each other.

> "Being apart from mi amor was like not having the left side of my body. Other people were just crutches; it wasn't the same," he explained.

For Jorge, it went further. He wasn't just a gay man in Mexico. He was a poor man, an uneducated man, and a dark skinned man.

> "Some people treated me worse than their dogs."

The way Jorge's body rocked to the sadness of his life story reminded me precisely of the expression that overtook avva whenever she talked about growing up in India. The emotion that stemmed from a life of poverty and discrimination was enough to melt the coldest spirit.

> "Will this help the case?" Pedro asked.

"I'm not going to lie, I just wanted to know for myself," I replied.

"Don't bother yourself with the boring details of two sad stories!"

"It's not boring! Was it worth the risk?"

Pedro, a man of well-calculated words to describe historical significance explained that gay rights had come very far in the years that he and Jorge were together in America.

"Even though it did not come far enough, I would do everything all over again."

"Me too," Jorge agreed.

"How did you know when to take that risk?" I asked.

I knew it was an irrelevant question. Pedro and Jorge did not have another option even though the opposition argued that they did.

"Submitting to the wills of society when society is so inherently wrong is not something many people must face," Pedro explained.

Neither of them had intended to be the poster children for highlighting the injustices gay immigrants faced in America. All they knew was how much they loved one another, and that their love was not a crime.

Chapter 8

New York moved faster than any other place I had ever been to, yet I felt like I grew so much as a person in its absence. For all of the classes, seminars, conversations, and traveling I did, nothing made me think more about my life and what it took for me to get there than that hour with Pedro and Jorge.

Being gay in New York was about as unique as having two arms. There were so many queer people in the City that individual neighborhoods had their own gay support groups, bars and gyms. The main LGBT center had specialized seminars for transgendered, lesbian, gay, bisexual, and bicurious individuals. The south Asians had their own queer alliances. The Latinos, the South Americans, the Africans, and the African-Americans did as well.

Yet somehow, through the rhetoric, we all forgot the basic truths: it was hard to be gay. It was hard to come out. For years, New York made me feel like a coward for only being partially out. It was why I came out to dad prematurely. Hearing Pedro and Jorge's words meant I was not crazy for still being in the closet to mom. I just needed to know when to take the risk since I was lucky not to have the risk forced on me.

"Sorry again you two," Barbara said as Carrie and I passed by.

"A 30-year relationship is unraveled in 15 minutes," Carrie said.

"I'm surprised they weren't thrown out of the country before now. Maybe they'd still be alive if they had been," I said.

Or maybe they would have died at the hands of a different set of vigilantes. Two days earlier, we received disgusting news: a white supremacy group in lock-up decided to take immigration policy into their own hands. With the help of a few corrupt security guards, they snuck in a gun through the prison walls and shot Pedro in the heart. He died within two minutes. Unable to withstand the pain, Jorge killed himself the next day by slitting his wrists with a pocketknife his cellmate snuck in.

I looked up at the dark evening skyline of midtown. It was one of those abnormally hot spring nights when the timing of the sunset hadn't quite caught up with the temperature change. Carrie and I stared down at the buildings' outline on Lexington Avenue as I hailed the lone cab that had the letters on its roof illuminated.

"You going to that thing for the Florida chicos?" the driver guessed.

"How did you hear?" I asked.

"From my gringo heffe of all people. Who'da think they fucking shoot the guy?"

The driver looked at me through the rearview mirror.

"They don't treat us right," he said.

It's not the first time someone had mistaken me as Hispanic.

"I'm not…" I started.

"I know you ain't queer. Me neither. I didn't like them when I first came here, but you see everything as a driver and you get used to it. It ain't right he got shot like that."

The driver was a few years older than me and from Mexico City. He told us how difficult it must have been for Jorge and Pedro in south Mexico back in the 70s.

"What brought you over here?" Carrie piped up.

"Shit, where I come from, you got two choices to make money: deal drugs or join a gang and deal drugs. My sister brought me here, bless her."

We pulled up a few streets away from the site of the vigil in Pedro and Jorge's honor. I handed the driver enough money for a $20 tip. Morose occasions always made me feel more generous.

"Light a candle for me?" he asked.

"I promise."

It didn't take long for Carrie and I to figure out that the majority of vigil turnout was not there in support. At least two hundred people were rallied behind various hate signs.

"God hates fags!"
"Support the troops! Kill the gays!"
"Mexico is not America's 51st State!"

Their constant buzzing in the background maligned any feelings of positivity that could have come out of this tragedy.

"Pedro served thousands of students loyalty throughout his career!"

"God agrees, the president agrees, gays don't deserve rights!"

I did my best to concentrate on the messages of realism and hope.

"Pedro and Jorge are symbols of bravery!" a gay activist proclaimed.

But the hatred was unrelenting.

"May God strike down the sinners and disobeyers of Christ," a woman told her congregation through a megaphone.

When the dialogue turned to election calls, Carrie and I decided to leave. We thought we were coming to a vigil to support Pedro and Jorge, not a political rally. After extinguishing our candles, we shuffled off in the lack of closure the hijacked vigil provided.

Chapter 9

"I'm going to head home," I told Carrie.

"No, you're coming with me to a bar on Bleecker Street."

Alcohol was the last thing I needed. It would only drown my sorrows in a heightened misery.

"We're seeing an Odri," Carrie said.

"What's an Odri?"

"No! Audrey! My French friend! The one I said I'd hook you up with!"

I thought I had dreamt that part amidst my life confession and the homophobic slur that sent us raging out of the Orlando bar. The public cries of hatred and semi-fake sympathy were taking a toll on my brain, and I told Carrie I was in no condition to meet anyone.

"A drink in their honor," she pleaded.

"There are better ways to honor Pedro and Jorge."

"Deepa, stop arguing! I am doing you a huge favor!"

Julie was out of town that week for work, and I admitted that I neither wanted to be alone nor make the effort to find someone to keep me company. I assured myself one drink in Pedro and Jorge's honor was an appropriate gesture, and reluctantly followed Carrie to the bar.

Carrie and Audrey ran toward each other with arms outstretched like a ten-minute song and dance number in 'Any Crappy Hindi Movie X.' I kept my distance so as not to intrude on their mini-reunion or be exposed to the Bollywood Invasion.

Observing from a safe corner, I could see that Carrie did not lie. Audrey was beautiful – her long chestnut hair hung freely over her shoulders and her dress tastefully formed a perfectly curved body. Even from back there, I could tell her brilliant blue eyes could both cut through steel or warm an entire ocean. It was incredibly intimidating.

Lacking the courage to walk over, Carrie practically pushed me to their table.

"Bonjour, ça va?" I managed to ask.

"Ah, vous parlez français? C'est formitable !" she said as she leaned in quite close.

Being one of the most coveted cities in the world, New York had a brilliant equalizing effect - if you lived there, people tended to stop caring where you were from. Still, the idea of this beautiful Parisian woman taking any interest in me, an Indian-American from Maryland, was shocking. Audrey was already transmitting a new energy to me, and I couldn't figure out whether to deflect it or absorb it.

"How was the vigil?" Audrey asked in perfect English.

"It turned out to be a well-disguised political rally," I replied.

"I spent a summer in New Orleans after hurricane Katrina, and so many 'vigils' were the same way," Audrey offered.

Mom's hatred of New Orleans was far more intense than Orlando. Somehow that only piqued my curiosity of the city.

"I love New Orleans! My mom lived there right before I was born!" I exclaimed.

"I never knew that," Carrie replied.

I told Audrey I also volunteered there after Hurricane Katrina. It was such as fascinating city - a unique cultural experience in the actual

United States. I didn't get why mom ever left.

"What is unique about the culture?" Carrie wanted to know.

"Have you ever been to that bar under the bridge…?" Audrey asked.

"Bridgista! Yes!"

"I'm going to get another drink. You guys want anything?" Carrie followed.

Carrie might as well have been talking to a rock; it would be more engrossed in what she was saying than we were. I took Carrie's quick absence to ask something I certainly didn't anticipate having the capability of upon first seeing Audrey.

"Have you ever been to Comfort?"

"No, what's that?" Audrey replied.

"The best Cajun restaurant in Harlem. Maybe we could go sometime?"

My breath stopped for a split second as I questioned whether I misheard Carrie both times. Maybe Audrey wasn't gay after all. Maybe Audrey thought she was completely out of my league. Maybe I could take back what I had just said…

"It's a date," she replied.

Audrey was standing across the street. The seconds I had to wait for the cars to clear a path to let me through to her felt like years. Moments in between us seeing each other were dragging on with no mercy, yet time had flown since we first met. That night was already our fifth date.

"Is that a bad thing?" she pretended to scoff.

"Eet ees so aaard to spend time wiz youu!"

"Great-T, I vill go zen,"

I complimented her on her fake Indian accent.

"I have an excellent teacher."

Our conversation picked up precisely where we had left off last time - I had a question that got lost in the wind after a post-dinner kiss that left me completely breathless.

"When you said your mother is a doctor, you said 'médecin' using the feminine article. Isn't it a masculine noun?" I asked.

"That's a great question."

I was right, but some people in our generation in France were making it feminine when speaking of a woman.

"It's like a gender revolution with words. My mother actually did it when she was young before it was as common," Audrey explained.

"That's amazing."
"My family is really great with gender equality."

I managed to avoid offering any information on mine. Explaining mom's situation to the outside world was complicated when I didn't completely understand it myself. The ironic part of mom being so supportive of my career was that I could never truly empathize with what it took to make her that way.

A perfect sunset casted a warm glow over the shimmering water shadowed by the Williamsburg Bridge. Gloria always complained that my romantic appreciation was limited to a few candles and drunken Karaoke song dedication. Maybe it was just being in bad company that stifled my passion. I had seen that view at least a hundred times. That was the first time I noticed its serenity.

My prudishness in physical affection for anyone in my life of a plutonic or familial nature was usually countered with moving too fast in a relationship. By the second date, I had nearly always slept with the person and we usually spent every night together within two weeks of meeting. Audrey and I had only kissed a few times. It was a strangely settling feeling to go so slow with someone I found so perfect.

"I love the ease of our discovery," Audrey suddenly said.

"Discovery of what?"

"Of each other. Usually I rush through this part, go straight to end."

Our hands reached for each other at the same time, instantly sending the electric jolt straight to the heart Jorge had described a few months ago. If I had said those same words back then, it would have been a scripted effort. Now it was completely different.

"Have you decided whether you're staying in New York for your doctorate?" I blurted out.

She had casually mentioned two nights prior that she might be returning to Paris within the year. It had been pounding on my mind ever since, but I knew it was too soon to discuss. I had no right to be a part of that conversation only weeks after us meeting.

"Why? Do you want me to stay another three years in the city?" she teased.

"Of course! Is that a question?"

By the way her face relaxed, I could tell she half-held her breath. Perhaps it was something that needed to be stated aloud despite its obviousness. It was a hard decision for her, though. She liked her program at The New School, but the psychology that she wanted to practice was not even called 'psychology' in the States.

"It's 'therapy.'"

Audrey didn't believe in using pills as the cure for most patients. She aimed to help people through talking and assisting them to analyze their problems. In France, medicines were used as the last resort, not the first solution.

Her hand was starting to become too warm; the subject tapped anger. Unfortunately my work only involved heavy subjects. I spent that day on a case about a group of Vietnamese immigrants who had been smuggled in by Chinese tradesmen as slaves.

"How are you doing otherwise?" she asked.

I knew she was asking about Pedro and Jorge. There wasn't much time to process what had happened before I started the new case.

"It's such a tragedy to lose your partner like that," she said.

"They were fueled by such a deep…"

"Passion?"

"And commitment."

Part of me was relieved Jorge had committed suicide. I could only imagine the homophobic backlash he would have encountered if the US authorities shipped him back to Mexico.

"I'd even be worried for his safety in most of the US," I followed.

"It's 2008, that's crazy!"

"Most of the world is still quite anti-gay."

She didn't agree and explained her opinion that most places had opened up considerably. Perhaps not as much in Africa and…

"Asia. You can say it," I offered.

"Yes, okay! Asia."

"And most of America."

"There are always the extremists."
"These are not the extremists."

Any gay person in the 50 United States could recount the sheer hatred of the LGBT community the Republican Party used to fuel their political base in the 2004 election. Suddenly America wasn't about the economy, war, the Constitution or the world. It was about making sure gay people couldn't marry whom they loved, openly serve in the military, or adopt a homeless child. Every LGBTQ person felt the wrath.

"That hatred won the election. I still feel it outside of major cities."

She looked appalled at the notion. I wished her reaction were founded.

"You are too negative about this, Deepa!"
"We're a detested group of people in this country!"

"You must focus on the positive."

Her face showed worry lines I did not yet want to discover. The sourness of our first fight created tension inside my stomach. Ruining any of our precious time that may be limited was certainly not worth an argumentative point in my favor.

"Did I tell you that you look incredible?" I said.
"That is nice of you to say," she stoically replied.

I squeezed her hand, hoping it was the valve on which to put pressure to dispel the bad vibes. The effects were minimal at best.

"Audrey, I'm so fortunate to live in a world where we are allowed to be together."

The lack of complete sincerity hurt my mouth as I pushed the words out. Pedro was right in saying America had not come far enough.

Chapter 10

"What are you doing for your birthday?" Carrie asked to avoid the real topic.

As with most NGOs, The Justice Coalition's funds for the immigration unit ran too low to keep Carrie on after her initial 6-month contract. My birthday was not my favorite subject, but since we were at Carrie's goodbye lunch, I had no choice but to comply.

Mom said how my birth was the first day in her life she knew everything would work out in the end. That meant I had to spend every birthday with her.

"The day is symbolic of our freedom, Deepa."

As I grew into an adult, I could see the love behind the gesture. I just wished it were an *option*. If my birthday was a workday, I was expected to use one of my vacation days to be with her. In fact, the only time she had come to New York other than my birthdays was for my college graduation.

"She spent the entire time alone on the opposite side of Washington Square Park," Brian said.

"She didn't want to see my dad and his obnoxious new wife."

"Your dad got remarried?" Carrie asked.

"For a few months," I muttered.

"What happened?"

Dad divorced his second wife, sold his condo, donated half of his money to charity, gave nearly the rest of it to mom, and moved to an ashram in north India New Year's Day. The timing was too coincidental of me coming out. I was sure dad took one look at his life scorecard and left after tallying the total.

Work: +5
Wife: + 2
Salary: +10
Deepa: -100

Total: failure

Result: Do not pass go. Do not collect two perfect grandchildren.

"He didn't take the news well?" Carrie pressed.

How was I supposed to answer? Dad was a doctor; I wanted to believe he knew homosexuality wasn't something one can control.

"All he said was he led a superficial life full of material possessions and it was time to release his mind to God."

He sent me an email every now and then to check in, but we didn't talk much after he left.

"At least he still loves your mom," Carrie offered.
"No, he gave her the money out of guilt."

I preemptively answered the question that always followed this conversation.

"And yes. Him leaving is another reason I haven't come out to my mom."

"And she's crazy!" Brian screamed in the middle of the restaurant.
"All this charm, and yet you're still single?"
"So what about your birthday?" Carrie repeated.

"I still have a few months to figure something out."

The end of August was one of my favorite times of the year. After the mass exodus of tourists and the mass influx of students, the city mostly returned to its normal order of residents. The excitement of the summer was still present, but the oppressive heat mostly dissipated, paving the way for Manhattanites to come out of hiding from their obscure connection to a summer beach house in the Hamptons.

I ordered a beer at the bar below my apartment, giving myself a few last moments of peace before dialing. The phone range precisely three times before it was answered. Mom loved to keep people waiting just so.

"Hey mom."

"Hi Deepa! How are you, dear?"

"Good. I wanted to talk to you about my birthday."

"Don't worry, I already made a reservation at our favorite Greek restaurant."

"Actually, I was wondering if you'd want to come up the following weekend instead?"

I recognized a pattern of two short breaths and one long sigh. She had now entered pause of the third persuasion: 'I'm waiting for you to reconsider.'

'I'm waiting for you to reconsider' first made its appearance around 1998 when that same cute, red-haired Amy invited me over to her party. Unfortunately, this conflicted with the Emily Dickenson speaker's panel for which mom had already purchased tickets.

Naturally, being a teenager and thus being unable to control my hormones, I accepted oh-so cute Amy's offer without talking to mom, exposing me to my first encounter with a pause of the third persuasion.

"You don't want to spend time with your own mother anymore?"

"Of course I do! But my birthday is Wednesday and I have to work!"

"So do I, but I am still willing to make the arrangements!"

"I have to go to my job that day."

"Why can't you just take the day off like you normally do?"

Because my fantastic girlfriend said three times she had already made plans for the evening. Because I was hoping to find an extra $750 and join her in Paris for Christmas if she officially invited me. Because I thought spending my birthday with her was a good step in that direction.

"We'd get more time together if you came for the weekend."

"Honestly, Deepa, I'd strongly suggest you reconsider."

"Just come the weekend after!"

"This is very disappointing, Deepa. I'm very disappointed with this situation."

Repetition was not a good sign.

"If you don't want to come, that's fine. I have to go."

"I'd strongly suggest you recon..."

I ended the conversation before she finished her sentence. For the first time in my life, hearing my girlfriend's name brought me more happiness than anxiety. Devout adherence to mom's ridiculous demands was fading.

Chapter 11

As if to answer my monetary prayers, I found out the following week that I got a promotion *and* a sizeable raise to go with the title. Barbara dropped a few hints the move was mostly due to having to get rid of money in the budget that was of too little value to keep Carrie on. I didn't care about the reasoning. Getting that promotion meant going to Paris for Christmas was now an actual option.

Mom reacted to the news with an unusually indifferent tone. Pause of the third persuasion made an appearance four more times. The sting of my birthday disappointment had clearly not worn off.

Barbara, on the other hand, took my promotion to mean she should keep me in the office way past normal hours on my birthday. I called Audrey three times to apologize for the delay. She feigned an air of understanding and told me to not get fired.

"Deepa, assign each of these 200 case files an arbitrary color and use the colors to arrange the files in alphabetical order. Then put them back," Barbara said.

"Yeah…no. I'm leaving."

"As you wish."

"Am I fired?"

"Not at all. Happy Birthday."

"SURPRISE!" several people shouted.

It took me a few moments to realize that my apartment was full of an assortment of my friends from every New York stage of life. Audrey was standing in the center holding a huge chocolate cake.

"Joyeux anniversaire ma chérie," Audrey whispered through the crowd.

I looked over to Audrey's right and saw Sonia, one of my department colleagues. Sonia told me Audrey had called to keep me at the office longer than usual. Barbara was all too willing to invent stupid assignments.

"Just wait until you see the surprise!" Audrey told me.

"I see it! This is the first surprise party anyone has ever given me!"

"Cause your damn mother wouldn't let us!" Brian screamed.

Before I could tell him to shut up, he leaned over to tell me something.

"This one's a keeper," he nodded in Audrey's direction.

Audrey grabbed my hand and led me up to the roof of the building where I saw heaps of Cajun chicken, collard greens, and mini po'boys staring back at me. The word "Comfort" was written on the take-away bags in a perfect testament to how I felt at that moment. The woman that made it happen was clearly a natural entertainer and a master at creating the perfect environment.

There was just one thing she wished she could have made happen.

"I wanted to call your mother and invite her to the party," Audrey told me.

I silently choked on my food at the thought of her calling. Audrey still didn't know I was not out to mom. Mom didn't even know Audrey existed. When Audrey asked for mom's number, poor Julie had to pretend to unsuccessfully search for an entry that was clearly listed in her phone as: 'Deepa's mom.'

"Audrey, do you love ponies?" Brian asked.

In all of his dramatics, Brian was brilliant at reading body language. He ran over as soon as he saw the look of shock on my face. His tactics involved a brand of repetition and confusion not far off of mom's; I knew by the end of the conversation, Audrey would be so disoriented she'd forget what she was trying to say.

Along with 20 of my best friends, I spent the evening eating and drinking on the roof against the brilliant backdrop of an East Village sunset. There was enough food to feed each of us several times over, so we divvied the rest up to distribute to a few homeless people in the neighborhood.

Julie found recruits to help her clean up so I could go back to Audrey's place.

"This is the first birthday I have seen you smile. Just enjoy!"

I didn't need to be told twice. As though the world didn't want me to waste a moment either, Audrey and I found a cab seconds after landing on the street.

"Are you having a good birthday?"
"The best!"
"I still have to give your gift."

She was amazing. I leaned over to give her a kiss, prompting the driver to cough a sound of homophobia.

"Oh my God, it's two girls kissing!" I mockingly shouted.

Audrey looked at me with amazement.

"I've never seen you so..."
"Happy?"

The driver looked like he was going to vomit with our continual displays of affection. As we stepped out of the cab, I made sure to hand him a large tip, though this time not out of moroseness.

"Why would you do that?" Audrey asked.
"So he feels conflicted about hating us."

She handed me my gift after we made our way inside. It was presented in a neatly wrapped box, which I was careful to open without ripping the paper. The first girl who ever broke my heart was that famous red-haired Amy. After mom convinced me to cancel going to her party (pauses of a second persuasion are certainly persuading), Amy came to my 14th birthday party a month later. I was so excited to see what she gave me I tore open the gift with all the passion in the world.

"I spent an hour wrapping that!"
"I'm sorry, I was so excited!"

Traumatized by gift-wrapping love aches, I took my time unsticking each piece of tape.

"It's paper, not a baby!" Audrey exclaimed.

What did that mean? I was glad I wasn't born in France. Beneath the paper that was now also torn with all the passion in the world was a gift of great thought.

"A Barack Obama shirt!"

It was a dark hunter green with Obama's face in relief. Beneath his portrait, the word 'Progress' was written. The subtly of the design was paired with a precise fit around my chest.

"Do you like it?"
"It's tasteful, it's elegant, it's perfect."

Just like its buyer.

She handed me a second object that fell out of the box - a compilation CD by one of the greatest French singers of all time and a certified icon in French lesbian culture. Audrey's mother had sent it direct from Paris, as it included my favorite song. The title track translated to 'I Wish She Still Loved Me.'

Chapter 12

> "This is precisely the example of American luxury I imagined when I moved here!" Audrey exclaimed, stepping inside.

As the elevator carried us up through the floors of the Harlem building, the air thickened with an unmistakable rise in anticipation. By the time the doors opened straight into the apartment, we both knew this would be a night that would live in either inspiration or sorrow.

Dan perfectly timed his arrival and ushered us into the massive kitchen lined with every possible home cooking utensil. His boyfriend waved at us from his perch by the custom icemaker. A woman was finishing her pesto in the smaller of the two food processors.

I stood back for a moment and watched in amusement as Audrey took in the excess of what New York life could offer. Behind me, Dan explained a few of the highlights. He finished his introduction and gave me a compliment I hoped to be hearing all night.

> "Nice shirt!"
>
> "Thanks! My girlfriend gave it to me!"

Julie wandered in after hearing the rambling.

> "They've already tallied the votes from 12 states!"
>
> "I still don't understand the American election process," Audrey said.

Julie pointed out that my plan of alternating between French and

English had already resulted in 100 days in English and 1 day in French. Audrey maintained an impeccable sense of modesty and assured we spoke English because it was difficult when we were around people who didn't understand French.

"Explain the process en français. You must to tell everyone if you come to France with me this Christmas," Audrey said to me in conclusion.

The world stopped for a few seconds as I desperately prayed no signs of reconsideration polluted the feeling of euphoria her words brought. It was the first time she had suggested that I come.

"Obama leads by 15!"

Audrey smiled at my brain being completely lost in post-election victory thoughts.

"You are obsessed with this election, no?"

"He will do a lot for gay rights. It will bring security and happiness to so many."

I caught myself from saying it would do a lot for us.

"Just don't mention that excitement to your moooom," Brian said, walking up.

"Why do you hate her mother?" Audrey asked.

"I don't hate *her,* just her homophobic ways."

"Perhaps it is just you. She gets along so well with Deepa," Audrey said.

In the sixth grade, I dedicated nearly a week to the wonders of watching movies frame by frame. At that moment, time slowed down to the same speed, and I watched in horror as Brian prepared to defend his gay honor. Before I could catch his eye and silently beg him to keep quiet, I heard the truth I had been avoiding for months.

"Deepa's mom doesn't know she's gay!"

Audrey usually shimmering face now looked like it had suffered a brush with death. The color drained out as though she were an open faucet. She whispered she must use the toilet and rushed off to avoid the impending disaster.

"Idiot!" I screamed at Brian.

"You didn't *tell her?*"

"I couldn't find the words…it always gets too close to an argument."

It was the one part of our relationship that I had come to despise. Audrey's cultured parents lived in the heart of Paris. Her mother had been a gender equality fighter from a very young age. She had a sister who was happily married to offset the parental dreams of a stereotypical family. Audrey was born into an easy coming out situation. So easy, she viewed the issue with unnecessary inflexibility.

"Audrey?" I quietly asked, tapping on the bathroom door.

"Leave me alone."

"Audrey, please come out."

"LAISSES-MOI!"

Her violent shouting scared me into backing away. In half-fear, half-hope, I waited for nearly 20 minutes. She pressed her hands to the door, repeating for me to leave.

Brian escorted me back to the kitchen clearly full of an uncommon shame. He had no idea. He was so sorry. She emerged half an hour later, still reminiscent of a ghost, and told me she would go home. Alone.

"I'll come with you."

"No. You stay and be a part of this."

"Please don't go Audrey. Please don't do this."

"You do not know what I am doing. I do not know either. Just stay."

She walked over to be swallowed by the piece of American luxury.

On any other night, on any other occasion, her departure would have been followed. And I thus debated the tone, the intonation, the speed, and the body language that accompanied her words to decide what to do. But the anxiety in the air was quickly becoming optimism, and I found myself torn by the idea of leaving this remarkable moment.

"He's up by 40! Now 50!"

What if she left me?

"65! We're making history!"

I couldn't lose her.

"Oh my God, he got Ohio!"

At the sound of that announcement, I rushed into the TV room and stared at the screen in total amazement. Every candidate who had won the US presidential election in modern history had won the state of Ohio. Even though thoughts of Audrey continued to rip apart my mind, this scene was so inspiring.

Inside stood the liberal, the progressive, the jaded, and the tired. After eight years of torment by a neo-conservative administration, it was their night to usher in a new era that used 'freedom' as muse, not an empty show of patriotism. Outside, we heard the calls of joy in a hallmark neighborhood. As the night progressed and the lead in our favor grew wider, I couldn't help but be swept up in the historic Progress.

When Obama hit the almighty count of 270 electoral votes, I found myself in a flash flood towards the streets of New York City. Two jumbo screens and the hope of a collected nation lit up the corners of 125th Street and Adam Clayton Boulevard with a display of final victory. A young man lifted his little daughter in the air, bouncing up and down with an uncontainable excitement. He leaned over to his wife and shouted,

"Our baby is gonna look ev'rybody straight in the eye! It ain't a curse to be black no more! You hear me, baby girl?"
"I hear you, daddy!" his daughter shouted.

Somehow through all of the motion, I felt my phone vibrate in my pocket.

"We did it!" I shouted.
"I've lived so long to see this moment!"
"It's a celebration of an impossible victory."
"I can't wait to see you! I love you!"
"I love you too! I love you mom!"

No pauses, no sighs, no criticisms or lies. That snippet was the best conversation I had had with my mother in years. The unifying power, the new era, had begun.

We celebrated in the streets until the early morning. In perfect keeping with my past bad habits, I downed six shots of tequila and could barely hold myself upright from the drunken bitter-happiness coursing through my bloodstream. A still guilty Brian hailed a cab and accompanied me home.

"She won't let this stop you two," Brian said.
"I dunnn…she'sss gotss suppor-ive family. She'sss not understand..."

"Well said, drunken Mary."
"Fuck you. The room ishh spinning, why is so fassstss?"
"We're here."

"Oh, rights…cab."

He paid the driver and took my keys from my hand. Carrying me up to the apartment, he laid me down in bed. It was the strangest feeling of déjà vu.

"Deeepaaa…"
"Yesh?"
"WE WON!" he shouted.

I threw my fist in the air and fell asleep with a drooling smile on my face.

I called Barbara the next morning as soon as my stomach had stopped shaking. Apologizing profusely, I began to lie about a particularly incapacitating case of food poisoning.

"Too much to drink or too high?" she asked.
"The first."
"The office is practically empty today. Get some rest, see you tomorrow."

Best boss ever, best victory ever, best…girlfriend. Near alcohol poisoning temporarily made me forget the traumatic portion of yesterday. There were no calls or text messages from Audrey. Her phone went straight to voicemail. I left a long detailed message.

"Our relationship is the only thing that has ever made caused me to be grateful for my orientation. I need you Audrey. I…value your opinion."

I couldn't bear to utter my first confession of love through the phone. I spent the next hour trying to map out the response to the cavernous questions that were surely to follow.

"Why haven't you come out to her? Why didn't you tell me before?

Why are you so scared?"

I stopped at the corner deli to pick up flowers and a copy of the only newspaper left - a tabloid. Her studio building was coated in a ghastly shade of grey. As I raised my fist to knock on her door, I saw the giant pulsating bulge that was my heart beneath my shirt. I couldn't tell whether the persistent feeling of nausea was from alcohol or nerves.

She quietly whispered for me to step in. As I gave her the flowers, I tried to make contact, praying even the softest graze of our hands would convey the care my inner core breathed for that woman. She was too skilled in the art of persuasion and took the flowers with caution to avoid any physical touch.

"They only had roses. I'll bring you lilies later."

Please Audrey, agree there will be a later. Silence.

She asked me about the rest of the night. I told her of the awesome power of the hope and the promise. This was something that so many people had been waiting for after centuries of discrimination in a country that prided itself as a land of opportunity. Now that promise had taken a great leap forward.

"It is really remarkable," she agreed.
"For immigrants."
"And black people."
"And women."
"And children."
"And gays."

We discussed the Progress for a full hour before bringing ourselves to the sensitive issue at hand.

"Are you mad?"
"Not mad. Just sad."

The last thing I wanted to do was cause her pain. I tried to explain everything. The emotional damage an arranged marriage took on mom was deep-seated. Never wanting to compromise her daughter as such, she shielded me from the judgmental, constant queries of society. Mom's ultimate conclusion, however disappointing, was not ambiguous in nature.

> *"Be yourself, find who you are. Don't get married Deepa, not until you have found the right* ***man****."*

Mom never got along much with anyone. She never went back to school, or started a career. She never took up any hobbies, or found peace with her past. But she raised me with love, and she raised me with care.

She guided me past the monsters and demons to my first steps of kindergarten. She volunteered for the role of sound master when I rocked to the beats of techno music. She strolled with me in a gorgeous kimono through the Japanese gardens we created in our minds when I chose a year in France over a summer in Tokyo. She never questioned when I asked to take a trip to New York over prom, and she put me on the highest pedestal when I accepted a job that paid less than $35,000.

Our convergent minds split ways through the years. But the immature gestures, the dramatic motions, and the continuous need for positive reinforcement were the small prices I paid to look at my mother, to hold her hand, and to thank her for always being strong enough to let me be who I was.

My one condition to rewrite was this - my orientation. Through her pauses of various persuasions, in her sighs of inner reflection, and her visible disappointment with the world's grand operations, mom had never wavered on her disapproval of queer people. My vagueness in appearance, my disinterest in dating, and my successful employ of pronouns carried me successfully until I moved away. She didn't know, and I was terrified to tell her. I was terrified to lose her.

"Deepa, you will not lose her if you tell her you are gay."
"I don't know, Audrey, who is to say?"

She tried to argue about pinni, who Audrey met last month.

"Your aunt doesn't care, and she is your mother's sister."

But pinni lived a life that was ripe for the picking. She was allowed to choose her own path, to define her own future, and find her way to happiness. Pinni lived her life as an open book, and as a result, had many diverse people write themselves into her life. Save the memory of her father, it was as though mom had severed her ties to anyone who was a part of her life before I was born.

"There will always be something your parents do not understand about you."
"How would you know? With Paris, your sister, a revolutionary mother?"

"Deepa, I know you think that it was easy for me to tell my parents, that I come from a family that understood everything before I did.

Of course that was what I thought. Audrey argued that her mother was progressive on female equality issues. For Audrey's mother, homosexuality was not the same. Audrey had to tell her parents she was gay just like everybody else.

"It was hard and I was scared. But I did it, and it worked out."
"It won't for me. Look at my dad!"
"You really think that's why he left?"
"Why else would he leave right after I told him?"
"Maybe it was one thing that made him upset. But Deepa, your mother is not your father."

That was a good point I had never wished to acknowledge. She wrapped me in a protective embrace, trying desperately to block out the complicated, harsh world.

"You are close to your mother. Why are you so scared?" she asked.

"My gut tells me mom will not be okay with this."

We tried to untangle each other from a mix of support and frustration.

"Do not let fear dictate your life," she said.

"Life has dictated my fear," I replied.

"If your mother wants you to be who you are, she must accept who you are."

"I know it's not time to take that risk."

There were tears forming in the corners of Audrey's gorgeous blue eyes. This conversation struck a chord that upset the very fundamentals of her being.

"Deepa, I can work out so many things, but I cannot live a half-lie. If you can't take this risk..."

"I couldn't handle the world if I had let you go," I whispered.

"Please, for you, for me, you must come out to your mother."

Her tears hit the ground like bombs in an ocean.

"I love you," I barely uttered.

"I love you too."

"I do this or I lose you?"

"Or we lose each other."

Chapter 13

"Over here!" I waved at pinni.

"Not our typical venue," she commented.

She stammered that it was cute, though at the sight of the restaurant decorations, her words lingered in the air like a thick smoke. The faux wood walls were covered in random pictures of France and Belgium - not typical touristy shots. They were intimate scenes of a 19th century family, recognizable only through the landmarks that stood centuries' test of time. Our tiny round table was met with two mismatched chairs that could be described as either vintage or garbage.

I called yesterday and asked her to meet me at my favorite hole-in-the-wall crêpe shop in the West Village. After the life changing experience of studying abroad in France, I found myself in mental limbo between two continents. This crêperie was the perfect resolve; it had always been an excellent place to talk and to think. Out of her normal pristine corporate element, pinni sat with an unusual self-doubt and waited for me to speak.

"What do you remember about the few years my parents were married?"

I was not there to mince questions. She was not there to mince answers, and recounted the vague details she knew of mom's existence in Orlando. Just when mom had sourced what she had been looking for in life, dad forced her to uproot and move. Mom restarted in New Orleans and ended with a deep hatred that could only mean a great happiness in between.

"What did she love about NOLA?"

"Are you thinking about moving?"

"No, I just want a better sense of her experiences before me."

Pinni let out a rush of air. No one had ever asked that question before. Who else would? I was my mother's only child.

"I met one of her close friends from New Orleans, Jeff."

"Jeff?"

I had never heard of a Jeff.

"He was really great. Smart, good looking, very nice and supportive. Your mom had a crush on him."

"Did anything ever happen!?"

It was a strange thing to ask your aunt that about your mother. Pinni looked equally uncomfortable by the question as by the answer.

"No, I don't think he was interested. Your mom thought he was, though."

"Where is he now?"

"I don't know. They lost contact after the divorce. She was a mess by the time she moved."

That was one detail that struck me by surprise. Mom spoke more emotionally of her smartphone than she did of my father. Even with the anticipated turmoil of ending a four-year marriage, mom being so traumatized with her New Orleans departure made no sense.

"Why do you want to know all of this?" pinni asked.

"Audrey and I..."

"Is everything okay?"

"For now. Audrey wants me to come out to mom."

"When?"

There was no explicit deadline. It went without saying that Audrey would not let our relationship progress until I took the risk.

"What do I do?"

Nearly four years ago, I had asked the same question. Without hesitation, pinni told me to come out to dad.

"He's a doctor, he'll understand."

This time, she chose her words carefully.

"I can't tell you whether to come out. This isn't anything I've experienced before."

Last time she told me she could easily relate. When she met Amir back in grad school, they dated in secret for nearly two years. After listening for the meaning behind avva's words, pinni decided to take her risk and announce to the world - avva included - that she was in love with an Iranian and they wanted to get married.

With years of avva's confessions of guilt and devastation at her older daughter's life, pinni became confident with the idea she had found someone she truly loved. The idea that avva would one day have a supportive family was enough to convince avva that it didn't matter who pinni married.

Between pinni's own story and the talking heads of New York, I took the risk in coming out to dad and watched it blow up in my face.

"Will it be the same with mom?" I asked.

"Honestly, I have no clue."

The once close relationship pinni had to mom had died long ago; mom was not the same person pinni knew growing up. She was not the same person pinni visited in New Orleans. That spirit had died slowly.

"She has never reacted well to these topics," I reasoned.

"Obama's support of gay rights will be a good way to set a positive tone."

"What about avva?"

"I doubt she even understands what 'gay' means."

Pinni caught my eye and realized what I needed to hear was a similar speech as when I came out to dad. This time she sounded more realistic. That gave me confidence.

"Mother excluded, you have a great support system in this," she assured.

"It's just so difficult."

"Love always is. Relationships and marriages involve more than the commitment."

"I know. It's not just the marriage. It's the circumstance of marriage."

"How was dinner with your aunt last night?" Audrey asked me.

"It gave me a lot of answers; now I have even more questions."

"You can never have the complete information."

"I at least want some indication."

"You know you have to tell her."

"A lifetime of hatred doesn't dissipate with a mere warning."

Audrey wrung her hands a few times and apologized for being pushy. Rewriting the inner workings that had been hardwired in mom's brain would not happen overnight. I knew it was a bad period of time to begin the process.

"Why do you say that?" Audrey asked.

"Mom will blame you, or the election, or New York."

"There will always be something to blame, Deepa. We cannot live our lives by this standard! Your mother wants to know that you are loved."

Audrey told me how important our relationship was and how important it was that mom understood what our relationship really meant. The worry lines first discovered by the bridge on date number five were appearing too frequently.

"I promise she'll know by Christmas."

It was a promise that I still didn't want to make. But Audrey was my soul and my world. This was the choice that she was making, and therefore the risk I had to take.

The atmosphere turned a murky lukewarm. Audrey settled into bed and pulled the covers up to her chin. The worry lines left traces of resentment that I couldn't stand to watch expand through the night. I fell asleep on the couch, letting my brain slip into the unencumbered world I created as a child.

Chapter 14

"Passport, boarding pass, camera, both phones. Got everything?" I asked Audrey.

"Oui, tous."

I reached out to adjust her scarf so it completely covered her neck. She had the habit of placing it so that it served the sole purpose of decoration underneath her pea coat.

"This is going to be the longest two weeks of my life," I told her.

"I will call you twice a day and tell you everything!"

A pile of snow I kicked splattered into a million pieces and left a dark mark on my shoe. I wished I had a camera attached directly to my eye that would have allowed me to zoom into microscopic levels. Kicking snow would be so much more interesting if I could see the individual flakes burst out into freedom.

"Keep in touch on your new adventures!"

"I'm gonna start the meter, ladies!" the cab driver shouted, honking his horn.

I wrapped Audrey in a giant hug and held her there for a solid minute, forcing my brain to make a copy of the feeling in case I got lonely without her presence. She held my gaze as though trying to sort through the disorganized files that made up my thoughts and feelings. I knew which one she was searching for. It was password protected.

"If it goes very badly, remember to come to me in Paris."
"I'll come next year, I promise."
"I have already told my parents!"
"Je t'aime."
"I love you too."

"God, I hate Christmas," said the driver.

I decided to take the train to Maryland after three consecutive years of experiencing the brattiness of New York City children at the airport Christmas week. At gate 12, I'd see little Johnny complaining to his mother about being dragged away from presents for the sake of her African adventure.

"Mom, I don't want to see a damn lion!"

At gate 15, the father of an already elitist 10-year old girl tried to convince her how much fun it was to visit the rest of the family in Central Michigan.

"It's a really lovely area."

> *"Really dad, nicer than our apartment on the Upper East Side?"*

The train had its own issues, though the sheer amount of time I had to lose myself in my own thoughts was a calming effect before facing the next eight days. Mom greeted me at the station with her usual mix of welcome and dramatics.

> "I'm so happy to see you! It's nice you've finally made an appearance!"

She scolded me for missing a birthday avva was not sure of and never celebrated, my own day of birth, Thanksgiving, and a smattering of weekends she had planned for mother-daughter exploration of her newfound hobbies. I smiled in return with my usual charades of regret.

It only took us ten minutes to pull into the driveway of the house avva bought less than a year after I was born. Despite the lack of opportunities, the blatant and subtle forms of racism, and the horrid weather, avva said it was surprisingly difficult to leave the tiny town in West Virginia she had longed to escape for so many years. After my grandfather's funeral, she experienced a sense of community she had only felt in India.

> *"In India, we live to please the community because the community is all we have to take care of us."*

Pinni was in college at Georgetown and the only reason avva had stayed in West Virginia was my grandfather's practice. After he died, avva cashed in every asset to her name for the down payment on the house in Maryland, and gladly let dad help with the mortgage after.

The two-story brick house 5 miles outside of DC area had quadrupled in value since it was purchased. Avva, a certified financial wizard, supplemented dad's support with expert investing and getting a job as an accountant at a local bank, where she worked for 15 years.

Between what she earned and the excessive amount dad sent, we lived very comfortably without ever needing mom to make money.

I padded upstairs to the familiar room that I had called home from ages 1-17. Mom wouldn't let avva change a single thing inside the square box interior that was heartedly decorated with memorabilia of every interest I had growing up.

> *"My daughter will always have her own space in this house!"* mom proclaimed.

Before going downstairs to my alternate reality, I called Audrey for a quick taste of her soothing voice. She was somewhere over the Atlantic Ocean, so I had to settle for a very old voicemail message of broken English.

> "You have reach me, Audrey. Thanks to please left your message after the sound. I will to return this from as soon as possible."

From the center of my bed, I could still see the outline of the celestial sticker packet I found in a box of my favorite childhood cereal. After sucking down two bowls of the sugary fuel, I spent an afternoon using my bed as a catapult to build 'Deepa's constellation.'

Most mothers would have dragged their kids straight down. Mine climbed right up and helped me determine the newest galaxy. I spent six years staring up at the sky we created together, foiled only by a necessary paint job after the stickers were recalled for Mercury poisoning.

> "Deepa! How are you, beta?" avva asked me, once I returned downstairs.

I smiled at the word, 'beta.' My software engineer friends all thought I was some kind of Android running on a beta version. It was easier to let them think that rather than explain the Hindi language word my Tamil and Telugu speaking grandmother had picked up from her late husband.

"Hi avva! I'm doing well, you?"

"Still a tired old lady, but much to thank God for."

Avva sat me down to hear all of the latest updates with my work. Mom and I managed to lie to the accounting czar about my starting salary. Thinking I made a comfortable living, avva was elated to hear that I had chosen to work in immigration rights.

Pinni appeared in tow with Amir and their kids, Sahra and Malak. It was always strange to see her outside of her exclusive regalia of the professional. Amir and I chatted politely for a few minutes. He loved to use his eyes to indicate when he was using a euphemism for anything 'gay talk.'

"How is the 'personal life'?" ::glance at French painting::

With avva in the room, I didn't want to spend extra time on relationship subjects, and steered the conversation to innocuous New York topics - the vending machine ate my metro card, an interesting movie just opened, I discovered a new candy store, and

"I'm hating the transition back to winter."

"It's better than being stuck in a perpetual oven like I was at your age! You get to live your life so freely in New York," mom called out.

For all her support of me, mom loved to bring up the depressing life of her mid-20s.

"I was pregnant with you, my life was in shambles, and..."

"Time for dinner!" avva shouted.

"Thanks for interrupting my story. It wouldn't have happened if..."

"Enough!" avva shouted, again interrupting mom.

The passive-aggressive battles of the two generations of women thus commenced. I used to play out battle scenarios in my head as a kid at the dinner table.

"In the right corner, we have mom weighing in at 125 pounds. She will be testing out her new custom made guilt rays flown in directly from West Virginia! And in the left corner, we have avva weighing in at 115 pounds. We expect to see another appearance from the poverty cloak and competition sword!"

To make up for a Thanksgiving spent apart, avva insisted we go around the table and give a word of thanks before eating. Rejoining reality, I heard Amir was already in the middle of his list.

"Thank you for an incredible wife, two amazing kids, and a buyout bigger than I could have ever hoped for when we started that humble company."

Pinni gave thanks for her promotion as a Vice-President at McKinsey, a great family, and a niece who forces her to go to restaurants that have more character than attitude.

"So you *did* like the place?" I coaxed.

"What place?" mom asked alarmingly.

Mom always got upset at the idea that pinni and I had dinner together on occasion. She used the opportunity to cut pinni off and start in on her list. Mom's mockery of the 'Giving Thanks' ritual went without criticism because she always ended on a note no one could question.

"Thanks for getting me out of that God forsaken marriage, thanks for my headphones that drown out stupid comments, thank you for peanut butter cookies, and thank you for the most wonderful daughter a mother could ever ask for."

We'd leave the honor of finishing to avva: thanks for never leaving question as to whether there will be food on the table, thanks for keeping us in good health and with enough wealth to last a lifetime.

"Amen," avva concluded.

The rest of us stifled our laughs. When she was a little girl, avva saw an old American movie in India. The word 'amen' had been with her ever since.

"They were so sophisticated, thanking God no matter what their wealth!"

She was elated when she found the perfect occasion to use the word.

The table was covered with our usual mix of Indian food and American side dishes. Every year at school when I had to describe what I ate for Thanksgiving and Christmas dinners, I got a round of snickers.

"Chapatti, vegetable korma and mashed potatoes."

Now I wouldn't have it any other way.

Mom broke the comfortable silence.

"Good thing you didn't bring that horrid friend of yours this year."

"Gloria? We don't talk anymore."

"She was very unpleasant."

"Deepa, congratulations on getting that promotion!" pinni called out, trying to control the conversation.

Grateful for the diversion, avva and Amir chimed in their sounds of encouragement. Avva stood up with her tiny stainless steel water glass straight from the slums of Chennai and dedicated a small toast in my honor. I loved her clashes of cultures.

"What's a promotion?" Sahra asked pinni.

"It's the thing mom got, dummy. It means you are more important at work," Malak told his sister.

"Alpa didn't really get a promotion. Deepa did, not Alpa," mom heatedly said.

Continuing on the 'East Coast Mom Pacify Highway,' pinni reiterated her elation in my promotion. I mouthed a quick 'thank you' before staring down at my plate in embarrassment for mom. This was certainly not Progress.

"Deepa, what happened to Mr. Ramirez?" avva asked.

"Unfortunately he died not long after his partner."

I cursed myself for using that word; Pinni and I held our breaths in unison waiting for mom to comment on what Jorge and Pedro being 'partners' meant. Thankfully, mom pretended to be engrossed in her string beans.

"Immigrants never deserve to be treated like this," avva continued.

"But they broke the law!" mom finally shouted.

"What choice did they have?" I asked her.

"To not break the law! They violated the law doing what they did."

The ides of repetition started to make way. Mom took out her frustration by stabbing her macaroni and cheese with a fork. Sahra and Malak liked the looks of it and followed in motion. Now we had three people stabbing macaroni and cheese and one awkward discussion.

"Sometimes the law isn't what is should be," avva sternly reminded mom.

"Your case was different!" mom exclaimed.

"How? Pedro had to lie to get Jorge in the country. They struggled to find a way to stay. The same thing happened to mom and dad," pinni pointed out.

Mom waved her hand to commence a very predictable two-part argument sequence.

Part One: "It's just different!" "It's just different!" "It's just different!"

Part Two: "It's just different, dissimilar, unalike, atypical, *unnatural.*"

She emphasized the word 'unnatural' to make the obvious point that it was not a synonym for 'different.' My mind flashed back to all the examples of her homophobia: the stares at the happy same-sex couples in DC, the commentary on TV shows with gay characters, and the clear hatred of the word *lesbian.*

"Why don't you approve? Because they were gay?" I heard myself say.

"Just drop the subject. Gay is not a happy word," mom said, sardonically chuckling.

We were all too shocked at how fast the conversation went from bad to terrible to respond.

"Geez, no one got my joke."
"We got your joke, mom. It wasn't funny," I replied.

Mom looked aghast that I would dare take that tone.

"What has gotten into you? You are so short-tempered with

everybody," she said.

"Not with everybody, just with you. Someone pass me the mashed potatoes."

Happy holidays, amen.

Chapter 15

"How is it going?" Audrey asked me.

Giant dead oak trees lined the street. Tim Burton must have used something in this vein as a muse for his life's work. Even in broad daylight, the giant arching branches, the large knots on the trunks, and ghastly gray overtones gave the appearance of a soul sucking entity.

"Mom is stressed out having my aunt around all week."
"Why?"
"Seeing a slice of my aunt's perfect life is always tough for mom."

Audrey was eager to meet mom for this reason. When Audrey's perfect older sister announced she was getting married to a tall, handsome, stable guy, the look her parents bestowed on the world was one Audrey never forgot.

"We have two daughters: one successful, one gay."

Even though same-sex couples had options in France, her parents didn't seem to care.

"I could still enter into 'Pacte.' You know this term?"
"Yeah, it's the civil u--baaa--nion."
"Why are you breathing like that?" Audrey asked.
"It's nothing, keep going."

"I think my parents are just sad sometimes…"

Clang clang clang clang clang. My teeth involuntarily became a percussion instrument.

"Deepa, are you outside!?"

"No! Okay, yes! I just wanted to take a walk."

"It's -4 Celsius today!"

"Maybe in Paris, but here it's real-aaaahhh-ly nice."

"That's the temperature for DC today! Are you hiding from your mother?"

Of course I was. After the Gloria debacle, I couldn't pass off the same excuse.

"I'm just talking to my cool French friend!"

Who else but a significant other would call three times in the first 48 hours of a vacation to visit family? The simple solution would have been to ignore Audrey's incoming calls. But the solution was too hard to execute.

"Deepa, this makes me so sad! Why should you have to freeze outside just to have a conversation with your girlfriend?"

"I would do the same thing if you were my boyfriend."

"That's bullshit!"

It was. It was total bullshit.

I did my best to control my loose teeth and vibrating body in the misery of a DC winter. She babbled about wholly unimportant things, like shoes, her tiny rodent dog, and the declining quality of Parisian chestnuts. To be sure I stuck around to listen, she dropped in an occasional,

"I love you. I miss you."

Just enough to keep me from throwing down my phone in a shivering defeat. It was a ploy to get me back inside the house, but I was stronger than she thought given the situation…because I hadn't gone to the gym in months and had a layer of fat to keep me insulated.

It was only when I realized my hand was firmly frozen over my phone that I conceded to the antics of my clever girlfriend.

"I should go inside or I'll freeze to death."

"That was mean to keep you on the phone like that."

"Where's the sorry?"

"It was just a statement."

Touché. That was the same ending I used when I told her that her 'euro trash' costume for Halloween was more likened to a prostitute. We exchanged our melodramatic proclamations of love before parting with our lines of communication for the day of Christmas. I hated the time difference. It made the blackout period 30 straight hours.

"Merry Christmas, mom!" I exclaimed as she opened my gift.

She was very careful to remove the paper without ripping a single shred. Perhaps I wasn't the only person traumatized by dear Amy. I retrieved my best stupid grin as she revealed a two-foot long frame containing my one extra copy of the November 5, 2008 Obama victory edition of the *New York Times*.

"This is beautiful, Deepa! Thank you! How did you get a copy? I thought you were out late that night?"

"I had to go all the way out to the end of Queens."

This was one for which I deserved zero credit. In my veiled queer identity, producing credible sounding lies had become second nature.

> *"Why do you think there are so many closeted gays on Capitol Hill?"* Brian always said.

The truth was that despite her severe sadness on election night, Audrey woke up early the next morning and got me a few copies of the paper while I slept in a drunken stupor. I had two copies professionally framed - one for mom and one for myself. A pay raise and no real plans for Paris had some advantages.

Sahra opened the gift I got for her - a 50-piece set of oil pastels. I figured she could use 25 of them to draw and the other 25 to throw at her brother. She absolutely loved the idea. It was a nice feeling reminding a kid who had everything that there was still something to look forward to.

"Are you going to draw me a picture?" I asked her.
"Yeah! I'll draw one of you in Paris!"
"No dear, Deepa studied abroad in Lyon," mom told her.
"I knoooow, but she's going to Paris with Au…"

"I might go to Paris next year with a friend," I told mom.

Mom gave me a strange look for cutting off my 10 year-old cousin, and continued distributing gifts. 'Santa's aide' (mom hated the word 'elf') was mom's favorite role of the year.

Pinni offered to make everyone hot chocolate. I jumped up to help. It was the perfect opportunity to chew her out for babbling my life secret to a child. Sahra had a mouth the size of Mount Everest that was as equally poorly regulated as the Nepalese climbing authorities.

"You told the kids?"
"Of course! We live in Manhattan. Half of the city is

gay! These days they know what gay means before they know what sexuality means."

Pinni tried to pass her blunder as a further incentive to actually come out to mom before leaving.

"What if avva finds out?"

Pinni gave me a bemused expression. It was the same look as when mom surprised me with my first car after letting me beg her for a ride to Baltimore to go to a party.

"It's not funny pinni, this is my life!"

"I know, Deepa. I do take this seriously. That's why I threatened to take away their ski trip this January if they tell."

I thought about going to the store to run off a few signs that prominently displayed our new family status.

"Rich people problems in progress."

Mom wandered in to see if I wanted to open her gift. All I really wanted for Christmas was a note on pleasantly scented paper that proudly proclaimed mom's unconditional love for her gay daughter.

Instead, I followed her back to the giant tree she had hauled in from the neighbor's yard. Mom took on Christmas decorations like a finely trained soldier. Navigating through the train set and floor ornaments, she found my gift in the back. It was a large envelope. In the background of my naively pulsating heart, she said it was a combination Christmas/birthday gift. If it was the note I prayed for, it was the last damn gift I'd ever expect from anyone, ever.

I tore open the top portion of the envelope and slowly looked down into its depths.

"This is a ticket to New Delhi," I said out loud.

"You, your avva and I are finally going to see the Taj Mahal in March!" mom said.

Mom had a radiant glow evenly coating every inch of her normally defeated face. I couldn't remember the last time I had seen her so excited. Her wanting to get out of the house and return to India was a good sign of her Progress.

"We're *finally* seeing the Taj Mahal after all those worthless visits!" mom repeated.

Avva shifted uncomfortably at the word 'worthless' and launched into one of her famous explanations about how it was her duty and honor to visit her mother and sister until they passed away.

Mom's enthusiasm was so infectious! I couldn't help but let my usually serious demeanor switch back into childhood mode. We did our happy dance that helped made growing up with a single parent a (mostly) absolute pleasure.

Pinni came rushing in to see what the noise was about. Mom grabbed the ticket from my hand and waved it in pinni's face.

"We're going to Agra to see the Taj Mahal!" she bragged.

"That's great! When?" pinni asked.

"March 17th!" mom shouted.

The word 'seventeenth' was secret code for engaging lead shoes. I felt myself come crashing down from my last leap. March 21st was Audrey's birthday. Even if our trip was only one day in India, there was no way I would make it back in time. I couldn't miss the first of Audrey's birthdays that we were together.

"I can't go the third week of March."

"What? Why?" mom said, whipping her body to face me.

The turnaround time on this lie was too short. This was my in to the conversation I had avoided for 12 years. I should have asked mom to step into the other room so I could calmly explain my reason.

"Well…it's just I have this conference for work."

"We will reschedule. When would be good for you, beta?" avva asked.

"No! You'll have to miss it, Deepa. This is too important," mom said.

"Chee! Too important for whom, Pooja? This is her job, she must go to the conference," avva argued.

Pinni took the tension as a cue to usher the kids and Amir back upstairs to give us air. The way mom and avva were shouting they would use the entire supply of oxygen within minutes.

"The weather will be terrible from April until August!" mom exclaimed.

"I can't get off work if we go before mid-March. How about October or November?" I suggested.

"I am starting a lecture series in October," avva quietly said.

Mom flailed her arms, pulling out pauses of the third persuasion. Avva's shield was made of guilt-proof iron, and she refused to budge on the issue.

"Great, so the entire year is gone! Thanks a lot! I have been excited about this for a very long time!" mom shouted.

In another frame-by-frame mode, I saw the short-lived elation fall steadily back into mom's regular frown.

"What about my birthday? September is usually really nice in

India. I can definitely get the time off 9 months in advance," I offered.

Avva did an Indian head nod in agreement.

"That is fine for me. Pooja?"

"It's disappointing I will miss another birthday in the city, but I suppose that is the only solution," mom said.

"Cheer up mom, we're going to the Taj Mahal!" I guiltily encouraged.

Mom gave me a weak smile, but clearly couldn't control her severe disappointment as she stalked off. Avva looked at the expression on my face and mistook it for sadness at the disapproval.

"Don't worry. You go to that conference and make us proud, beta."

Chapter 16

"Bitch, it's Christmas. Why you callin' me?" Brian answered.

"Are you kidding me?"

"Of course. I hate it here. What's up?"

I told him about the trip to the Taj Mahal and how I blew the perfect entryway into 'the' conversation.

"Just tell her the truth!" Brian said.

"I can't let her down again."

"Your mom has serious issues if she's upset about a 6-month delay on a trip she has waited 40 years to take."

I wished Audrey weren't in the deep lairs of Parisian Christmasland. Brian didn't know what he was talking about.

"Oh please. I've known you for seven years. Your mom wants everything that involves you to be perfect, but her idea of perfect is so out of touch with reality that the world will never live up."

Gloria had said the same thing to me before. She even went so far as to write out a few examples in a flowchart. It was a work of genius, if not extremely offensive and slightly disturbing.

"What should I do?"

"What do you like about Audrey?"

I loved the way she always picked out the perfect wine. I loved the way she allowed me to explain American culture so she drew her own conclusions. I loved the...

"No! Not that small mushy shit, Deepa. What did you think of the guy I brought to Kelly's going away party last month?" Brian asked.

"Even during my existential crisis you turn the subject back to your dating life!"

"Just answer the question, Deepa!"

"I dunno! I liked the way he described his work and the way he dressed."

"See?"

"See what?"

Brian told me that a year ago, I would have said the guy's skinny jeans made him look like a drag version of the 'Little Mermaid' and asked what it was like to work in a company devoid of personality or emotions. He was right.

"Audrey has made you relate to the world in a more positive way. She's not going to change her mind and you have to come out eventually, Deepa. Audrey is just the catalyst you need."

"Hey mom, can I come in?"

She sat at the enormous mahogany desk she had three burly movers drag in during one of the hottest summer days. Dad had just sent her a large check for her birthday. He never learned when her birthday actually was.

Part of the reason Barbara's ever growing pool of papers gave me comfort was because it was similar to mom's style. Mom would print off hundreds of academic studies related to urban design and architecture. What she planned to do with all the printed knowledge was unknown.

"What are you reading?" I asked.

"It's about urban development challenges in 1850s Paris."

"That's interesting. Is that?..."

Your latest random obsession? I decided to fill in the important part of the question from the safety of my own head. She smiled and looked past me out the window.

"It's hard to believe there are only four days left in the year," she said into space.

"Can I talk to you about something, mom?"

"I'm sorry, Deepa."

"That's okay, we can talk later."

I turned to leave, partially upset, but mostly relieved.

"No! Deepa, I'm apologizing for acting so crazy lately."

I didn't know if I was more surprised by the apology or the 'lately.'

"December is a hard time for me. The next one will be the 30th anniversary of your father and me getting married."

By the body language and the tone, my 'Mom Feelings Geiger' was giving me mixed signals. Was this a happy conversation of her personal life Progress or a regretful conversation on the lack of her life Progress?

"What did you want to talk about?" she asked.

Through all of the complaining, I often forgot how pretty mom was beneath her dark circled eyes and furrowed brows of analysis. It was the rare moments like this when we made clear eye contact that I could see old reflections of the happy mother of my childhood.

"Tell me about New Orleans. What was it like to go to school there?" I asked.

"I hated having to move there, especially since your father didn't consult me on the decision…not like he ever consulted me on any decision," she started.

I echoed my agreement even though I knew dad had apologized a million times for that very reason.

"It was a great city to study in. It's in the south, but people are progressive."

"Having progressive people is really important," I agreed.

"It made for a globally aware environment. Did I ever tell you I studied about France, about Lyon?"

It was surprising considering she never actually came to visit when I lived there.

"No, tell me about it now."

From the placement of key statues, to the historical significance of districting, to the class warfare of street layouts, we covered nearly everything I remembered about the physical aspects of the city. I had no idea everything was laid down with so much purpose. I had no idea mom *knew* all of this was laid down with so much purpose! She beamed with the knowledge that she had imparted new context to my understanding.

> "The level of development in the European continent - the history, the stories - it's fascinating to see how they play out in the end product," she said.

Her entire body became animated as she waved her arms to conduct the intricacies of her subject. With every new street, with every new passage, the ornate hall began to take shape. The lights shone down as though directed from heaven, the curtains fluttered at each breath of enlightenment, the instruments bellowed out their music with cause. As the performance came to a close, she beckoned me to join in as a co-conductor.

"Deepa, you wanted to talk to me about something?"

She held her baton in mid-air, waiting for my cue on which direction to move the symphony. I looked out into the audience waiting patiently for the completion of our song. They had been anticipating this for many long years.

"Don't keep us waiting! Let us know the ending!"

I held my breath as I marched to the dignified podium that looked upon them. Raising my arm to match her poised level, I said the words that completed her work of genius.

"We should stop in Paris for a few days on our way over to

Agra. I know you've never been."

Oh how the audience gasped at my twist ending! She looked at me to confirm the conclusion, to etch into stone the grand finale.

"I thought you were going with your friend?"
"No mom, I want to go with you."

Chapter 17

"I couldn't do it," I told pinni.
"What happened?"

I replayed the glory of our grand ensemble.

"Encore! Encore!" the audience screamed with such fervor!

"I just never found the right time or the right words."
"I wish I knew what to tell you, Deepa."
"Audrey will understand."

My attempt at false confidence had the strength of a cloud. Pinni stared straight through its transparent surface.

"You don't think so?" I asked.
"I just don't know when else you will have the chance to tell Pooja."

"It doesn't matter; Audrey had no right to give me that kind of ultimatum!"
"Perhaps not, but you still have to tell her."

Julie wrote me an email saying she had decided to stay with her family in Boston for New Year's Eve. At the time, I forwarded it to Audrey with total elation. Now I was regretting that move. Who would have thought I'd prefer to spend New Year's in an overpriced, crowded club instead of alone at home with my girlfriend?

I kept myself busy the last day of 2008 by pulling out all the stops to create a romantic atmosphere for New Year's Eve; I needed to soften the blow that I was a lying coward. Audrey called me as I was making the wine reduction for the pasta.

"I'm coming straight to your apartment!" she said.

By the time I hung up, the pasta was drenched in a giant pool of my sweat. I managed to finish cooking dinner without burning myself on anything, though that sounded like a decent exit strategy. When I dated the girl who turned me on to vodka sodas, I had actually considered the move. Brian made a nagging comment to snap me back to reality.

"If you are willing to inflict bodily harm on yourself, it's time to break up!"

I heard the door buzzer just 45 minutes after Audrey called. Leave it to the New York City taxi system to get Audrey to Lower Manhattan in record time from the outskirts of Queens.

"Wow, you didn't have to go to all of this trouble, Deepa!"

I didn't have time to clean up the counter, the sink was piled high with dishes, the soap dispenser was nearly empty, and the mystery sweater was still on the couch from our last party. Even so, Audrey eyed everything with such appreciation as though the room was the very definition of perfection.

I told her to take her time getting ready. Later, she emerged from the shower wrapped in an oversized robe.

"Alors, je suis vrai canon?" she asked.

She was referring to how "hot" she looked, and wore her fuzzy dolphin slippers to strut along a fake catwalk down the length of the apartment.

"Oh oui! You h'aare a totalE knock-OUT!" I replied in my best fake French accent.

"Great-T! Zank you wery much!" she replied in her fake Indian accent.

Her constant smiling helped me relax, and we caught up on the past few days without me dipping in and out of consciousness. Between the time difference and the general laziness of the holidays, we only managed to catch each other once after my freezing encounter with the Burton-esque oak trees. As of our last phone conversation, I hadn't come out to mom. Audrey was clearly dying to bring up the subject, but we both knew how quickly that could sour the mood.

My mind flashed back to this precise day one year ago. I spent the last few minutes of 2007 explaining to a stranger why I thought I was born gay. Gloria was right; I did have a problem with my sexuality. I was comfortable enough to not suppress it, but not enough to embrace it. It made me bitter; it made me lash out.

I looked down at Audrey resting her head comfortably on my shoulder. Her legs were crossed over mine. Despite the difference in our skin tone, the point at which she ended and I began was indistinguishable. She stimulated a part of my brain and a part of my heart that had laid dormant up until we met.

"5…4…3…2…1…Bonne Année!" she yelled.

The screen flashed over to president-elect Obama.

"My fellow Americans, from the great city of Chicago I want to extend my warmest wishes of gratitude for your support this past year. As we look forward into 2009, I want to reach out to every one of you – black, white, Democrat, Republican, Christian, Muslim, straight or gay…"

Audrey squeezed my hand as Obama said the word 'gay.' I could feel the Progress.

Her warmth and the emphatic release of our new president supporting our right to live honestly enveloped my entire body. Looking over at Audrey, I gently guided her chin so as to look into the depths of her gorgeous blue eyes. In their reflection, I saw the black of my own poised for the confession.

"Audrey, I have to tell you something."

Chapter 18

"You lied!?" Brian screamed at me.

"I couldn't bring myself to let either of them down!"

"You think lying to Audrey's face is the solution?"

The thought of living without mom or Audrey was as Jorge had described: living as a half-person.

"What can I say? I panicked."

"What exactly did you tell Audrey happened?"

"That mom wants to keep some distance while she figures things out in her head."

Brian congratulated me for regurgitating his mother's exact response from seven years ago. I remembered him standing up at the only LGBTQ Alliance meeting I ever went to and telling everyone his step-dadzilla was too stupid to figure out basic concepts like evolution or homosexuality.

Step-dadzilla had a complete breakdown and accused Brian of being a pedophile and practicing bestiality. After calling the cops, he almost had Brian hauled away to prison. Brian's mother defaulted as the negotiator.

Brian and I became instant friends after that story. Unfortunately, I didn't have a balance of two parents to calm the other down.

"What about your grandmother?"

"I doubt she understands the idea of sexuality."

"She's asexual?"

"No! Well, sort of."

In Indian society people don't get married because of love or sexual attractions. Westerners in favor of gay rights appeal to the emotional side of opponents by asking them to think about how they love their spouse.

"That love and desire is what gay people feel, just for someone of the same sex."

That was a conversation I knew I would never be able to have with avva or mom.

I saw the coffee shop empty out with morose and conflicted faces. We were already a few minutes late to the first day back to work. Before parting ways on our familiar landing floor, Brian warned me of introducing any more stupid decisions.

"And remember to cover all of your bases."

As expected, the next few months went by in blur of computer, train, and bed. The only weekend I managed to stay away from the office was met with a bowl of chicken noodle soup and a treacherous landscape of dirty tissues.

Audrey's studio, my office, and my apartment formed a giant triangle of inconvenience. To spend any time together, one of us either committed three nights away from home or we had to be satisfied with a mere drink like common colleagues.

"Deepa, you look horrible," Julie said in our first words all week.

"Many thanks…"

"Where is Audrey?"

"Dealing with her place."

"Great amenities?"

Oh, the works. Broken pipes, rats, noisy neighbors, and one of the apartments two flights below had bed bugs. That was a fantastic Saturday of playing detective, exterminator, comforter, and paranoid repellent sprayer.

"You guys should move in together," Julie suggested.

"Am I that bad of a roommate?"

Julie tapped her foot in annoyance. It was too late in the day, too late in the week to go phishing for compliments. That activity was best done Monday - Wednesday, from 10 AM - 4 PM.

"You know what I mean. I can find someone take over your room."

"Am I that easily replaceable?"

Stop. Still off hours. It was a phish out of water.

"Thanks for the offer. It's just…"

"Just what?"

"It would be stupid to give up this great apartment and move into that dump."

"She could stay here for a few weeks."

"Thanks for the offer, it's just…"

Julie gave me a look of annoyance now turned anger. I spilled my inner turmoil to her two weeks earlier in a coughing, sneezing, dazed

3 AM confession.

"You still haven't told her!?" Julie guessed.

No, and that was why I was afraid to move in together. Inevitably the conversation I had been carefully avoiding would no doubt transpire if I saw Audrey every day.

"How can your mother keep her distance if you go to India with her in September?"

"Well you see Audrey, when I gently guided you to meet my gaze on our first New Year's together, I actually lied about the ***one*** *thing that you said would be a deal breaker in this relationship."*

"Is that the only reason?" Julie demanded.

"Basically."

"Dummy, then tell her!"

"It has to be clear this lie was out of a genuine fear of losing mom."

"That will happen anyway if you don't have a visa to go to India."

Every time I tried to fill out the visa application form, some refugee got thrown in jail, a boat of illegal immigrants washed up in Florida, or Barbara panicked because she dreamt the world ran out of coffee beans.

"I haven't even printed off the damn thing."

"I'm an incredible friend, right?"

Hey! No phishing!

Julie walked over to her gigantic purse, which engulfed her whole as she rummaged around the basement level. After a few crashes of overstuffed file cabinets, she reappeared and waved a gigantic envelope as though I were her puppy and the envelope were a bone.

"I took the liberty of filling out all of the parts I knew."

"Oh my God, thank you so much!" I exclaimed.

The envelope contained an application form that was mostly filled out, and correct. Attached was a print out of passport photos I had sent to Julie when we were in college for our trip to China.

"You *are* a fantastic friend!"

"Deepa, in exchange, you have promise me something."

Julie walked to the door of my room and peered around, flipping through her mental memory book of being roommates for five years. Together in that apartment we had battled the all-nighters of school, the mistakes of young love, and the realities of transitioning into adulthood in an overpriced yet tantalizing city.

"You have to tell Audrey. Coming out to your mom is your decision, but lying about it is a whole other issue."

This was a memory I hoped would get tucked away in the archives. I promised to take care of everything. Julie looked truly undecided between believing whether my promise was truth or fiction.

Chapter 19

Audrey's housing situation deteriorated further when her landlord announced her building had significant pipe damage and would be shut down by April. Residents had four weeks to figure out alternate arrangements. On the upside, security deposits would be returned. On the downside, lives would be ruined.

As many foreigners did, Audrey moved in to her studio under an illegal sublet, and had enjoyed a rent controlled price established around 1975. With the budget she had, her only options were to move in with strangers to stay within sanity's reach, or move to the ends of the City to retain the notions of privacy we had become spoiled to enjoy.

"These arrangements were too good to last forever," I sighed. "If only there was a way for us to live together."

We had benefitted greatly from the process of 'discovering each other,' and she dropped many lines to suggest we were ready to move in together. As much as I loved the idea of coming home to her, my secret followed me around like a bomb close to detonation. Mom meant we were not ready to move in together.

"I can come to Queens on the weekends. Roommates are an option; it's nice to have company," I told her.

"We'll make it work," she agreed with disappointment, unsure why I wouldn't concede to the ideal move.

For two weeks, I helped her search through every nook and cranny of Manhattan, Brooklyn and Queens. As the lucky beneficiary of a well-priced, well-located apartment, I forgot how difficult the process was of narrowing down places in that labyrinth of a city. The best options we found were still pathetic:

Apartment 1: Lower Manhattan, two roommates, practically condemned, room about the size of my head.

Apartment 2: Brooklyn, three roommates, one of whom may be a serial killer.

Apartment 3: Queens, no roommates; we'd essentially be a long-distance couple.

Apartment 4: Hoboken, New Jersey, one roommate with the

following kitchen requirements: no dairy, no meat, no gluten, no sugar.

Apartment 5: Brooklyn, four roommates, two live-in partners, one bathroom.

Audrey agreed to take the one bedroom apartment in Queens, and was set to sign the lease just a few days after her birthday. She spent a few nights with me, though the noise of my neighborhood kept her in her broken studio most of the week.

"We can make this work, right?" we both questioned.

"Ah, I am so -appy to get out of that fucking apartment!" Audrey exclaimed.

Up until we started dating, I hated the way French people drop the beginning 'h' in English words. Turning to look at her shimmering face, I could now see how deaf I had been for all of those years. What else could describe her total elation?

"-Appy."

My gaze was fixed straight ahead at the road. I debated whether I would have rather been in India to take away the hanging doubt that was so hard to stuff into this motorized vehicle. The previous week, I took a timed ride out to Audrey's new apartment from my strategically placed office building. At the end of my run, the clock read 117 minutes. Rides two and three came in at 112 and 124, respectively.

"What are you thinking?" she asked.
"How much I love cheese."

Her bemused expression deflated the doubt that remained. Over the years, I charted the random thoughts that populated my brain and the rate at which I verbally said them. As my relationships progressed, the chart lines moved in a direction of divergence or convergence. The better the relationship, the closer the lines got.

"Really, what are you thinking?"

"Um…I was just…have you decided whether you are going to do that year of independent research here or back in France?"

I could only hope that Audrey was the second person who reached that convergence. My whimsical years of childhood had already awarded the first.

"The program in France is much better suited to my interests."

"We can work out something long dist…"

"BUT, I filed my application to stay here."

I jumped up in victory, causing the steering wheel to jerk the entire car to the left. Audrey reached out to steady the deadly swaying.

"So you want me to die?"

She was phishing. I didn't care.

"We'll reach that convergence. Just be careful, it's not permanent."

"I have no idea what you are saying sometimes. Where the hell are you taking me!?"

Dan's father died with two explicit instructions:

1. Marry a beautiful woman
2. Clean up the God damn beach house

Queer as the West Village during Pride, Dan failed on the first account. The previous week I had offered to help with the second in exchange for exclusive weekend usage rights. The beach was freezing, the town was dead, and it was as quiet as the French countryside – it was perfect. As we entered, Audrey let out the gasp for which I had very much hoped.

Using images of our well-documented journey, I reopened my toolbox of graphic design skills. With the help of a thick curtain, I blocked out all of the light in the main room, save the warm strokes of a few jasmine scented candles. The black and white chronicle of our lives thus far was washed in a stunning sepia-like glow.

"It's beautiful, Deepa."

"I have another present. It's very small."

Timed runs from my apartment to Audrey's new planned abode also took around two hours. We had aimed to grow into each other, but life doesn't always work out the way plans are established. If this lie to mom was my only real barrier to my domestic bliss, something had to give.

In between my Long Island house cleaning, I took a day trip down to Maryland to see mom. We started the conversation by outlining the forthcoming memory blocks of all things Parisian, of all things north Indian. She as the architect, and me as the builder, it would be a lifetime of happiness on which to reinforce our foundation.

"I'm hopefully moving in with someone," I then told her.

"Is it a friend from school?"

"I met her through a colleague. We're moving into a one-bedroom apartment."

An earthquake erupted, shaking mom so violently she spilled half of her tea on the kitchen table.

"Rent is expensive in New York. Many friends split one-bedroom apartments."

"Mom. I'm moving into the apartment with Audrey,

my…"

"Roommate. Yes, I heard you."

The architect told me to take a step back.

"Do not do this, the public cannot know this, the building will collapse."

Her decision was swift and it was final.

"Yeah. My roommate. Audrey."
"We'd better get you back to the train station, dear."

Audrey was still waiting for her small gift. I tried to turn my deception into truth, but it was like molding steel as clay. My only other option, the one I know would work, was to move forward with my soulmate and explain the truth of the matter when the correct time presented itself. I knew we'd live happily together, and my falsity would become a distant, laughable memory.

"Audrey, if you hate the idea, I totally understand."

She looked down at my hand and gasped at the small gold box. I steadied myself as she carefully removed the cover.

"It's a key to your apartment?" she asked with distinct disappointment.
"No, it's the key to an apartment in Brooklyn."
"I don't understand."
"I signed a lease two weeks ago…for us. I want us to move in together."

I held my breath to tread the approval water.

"I love it!" she screamed.

Treading was not necessary. The water was at waist-level.

"Where is the apartment? What does it look like? When can we move in? Can we get a téléphone fixe?"

"Right off of the Bergen F train stop, modern and sleek, and yes, I think a fixed landline phone is a splendid idea."

She told me this was the best birthday she had ever had.

"Even better than the one when that boy threw up all over your new dress?"

"You're quite close."

Chapter 20

It was a strange feeling moving out of the East Village after seven years. Manhattan was one of the few places in the world that outpaced the change of the most frequently changing people. Somehow, through all of the rent hikes, the gentrification, and the influx of attitude, I was able to thoroughly savor that lifestyle. Audrey ushered in a new era to my life, however, and I couldn't wait to move forward.

It only took us two days to distribute our collective belongings into a perfect symbiosis. The gimmicky appeal of the modern-style stainless steel appliances and shiny hardwood floor said that we had become sell-outs, but that was a compromise worth making. They contrasted perfectly with the black furniture we discovered on our first decorating adventure. With a few splashes of color, we achieved the effect of 'cool lesbian couple.'

"We make a great team," Audrey said.

"Indeed we do. I love that shelf we bought."

It was an asymmetrical unit that a certain ex would have said was the product of a stroke.

"Oh, I forgot! I bought a fixe!"

"A landline phone."

"Yes, a landline. This will make it much easier for me to call France."

Two years in the States was enough time to justify not carrying a computer around as a phone for cheap Internet calls. Unfortunately, I was a dud at operating the antiquated system.

"How do we record a voicemail message?" I asked.

"Are you joking? Remind me to teach you before September," she said.

"Why?"

"Because my parents only use a landline...I was thinking we could go to Paris for your birthday."

My brain split in two. We had been in the apartment for less than 48 hours and the conversation of death had already surfaced.

"September is a perfect time for Paris. Which is why I am going with mom. Oh yeah, I still haven't told you."

"I forgot to tell you though. I'm going to India for my birthday," I replied.

That part was indeed true.

"Ah that's too bad about Paris, but India will be great! For work?"

"Yeah, Barbara is sending me to a human rights conference in Delhi. I'm sorry I didn't tell you sooner, it just got crazy with the move..."

"No problem, I know I can trust you."

Our schedules were polar opposites:

'Student v. Professional'

But we read each other's minds and knew how to make it work. The apartment was big enough that she could carry on raging debates of psychology well into the night, and I could wake up on time the next morning to ponder the all-important question:

"Bagel or toast?"

Lesbians have a tendency to disappear when two find each other and so much as think about love. Audrey and I both lived in the city to enjoy the city, however, and we made our own 'Pacte' not to bring each other down. Some nights were surely spent alone in the comfort of each other's arms, but mostly one or both of us were out to live our lives in the vast expanse of the urban paradise.

We had a housewarming party a few weeks after we moved in. To compliment my Chelsea Market cheese excursion, Audrey paired my favorites to three types of wine, and the finest meats and bread my credit card would allow. We stood back in proud wonder as Audrey's international friends blended effortlessly with my artsy, progressive New York life companions. The verdict was in: our life was nearly perfect.

Chapter 21

Audrey's parents visited the third week of May for her graduation from The New School Masters of Psychology program. After dealing with a stingy customer service, I cashed in all of those overtime nights from the winter. For two days, Audrey and I cleaned up our first few months of apartment filth and mapped out a treasure chest of her parents' favorite foods. They were not stubborn people, just French.

> "This apartment became so dirty in just two months!" she cried on day two.
>
> > "This guy once told me the reason New York is so dirty is because it carries the emotional dust of the world."
>
> "I think it's because of poor funding."
>
> > "At least people clean up their dog shit here."

For a society so concerned with cleanliness and order, how many times during my year in France did I jump around on the sidewalk to avoid dog turds? In a country that functioned with poise and grace, they were literally the black dots that maligned the pristine face.

> "Ahh, Deepa don't say things like this to my parents! They think France is the best country in the world. It is really important to me that you get along."

She looked at me with an intense expectation. That didn't help quell the anxiety that was brewing inside. It had occurred to me the previous week that this would be the first time I'd meet a girlfriend's parents in any formal capacity. Gloria once dragged me to one of her father's drunken backyard Bronx barbeques when we first started dating.

> *"Are you girl from ER!?"* he screamed in my face.

I wasn't sure whether no frame of reference would work in my favor. All I knew was that I couldn't screw this up. First impressions were everything.

We decided to take the subway out to JFK to pick up Audrey's parents. From our part of Brooklyn, the ride was one of my favorites in New York City. Together we sat on the train observing the fine details of the New York City masses. There were so many influencing cultures.

"What does my father do for a career?" Audrey quizzed.

"He is a professor of economics at Université Sorbonne Nouvelle, Paris III. Your mom is an orthopedic surgeon at the nearby St. Germain hospital."

"And my sister?"

"Your sister, Cécile, is three years older than you and a marketing executive. She is married to Nicolas, a successful software engineer."

"And the dog?"

I snickered.

"Your dog, Pépite, is a bichon."

I couldn't help but fall into a small pool of hysteria. What better stereotype for this dark-haired, tall French family than a tiny rodent *Bichon* named *Pépite*?

"Don't make fun of chère Pépite!"

"Sorry! I just think small dogs are lame."

She told me we were getting a small dog eventually, so I'd better start liking them or else it would be an awkward dynamic.

"When do you envision getting this small dog?"

"Perhaps in 2 or 3 years. Once we can move to a bigger apartment. Are you sick?" she asked.

"No…I'm just excited to think about the future."

It was nice to walk inside the expanse of JFK airport and sit idly by, recreating all of the stories the buildings contained. I imagined the anticipation and fear avva must have had setting foot on the other side of the world - her new life - for the first time. Mom must have been so nervous bidding farewell to her childhood here. Now there I stood, awaiting the beings that bore the reason I was a better person.

Audrey stopped to buy flowers for her mom.

"It's the one gender stereotype she lets apply."

I spotted Audrey's parents a mile away. Audrey was clearly her mother's daughter, with the same flowing chestnut hair, a perfectly curved figure, and an identical poised walk I imagined old French royalty doth bequeath. Her father was a tall man with a slight slouch, and simple features that formed an unyielding face. Their clothes were impeccably in place and they walked in harmony straight into the arms of their loving daughter.

Back at the apartment, Audrey showed her parents into our bedroom. They examined every inch of our place. By the way they subtly pointed and found each other's gazes, I could tell they had developed their own mental language for comparing notes.

From my year of living with quintessential French students, I could guess the level of detail at which two older Parisians examined a property. Compared to the American level of scrutiny, I only hoped my efforts sufficed.

American: Is the bathroom clean?
French: Precisely how many bathroom tiles have a disagreeable substance between the crevasses?

American: Do all of the appliances in the kitchen work properly?
French: Are the utensils arranged for maximum efficiency? Are the cheeses, yogurts, and creams stored separately?

American: Is the apartment nice?
French: How many trains, buses, metros, and trams in the vicinity? How good is the grocery store access? What is the historical significance of the neighborhood?

Audrey's parents completed their detailed inspection and returned to deliver the verdict. Thankfully, there was only one complaint.

"There should be a bidet."

Audrey rolled her eyes. Apparently this was ridiculous by current French standards.

"Even in France it's just for decoration," she argued.

"Perhaps you have become Americanized," said her father, eyeing me a bit too coldly.

I told Audrey I would be absolutely fine if she spent the first night alone with her parents, at least for dinner.

"My father suggested the same thing, but he would never do so if you were a guy. I chose to be with you, he has to accept this," she replied.

She never squandered an opportunity to assert her sexual identity. I looked away with guilt as the words came out. Apparently my guilty face screamed anything but.

"Oh Deepa, I'm so sorry. Your mother will accept you. It will get better."

I was fascinated with the dynamic between Audrey and her parents. They formed a perfect triangle in debates and discussions.

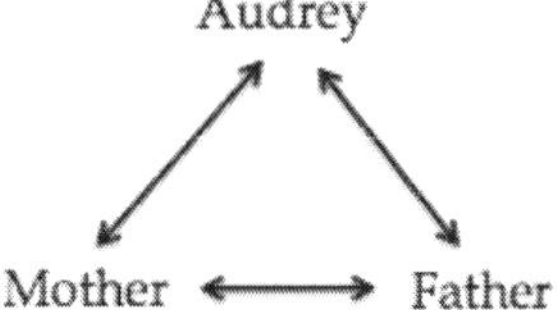

My entire life had been a straight line between me and mom or avva. One of the two would be a firm other side of the conversation before the other would inevitably interject in the middle.

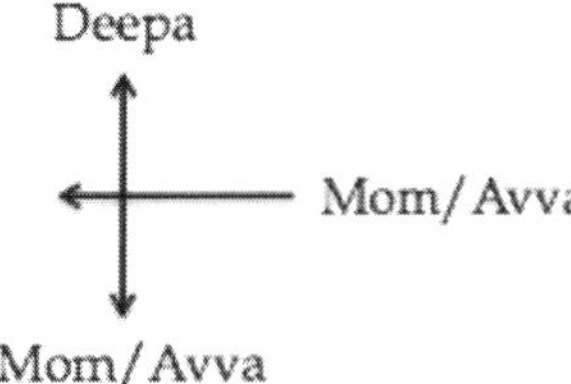

Most of my friends growing up in Maryland had parents who were divorced. Previous girlfriends never won many of my genuine affections, and no one in New York dared to ask friends around on touristy family visits. This was my first intimate look at how a two-parent family functioned.

People always asked me if I wish I had grown up in a proper nuclear household. To be honest, it seemed boring. Audrey's parents were different. They disagreed respectably, they supported each other fervently, they were assertive without being abrasive, and they had most certainly found every type of conversion. It was an encouraging window into my future.

Unfortunately, Audrey's father hated me. Hate was a strong word. Hate was the Westboro Church on gay rights. Hate was a native New Yorker's feeling towards a Boston-based sports team. Hate was my feeling of the George W. Bush administration. Audrey's father hated me.

Despite my best efforts to avoid one-on-one contact with either parental unit, Audrey's mother managed to corner me at breakfast one morning while I contemplated another important question.

Waffles or pancakes?

"Your parents grew up in India?"

"No, just my father."

I explained my hatred (hate was the right word) of the new Bangalore city developments.

"They call it the Garbage City."

"And your parents want you to have an arranged marriage?"

"Not at all, my mother is very against it."

"She is accepting of your sexual orientation?"

On the scale of acceptance, I believed the best I could hope for was constant, total denial.

"She is getting used to the idea," I lied.

"It was the same for me too."

"Really?"

"Of course, it is not an easy thing to hear that your daughter is a lesbian."

She explained that for her, as a straight mother, it was very disappointing to know her daughter would go through something very different than what she had to find love. Even having a straight older daughter did not lessen the feeling.

"I could not connect to my own child about something as fundamental as love."

"In Indian culture, a partner is found for you. The love may or may not come later."

Audrey's mother scrunched her nose in a moment of negative reminiscence. The first Indian she ever had met was a resident at her hospital. His parents were from one of the last surviving French speaking villages of the formerly French-colonized Goa. He was a young fellow, a quiet fellow, and very set in his ways.

"He spoke of his wife as though she were a furniture purchase. 'She must be durable, comfortable, and easily transported.' "

"Wives in India are often treated like a long-term investment purchase. American ideals combined with Indian execution..."

"It must be hard for your mother, then."

This woman was perceptive, just like her daughter.

"I fought throughout my youth for gender equality," she said.

"As with the using the French feminine article when describing a doctor?"

She was happy to hear Audrey spreading the world of the mini revolution. I was envious of the connection they shared. My relationship with mom had simply faded with time.

"I demanded people show me respect as a female doctor, even if the French language didn't have the correct words."

"That is very eloquently stated."

"It was Audrey who first described it this way when she came out to us."

Audrey's mother explained that as a straight woman, being in 'radical support' for women's rights was not the same thing as two women falling in love and building a family.

> "Audrey helped me realize that it is very much the same struggle."

Her mother gently laid a hand on my shoulder and thanked me for making her daughter so happy. It had been a long time since her precious baby girl had been at ease with the world.

> "As a mother, it makes me feel better knowing my daughter is growing into her own person."

Chapter 22

Under a brilliant blue sky, cotton ball clouds, and a perfect temperature, Audrey decided that she didn't want to go to the big, indoor final university commencement the next morning. Without the need to rush to dinner and back home, I awkwardly played the third wheel of her parents as we admired the backdrop of the department ceremony location - a Gothic-style church that oddly poked out from the busy streets of Greenwich Village.

Audrey found her friends for their dramatic end of program goodbyes. She was flushed at the culmination of this stage of a most promising career.

"She looks so happy, it's amazing," her father said.

Her mother peered around and gave me a wink.

"You are making our daughter quite happy," she repeated.
"It's probably just the city," he said.

Audrey galloped across the churchyard and excitedly explained the feelings of a bittersweet ending. Her father asked where she wanted to go eat, careful to adjust his body so that my invitation was in question.

> "There is a fantastic Italian restaurant in the East Village," Audrey replied.

Audrey turned, waiting for me to say that was my old neighborhood of seven years. Her father's back to my face was enough to make me hesitate, so Audrey declared me available for a tour. Her father's reaction made me feel as though Audrey and I were at a theme park rollercoaster.

> *"Please proceed in an orderly fashion. No drinking, no eating, and certainly no fighting. Priority seats available for the vision impaired and disapproving."*

I saw Audrey's father stare at our piano keys display of handholding affection. The laser beam that accompanied overprotective fathers burned a hole straight through my right palm. Audrey was unharmed.

> "Don't let it bother you, seeing me with my girlfriend is still new to him," she whispered to me in English.

Audrey called the restaurant and took the first available reservation for eight o'clock. With two hours to kill, we decided to wander west to the Meatpacking District before heading back to the East Village. I was embarrassed to show her parents our gross, polluted Hudson River in case it was viewed as my attempt to one-up Paris.

> "This is a filthy body of water, nothing like the magnificent Seine," her father immediately commented.

Worried about the failure to appease Audrey's parents, I suggested alcohol might best celebrate Audrey's achievements. Once settled at a table, Audrey's father questioned my level of French culture exposure.

"Have you been to France?"

"Of course. How do you think she can speak French so well!" Audrey exclaimed.

"It passes," he answered back.

"I studied abroad for two semesters in Lyon," I offered.

"Ah, Lyon! I grew up near there. How do you find the city?"

I did my best to balance out potential competing interests. It was surprising he even wanted to know my opinion.

"It's very pretty, but I prefer Paris."

"Why don't you like Lyon?"

"It just isn't as open or progressive…the people, I mean. There is not the same level of diversity."

Audrey looked alarmed at my response.

"The important thing is that Deepa speaks French and she loves Paris."

"Yes, Paris is the best city in the world," he thankfully agreed.

"My husband has not seen much of the world, but Paris is a great city. When will you come to visit, Deepa?" her mother asked me.

"Septem…September was my plan, our plan, but I have to go to India for work. Perhaps Christmas?"

"We will be in Luxembourg for Christmas. You cannot come," her father snapped.

"No problem, I understand."

"Family is important," he continued.

"Supporting and understanding family is important," Audrey added.

"They are all important!" Audrey's mother shouted.

Mercifully, the waitress interrupted the conversation. I waited for everyone else to order before requesting the same drink as Audrey's mother. It was the safest move given the situation. She was the only person Audrey's father did not question.

"Would you like to stop in Paris on the way to India?" Audrey's mother asked.

"Yes! That is a great idea! What do you think, Deepa?" Audrey eagerly asked.

"It's not possible, we have to go back to Lyon to help my brother after his surgery and Deepa hates Lyon," Audrey's father replied.

Her mother angrily explained that Audrey's uncle was having minor surgery on his hand. It did not require they be there all month.

"No! Don't rearrange anything for me," I exclaimed.

"Yes, she is actually right," he backhandedly agreed.

The three started in on a triangular fight.

"There is no need to argue," I desperately chimed in.

"Supporting family, remember Audrey?" her father snapped.

Audrey looked at me as if to say I was shooting myself in the foot. Her mother caught the glance and soothed the storm once more.

"Deepa, you are welcome to stay with us when you can come," she politely offered.

Practically slapping him the face for bad behavior, she demanded her husband repeat the same thing. He looked at Audrey and saw the emerging sadness on her face. This was supposed to be her special day.

"Yes, you are welcome to our home, Deepa," he reluctantly replied.

I sucked down the rest of my drink before excusing myself to the bathroom to send Audrey a text to come join me. Without asking, I told her I would leave the solid family triangle less I cause a major breakage.

"You don't have to! My father does not have the right to treat you differently..."

"Stop!" I pleaded.

This was the first time that I forcefully challenged her judgment. There were a thousand reasons why her dad may not have liked me.

"Who is to say it's because I am a woman?"

"What other reasons could there be?" she asked.

"My race?"

"Is that better!?"

"No, okay! Maybe he's just scared of losing his little girl?"

She pursed her lips at the thought. I was on to something.

"He might not see 'that gay girl who is with my daughter.' Maybe it's 'that person who took my daughter away from me.'"

For the first time since we started dating, she gave me credit on something 'coming out' related. I told her parents I was feeling under the weather, and bowed out after paying for the drinks. Her father looked elated to see me go. I didn't care. I had a call to make.

Chapter 23

I walked to the highline and chose one of the last free seats overlooking the Hudson. Against the gentle splashing waves on the pier, I saw thousands of happy couples walking, children eating ice cream, and relieved students celebrating the culmination of a lifetime of work. It was a soothing backdrop for the titan of a storm I was about to unleash on my life.

Every gay kid dreamed (or had nightmares) about the day they came out to their parents. The few gay characters that were depicted in movies and on TV always had a dramatic story of catastrophic proportions. In reality, most of my friends, save Brian, had a relatively calm discussion. Even my coming out story to pinni entailed all of three lines:

> "I'm gay."
>
> "I would have guessed. Got a girlfriend?"
>
> "No, just dating. Pass the ketchup, please."

As I heard the explanation 'maybe he is scared of losing his little girl' come out of my mouth, I realized I wasn't just talking about Audrey's father anymore. The pronoun 'he' was off, but pronouns had been established as inaccurate in these matters. In a strange epiphany, that angry, jealous, irrational man made me realize how ridiculous I had been.

Everyone in mom's life dealt with the symptoms of her actions, not the root cause. I knew then that if I addressed the underlying issue of her fear in losing me, it would be okay. I was tired of lying. I was tired of sacrificing my relationship with Audrey for mom's prejudices. It was time to take the risk.

Mom picked up on the third ring, just as expected. We exchanged mundane life details – the weather, the television, the 'work' and the family.

"Deepa, are you okay?"

"Everything is fine. Are you free next weekend?"

"You are always welcome to your own home."

Her words hit the drum of my pounding heart with a weird reverberation.

"We can discuss hotels when you get down here!"

"You go ahead and book whatever you want. The important thing is that we get to spend my birthday together."

I sounded suspicious. She asked if I needed money, if I was in trouble with the law, or if the pressures of work finally forced me to cave into quitting. I yearned for a return to the days when a few simple words could be read for all its hidden meaning.

"It's nothing bad, I…I just love you, mom."

"I love you, too. Call me when you book the ticket down here."

"You're going to see your mother next weekend!" Audrey exclaimed.

"Shh, you'll wake your parents up."

And her father would have stared me down with his monster green eyes, forced me to confess my innermost secret, and destroyed the fragile bridge we had created to our palace.

"She is just scared to lose me. I called and explained how I miss her."

"This is such a big step!"

Audrey thought this step would lead up. My hope was mom and I would stay level.

"It's 2 AM, you should go to bed," I said.

"Aren't you coming?"

"I have some work to finish."

"An insomniac consumed by work. Perfect, I live with my father."

She left me to wonder if she appreciated the irony of her statement. I looked at her angelic silhouette as she arranged her body in her favorite sleep position. So much as a hint of her shadow made me question the risk. In all of the misery and all of the deception this lie had created, my biggest regret was the fact that I could not decipher between my fear of losing her and my need to be wholly honest.

For three hours I researched resources for parents and family members of LGBTQ community members in the DC area. That wasn't the first time I had done the search. In 1999, my findings included a few text heavy webpages. In 2004, my search led me to websites with online newsletters and event pictures. Now, in 2009, my search yielded blogs, social media groups, smartphone apps, and links to more than 20 organizations in the DC area alone. I was starting to see the benefit in being mainstream.

At around 6 AM, I finally emailed myself the extensive list I pulled together. The sun would be up in less than an hour. Quietly changing, I emerged from the bathroom and crashed into the intimidating relationship enemy I had been so careful to avoid.

"Ow!"

I managed to stifle a full scream.

My night vision finally made an appearance, and I saw the angry man covered in a milk moustache. Trying my best to walk around his demonic child-like persona, I made my way back to the pull out bed.

"I have a stomach ache from that terrible restaurant. I came to get a glass of milk," he announced, forcing me to come back.

"Good luck. American milk is not nearly as good as French milk."

"You speak the truth."

Brilliant, this man connected to people by complaining. I told him I was going to bed. He tried to correct me.

"You mean back to bed."

"No, I am going to bed for the first time."

"What are you doing this late?"

I hesitated to tell him, thinking he'd say I approached this the wrong way, or my analytic skills were like that of a monkey, or that I should have just asked Audrey.

"Just research."

"About what?"

"Resources for family members of LGBTQ people."

"For me!?"

"No! For my mother!"

"Ah yes, I did a lot of research on the subject after Audrey came out."

"Really?"

"Of course, I am not an imbecile."

"I didn't…why would you say that? What have I done to make you so mad?"

In the darkness, I saw him lower his head to the floor. I'd be damned if all that was needed to weather his hostility was to simply call him out directly.

"I'm sorry. This is just how I become when I am nervous," he admitted.

Doubt was ringing in my ears. I was not an instinctual person, but I could feel another trap of humiliation being set.

"Audrey called 20 times to tell me how to act here," he said.

He seemed genuine in his apology, though I had little experience in the way of fathers.

"You did a lot of research on support groups?" I asked, changing back the subject.

He did quite a lot. Having been in Paris a long time, he had been exposed to many gay people without ever having a problem. But it was different when it came to his daughter.

"Deepa, can I ask you something?"

My top three guesses were:

1. Why aren't you good enough for my daughter?
2. When will you sign up for proper French courses?
3. Why aren't you good enough for my daughter?

"Sure," I answered.

"I have many colleagues who work in human rights and immigration, but I have never heard of a conference for this in Delhi. Are you cheating on my daughter?"

"No! I would never, ever cheat on Audrey."

"What then? Are you going with your mother?"

I realized too late that the silence I used to formulate a response was the very thing that answered his question.

"Deepa, it is okay. I only thought this because you were very eager not to come to Paris. I thought you are not speaking to your mother?"

"I'm so sorry I lied. Please don't tell Audrey!"
"No, of course not. But…why?"

The silence and the lies were not working.

"She wanted me to come out to my mother so badly. I wasn't ready. I panicked."

I expected a long lesson on the art of communication.

"There are a lot of good things about my daughter, but she is too stubborn. She should not have pushed you like that."
"I shouldn't have lied," I added, preemptively scolding myself.

"These circumstances make us do crazy things."

He and I awkwardly faced each other for what seemed like an eternity. Feigning a yawn, he told me he should get more sleep before the demands of his wife kicked in. Completing his change of character, he patted me on the hand without a hint of negativity.

I finally crawled into our pullout bed. The love of my life was snoring softly by my side.

Chapter 24

It was nearly 8:30 PM by the time the train pulled into the station. Mom guessed well and was standing almost directly in front of the door as it sprang open. She greeted me with the kind of warmth that precedes a volcano.

"You should have called. I've been waiting here for half an hour."

"Spending an extra 3 hours on the train was hard for me, too."

"You should have called. I don't appreciate waiting."

My comment sailed way over her head. That weekend wasn't the best for a second attempt.

Through the torrential downpour that reduced our car ride to a slow jog, we sat in near silence to cool down from our bad start. Despite her love for confined spaces, the concept of a garage door still had avva beat. I parked behind her car on the driveway and we made a mad dash for the door, completely forgetting my bag.

"I called you earlier. You didn't pick up. I left a voicemail," mom said.

"Sorry, my phone is dead and I left my charger in New York."

Fortunately the phone call in question related to a most happy occasion: hotels for Paris and Agra. She booked them, and they were grand.

"Also, your father called. He forgot about an investment account he opened up while we were together. Honestly, it's a ploy to get us to come see him. We only have a week there..."

Impending negotiations of sensitive matters take wit, courage, and sharp skills. Indeed, it was this method by which I had organized the statistics, the reports, and the conclusions. But standing there in uncertainty, I heard my love in her final bids of warning.

"Do not prepare as though your mother is just a presentation."

A strange sense of light-headedness slowly lifted me up from the floor. Images of my whimsical childhood adorned the four walls of the room. The memories of mom and I recreated our enchanted journey of a beautiful convergence. The gash that plagued us since would only be mended by our original approach. The enemy was impressive, not impossible.

"Deepa! Hello, come down from outer space!"

"Mom, you know how much I love you, right?"

"What's wrong?"

It was not her normal reaction - she usually took well to compliments of any kind, but even I couldn't blurt out something so ominous without suspicion.

"I love you; you are the best mother in the world."

"And you're my angel, Deepa. Seriously, what's wrong?"

"No matter what happens or who comes into my life, I'll always be here for you."

Even if it was a statement worth saying, it was something I had yet to say. Between all my travels, moving to New York, and being so independent for all of these years, I had never once imagined a scenario where my love for my mom would be questioned. Her acute understanding of this fact was enough to make her nearly faint.

"Deepa, stop. I don't need to hear this."

"We need to have this conversation."

"After everything I've been through…"

"I'm gay," I heard myself say.

The reaction of panic was instant; she was not prepared to absorb the reality that was delivered. To her, it would split the appearance of tranquility that was so well maintained under storms of denial and wars of lies.

"What did you say to me?"

"Remember how I said I was moving into a one-bedroom apartment?"

"I did not raise a gay daughter."

"No one raises their daughter to be gay. There are several reasons why someone could be gay. Studies have found undue stress during preg…"

I launched into my academic explanation before realizing I had gone completely off track. For as much as mom absorbed herself into studies and literature, the basic line she needed to know was that I would always be there for her. My attempts to correct the mistake were a futile effort.

"Stop! Stop talking, Deepa. I can't hear this right now!"

"I love you, I'm here for you, but we need to have this conversation!"

Her first true acknowledgement of my words came in the form of barely audible whisper.

"Get out."

"What? No!"

"I want you to take the keys to the car and get out."

"Look, I'll go to the car but just to get some info on support groups."

"GET OUT!"

I begged for her to reconsider. A few minutes to cool down were warranted. Banishment from my childhood home was too harsh, too permanent.

"Let's start over, we'll talk about how you feel," I pleaded.

"GET OUT! GET OUT!! **GET OUT!!!**"

Centuries of discrimination were mounting against my reasons. She had no patience for the uprooting of her expectations.

"Mom, stop saying that! I know if we just sit and talk, this will all make sense!"

I reached out in a final attempt of loving gesture. I had hugged my mom more than anyone else in the world, Audrey included.

"Don't touch me! Get the hell out of my house!"

"I haven't done anything wrong, mom! It's me, your daughter!"

A force far stronger than any human physical power was at her disposal. I had no chance at negotiating a peaceful recess. As she pushed me out the front door back into the pouring rain, she cupped both of her hands over her mouth at the sight of our broken family. The sobs rushed out as though she were mourning the death of her child. Before slamming the emblazoned door in my face, I heard her say one lone sentence.

"You will never understand the pain the words 'I'm gay' have caused me."

Chapter 25

There was only one place in the world I felt safe given the situation. I managed to get myself on a flight back to New York that departed just two hours after I reached DC.

Shining streaks of travelers shot past my eyes in a blur as I pushed through LaGuardia airport with uncharacteristic speed. I was at her apartment in less than 30 minutes.

"Oh my God, Deepa! What happened?" pinni asked.

I collapsed in the doorway unable to hold up the remains of the fraction of the person I had been a mere 12 hours before. Sahra was woken up by the commotion, but immediately retreated after seeing me crumpled on the floor.

In a rush of incoherent explanation, I told pinni everything – the single blemish that had wrought my perfect relationship, an epiphany borne out of the unlikeliest of places, a miscalculated risk, and a final ending that was delivered in a most offensive fashion.

"You flew straight back here?"

"I couldn't call because my phone is dead."

I woke up the next morning to the sound of my own belabored breathing. Every inch of my body ached and I could barely see through the clouded contact lenses that normally made my perfect vision possible. After a long shower and a few pampering tricks straight from pinni's personal collection, I felt physically capable of making it out of her apartment.

Instead of using pinni's charger, I decided to take my phone's deadness as a sign to go home and immediately face Audrey. Pinni walked me down to the street, hailed a cab, and handed the driver a $100 bill. She also had the habit of giving large tips in battered situations.

Before summoning up the courage to face my own lies, I cleaned away any stray tears and put on a brave face. Though unsure of how I would approach the coming scene, I was certain I did not have the right to use my emotional turmoil with mom to win Audrey's affections. Pity would inevitably subside and be reborn into anger.

In a bizarre entryway into the frightful episode, I saw Audrey curled up on the couch. She had the curtains drawn so tightly shut that no light shone through. The apartment looked stripped of life.

"Salut chérie, I'm home early. My phone died and I forgot my charger," I managed in a steady voice.

Audrey was coated in a thick substance that repelled close contact. I walked past her without even a hint of a touch.

"Audrey?"

"You have a message on the answering machine."

Letting in a tiny sliver of light, I slowly brought myself to look at Audrey's face. The mascara she was wearing covered her cheeks in a dark film. Her normally angelic eyes were red and puffy. I knew what was coming.

"One new message: Deepa, it's mom. Your phone was turned off. I got scared and called Julie. She gave me this number. Why didn't you tell me you got a landline? Anyway, I found a hotel for us in Paris and Agra! I'm so excited, can't believe the trip is only three months away! Okay, hope this message reaches you before you get on the train. If not, I'm sure your new roommate will call and let you know. Her name is Audrey, right? Love you!"

I faced the window at the message's completion. A bullet had just pierced my heart, and I was sure the remainder of my spirit splattered over the glass.

"Turn around, Deepa."

"Audrey, please, I was going to tell you."

She buried her face in her hands and started sobbing. Through the corner shadow I saw her rocking back and forth. I had never seen her do anything of the sort. After seeing mom do the same thing just 12 hours ago, it was downright terrifying.

I was too scared to speak. I was too scared to move. I was too scared to breathe, to feel, or to live. Finally, she started her lines of questioning.

"Your trip to India is not for work?"

"No."

"It is with your mother?"

"Yes."

"When did you plan this?"

"Over Christmas."

"And you are stopping in Paris on the way?"

"Yes."

"You weren't going to ask me to come?"

"No."

"Does your mother think I am your roommate?"

"I'm not sure."

"Did you come out to your mother over Christmas, Deepa?"

"No. I lied."

Audrey clenched her fists and slammed her eyes shut at my last answer. She stood on the edge of a cliff, waiting for me to push her over.

"I didn't mean to lie, Audrey. It just happened."

"How, Deepa!? *You* started the conversation!"

I tried explaining the complexities involved in disappointing one of the two people in my life I couldn't bear to hurt or let go. Lying wasn't the solution, but it was the only thing that could be done given the battle both she and mom left me to solve on my own.

"You accuse me of forcing you! I am here to support you!"

My calm instantly broke at the word 'support.' My words came out in a waterfall of acid.

"Fuck you! Support me? *You* didn't want me to come out

when *I* was ready! *You* wanted me to choose between you and my mother. Well I am sorry, Audrey, but that is not a decision I could bear to make."

She was taken aback by my sudden aggressiveness, and let out a guttural scream that echoed how unreasonable she thought I was. Her training as a therapist wanted to reduce the conversation to a teacher and a student. We both claimed to be the former.

"Deepa, do I…do I make you happy?"

I closed my eyes and willed myself to respond with patience. It would have been all too easy to ruin everything we had built in the last year.

"More than anything."

"I could tell there was something that was eating at your soul. I could tell that you were not completely comfortable with being gay," she said.

"When have I ever hidden our relationship here?"

She tried to argue that all of my friends said how unhappy I was until we started dating.

"That doesn't mean I wasn't comfortable with being gay."

But I knew she was right. I knew Gloria was right. I knew they were all right.

"Deepa, I understand that feeling. It wasn't easy for me in France. Men are more aggressive there, and they never believe me when I say I'm a lesbian."

"Why are you telling me this?"

"Because it is the real reason I came to New York. Not being accepted for who I am was destroying me inside."

I knew that feeling, too. I knew that feeling of being criticized, tormented, and shunned by both family and strangers for simply being who you are. It made one an angry, bitter person.

"If we cannot be honest about who we are, it will destroy us," she continued.

Even so, it was not enough to justify the relationship I had just lost.

"Audrey, I was fine with living our life here and another life there. It was worth it to keep my relationship with my mother."

Her English was too perfect to not recognize the tenses.

"Why are you using the past to explain the present?"

"I came out to my mother last night."

"Oh my God! What happened?"

"It doesn't matter. It wasn't the right decision for me."

"It *was* the right decision."

"You're ***wrong***, Audrey. You made me destroy my relationship with my mother."

She became livid at the accusation that anyone but mom was responsible for mom's homophobia. Regardless, it didn't change my gross error.

"You lied to me for six months!"

"I wanted to tell you the truth so many times. I'm so sorry."

"One apology is not good enough. I am in New York for *you*."

"Don't act like this is second best!"

She argued that the career she wanted to forge, her closest friends, her real life, was in Paris. She thought she could build a life in New York with me.

"But you are willing to lie about something so important. What happens in five years? In ten years? Will you lie about something bigger?"

"I wasn't sure how you felt about me back in December."

"You're lying again. I was so confident. Not anymore, Deepa. Not after this."

She walked over to the kitchen table and picked up a bag from the floor. It was not the same kind of overstuffed daytime menace that Julie always carried. This one was for the long-term, for departing.

"Audrey, NO! Don't do this!"

"Let me go, Deepa."

"Where are you going, Audrey? Please talk to me!"

"I have tried to talk to you. I can't be here right now."

"When will you be back!?"

She stared down at the floor with an untimely stillness.

"Audrey. *Will* you be back?"

Her silence spoke louder than any words could say. My lie had finally driven her away.

Chapter 26

The impact Audrey had on my life felt large enough to fill the universe, yet all of her worldly possessions fit in a few suitcases. It took her friends less than an hour to empty her material contents from my life. Although her friends seemed sympathetic, their loyalty laid unyielding to my better half.

"She's a wreck, too," is all one of them was able to offer.

In a cruel ending to the happiest story I had ever told, I lost the two women that meant more to me than life itself. They shut the door in a betrayed silence and left me to drown alone in the aftermath.

Part IV – *Narrator*

Chapter 1

From the back hallway, Lakshmi hears Pooja slam the front door with a deep-seated rage that has been festering for 25 years. As she looks at her daughter coated in a mix of tears, panic and anger, Lakshmi feels a sadness creep over her body - a sadness that was anticipated, yet impossible to prepare for.

"Pooja?"

"Leave me alone!"

"Beta, can we please talk?"

Pooja scoffs at the notion that a conversation with her mother will do anything but rub salt on the now pulsating wound of the past hour. In a deafening quiet, she turns and storms to her room without so much as acknowledging Lakshmi's trembling body.

After hours of hoping Pooja would change her mind, Lakshmi concedes at 5 in the morning and retires to her own room. Inside her nightstand sits the green and gold broach she gave to Pooja the Christmas Alpa received acceptance to Georgetown University.

Bringing the broach to her heart, Lakshmi closes her eyes and allows her mind to transport her back to the perfect days of Philadelphia, back to the pristine period of her and Shankar's life that was met with total professional *and* personal satisfaction.

In the years she and Pooja have lived together, Lakshmi's one wish was to see her daughter live that same perfect balance in this world. It had taken much contemplation and many conversations with Alpa for Lakshmi to understand her choices had failed Pooja. Seeing the one person who made Pooja happiest - Deepa - cut out from Pooja's life scares Lakshmi in an intense way that only a survivor of extreme cruelty and poverty would understand.

Too exhausted to leave, too unnerved to sleep, Pooja paces around the 10′ x 10′ space that contains the contents of her existence. Below, she hears Lakshmi's mirrored anxious pacing as though begging Pooja to return downstairs.

Flashing before her eyes, Pooja sees a reel of the numerous moments of regret in her life; raising her daughter is not contained in any of the clips. Deepa did well in school, she was popular; she was a strong woman and a good daughter. Deepa had become synonymous with Pooja's pride.

The idea of a perfect daughter had always been enough to convince Pooja it was normal that Deepa did not want to go to prom, that she never talked about boys, and instead brought home that despicable Gloria, who was otherwise inexplicably close to Deepa. When the signs of Deepa's sexual orientation became obvious, the denial in Pooja's heart was reborn from her days in New Orleans.

Just weeks after Deepa's graduation from NYU, Anand flew back to the East Coast to deliver to Pooja what he called a lifetime of reflections.

> *"It's only a letter?"* Pooja asked.
>
> *"Little happened since we split."*
>
> *"You accomplished all of your goals."*
>
> *"Only professional."*

As she has done so many times before, Pooja walks to the top shelf of her left bookcase where she keeps this life reflection of her ex-husband. Pulling it out, she rereads the words for a wind of assurance.

Anand met his synthetic doll of a second wife at an Indian fundraiser in San Francisco. It was to help the baby seals of Norway, or some equally transparent, fake cause. The doll was one of the organizers. Anand used that as a reason to find the woman as one of substance.

Having recently made Chief of Neurosurgery at the preeminent hospital in the country, Anand couldn't help but feel he had already reached the pinnacle of success. He proposed just three months after meeting, and even had the nerve to bring the doll to Deepa's graduation.

> *"She's a puppet,"* Pooja remarked to Anand upon meeting his new wife.

> *"Don't be bitter."*
> *"Open your eyes."*
> *"Open your heart."*
> *"I'll be at the other side of the park."*

Within a few weeks of being back home, Anand began to see the validity in Pooja's assessment of his new life partner. Gradually, he worked up the courage the approach the plastic person.

> *"Why did you want to marry me?"*
> *"The luxury, the status, and the parties!"* she replied.

Anand moved to America to conquer the world, to leave behind a life dictated by superficial motivations. The person he chose to share his life's accomplishments possessed the emotional and mental depth of a puddle.

Before handing her the reflection, Anand apologized to Pooja one last time.

> *"Pooja, I'm so sorry. I wanted an equal, a partner."*
> *"That's what you want, not what you wanted."*

At the end of his four-page reflection, Anand wrote the one line for which Pooja had waited since the divorce.

> *"I finally understand what you meant."*

Every time she reads that letter, Pooja knows she made the right decision to leave Anand. Pooja knows eventually Deepa will also understand Pooja is right about their situation at hand.

Chapter 2

Alpa convinces Barbara to sign Deepa over on a temporary consulting contract under McKinsey. This buys Deepa a month of recovery; Deepa is sure it will take a lifetime.

By week two, Deepa is able to emerge from her catatonic state enough to make small trips alone. On her first outing to the pharmacy, she notices someone left 9-volt batteries on top of the last package of toilet paper. Remembering the answering machine also uses 9-volt batteries, Deepa finds she is slowly sinking to the ground.

This happens every time she tries to go out. No matter how weak or ridiculous the connection, Deepa inevitably finds something to associate with Audrey and is set off in another downward spiral. The word "pineapple" sends Deepa into cardiac arrest on command, as the citrus is Audrey's favorite pizza topping.

"Deepa?" a familiar voice calls.

"Fuck..."

"Girl, I haven't seen you in forever! Why are you on the floor like that?"

"It's nothing, just leave me alone."

Deepa landed face down in a pile of paper towels. If this were the subway, people would step over her body and let her lie in peace. Since this is an overpriced pharmacy in an overpriced neighborhood of Brooklyn, Deepa is forced to pick herself up to avoid getting arrested. Gloria manages to catch Deepa's arm in the midst of her next crumbling.

"I know nothing. This ain't nothing. Que pasa?"

"How much time do you have?"

"All the time in the world, baby. Let's go back to my place."

Gloria is much stronger than Deepa following Deepa's almost muscular atrophy from two weeks of nearly no movement. Guiding Deepa through the aisles and down Bergen Street, Gloria stops in front of a building less than three blocks away from Deepa and Audrey's apartment.

"You live here?" Deepa asks.

"For the last six months. Bad breakup?"

"Have you been stalking me?"

"Don't flatter yourself. I can still read you like a book."

Gloria snatches away the dark sunglasses that have been shielding Deepa's eyes from the world. It's so bright outside. Eventually, the white dots floating around in her eyes subside and Deepa's vision comes into focus. In every corner, she sees pictures of Gloria and an attractive black woman.

"Still think I'm stalking you? What do you have to say?"

"You guys suck at taking pictures."

Gloria catches her mouth in her hands, eventually coming up for air in between fits of giggles. Deepa can't help but burst into laughter as well; everyone has been exceeding morose around her.

"What happened?" Gloria asks.

"I never cared about relationships before meeting Audrey."

"Really bitch, that's how you start?"

"Sorry."

Against her initial judgment, Deepa tells Gloria everything about the extended lie and losing Pooja and Audrey in less than 24 hours.

Gloria listens with a care that she never displayed while she and Deepa were together. They really did make a terrible couple.

"Why aren't you fighting for them?" Gloria asks.

"Because I'm devastated! Because I feel like dying!"

"This is what I hate about you, Deepa!"

Trying to avoid hearing Gloria's enumeration of all things wrong, Deepa makes an attempt to leave. Still lacking any sure footedness, Gloria again catches Deepa in mid-sway and drags her over to the living room couch. Being held in someone's arms opens up another box of emotions, and Deepa can't help but babble the melodramatic thoughts that come to mind.

"I loved the way Audrey spoke of passion with such nonchalance and nonchalance with such passion. I miss how mom would tell me to follow my dreams instead of following money…"

"Deepa, enough! For all of your detailed thinking, you always lacked action to back up emotion!"

Failure to acknowledge the good, the choice to remain in a pity party, and no efforts to correct the bad were among the reasons why Gloria decided to fall out of touch with Deepa.

"How am I supposed to right these wrongs?" Deepa asks.

"Start with your strengths."

"I can barely hold myself up."

"Not literally."

"Figuratively?"

"Baby, you won me with your words. This will be no different."

"That's the shortest Brooklyn stint I've ever heard of," Julie says to Deepa.

No stranger to bad break ups, even Julie stumbles in words of consolation. Julie's relationship woes pale in comparison to Deepa's debacle.

"What do you want to do for your birthday tomorrow?" Julie asks.

"Unpack?"

No mood can describe Deepa's current state, least of all, fun. The world still feels numb against her fingertips. Her brain is moving on automatic pilot.

"No answer from her?" Julie asks.
"Who?"
"Audrey."
"No."
"And your mom?"
"No."

Deepa's new strategy to conserve what little energy she has involves having other people ask questions such that responses can be whittled down to one word whenever possible.

Within weeks of their breakup, Audrey discontinued her cell phone service. Gloria's observations of Deepa's normal fluidity with words is not holding true through a shattered heart. Before Deepa had the ability to string together even a basic sentence,

"Please come back to me."

Audrey virtually vanished. Deepa took that as a sign to find the correct written words before any attempts at contact, and thus spent countless hours searching through the archives of great poets, of

Pulitzer novelists, and of world leaders who used their ideas to inspire generations.

Meeting Jorge and Pedro Ramirez first alerted Deepa that the intersection of being a common Indian and a common gay woman is infinitely more complicated than the individual groups. Loving a gay French woman makes the search for the perfect words still harder. Deepa can't find the way to properly articulate her and Audrey's convergence.

During one particularly long attempt, Deepa came across an online conversation dated August 28th.

> Audrey → Jessica: Thanks Jessica! I am all settled. How are you?
>
> Jessica → Audrey: I'm good! Started my research program. I miss you!
>
> Audrey → Jessica: I miss you too! Come visit me here in Paris! Bisous !

By September, Deepa and Julie are once again roommates.

Chapter 3

"I'm going out for my seminar," Lakshmi tells Pooja.

"That's the third time this week!"

"It is good for me to continue to learn. Will you be going anywhere tonight?"

"I have a lot of work to do," Pooja curtly replies.

Lakshmi lingers by the door in the hopes Pooja will ask her the simplest of questions,

"What is the seminar about?"

To start a conversation Lakshmi has not yet found the courage to commence. It has been four long months since the unofficial ban on communication with her granddaughter, and the silence is weighing down on Lakshmi's aging heart.

Pooja shows no sign of budging, so Lakshmi pushes herself out the door in a somber march. Only the knowledge she is moving in the correct direction keeps Lakshmi fighting without a timeframe to accompany the motions.

Most of Pooja's days have been marked with alternating cycles of anger and depression. The latest manifestation of this discontent is the total indecision of how to decorate the house. Before Pooja heard Deepa utter those heinous words,

"I'm gay,"

the walls were littered with pictures of Deepa, Pooja, Lakshmi, and every combination therein. At this current hour, Pooja decides those displays are entirely inappropriate, and she begins removing all signs of a photographic past. When she made the same effort back in New Orleans, it was permanent. Cutting out her daughter could never be as straightforward.

Each oscillation of indecision adds another layer of volatile misery to the situation. In the back of her mind, Pooja knows she needs to talk to someone, but the vows of silence she took before Deepa was born makes the idea of confessing her soul to a stranger nothing short of terrifying.

Instead, Pooja continues to her escapist reality of the Internet, where new identities are encouraged and rarely verified. Sentences can be typed out and reviewed before being sent. No one online criticizes her judgment, her choices, her non-choices, or her life. Pooja gets more than what she gives to the online world, and at this moment in time, she has very little to give. The Internet helps remind her it is still worth living.

Her mind still swirling with the disappointment that Pooja has chosen another night alone talking to strangers on the computer, Lakshmi barely notices when the tiny phone in her purse starts vibrating. She answers once safely inside her car.

"Hello?" Lakshmi asks.

"Hi mom," Alpa replies.

"Hello beta, how is Deepa?"

"Better, thanks for asking about me."

Alpa is being sarcastic. It is the one thing she and her sister have in common. Lakshmi discusses Alpa's tiring work schedule for a few minutes before reminding Alpa to take a vacation. The reminders do not go very far. Lakshmi has been telling Alpa the same thing since Alpa was 25.

"How are the support groups going?" Alpa asks.

"I find garages very redundant."

"Your car roof is more secure than any you saw until coming to the States."

"Who needs a roof for a roof?"

Alpa is accustomed to her mother's obtuse methods of relaying how far Lakshmi's situation has evolved in one lifetime. Alpa knows this means Lakshmi is not yet ready to explain what dots the sessions are connecting.

"I called Pooja yesterday," Alpa offers to change the conversation.

"She has not risen from behind that computer in days."

"Hamed is coming for Thanksgiving. You both should come, too."

Lakshmi lets the pang in her stomach subside before replying.

"I will respect the wishes of my elder daughter."

Both Lakshmi and Alpa know this means they will not be seeing each other for the holiday. Hamed, Alpa's brother-in-law, had always been a contentious force with Pooja. Least of all, this year Pooja will not stand for such confrontation.

"Beta, I must go. The Bobby boy will be waiting only," Lakshmi says to break the silence.

Bobby is the session leader who took kindly to Lakshmi once he found out they lived in the same town in West Virginia for nearly 15 years. The high school in which the sessions take place is the same size as Lakshmi's former Chennai university. Very unsure of herself at first, Bobby has been invaluable, and Lakshmi does not wish to give the kind soul the impression she will not be coming.

"I'm proud of you, mom," Alpa replies.
"It is for Deepa."
"It will be for you, too."

Chapter 4

Alpa invites Deepa over for Thanksgiving this year.

"I'm staying home," Deepa replies.
"Are you having people over?"
"No, I'm spending it alone."

Alpa ticks her tongue in a Morse code-like way as though trying to send a message.

"Don't do this, Deepa."

"Do what? Be gay?"

"Don't turn into a hermit because life isn't working out the way you want."

Deepa can't help but think that's a terrible thing to say to someone who is going through such a difficult time.

"I don't feel like seeing anyone! It has been a hard year…"

"You know who says things like that?"

Letting Deepa recall the hundreds of moments Pooja used her difficult past as an excuse for not doing something, for not being nice to someone, or for blaming someone for her own errors, Deepa quickly sees where the conversation is going. Pooja never talked about the way she felt after the divorce. Is this what she went through? Is this the first step to a life of unhappiness?

"Point taken," Deepa concedes.

Looking up from a pile of oil pastels and cousins, Deepa sees Hamed peering down at her. Save the terrible pea-green inseam of his jacket, he looks as sharp as ever in a finely tailored Italian suit.

"Are you free for a tea before dinner?" Hamed asks.

He explains one of his old university 'mates' owns a shop down the street.

"Brits refusing to celebrate Thanksgiving," he says.

Sahra and Malak are busy drawing giant orange and red circles on sheets of paper. Deepa tells Hamed they should go now before the cousins migrate to using her pants as their canvas. The cousins like to experiment with mixed media, especially media Alpa has explicitly forbidden them from using.

"The shop has this delightful cinnamon-infused black tea.

Fancy trying it?"

"Sure," Deepa replies, suppressing a scrunched nose.

The two orders of tea and biscuits barely reach the table before Deepa blurts out the pressing question on her mind.

"What kind of conference would bring you to New York for a month?"

Deepa couldn't shake the feeling that Alpa actually flew Hamed over to talk, as Alpa's offer to fly Deepa to Paris was met with panicked indecision. The timing was too coincidental. To that, Hamed assures otherwise.

"Pompous bastards are calling a brainstorming session for a new LGBTQ writing collaborative a conference," he explains.

In swift British efficiency, the bill makes an appearance a few seconds later. Deepa motions to throw in $5.

"Nope, I got it. This place is a rip-off. Just supporting my friend."

"$17.50 for this?"

"Better than London!"

New York: Where Londoners go to find a bargain.

Even Hamed looks dumfounded as he settles down $20 to cover quite possibly the worst tea of all time. His next subject of conversation does not pick the mood back up.

"What happened with the Ramirez case?" he asks.

"It had a tragic ending."

"Poetic injustice."

"Exactly. Anything specific you wanted to know?"

"Not really…Alpa said the case really made an impression on you."

Deepa stares down at the biscuit that costs more than Lakshmi's father made in a week.

Through countless hours of psychoanalyzing every move, Deepa has thought about the Ramirez case incessantly. Pedro and Jorge's decision to sacrifice everything to stay together made little sense at her first glance.

"You feel differently now?" Hamed asks.

"I now know what it's like to have someone that is worth the sacrifice."

Hamed makes a sudden shivering gesture, saying it's unsettling to think about the millions of people who have to be completely closeted, even in modern-day.

"Jack and I have been together for ten years," Hamed follows.

Deepa gets the impression that Hamed is no Pedro and Jack is no Jorge.

"Your parents never knew?" Deepa asks.

"The only thing I know is what they didn't want to know. Have you spoken to your mother at all?"

This time, Deepa swore to follow Gloria's advice, to be proactive, to use her strengths.

"As of last count, I've sent 20 emails, 33 voicemails, and 7 letters by post."

"Nothing?"

"Not a hint. Do you regret not coming out to your parents?"

"When I see other parents reacting like this, not always."

Hamed's situation was much different, though, Deepa knows. His parents came from Iran to England in the 80s. Having met her before she died, Deepa can still recall Hamed's mother's flare for the dramatics.

"I was afraid she would kill herself if I came out," Hamed says.

Deepa knows this is not a claim she can make about her mother.

"And your father?" Deepa asks Hamed.

"He was quite senile before I told him. I doubt he understood. Yours?"

On the slate of subjects to dance around with caution, why Anand moved to the ashram ranked high on Pooja's list. Deepa still does not know more beyond the cryptic explanation Anand offered.

"He moved shortly after I came out to him," Deepa says.

"Because?"

"He became the person he despised. My being gay had nothing to do with it."

"Is that what you believe?"

Deepa thinks back to when Audrey first asked her that question. It was after they saw Audrey's favorite play for the fifth time.

"Imagine revealing only half of your face to those you hold closest?" Audrey remarked.

Audrey and Deepa both instantly made the connection to Deepa's father.

"I didn't know then, I don't know now," Deepa finally replies.

"Did it affect your decision to not come out to your mother?"

"How could it not?"

Hamed echoes that it's hard balancing complex cultures in a world whose views towards homosexuality are constantly evolving.

"Those intersections are poorly defined," Hamed finishes.

"Yes, it's so hard to navigate. Do you think my mom will come around?"

"I do. I can tell she knows the power of love."

Deepa had never considered love was behind the hidden half of Pooja's face.

Chapter 5

"Pooja, can you please bring me the forks?" Lakshmi calls out.

"Aw, they're so cute!" Pooja screams in response.

As a child, Pooja was always very coy in letting Lakshmi know she was not paying attention - some things never change. Today is not the day, however, to tell Pooja to be kinder. Lakshmi knows Pooja is especially missing Deepa right now. The plan six months ago was to gather around a giant table with all the family listening to Pooja recount their dream journey to Paris and Agra.

"We're going to have to throw out half of this," Pooja says to Lakshmi, walking up from behind.

Biting her tongue, Lakshmi does her best to concentrate on the positive aspects of her life, despite the strain of not seeing her granddaughter for a second Thanksgiving. Pooja had refused to entertain any conversation on the subject, leaving Lakshmi to do the food order alone.

"I will not be throwing out this much food," Lakshmi replies.

"Or what? The poor people in Chennai will starve?"

It takes Lakshmi a few seconds to register Pooja's vile comment. The subjects of disagreement between the two generations of women are endless, though Pooja has never made a mockery of Lakshmi's struggles growing up in poverty.

The words "I'm sorry" hang on the tip of Pooja's tongue before she finally manages to sound them out in audible form. There are far better ways to articulate the ridiculous scene unfolding. Lakshmi's perpetual grandiose image of America is shown by the black pantsuit she wears. She contrasts sharply against Pooja's pajamas. The younger of the two didn't find reason to change clothes from bed this morning.

"Thanks for my headphones, thanks for the money, thanks for the Internet," Pooja says as grace.

The lack of Pooja's usual ending is acutely noticed by both women present.

"Thank you for this day, another special gift from God. Amen," Lakshmi finishes.

"This day is far from special."

"We could have gone to visit Alpa."

"There is unwelcome company."

Until recently, Lakshmi hadn't understood Pooja's constant disdain of Hamed. A flash of nausea overtakes Pooja as she recalls her most vivid memory of Hamed's 'good friend,' Jack. When Alpa called Pooja with the news Hamed would be in town for the holiday, Pooja immediately spotted the trap.

"What were you watching on the computer?" Lakshmi softly asks.

"A video of cute puppies."

"That's nice."

"You're lying. You hate dogs. You always have."

"Your father helped me li…"

"Don't bring up dad!"

Speaking of Shankar's good qualities had always been neutral ground with her daughter; Lakshmi is taken aback by the sudden shift on the subject's limits.

"Your father died before his time. I miss him dearly," Lakshmi offers.

"You could have showed it more."

"One cannot agree with their spouse about all decisions."

"Or any decisions, especially about your own daughter."

Both women falter on whether to make eye contact; they have almost had this argument more times than either cares to count.

"Pooja, I have apologized for 20 years. What else can I do?"

"How dare you throw this back on me!"

The leak in this bottle is too wide to withstand the pressure. Thanksgiving and all, Pooja screams at Lakshmi about the argument the night before Shankar died.

"You cheated dad out of his income!" Pooja shouts with an almighty fury.

"That is not accurate!"

"It's not a coincidence he died the next day!"

Pooja feels an armor of truth build around her body as she stares her mother down.

"The fight was about your mistakes, Pooja! You lived beyond your means!"

"You hung me out to dry! You paid for all of Alpa's education!"

The protective barrier strengthens, making Pooja feel invincible. Lakshmi knows in the end Pooja too had her education paid for, though not in the guilt-free entitlement Alpa enjoyed.

"I did not cause your father's heart attack," Lakshmi says.

"You destroyed my life, mom. Look at what you did!"

The argument has reached a confounded place such that Lakshmi no longer knows to which point she must respond. Long ago, she understood the futile nature of arguing battles past.

"What about Deepa, Pooja?"

"What *about* Deepa? She's *my* daughter."

"You are pushing away the best part of your life."

Pooja reconciles this effect by knowing she at least had the strength to acknowledge Deepa's potential. Her job as a mother is to steer her child in the right direction.

"Imagine what would have happened if I had actually run away?" Pooja counters.

Lakshmi feels the color from her face drain away. Swept away in the flow is the orientation of events on the fateful night she first told Pooja to have an arranged marriage.

"You were going to run away?"

"YES! Dad is the one who convinced me to stay!"

The reasoning for Pooja's destiny had always been clear in Lakshmi's head.

"Pooja, I have had a very difficult life..."
"Enough mom, just STOP!"

And stop Lakshmi had, thanks to her late husband. Shankar was the one to recognize Pooja's suffering; Shankar was the one to ensure their younger daughter would make her own choices.

"Beta, it is your decision to not speak to Deepa."
"Of course it is. I know that."
"But you must ask yourself *why*. Otherwise you are doing to Deepa what I did to you."

Suit perfectly in place, Lakshmi turns and leaves the room. Pooja sees the remnants of her protective armor dragging on the heel of her mother's shoe.

Chapter 6

The brutal Thanksgiving argument marinates for a month before Pooja brings up the subject, which happens just after seeing Lakshmi take a small tumble on the stairs.

"I am getting old," Lakshmi remarks.
"You should be around family, it's Christmas."

Not having many friends to share the experience, Pooja never used her computer-savvy to join any form of social media. Finally armed with a reason, it takes her all of ten seconds to find out Jeff is now a professor at Emory University. A few clicks flood her screen with the highlights of his now impressive accomplishments. On a page of selected works, Pooja feels her heart plummet at the sight of his memoir, titled *My Roommate, My Partner, My Husband.*

Jeff is the kind of author who writes precisely as he speaks, and Pooja is only able to get a few pages in until echoes of his voice take over. Overwhelmed, she comes up for air less she loses her courage. Eventually, Pooja settles on the simplest possible email.

> Dear Jeff,
>
> Remember me? I came across your website and thought I'd say hi. Hope you have been well.
>
> Pooja Deva (formerly Suresh)

It takes an hour to compose the message. As an English professor, Jeff will certainly notice any grammar mistakes. Then again, effective writing is sometimes best harnessed through creative use of punctuation.

e.e. cummings [For Example].

Pooja's attempts at self-sabotage do not prevail; no error or bounce back message appears in her inbox after more than an adequate period of staring. It would have been the perfect scenario on some level.

> *"I tried to make peace,"* she could tell herself.

He responds several days later with a more detailed reply, taking it a step further in inviting further conversation.

> Hi Pooja!
>
> So nice to hear from you! I am doing well, thanks. Where are you living these days? If you ever find your way down to the Atlanta area, I'd love to get coffee sometime.
>
> Sorry for the slow response, been busy with work.

Jeff

They write back and forth before Pooja says she'll be down in early February.

"Are you going to be in town?" she leads.

"Sure will! What brings you down?" he responds.

Using her daughter's default work excuse, Pooja lies and says she'll be in Atlanta for a conference. The numbers of her credit card barely make it on to the screen as she steadies her hands enough to type. A brain lapse immediately follows and she almost forwards the flight confirmation to Jeff as she has done so often with Deepa.

Pooja can't help but smile as she uses the calendar function of her phone for the first time in ages. A date, place and time is secured and confirmed. It's amazing how much it took to get to here.

"Are you ready?" Lakshmi asks Pooja.

"All set."

All of Pooja's attempts to pack lightly for the trip were foiled as soon as she realized she needed everything to go perfectly. Her enormous suitcase takes up so much room in the car trunk that she fails to notice a tiny overnight bag that is already stuffed in the back corner.

"Are you nervous?" Lakshmi asks.

"Why would I be nervous?"

"No reason."

"You don't know what I'm doing."

This much is true. Pooja had not offered and Lakshmi had not asked the nature of Pooja's trip down south. A mother knows, however, when her child makes a transformation. Lakshmi is just not sure whether the transformation has already started or is soon arriving.

"Have a safe journey, beta," Lakshmi wishes her daughter at

the airport.

"Hey, that broach."

Pooja is staring at Lakshmi's tiny frame. On top of Lakshmi's black suit of the day sits the same green and gold broach.

"Yes, I am delivering it home."

"I thought it was garbage," Pooja replies.

"Far from it."

The thought the cheap tin had any real meaning had never crossed Pooja's mind. On another day, she would have pried further. Today, other issues are simply taking all of her mental bandwidth.

"Have a safe journey, beta," Lakshmi repeats.

It took Lakshmi time to realize the significance of the jewelry that lay on her chest is not meant to be shared with her daughter. Relieved at the pass, Pooja sets off to confront her past.

Lakshmi reaches the tranquility of the Appalachian Mountains. The size of the giant formations served well as a calming effect to the turbulence the area residents often wrought on Lakshmi's family. Even today, these mountains are her home.

The crisp spring air invites Lakshmi outside, and she stretches her feeble legs. Her old memory fails her on occasion - how to turn on the computer, where she put her glasses, what are the neighbors' names. It has no troubles finding Shankar's resting site, though. She is guided by something far more powerful than the mind.

Pooja was several months pregnant when she, Lakshmi and Alpa gave Shankar's ashes to the earth. At the time, Lakshmi was sad they could not go down farther into the thicket to lay Shankar as Lakshmi had laid her nana down. Now she is grateful to only have to walk a few steps.

With a light kiss, Lakshmi bends down and places the broach in the riverbed. Just as the blue and black water returned Shankar to the depths of the earth, the water washes over, absorbing the broach into the delicate landscape. Lakshmi bends her head down and feels a few tears fall from her normally dry eyes. The eulogy she could not bear to say before comes out in soft whispers that are swept away by the wind.

> "Oh Shankar, oh nana, even when society publically shamed you, you had the insight and the courage to listen to me, to amma, to the women of your life. You are the reasons I survived to raise a beautiful family. I am so thankful I am able to pay my respects before my gratitude dies with my humble body. I carry a piece of each of you in my soul on to the next day, on to another special gift from God."

Chapter 7

"I'd like a small skinny latte with extra reduced fat milk and a shot of ginseng and hazelnut. What about you, Deepa?" Brian asks.

"A small coffee."

Brian squeals as a mother pulls away a hyperactive girl, leaving a highly coveted table open. Children in coffee shops are like trucks on the highway - they slow down 99 percent of traffic and leave the road open for one lucky car to skip ahead. Of course the day Deepa feels like leaving, she's the lucky car.

"You seem more listless than usual," Brian says.

The topic of persistent silence from Pooja and Audrey has become staple enough that people automatically assume Deepa is a depressed half-human. As cool as she tried to play her efforts, Deepa told Brian and Julie during a particularly emotional, drunken holiday party how broken she still feels.

"Isn't Audrey's birthday is coming up?" Brian prods.

"Next month."

Knowing that words of sympathy roll right off of Deepa, Brian merely offers a moment of silence.

"Well, let's get away! Let's take a vacation!" Brian suggests.

"It's cold."

"San Francisco? The weather is the same there year-around."

"Reminds me of my dad."

"Miami?"

"Reminds me my failed relationship with Gloria."

"Hawaii?"

"Reminds me of a vacation Audrey and I once planned."

"Austin?"

"Reminds me of mom's preferred type of Tex Mex."

"Jesus, Deepa!"

Recognizing a losing battle, Brian walks up to the counter to pick up their lopsided order.

"Hey!" Deepa shouts, running over beside Brian.

"No! Our table! Damnit, Deepa!"

The coffee shop hawks immediately pounce on the in-demand real estate. Deepa barely notices with a sudden moment of recognition.

"What is that song!?" Deepa asks the barista.

"My buddy works in Paris. I promise I didn't steal it! Oh God, are you the police?" the barista asks in a rush and tumble.

For the first time since she can remember, Deepa feels uplifted by a sound. The song playing is a new edition by the same French artist of Deepa's birthday CD.

The strung out patrons snap their heads up to remind Deepa how valuable their paper reading time is. Fortunately, the barista, the one who controls the coffee, is on her side.

"What's she saying?" the barista asks.

Deepa is only able to make out the basic premise at first. Much to the dismay of the 'iced skinny mocha with caramel and vanilla extract' woman a few feet over, the barista stops making drinks to bring over paper and a pencil on the condition Deepa leave him a copy of her translation.

Careful to look up a few key words, Deepa confirms she has not confused something critical. In high school, she had the most comical mistranslation:

"My presentation will be on Mozart, the famous ***Ostrich*** *Composer."*

Making good on her promise, Deepa scribbles down a copy of the translation before jetting outside. A confused Brian still stands in the corner as Deepa shouts out a quick line of explanation,

"Last mail collection is in 30 minutes!"

New York postal workers are some of the meanest people on the planet, but Deepa manages to dive through the doors with a few seconds to spare, postcard of the Brooklyn Bridge in hand. Her sense of urgency is enough, even by New York standards, to stop the employees from kicking her out.

Though she has long ago memorized the contents, Deepa pulls out the most valuable piece of paper in the world. It has the address of

Audrey's parents' place in Paris. Audrey wrote it down and stuck in Deepa's bag before Christmas '08, thinking they would write each other while apart for the holiday. Deepa fits everything on the postcard by writing in microscopic font.

> In the distant horizon
> I walk towards your shadow.
> The soul you carry
> Was mine to share.
> The soul you left
> Cannot bear to move forward.
> A river that echoes water,
> Does not flow without your presence.
> The blue, the black that remains,
> This is our battle.
> I walk towards your shadow,
> My love.

With a soft kiss, Deepa drops her last hope into the blue and black mailbox. She knows she will never find better words to say to Audrey than the words that have found her.

The sun is teeming at the surface of the tall buildings on the opposite side of Houston Street. A quick survey of the scene reveals no one who resembles Deepa's impending, admittedly boring date through the crowd of late commuters, hipster explorers and the occasional lost tourist. Online dating is such a pain.

By the end of her second beer, Deepa realizes the girl is not coming. The only thing worse than going on a date with a dull, unappealing person is getting stood up by a dull, unappealing person. Finally bringing her feet to the pavement, Deepa feels the two pints of liquid she consumed slosh uncomfortably in her stomach. Just moments after paying the check, her phone goes off. It's from an unrecognized New York number. Of course the stupid date decides to call now.

"Hi. You're like an hour late, so I'm going home," Deepa answers.

Deepa pauses after the last word to allow enough time to hear which lame excuse, like a subway delay or a late night at work, will be the reasoning. Those are the perfect, uncreative, impossible-to-dispute New York City defenses.

"Deepa?" the woman on the phone says.

Deepa nearly drops the phone. This time, Deepa does nearly go into cardiac arrest.

"Um…how are you? How's the psychology?" Deepa replies.

How's the psychology? Drunk after two beers, it appears.

"Is this a good time to talk? I can call back later. I'll call back later."

"No, no, no! This is fine. Now is great. Are you in the city?"

"Yes. I arrived a few months ago. Are you still here?"

"Yes. Are you?"

"…Yes."

She lives in Astoria now. It's a good choice for a Parisian. The bakeries in that neighborhood are the best New York has to offer, restaurants flaunt their al fresco dining, and none of the buildings are massive structures designed to extinguish architectural diversity.

"Are you free tonight? It is no problem if you have plans," Audrey follows.

"No! I don't have plans. I did have plans, but she stood me up."

That's a good way to showcase attractiveness as a girlfriend.

"Can you meet me at that beach place in Queens? What is it called?" Audrey asks.

"I know what you're talking about. See you in an hour?"

"Okay, see you there."

The "beach" is a quaint area of Long Island City, Queens. During the summer, the carved out, sanded area is open to the public for concerts, food festivals, and fundraisers. Deepa finds it surprising Audrey would pick such an expensive place to meet, but she's not disappointed with the choice. The final moments of the sunset send out intense rays of color in every direction behind the massive skyline of midtown Manhattan. It's so…romantic.

Deepa does her best to talk herself out of thinking such a setting means anything. Audrey is probably dating someone by now. It's best to assume this meeting is for something insignificant, like getting clothes back or seeing how much money was returned on the apartment deposit.

"Deepa?" Audrey says, this time not through a phone.

Her efforts at practicing turning around slowly are futile; as soon as Audrey utters the 'D' in Deepa's name, Deepa whirls around like a trick pony.

"Hi!" Deepa says, a little too eagerly.

"Did you get a drink already?"

"No, I'm just having water."

A dry spell kicked in towards the middle of March. The two beers from the bar are the most alcohol Deepa has had in nearly a month. A drier Deepa is pleasing to Audrey.

"You used to drink too much."

"Thanks..."

"Sorry, I didn't mean...I'll go get something and come back."

So she can shift to watch Audrey walk to the bar, Deepa pretends to spot something on the side of the bench facing the other direction. A random guy across the way catches Deepa's gaze at Audrey and flashes an obnoxious wink. Some people never learn lesbians don't exist for the entertainment of straight men.

"It's pee. I'm moving because there is pee," Deepa lies.

One ignoramus is not enough to spoil the moment, and Deepa's attention snaps back to her favorite Frenchwoman. Audrey looks as radiant as ever in a simple long black t-shirt and a stonewashed pair of jeans. She has gained a little weight, though the effect is to merely accentuate the perfect curves of her waist and chest. As Audrey reaches in her bag to pull out money, Deepa catches a whiff of the subtle way Audrey's mouth curves when she is excited. It still turns Deepa's breathing into an enamored rattle.

Audrey and Deepa's mutual admiration for the other doesn't manage to translate to the conversation.

"When did you get back to the States?"

"Two months ago."

"Just visiting?"

"No, I said two months ago."

"Oh, right. What brings you back?"

"I will start a PhD at Columbia. I have preliminary research now."

"Wow, congratulations. But I thought you didn't like the programs?"

"Thank you. I changed my mind. Are you still working?"

"Yep."

"Okay."

Disappointed at the awkwardness that was never present when they were together, they turn their attention to the cups in their hands.

"I got your postcard," Audrey says to break the silence.

"I thought you've been here for two months? I sent that a few weeks ago."

"Yes, well my father actually saw the postcard and called me. The poem was really beautiful."

Deepa explains about the paranoid barista and his contraband demo. Mozart, the Ostrich composer draws out a little laugh. Deepa has missed that laugh so much this past year, it hurt to be happy.

Audrey compliments Deepa on what seems like a very good translation. She hesitates to add a question in case the answer does not match the expectation.

"Did you keep up your French for me?"

Instead, they settle on recapping the past. It has to happen eventually.

"Did you see Paris and the Taj Mahal in September?"

"I got the ticket cancellation soon after…"

Deepa holds back finishing the thought with any of the possible painful endings:

- you broke my heart.
- I broke your heart.
- we lost each other.

Audrey can hear the options above even though they were not said.

"And your mother?" she tepidly asks.

"Sorry," she quickly adds.

"It's not your fault."
"Yes it is. I pushed you. I'm sorry."

Deepa is unsure whether she deserves that apology. Audrey had always been honest about her need to not be in the closet to either of their families. Audrey and Deepa were allowed to disagree on coming out; Deepa was not entitled to question Audrey's reasons.

"And I should not have questioned your reasons, Deepa."

Audrey's father eventually recounted the conversation Deepa and he had that night in the milky dark. He told Audrey about his own challenges in accepting a gay daughter. Who was Audrey to question Pooja's process? Who was Audrey to question Deepa's hesitation? An ultimatum was unfair to hang over Deepa's head.

"I thought I was supportive. My father made me realize what that really means."
"There were a lot of cultural factors hanging in the balance."

Lying was not one of them. Lying was entirely Deepa's fault.

"I am so sorry, Audrey."
"That lie killed me inside."

And the fact that lie killed Audrey inside killed Deepa inside. Not having the option to legally marry did not diminish Deepa's implicit vow to support and protect Audrey.

Nearly a year later, Deepa finally tells Audrey what happened the last night Deepa saw her mother. Deepa felt nostalgia of the fantastic, whimsical childhood Pooja had so selflessly helped Deepa create. Even in the years that separated their convergence, Deepa still felt overwhelming moments of Pooja's care against the world. Nothing, not even Audrey, affects Deepa so deeply.

"In a split second that changed everything, I convinced myself that my understanding would be her understanding."

Pooja's understanding is entirely her own.

"I connected to my parents through their own experiences," Audrey says.

"My mother is under entirely different circumstances."

Audrey appreciates that now.

"Deepa, you found the words to reconnect with me."

"I haven't found the words to reconnect with her."

"Perhaps they are not for you to find."

Chapter 8

Pooja reaches the coffee shop first. She sits down among the students half her age before realizing the overpriced espresso does not come with full service tables. The menu is written in impossibly small text as if to signify the hipsters milling around are wearing glasses for purposes other than vision correction.

"What the hell is a chai coffee?" Pooja asks the cashier behind the counter.

"It's..."

"You know 'chai' means tea in Hindi? So that means tea coffee."

The cashier includes an evil eye with Pooja's small Americano at no extra charge.

"That'll be $3.25."

"How is this place more expensive than New York?"

"I'll get that for the pretty lady," someone behind Pooja says.

Relishing Pooja's panic at the voice, the cashier feels vindicated enough to give Pooja and Jeff a little space. As though mimicking Deepa's train preparation, Pooja turns around in slow motion to make eye contact with the face that broke her so long ago.

"Did you find the place okay?" Jeff asks.

"I have a GPS. I'm very good with computers," Pooja blurts.

"That is one thing I could have never known about you back in NOLA."

"Yes, we are old."

Jeff manages a chuckle in what already appears to be a tainted atmosphere. Pooja tries looking into his intense blue eyes for comfort as she did when they were younger. All his eyes offer now is uncertainty.

"What brings you down to Atlanta? What's the conference about?" he asks.

"Immigration human rights," Pooja responds without thinking.

"Decided on a career change from architecture?"

"No, I just find the subject interesting."

Scoffing at herself, Pooja can't believe the career she fought so hard to establish isn't even her instinctive fallback lie. Thoughts of Deepa permeate her brain.

"You're a professor here at Emory?" she asks.

"Yep! Been here about 15 years now."

"Where were you before?"

"UCLA for two years, UVA for one, George Mason for five…"

"You were in DC for five years!?"

Jeff is alarmed at Pooja's sudden onset of hysterics. The thought that this man roamed the streets minutes from her home makes Pooja tense.

"Why didn't you stay at Tulane?" Pooja asks.

The faux finish ceiling suddenly catches Jeff's attention. His head stays fixated upwards for a solid minute. Pooja did not fly all the way down to Atlanta to stare at Jeff's Adam's apple, and clears her throat to get the point across.

"I had some memories I needed to escape," he eventually responds.

"You mean me?..."

"No!"

He quickly changes his tone again after seeing Pooja's offended jaw lying on the ground.

"Losing you was very hard, Pooja, but I was referring to Charles passing."

"AIDS?"

"Car crash."

FUCK! Pooja's mind screams. She couldn't have said something more offensive if she had tried. Jeff's Southern chivalrous behavior hasn't worn off, and he assures Pooja it was a fair guess given the era.

"Would you like another coffee?" he offers.

"No thanks, I think I will save the money to buy a motorcycle."

"Ha! I see you still have that biting sense of humor."

He produces the first real smile since they sat down, and immediately Pooja feels the tension cut in half and deflate to the ground. Both are slowly sliding back into place as close friends.

"Can I ask why you got back in contact?" he asks.

"I randomly came across your website," Pooja lies.

As she has many times in the past year, Pooja silently thanks the Internet. These days, one can 'randomly' stumble across anything to bring up in a discussion or to contact someone. It was much harder to lie in the 80s.

Pooja's feeble excuse is enough to keep Jeff satisfied. He recaps his life at Emory, what it's like to be on a tenure track, and what it's like to once again teach rich kids as a man from a poor background. Chats with Jeff as the main subject were never to his liking, however, and he quickly reverts back to Pooja's (fake) conference.

"There was an interesting immigration case in Orlando. I think his last name was Rodriguez," Jeff says.

"Ramirez," Pooja immediately corrects.

"You've heard of it?"

"Yes…my daughter worked on the case."

"You have a daughter!?"

Pooja's heart races so fast, as though it is competing for an Olympic gold medal.

"Yes. She's 25, lives in New York and works at The Justice Coalition. I think."

"You don't know?"

"We haven't spoken in nine months. That's the real reason why I wanted to meet."

"Pooja, we never...you know she can't be mine..."

"Anand is her father, Jeff."

It's Jeff's turn to be embarrassed.

"Of course. What a stupid thing to say. But why her? Why me?"

"Jeff, you broke my heart, and as a result I rejected my gay daughter."

Jeff goes bug eyed at the assessment. Pooja questions if she is being ridiculous. The moment of doubt quickly passes.

"Pooja, for me, our connection was just plutonic."

"I was in love with you. I went insane when you left."

"I never wanted to let you go."

Jeff holds Pooja's hands and apologizes for something that was never really his fault. Though these kinds of situations have victims, laying blame is not the answer.

"Even plutonic, I really loved you, Pooja."

"It has been so long since I've seen a true friend."

"Tell me about her."

Pooja always smiles as she describes her daughter, her Deepa. Deepa is an amalgamation of so many different people.

"What part of her does she share with you?"

"With me?"

Deepa sees the world with the same curiosity as Pooja did as a child. When Pooja saw Deepa frolicking through the rivers of chocolate, the cities governed by music, and a globe that shifted at her touch, Pooja rediscovered excitement in the future.

"Together, we constructed our own world and marched to the beat of a drum no one else could imagine."

"What happened?"

"Our convergence parted."

Fantasies couldn't translate to the harshness of the real world.

"Deepa wanted to join the outside, the others. I didn't have the strength to follow."

"What does that have to do with me?"

"Everything and nothing."

"The words 'I'm gay' destroyed your first utopian society?"

"That's everything."

"Deepa made the only real choice to move forward?"

"And nothing."

Pooja dreaded the thought someone would be with Deepa the way Pooja had dreamt of being with Jeff. Pooja's pain became her homophobia.

"Her orientation doesn't change your relationship."

"No."

"Her love of someone else is what scares you."

"Yes."

It has everything and nothing to do with Jeff. It has everything and nothing to do with Deepa's sexual orientation.

"You need to talk to her."

"I can't."

"Why not?"

"I did the same thing to her as my mother did to me. We'll never recover."

"One year of no contact will not destroy a lifetime of good will."

Now a domain expert in reconciling with family, Jeff assures Pooja he will get her connected to the right resources. The right resources can help Pooja reconnect to her daughter.

Jeff glances down at his watch and sighs. He has a class starting in ten minutes.

"Do we have time to meet again?" he asks.

"The conference was a lie, dummy."

"I know. I was being polite, dummy."

They exchange every possible form of communication before verifying when they will next meet in person. Before leaving, Jeff swallows Pooja in a bear hug he was saving for this very occasion. He grabs his keys and walks out the door, leaving Pooja with the ultimate comfort that this time it is not forever.

Chapter 9

Making good on their original commitment, this time around, Deepa and Audrey decide to take things slowly. Ample time apart builds a kind of excitement that weathers with too much exposure. Even so, they find it strange to go at this pace. Their interactions are rich with a personal history a new relationship cannot offer. Both have to make an effort to refrain from saying previously innocuous statements.

"We'll do it tomorrow."

A lack of these statements is disappointing; it means they are not where they thought they would be. This is part of the battle.

Audrey came over tonight to cook dinner with Deepa. A talentless chef before she went back to Paris, she spent much of her breakup therapy learning how to use the kitchen. The menu for this evening hails from Scandinavia.

"Did you find the wine?" she calls out as Deepa walks through the door.

"They didn't have any good Rieslings. I got a rosé instead."

A rosé is not the best for her recipe. The wine store Deepa has been going to for the last four years is always a hit or miss in its selection.

"A great new store just opened in Gramercy. We can go there tomor...umm...we can go next week," Audrey says.

"What's in the dish?" Deepa asks.

"Sprinkle some flour and sugar over the garlic, and..."

Deepa is starting to regret agreeing to this meal. Garlic and sugar sound similar to the combinations Audrey thought worked when they first started dating.

A knock at the door interrupts Audrey mid-explanation. Grateful at the timing, Deepa runs over to answer. The peephole is dirty with the years of familiarity. When Deepa finally gets a visual, she nearly falls over.

"It's my grandmother!" Deepa exclaims in a panicked whisper.

Being a good psychologist, Audrey rushes over and sits Deepa down. In the chaos of coming out to Pooja, Deepa's relationship with Lakshmi became unspoken at best.

"Invite her inside," Audrey suggests.

"And say what?"

"That I am your girlfriend...or whatever you want."

Audrey and Deepa are just starting to reconnect. Now is not the time for Audrey to reassert her opinions.

Patience was never a virtue that graced Lakshmi's being. She is knocking rapidly on the door.

"Deepa? Are you there, beta? I can hear voices."

Summoning every speck of courage, Deepa paints a smile on her face before opening the portal to reality.

"Hi, avva!"

Lakshmi notices her granddaughter is sweating as her dear friend Alpa would in the hottest Chennai months. She gingerly takes her first steps inside the apartment, recalling how she calculated the expenses when Deepa decided to move out of the university dormitories. Deepa's rent is more than any mortgage Lakshmi has ever had.

"There is not much space," Lakshmi comments.

From Deepa's reaction, Lakshmi can tell this was not the best first thing to say. On the other side of the six-meter apartment, Lakshmi sees a brown-haired woman absent-mindedly stirring a pot and staring in her direction.

"Avva, this is Audrey," Deepa introduces.

"It is a pleasure to meet you," Audrey follows.

"What is your accent?" Lakshmi asks.

"It's French, I'm from Paris. Have you been?"

Deepa shoots Audrey an expression that to Lakshmi communicates constipation.

"Try a laxative," Lakshmi advises.

Asking for a moment of reprieve, Deepa whispers to Audrey in language Lakshmi cannot understand.

"Sure, I will give you two some privacy," Audrey agrees.

Following Deepa's cue, Lakshmi waits for Audrey to leave before offering an explanation of why she came, and came alone.

"Audrey appears kind. You have chosen your partner wisely."

"Partner? How do you know that word, avva?"

The story is still hard for Lakshmi to piece together. It started two Christmases ago, when Lakshmi approached her other granddaughter, Sahra, for a bit of information.

"Pooja was always insistent we never push you to get married," Lakshmi says Deepa.

"I know. She wanted me to establish myself as a person first."

"Still, I would sometimes press the little ones for updates."

As a New Yorker and a child, Sahra was terrible at keeping secrets. It took all of five minutes for Lakshmi to find out Deepa was in a relationship.

Sahra's main concern was losing her ski trip," Lakshmi says.

"How did pinni react?"

"Alpa forced me into a confrontation."

"Confrontation?"

"She phrased it differently. 'An intervention.' "

It was Alpa who first used a set of words Lakshmi found highly offensive:

- Gay
- Lesbian
- Sexual orientation

Not wanting to be any part of the discussion, Lakshmi tried her best to leave the room whenever possible. On her last attempt, Alpa stopped her with one powerful question.

"Do you want to make the same mistake you made with Pooja?"

Lakshmi had never been so caught off guard. How dare Alpa compare the situations!?

"This is different, this is sick," Lakshmi argued.

"This is **no** different. This is you not understanding," Alpa retorted.

"Too much New York has ruined your judgment."

"Mom, you have the chance to accept your granddaughter as you never did with your older daughter."

Lakshmi tells Deepa how many times she cried inside seeing Pooja cry outside. Pooja sacrificed everything for Deepa; Pooja felt like no one had sacrificed anything for her.

"That's not true, you did so much for my mother," Deepa counters.

"And she did so much for you."

"She took her empathy for me much further than you did for her."

This is precisely the point Alpa tried to make with Lakshmi. For all of the battles Lakshmi had conquered for her daughters, having the courage to understand Pooja's circumstance in life was not included.

"Pooja never found the words to tell me, how could she?"
"And you never found the courage to listen."

Alpa presented to Lakshmi a new choice with Deepa.

"Mom, if I connect you to the right resources, will you try to understand? For Deepa?"

It took every ounce of faith for Lakshmi to respond as Alpa hoped.

"Yes."

Lakshmi turns to face Deepa, gently bringing her feeble hands over to her granddaughter's.

"Deepa, beta, I have been going to LGBT support sessions."
"For me?"
"For us."

A river of emotion in Deepa immediately follows Lakshmi's confession. Deepa stares into the tired face of her grandmother, and sees her grandmother's struggles, triumphs, and losses.

"What finally convinced you to go?" Deepa asks Lakshmi.
"I was born into this world a Shudra, a peasant caste."
"You overcame all odds to be here."
"I did, though the costs entailed were pure injustices."

Lakshmi and her family endured the evils of society in exchange for Lakshmi's progression.

"Deepa, many people in India said I did not deserve an education. That does not mean they were right. I will not be a part of the many against you."

Chapter 10

Jeff tells Pooja one of his students just walked into his office with a question.

"Talk tomorrow?" he asks her.

"I have lunch with the girls. Anytime before one works!" she replies.

"Excellent, can't wait!"

A happy sigh escapes Pooja's lips as she stares down at her phone, which flashes, 'Call ended. Duration: 51:48.' She and Jeff have made it a point to talk every day since her trip to Atlanta. It turns out his renewed friendship and a newfound openness towards others constitutes the resources Pooja needs to move forward. This time the Internet is the facilitator, not the replacement.

Clanging plates grabs Pooja's attention, and she makes her way into the dining room. A confirmation of Lakshmi's old age is in front of her.

"Mom, you brought out three plates. Trying to set me up with a husband?"

"Very funny."

Lakshmi continues her place-setting efforts. Pooja walks to the study to her other form of progression. She knows she is getting ahead of herself with the depth of her urban planning research. First she needs to get in to the program at the University of Maryland. Then comes the thesis.

Out of the corner of her eye, she sees an unrecognized car pull into the driveway. From her Orlando days, she knows a Florida license plate means it is likely a rental. The mystery person enters through the back door as if this is their house. Suddenly, Pooja realizes this is indeed their house.

"Deepa!" Pooja screams in alarm.

"Hi mom," Deepa replies, flowers and forgiveness outstretched.

"What the hell are you doing here?"

The violent reaction from Pooja is involuntary. She immediately regrets not saying something else - the stories, the apologies, the explanations. Any attempt she tries to make at reconciliation is replaced by the same offensive question.

"WHAT ARE YOU DOING HERE?"

"Chee! I invited her," Lakshmi interjects.

Pooja feels her body turn into a sack of sand. She grabs the countertop to avoid crumbling into an amorphous pile.

"You KNEW what happened?" Pooja asks Lakshmi.

"I have come a long way in my understanding."

A tide of betrayal erupts from Pooja's body, nearly knocking down the other two women. The word 'understanding' was understood as irrelevant in the childhood Lakshmi offered her elder daughter.

"*How* could you do this to *me*?" Pooja screams at her mother.

"Mom, it's not *against* you, it's *for* me," Deepa offers.

In due time, Pooja knows she will know this. Her younger sister made the same logical argument when they were kids. But Pooja's animosity of the situation is constantly deflected to the recipient of the understanding - Alpa.

"What if that happens again?" Pooja argues out loud.

Neither of the others knows what she is asking.

"I can leave you if you want," an already scared Deepa follows in a hurry.

"Yes, that would be best," Pooja whispers.

Lakshmi had a feeling this would happen; instead of fighting Pooja back, she merely escorts her granddaughter to the car. Deepa's flowers and forgiveness are lying pathetically at Pooja's feet.

"It's too soon, why did you ask me here?" Deepa asks Lakshmi.

"Go to the corner of Chester Road and Bridge Place. If we do not call you in an hour, you can go," is all Lakshmi offers.

Back inside, Lakshmi sits on the ground to face her daughter. Pooja long ago grew accustomed to her mother's inability to properly express sympathies. Pooja does not realize positioning herself at eye-to-eye level is Lakshmi's best attempt at trying.

"Pooja, my life in India was extremely fragile."

"I know; that's all I heard growing up."

"I lost my father and my closest friend in the cruelest of ways."

"You've already told me the ending to this story."

"No, I haven't. Because the ending to my story is you and Deepa."

Lakshmi tells Pooja of Lakshmi's and her nana's walk to the decrepit cabin.

"Lakshmi, sometimes we do not live this life for our own opportunities. Sometimes, we live this life for the opportunities we

bring to others."

It is those words that sustained Lakshmi through every hardship life presented.

"I was living for *you*, Pooja."

"You were?"

"Beta, I have made many poor choices for you in the past."

Lakshmi takes a step back in her mind to recall how ill prepared she felt for so much of her life. Raising a family in a foreign land, leaving a life to which she could never really return, and facing the reality she would spend half her years without her life partner.

"Pooja, I cannot correct what has already happened. Only what will happen. You are an excellent mother. Deepa is so strong because of what you have done for her."

"I am still not ready."

This something Lakshmi recognizes is not true.

"One of my deepest regrets is not including you in your own life dialogue."

"Then don't do this to me now."

"Beta, I am not doing this *to* you. I am doing this *for* Deepa."

Coming from Lakshmi, the line of reasoning has deeper meaning. As a daughter herself, Pooja knows she has a right to retreat. As a mother, her responsibility to include Deepa in their life discussion is an entirely different matter.

"That era has passed, I drove Deepa away. She must hate me," Pooja concludes.

"Pooja, do you hate me?"

For many years, the answer to that question was yes. Through Pooja's depression, anxiety, and anger, Lakshmi turned a blind eye and told Pooja to quit complaining.

"Pooja, do you hate me?" Lakshmi repeats.

But Lakshmi is also the reason Pooja grew up with food, a roof, and a steady modicum of safety. Lakshmi is the reason Pooja could focus on being an excellent mother.

"Pooja, do you hate me?"
"No…I don't hate you."
"Deepa does not hate you, either."

In the midst of yoga breathing techniques Audrey taught Deepa, Deepa jumps at the sound of her phone ringing. True to Lakshmi's prediction, it only takes 35 minutes after Deepa's second runaway from the house. Deepa pulls into the driveway once more, praying these are the first steps back to a convergence.

"Want to take a walk?" Deepa and Pooja ask each other at the same time.

"Yes, this day should not be wasted," they both reply.

The two women fall into a rhythmic unison of small talk catch-up and petting dogs to lay a foundation to unfamiliar territory. Deepa takes the first round of explanation, apologizing for leaving a live bomb without instructions on diffusion.

Much to Deepa's shock, Pooja says the signs of Deepa's orientation were obvious. It wasn't the superficial elements of how Deepa dressed or her curiosity in certain subjects. It was the intimacy with Gloria, the disinterest in the opposite sex; it was the unease of the milestones that traditionally mark a girl's life.

"I should have approached you a better way."

"I should have listened to what you had to say."

Pooja explains the lifetime difference four years between she and her younger sister entailed. Beyond her education and profession, Alpa was able to choose a love and happiness that fit her needs.

"I vowed my daughter would have the same opportunity."

"Thank you so much for letting me be who I am."

"It took time, but I now know it does not matter if your life partner is not a man. Who you love is part of who you are."

The partner chosen for Pooja was not a soulmate. Her soulmate was not available to be her partner. Love, commitment and passion in all its complicated forms are neither predictable nor formulaic.

"I wish dad understood that. I drove dad away," Deepa says.

"My darling Deepa, your father had his own reconciliation to address. You did nothing wrong; you are not his reason."

Deepa offers to connect Pooja to resources needed to understand what it means to have a gay daughter. Pooja merely smiles at the suggestion and tells Deepa a former demon now turned angel has already started her along that journey. The process will be as long as it will be cathartic.

"How was your walk?" Lakshmi asks back at the house.

"Transformative," Pooja replies.

"Emboldening," Deepa says.

As the shadows the sun casts dance in the distance, these three fantastic women walk on to the patio for a long-deserved gaze of appreciation. Lining up their family from the slums of Chennai to the heart of New York City, they join hands in the security of each other. Together they direct the giant clouds to part above their heads. A brilliant rainbow created in their minds illuminates the path on which they walk. Three tunes of their generations are all that is needed to direct each other to the converging horizon.

Tomorrow starts another special gift from God.

Epilogue – *Deepa*

In the years since mom and I took our walk, she has approached the complex discourse in sexual orientation with the fervor of an academic subject. I am more comforted by the philosophy of her approach.

"No matter what, you are still my daughter."

Audrey came down to Maryland with me for my 26th birthday. Seeing mom, avva, and Audrey at ease with each other is the best gift I could have ever imagined. For many LGBTQ people it is a moment that will never happen.

Two years later, avva, pinni, Audrey and I gathered on the main lawn of the University of Maryland campus and cheered with the hope of every woman as mom accepted her Bachelor of Science in Urban Studies and Planning. Mom enrolled in a Masters program at American University the following year. She is now a professor. Avva passed away last year. I feel her in my soul every time I brag to the world about the courage of my family.

Barbara eventually promoted me to a head researcher on the immigration unit of the New York office. Against the backdrop of one of the most significant eras of gay rights in America, my job increasingly deals with cases that are as much LGBTQ as immigration issues. I love it.

New York State legalized gay marriage in June 2011. Audrey and I continued our promise to take our time to grow into each other, less I would have proposed to her at the law passage announcement. During our fourth New Year's in concert, she suggested we move back in together. We decided that the racial and ethnic diversity of Queens best fit our needs, and we have been there ever since.

"Are you ready?" I whisper to Audrey.

"I am going to vomit."

"I love you too."

I glance over at the giant banner that has become a symbol of inspiration.

> "Equality? Check."

The announcement of federally mandated same-sex marriage was made 65 days ago. I proposed to Audrey 64 days ago. She said yes before I finished my sentence.

We survey the crowd - nearly 2,000 sets of chattering, ecstatic voices are waiting alongside us to hear the words that honor decades of struggle.

> "By the power vested in me by the District of Columbia and the United States government, I now pronounce you wives, and husbands. You may kiss your partner," the judge says.

We catch the other's reflection as my wife falls into my embrace.

As we make our way down the steps of the US Congress building, I spot our amazing support system in the distance. Through the millions of people celebrating in the streets, and the thousands protesting our peace, pinni finds us and gives us each a single flower. Before I have a chance to say anything, I hear someone shout.

> "We're from Channel 10 News. Can we get your reaction on the events today?" a reporter says to us.

Audrey lets me properly thank pinni as she explains the significance as an immigrant.

> "I can become a US citizen and my wife can become a French one since both countries have legalized gay marriage!" Audrey exclaims.

The reporter and cameraman turn to face me.

"I'm incredibly lucky to be alive in an era that properly recognizes my relationship. I've known so many who have lost this battle."

"And how have your loved ones responded to everything?"

The reporter lingers on her words, on my brown skin. I grab Audrey's hand and direct the reporter a few steps over.

"I owe everything in my life to this woman!" I shout.
"And who is this?" the reporter asks.
"This is my mother, the bravest person I have ever met."

The reporter captures mom's shining face and finishes the interview with a final question.

"How are you and your wife planning on celebrating?"

I peer over at Audrey who happily motions for me to continue.

"In lieu of a honeymoon, we're taking a family vacation."
"Where are you going?" the reporter asks.

"Paris, Chennai and the Taj Mahal."